LAELA

and the

MOONLINE

Lisa Perskie Rodriguez

LAELA

and the

MOONLINE

gatekeeper press™

Columbus, Ohio

The views and opinions expressed in this book are solely those of the author and do not reflect the views or opinions of Gatekeeper Press. Gatekeeper Press is not to be held responsible for and expressly disclaims responsibility of the content herein.

Laela and the Moonline

Published by Gatekeeper Press
2167 Stringtown Rd, Suite 109
Columbus, OH 43123-2989
www.GatekeeperPress.com

Editor: Bradley Jay Dodge
Cover design: Jordan Elaine Boyce

Library of Congress Control Number: 2021953543

ISBN (paperback): 9781662924200
eISBN: 9781662924217

Dedicated to:

Danielle and Ivan, David and Tahereh, Mateo and
Lucas, Leyla and Gabriel
Beloved children, spouses, and grandchildren

Contents

CHAPTER 1

Stirrings

Laela awoke to the lapping of her curtains, her room bathed in cool, iridescent blue light. Her window framed the full unblinking sheen of Cor and the ark of the edge of Cora with its soft melon glow. She had forgotten to close the shutters and was reminded of how powerfully these giant orbs filled the sky and flooded a room with light.

The Treedles dedicated many odes to their twin moons, brother and sister, close in orbit and size, waxing and waning in synchrony. Some Treedles even prayed to one or both of the moons, though they knew they weren't the 'One.' For a tiny people so prey to forces hidden in shadows, these were nocturnal guardians—defenders of their sky-born communities. They were a reliable compass for nighttime foraging and illumination for gatherings and celebrations.

Tonight, Cor was peering into her room. Impassive and mysterious. Laela saw the moons as protectors and confidants, though not easily accessible to one's petitions. It was part of Treedle lore that the moons draw out one's deepest secrets and the answers to inner questions if one gazes with patient devotion. Laela wasn't prone to patience. Yet, she was drawn to gaze at them tonight.

She slipped out of her bed and sat on the spacious ledge that served as a window. It served as a porch rimming her bedroom and a perching place for sylvestrian visitors during the day. She could use curtains or shutters as needed to increase her privacy or keep out the rain. However, a broad thatched roof protected the room from intense sunlight and all but the heaviest downpours. Laela sat out far enough for the night breezes to whip her hair around her face and to have a panoramic view of constellations that marked the season of spring. The group of stars that formed a maiden pouring an arc of water from a gourd, a sign of spring, was just to the east beyond the moons. Tonight, the moons, in their ¾ phase, were another reminder that a new month would soon begin. The month of Hope. The rainiest month and an auspicious time for new projects.

Laela felt an uneasy chill beneath her skin, quiet but distinct as a chameleon changing colors, which warned her of presence and danger. She possessed hair-trigger alertness, an inner arrow that guided her to focus instantly on a threat. When she ventured through the layers of the treetops with Phips, her partner for hunting and exploring, she was the first to warn of an approaching raptor, a constrictor, or predator. Her lasso would be sliding out of her hands before she could utter a word. In turn, Phips was physically stronger than her and able to wield a slingshot or handheld arrow at lightning speed. Very coveted skills at the heights of Aerizon.

However, these days she found her senses diffused. Restlessness tagged her like an unpredictable shadow. Her thoughts meandered from slow and random to buzzing and intense. She was becoming more apt to say or do something that raised eyebrows or surprised even herself. Sometimes she lay awake for hours, trying to break from a trap she couldn't define. She wished she could just move, run, fly until her heart cleared like a bird soaring up in an unbroken sky. Escape. From what she didn't know. And the last thing she wanted to do was to spend the following day in a state of calm and quiet, grounded Treedle-style to reflect on a current act of 'immaturity' at school.

She looked at Cora, wanting to pose a question. She wasn't sure what questions to voice about the inevitable. Soon, very soon, she would become a woman, the oldest in her group of friends to do so. Too many 'manly' activities had delayed the onset of this event. The unstoppable momentum of the turn of life changes was converging together: the end of her schooling, choosing her path of service, the increasing pressure to find her lifemate.

"Surprises unfold in the predictable... You can never fully foresee the foreseen." She mused on the words of one of her teachers. If she couldn't fully grasp the present these days, what control would she have over her future, even knowing the predictable?

In a way both unsettling and reassuring, she knew instinctively that she would come of age in the month of Hope. She also knew that the very sweetness and light of this month would taunt in her about the hopes she couldn't yet express. She would leave her childhood behind, shed its comforts and pleasures, to embrace the responsibilities of womanhood and maturity.

This transition in Treedle culture marked a profound dividing line between a youth's unconscious simplicity and adulthood's well-defined roles. She would follow the strict rituals to guide her over this threshold; she would undergo the rigors of solitude and intense meditation in the Enclosure. And later, she would have to answer questions about her role in the community. She felt a mixture of excitement and dread about sipping the dream teas that would reveal her future and reflecting on them in the hours of stillness. But not even her talent for prediction allowed her to see beyond the passage of the 'Enclosure.'

As the moons, she was in a near stage of completion, at a peak turning point in becoming a woman. Her breasts had become round and tender—a sign she had at first longed for not to be a child. But the changes were more an inconvenience to her now. A hindrance for running and leaping hard. A distracting and weakening ache at times. Tara promised that she would see her body in a completely different way when she had her first child. But hopefully, she might be the last young woman of her age to mate and give birth. Laela wasn't particularly looking forward to either. She longed for something else. More and more daring adventures with Phips. A releasing of restraints. Exploration of frontiers.

Laela reached into a pouch she always kept around her neck or in her tunic pocket. She needn't sleep with it, but she had tonight. She pulled out the coil of line, moonline, the most precious of the spider-woven tensile cords used as both a tool and mechanism of defense. Stronger than Mergon metal and with the capacity to pull up a large log without breaking, it was incumbent for every Treedle to have one on hand. Laela also used a smaller piece of line to play with, and now she swung hers in spiral patterns and tried to fish the center of Cora with it. Even the silvery brilliance of the coiling line arching and flashing gracefully within this orb didn't ease her unease.

She watched as the first blushes of morning light swelled into the certain blue of day, eclipsing the moons—an invitation to get up and about. But not for her. Today she would stay at home all day. She sank back into floral-scented pillows; her mother filled with bird-down and petals from their garden and herb nurseries. The inviting softness of her bedding was the work of aural spiders, trained to fabricate every kind of thread from feathery cotton fibers to metallic-like cords.

With a slicy woosh, Macecle swung through the window, his long, tapered fingers stretched around a tree vine. Still hanging on to the vine, he jumped onto Laela's chest and dangled a large calipsoberry, good for morning digestion, over her mouth. Laela accepted the berry and stroked Macecle's peppery chocolate-tufted cheeks. Macecle tickled her with his dark brown and ash striped tail and poked her cheek back mischievously. Macecle, her totem, accompanied her as her most valued protector. All Treedles bonded with their totem and other animal friends from the time of their birth. Survival at the top of a towering forest required them to weave a web of connections among peaceable animals, edible plants, and one another.

Laela's mother knocked on her door, "Laela, are you awake now? I have some breakfast for you."

Laela opened the door to the smell of steamed grains, honey, and nuts mixed into a porridge and a cup of bulbnut milk, which she never tired of eating. But this was, of course, a pretext for the mother-daughter 'talk' to follow. Tara didn't smile at her but looked at her with calm, appraising gray-lavender eyes. Laela had arrived home early from school, let her mother know she was suspended for an 'incident,' and asked if they could discuss it tomorrow as she would be staying home the following day. Her mother answered, "If you think it should wait, so be it."

"Thanks for breakfast in bed, mom," Laela said with a false note of cheeriness. "I think it is time to share the letter with you from Miss Adel." She handed a stiff envelope to her mother. "I didn't give it to you last night to not disturb your rest over something really rather silly. And I told Miss Adel I'm sorry, right away."

As it was her 'responsibility' to discuss Miss Adel's message with a parent, she chose to do so with her mother after their mutual night's rest before responding to it. Laela was still irritated that a woman of Miss Adel's age wouldn't brush off a kind of joke, especially after they had apologized. Also, she felt too old to still be in school anymore, let alone be suspended from it. But these were the last days of it, thank goodness.

While Laela ate her breakfast, with Macecle helping himself to some nuts, her mother sat in the hammock chair by Laela's bed and read the note. Her mother closed her eyes and breathed softly while Laela finished.

"So, Laela, how do you feel about what happened," Tara asked, "Do you think you deserved to be suspended from school?"

Miss Adel had written about not caring for her hurt feelings as much as Laela's apparent lack of sensitivity to others' feelings. Treedle Basic Education's whole purpose is to become a caring community member, an upholder of the principles of the 'One' in every aspect of life. So humor is not funny if it is at the expense of someone else's dignity. To make fun of a person is usually a way to reduce them and make yourself feel superior: the targeted other and you, the better, the more clever one. Also, wasting time and wasting resources on our school parchment isn't a Treedle virtue.

"Ah, mom, Miss Adel 'overly' interpreted this. She fusses over the smallest things. Maybe what I did wasn't pleasant, but she keeps repeating the same things over and over in classes. We have more than memorized her words and stories. I know them backward and forward now! She doesn't understand youth—our real needs sometimes. She doesn't interest us in learning new things. To be honest, she's like a burli-parrot (one with a bright feather fan springing from the crown of its head), and I drew a picture of her while she seemed to be almost babbling. I drew her with a bubble coming out of her mouth, saying blah, blah, blah.

Okay, as I tell you this, it does sound kind of bad, but I did it while giggling inside. We never imagined Miss Adele would see it. Only Phips, and he's as close to me as my heart. Oh, and he helped me draw it. Not, of course, to involve him in blame too." Laela stopped, disappointed at herself for bringing Phips into this. She usually wouldn't blurt out such information about a friend, especially such a close one. Her comfort was that her mother wasn't a person ever to repeat others' secrets or faults. She continued, "The situation for us isn't easy. Mama, really they should let us finish school much sooner. How can boredom be educational? We want to get on with 'life.'"

Her mother replied, "You sound angry, Laela. Were you angry when you made this joke?"

Laela answered," Maybe frustrated more than angry. Something has been building up inside me."

"And do you think that outside of school you will never be faced with boring and repetitive tasks? And outside of school, will it be okay to mock members of your community, especially your elders?" Tara eyed her firmly. "Laela, a more important question, for now, is if you would accept to have someone draw a picture of you as a most unflattering animal. A picture that wounds your pride?"

"I have a good sense of humor, mama; I would laugh." Laela retorted.

"Laela, be honest with yourself. If someone criticizes any of your 'creative' ideas, you become quite rattled. If someone doesn't take you seriously, you are the first to take offense. You were mocking Miss Adel. I don't hear any reflection about that in your words."

Laela felt a kind of jolt at her mother's frankness. Her mother usually gave advice so delicately that she wouldn't realize until later that she was correcting behavior or recommending another course of action. She got up to hand her mother the breakfast tray. Laela preferred to move around when she wanted to think things out.

"Mama, can I work some in the garden and then reflect about this in the afternoon?"

"Yes, but I hope that you will honor yourself, our family, and Miss Adel with some careful thought on this. Hurt to the heart is never little."

Laela nodded. There was no one whose approval she desired more than her mother's. Her mother was a kwanai or 'healer' who treated both the mind and body. Her mother always chose her words carefully as she said that stories are even more potent than the remedies she prepared from the herb gardens.

Her father was a scholar and dedicated most of his day thinking and writing in a quiet tree loft study. Her father would know volumes about intentions, but she and her mother rarely involved him in day-to-day concerns. Few Treedles spent full time practicing the art of philosophy. Her father was responsible for providing expert advice for the Treedle Elders and the Community Council, of which he was a member. He had a safely guarded library with a number of parchment scrolls and books with historical records of Treedle law and regulations for community life. Her father, Alvaro, appeared mostly at meals and never made small talk. Laela feared her father, but not in the way of danger or hurt, like with animals. She feared his disapproval or not making sense to him.

However, Laela felt her mother could outshine any of the most studied Treedles and was a philosopher of experience, an intuitive healer. Her mother spent hours every day in the gentle but demanding work of caring for the nurseries and creating herbal medicines, soaps, perfume scents, and candles from bee's wax. Treedles of all ages sought her mother out for consultations on problems ranging from trouble sleeping to a broken heart, often leaving no need for any other remedy. Her mother was a balm to her ardent nature, honey, to an unspoken wound. As much as she admired her mother, she would never be like her.

Laela's thoughts returned to that change in her life that would represent a beginning and an end, a force of nature over which she wouldn't have control. One that would change her permanently. Laela took a mirror apart from a simple telescope apparatus she had to study the stars at night. It was a precious possession, and few existed in the known world. Although vanity and self-admiration were highly discouraged in Aerizon, she occasionally used them to examine her face and body changes. Today, she stared into it for reassurance and to see her sameness. Her face was agreeable to her. An oval face, with large round, upturned eyes. Rarely smiling, alert, with a flexible and robust mouth—lips and tongue that could twist into acrobatic shapes to make calls and whistles at different frequencies through the forest.

Laela's body frame was small and light. Treedles rarely grew over half a meter tall. Many ages ago, her people were forced to emigrate far from an ocean land engulfed by vast floods, ultimately settling in the towering and strongly branched treetops of the forestland of Aerizon. Four clans with different shades of complexion: lavender, olive-green, rusty-copper, and golden-brown emerged. Three of the Treedle clans had a basic pearlescent gray undertone to their skin and hair, ranging from a chalky to an iridescent hue like the nacre of the inner shell of mollusks. These gray tints subdued the distinctive hues of their clan colors. All but one clan shared the same wiry hair that could look gray or silver depending on the light or shade in which they stood. These silvery-gray colorings had originally helped them blend in the sands, grasses, and corals of their ancient native land. The color-adaptive capacity of their bodies had enabled them to thrive at the forest heights as well. They could quickly submerge and camouflage themselves with objects nearby.

Laela's skin was suffused with lavender, which appeared pale lilac/gray in the bright sun. Her coloring heightened into a vibrant, deep lavender in her thick, petal-shaped eyelids. Her eyelids curved up with a dramatic flair, accentuating the inquisitive brightness of her pale gray-lavender eyes. Striking to see on any Treedle, these signature, large, thick, leaf or petal-shaped eyelids protected their eyes from the sun and indicated their family ancestry from a distance. The shape and the color of a Treedle's eyelids were signs of each of Treedle's three main clans. The long-ago estranged tribe of the four, the earthy-colored Mergons, had evolved in ways that fit the forest ground, a great distance below.

In ancient, peaceful times, Mergons had been service providers of all kinds but now were feared as warriors and usurpers of lands and enslavers of peoples. Tribal Elders regaled the Treedle youth with cautionary tales of the dangerous Mergons, who had evolved differently as ground people originally from the same race. They had lived farthest from the sea on higher hills, and when the floods arrived, they escaped to forested hills. They didn't join the other three clans in gradually building a treetop civilization in the lushest and tallest tropical forest of Aerizon.

Laela brushed her hair with a wooden brush Phips had made for her and tied her hair up in a bun on top of her head with brightly colored cotton bands that Oti had woven and dyed. She and Oti first met at school at age four. Oti sat beside her one day, smiled bashfully, and offered her half of a coconut sweet. From then on, they became—in short order—friends, confidants, and sisters.

If yesterday had gone as planned, she and Oti would meet Phips at his house late afternoon to talk until early evening. Tara consented if Phips accompanied her home. Phips' house had the best views of Aerizon and its sunsets, orange, fuchsia, pink, and purple waves of light cascading across the sky. Phips and Oti wanted to tell her 'something.' She knew well what it was and that the joy would be in the telling and not the news.

Phips' house was the ideal setting for sharing secrets or for playing. His family was among the most expert builders of the Bouder Clan. Phips would unveil the new wing of the house that he had barred both of them from seeing. His craftsmanship was developing to a state of artistry. He experimented with unexpected architectural forms—new shapes of resin windows- arched, encased, multicolored pains, suspended stair-towers with weavings of metallic cords and wooden steps, shingle textures, stained boards, and situating rooms for the most captivating views.

Laela felt fortunate that each of her best friends was from a different clan. It opened a more expansive world to her. She could spend many hours absorbing the smells, sounds, and vibrancy of the clan life in other neighborhoods of Aerizon. All were Treedles and citizens of one land, but each clan had very distinct characteristics and customs. The clans were denoted by their skin color and their extended communities' main occupations.

Laela sighed heavily, thinking of the loss to her when these two would join for life. They would remain friends, but the relationship would shift entirely. Oti would still be quietly and steadily present. But, Phips. She wouldn't be able to call on him any time, sneak off to hunt together, trade tools, or experiment with new ways of climbing, swinging, and traversing the forest.

She envisioned Phips standing on a branch exposed to the sky. Laughing. His skin was glowing burnished red-brown as if stained with wine resin. He exuded a powerful and noble presence with his broad shoulders, angular forehead, and well-articulated muscular hands. He would raise his prominently arched, russet eyelids in quizzical ways that made her laugh. His humor was a secret until you knew him.

He was becoming more serious, almost by the day now. He promised to bring much pride to the Bouder clan as a gifted hunter and inspired artisan and builder. He was blunt and truthful, valued Bouder qualities, but he was becoming more thoughtful about what he said or did. He was becoming a man.

Oti was no less strong or accomplished than Phips and wise as an elder. A Texare, she had a round face, and her almond-shaped eyes slanted up like half-moons. Her skin was silvery-olive like the underside of tender tree leaves. Oti's fingers were long and tapered, which favored her artistry with textiles and weaving. Hours with Oti could flow by gently, and Laela would never tire of her presence. Phips had found an ideal mate.

Laela mused to herself about how to make this day profitable. She settled on a project to improve her current kit of helpful outdoor gear. Courtesy of the team, Tan and Gibble, she had a lightweight camouflage jumper whose metallic-thread mesh helped her blend into any setting and protected her from volatile and sharp objects. She added extra pockets to the jumper to carry longer ropes for lassos and thin, translucent lines for tying and sewing. Today she was thinking of designing a sack with shoulder loops to carry heavier loads when hunting and foraging. She would need Tan and Gibble to spin two different kinds of lines for this.

She picked up a tray where Tan and Gibble were sleeping, nestled in leaves, and headed for the gardens. She shuffled them awake, "Come on, buddies. Time to work!"

CHAPTER 2

A Seed of Good

Laela opened a tunnel hatch into a netted walkway below her room that Phips built for their home. It led to the most extensive gardens of Aerizon that were distributed over a series of circular and interconnecting wooden decks. Affectionately called Joy Park, it was situated at the heart of their community and close to the town market and a small theater.

Her mother's life project was tending to private medicinal gardens and nurseries and overseeing the public parks—always open to the community. Her family had a private entrance as caretakers of the gardens. There were two other public entrances on different sides of the central park. Visitors entered through an initial door into a netted walkway and then opened a flap door to enter the garden. The double doors helped ensure that butterflies remained within where it was safer to breed and feed. The number and variety of butterflies, who fearlessly danced on Treedles' fingertips and through the flowers, brought endless delight.

The decks were built around the broadest and sturdiest trees and set into the firmest nooks in their branches. They were supported below by strong buttresses and anchored to the tree trunks with nails and metallic cords at key points. The west side of the gardens, from which the strongest winds blew, was shielded by a wooden wall made from rough-hewn logs. Meandering paths led around small sloping moss and grass-covered mounds and a shallow, pebble-lined fishpond. Lush fronds and ferns lined the main paths, making a canopy of fresh greenness. From around the bends, pops of color and luxurious hillocks were overflowing with foliage and fragrant flowers. Each surrounding garden area contained different beds and patches of flowers, trim bushes, and miniature fruit orchards. The roots of larger plants grew below the flooring as holes cut out and wire bulb-like containers were created to hold their needed soil.

An armature of sleek metal ribs arched overhead, encasing the garden and forming a cupola on top that was covered with fine, translucent netting. Smaller netted domes and spires flanked the central garden area. The effect from afar was of a light, air-borne cathedral with surrounding chapels.

Extended family members and various regular helpers tended to the daily upkeep of the garden. Today, Laela would water the earthen floor to moisten it and make small puddles for those birds who needed the wettest areas. She would prune bushes and gather flowers for baskets for the elders who couldn't visit the gardens.

She stopped to greet baby Lucas, who was hanging in a basket, just inches above a moss and violet garden, cooing to himself. Laela bent over, and Lucas rewarded her with a smile that opened his creamy, pale face with its lavender-rose-colored cheeks into a full blossomed giggle. The sweetness in his nature was evident from birth. He easily interacted with others and required little attention to thrive. With his lithe limbs and sculptured chest, he promised to be a strong and gentle young man. She stroked his soft gray curls and offered him a bright blue gorsli feather from her pocket to hold.

She would play with him more after finishing the essential garden chores. They would escape the mid-day sun in a hammock under giant frodi leaves.

Laela's mother had systematically planned this garden to become the largest butterfly, hummingbird, flower, and herb sanctuary in the airborne kingdom. There were butterfly bushes and star flowers in vivid hues of purple, yellow, white, flaming red, eye-popping pink, and twilight blue. Then there were the signature orchids, lavender, fuchsia, butter yellow, and cream-colored ones. The orchids in the upper reaches grew attached to the trees' trunks, securing the sanctuary on four sides. Laela's family fashioned little bark trays, and some of the orchids remained inside, while others surrounded the tree trunks on the outer sides of the netted garden.

First came her primary task. Laela walked over to a spacious mulching station hidden by a rock garden where Tan and Gibble could work without being disturbed. Tan had shrunk almost in half, and the trailing sack that accompanied her production of line was a wisp between her two longer lower legs. Gibble lay squinched up by a rock, his eyes almost shut. The two were in bad moods and utilizing their limited but very expressive high-sonic vocabulary to bicker again. Tan complained about Gibble's lazy and inconsistent munching and fetching habits and his reluctance to feed into her the needed masticated bundi leaves for producing the wiry, tensile-like moonline.

"It isn't me who is depending on you; it is our Mistress, lazy lump!" Tan signaled to emphasize with her knotted feet and wagging feelers and with words that Laela interpreted as "Goodness, all you have to do is drag your stomach around and eat. Is it too much to ask you to do your job and just pass the mulch to me?"

The spiders' moonline was six times stronger than the best metal wire produced by Mergones. The threads they created for clothing could be stretched to twice their length without breaking. The gossamer they made for clothing and textiles was soft as a caress on the body. Certain weaves of silk in layers could help keep a Treedle either warm or cool as needed.

Tan and Gibble were the spawn of the best spiders and feeder-worms on Oti's breeding farm. The large round aural spiders, like

Tan, were almost as flat as coin and semi-translucent when their stomachs were empty. They had a bag-like storage system attached to their spiraled digestive system that contained small and large ducts. Tan had eight different spinneret glands to produce the various kinds of lines or threads required. Each type of thread required a given mixture of leaves and insects that the feeder worm fed to the spider.

The spiders mated with a feeder worm for life. This gave a duo much time to practice! When Tan and Gibble worked in synchrony, they produced some of the best threads and lines in the treetop community. With the worm's companionship to break down food, the spiders could produce more rapidly as they would have to break down prey into a liquid globule to suck them into their stomachs. Tan could also emit a gel-like substance to be used as glue, which involved spitting out the digested leaves of the bundi tree before turning them into threads. Even the waste that Tan excreted was valuable for its healing properties for skin wounds. They collected this in small resin containers for Laela's mother's healing room.

Laela set the two in a nice cozy corner with some moss and branches for them to repose on, surrounded by a large pile of bundi leaves she had recently gathered in the large gathering sack made with course, sturdy but stretchy 'every day' threads from Tan and Gibble. Gently nudging Gibble, she said," Now, Gibble dear, get inspired and eat steadily. We need metallic silk lines for a very special sack. I'll be able to gather choice leaves for you and carry much more food for the family." She added cheerily, "This is an important job, so be a good team!" She picked up Tan and tapped out a pattern on her back to clarify which line was requested.

Once Gibble got engorged to four times his regular size, he would wobble over to relieve his stomach by feeding Tan. He always looked most content just after letting go of his excess cargo, with enough to satisfy his more minimal nutrient needs. Gibble's favorite activities were resting and chattering or combining the two.

"And Tan, be patient and enjoy the feeding and company in the garden. Lucas's cooing should be music to your ears." Tan's miniature ears were especially attuned to high-pitched voices.

Looking about her, she noticed dead leaves to sweep and some drooping flowers that could do with watering. The gentle motions of sweeping and tending always put her in a reflective mood.

When they were 'startlings,' Miss Adel used to bring her class to learn to water and weed the gardens from their beginning school years. She encouraged them to observe the work other creatures do in the gardens. "Now watch the bees, butterflies, and hummingbirds. What are they doing?"

"Buzzing in circles, flying, dancing, moving their heads and beaks, and landing on the flowers." the children cried out.

'Indeed,' Miss Adel nodded. "But they don't just hover over the flowers to admire their petals. What else are the bees and hummingbirds doing today? Look for clues."

The students agreed that the birds and bees were most attracted to the stamens and sticking their noses in them. Were they snuggling, sipping, or eating?

Feril pointed and said, "They're getting something yellow on them!"

"Yes, and what do you think is stuck to their bill and feathers?"

"Fairy dust?" Nivea queried. "Yellow dirt?" Tomi ventured.

"Now, class, look closely at this bee that was just on the lily's anthers and stamens." Ms. Adel had expertly caught one in a thin glass jar so the students could see the yellow dust on the bee's feet and belly up close. "This yellow dust is called pollen. Pollen is needed for the flower to produce seeds for her babies: fruits and more flowers. When I release the bee, she'll fly to a flower that needs pollen to grow seeds. Later the flowers will fall, and fruits will appear, and you will eat delicious fruits because these bees have worked so hard."

"They seem happy like they're having fun," one of the girls said, tracing a finger in the sky to follow a bee's bouncing movements.

"The bees and birds are happy and tireless in their work because they're 'sowing seeds of good.' And just as they get nectar and food from the flowers, they're helping the flowers produce food for us!" Ms. Adel fluttered her hands and twirled with delight.

Ms. Adel often used the relationship between the butterflies and flowers to teach children how reciprocal relationships work in nature and among Treedles. Bees and butterflies are attracted to the tall colorful clusters of flowers, like dizzy lovers. They land on them and sip out the hidden nectar from one flower, unaware that they're dipping their feet with the flower's pollen. As they move to feed on other flowers, they impregnate them with the pollen they carry. Pollen slides down the feminine pistil and fertilizes hidden ovules, initiating the flower's death, the life of the seed, and the fruit's birth—the feeding of one giving life to the other.

"Life depends on our complementary roles and also on our sacrifices one for the other," Mr. Henri would tell the 'explorer's class.' Then he would proceed to the lesson on birds and the bees' mating. It started with 'Mr. Stamen and Mrs. Pistil.' Every generation heard the same story. It was easy to grasp impregnation through flowers, but Laela and Oti often giggled about how 'mating' and procreation appeared to be anything but gentle in the animal world. They would tease each other, "May it be like the flowers for you when you mate!"

Laela passed by a berry tree in full bloom and picked an incredibly lush berry blossom that quietly fluttered to the ground. It was still fragrant, still a vibrant flower. But it had fulfilled its perfection and would wilt away in the dell of death, formless and forgotten. Laela cupped it tenderly in her hands and thought how quickly her childhood was giving way to the season of maturity. She ached to think of her own life after the promising time of flowering to a beyond in which she would be submerged in the predictable rhythms of Treedle womanhood. Rocking cradles, stirring pans, comforting babies and men. She had no interest, no desire to fulfill the roles that awaited her. Nor did she want to become an apprentice to her mother, whom she adored. What would life be like for her then?

She tiptoed in her mind around the taboos spoken and unspoken for women. There were questions she was even still afraid to explore—even in the quiet of her mind—as she didn't like to shirk from the truth or its consequences. Those around her noticed her hobbies and pastimes weren't common to girls on the brink of womanhood. Her parents warned her about rudeness and disrespect. She seemed to need many more reminders about this than other girls. They counseled her frequently on courtesy and the careful choice of her words.

But on the other hand, she felt extreme sensitivity, even pain, and tenderness in the hidden recesses of both her breast and heart. Were men this sensitive? She didn't want to be a man, yet why did she most long do what men do? How terribly sinful or unspeakably divergent would it be to cherish the dreams of daring to be herself, a girl with big dreams? Why did history rarely tell of brave women: explorers, women who leave an indelible legacy, who write epistles, and those who change the course of events?

Why must a woman be a shadow or, at most, a valued servant in their world? In the end, it seemed to her that mothers and daughters were ultimately raised to be servants to men. A woman was valued more than an animal but not as much as a man, though they praise Treedle women to kingdom come. While no one claimed it an outright law, every custom guided women to their place in the home—their ultimate realization: motherhood and caring for the next generation.

Only Laela's mother, of all the women she knew, had found a graceful way to expand her work outside the home, her garden into a project that permeated the community's life, and herself into the only female apothecary presiding over the largest store of medicinal herbs in the land. Tara was so gentle and self-effacing that her influence had spread, unnoted, until it became as pervasive and imperceptible as air. She threatened no one and served everyone.

Well, service is undoubtedly worthy, but could it be that women could serve the community in ways men do?

Laela stopped, suddenly too tired to continue working, and laid back on the moss under an arbor of vines and flowers. These questions played and played in her mind without an answer. Tara could be a model, but then Laela was nothing like her, really. "How will this me, this demanding yet very delicate me, survive?"

She pulled out a light silk scroll with teachings from the 'One' that most Treedles carried in little water-proof pouches. Every Treedle should study Writings of the 'One' in the morning and evening and always keep the 'One's' words near. The lettering on these scrolls was inscribed with the finest penmanship in long-lasting ink by Treedle monks.

She preferred to do her devotions sitting in the garden. She saw the 'One' as a friend but also as a powerful sovereign holding the universe in the palm of His hand. She would approach Him in different ways. Sometimes in simple conversation and sometimes with all her heart, stretched wide and open, in complete lowliness to beg Him for assistance. Especially when hunting.

She closed her eyes and let her finger slide through the scroll, and stopped at the verses:

"Be kind to others and a balm to their hearts."

"What you give is who you are. Your heart is your treasury. Keep in it the pure golden light of love, the stamps of good thoughts, and the seeds of good actions. Your generosity toward others is your wealth."

"Giving is wealth..." She felt that she must find a way to give and to be herself. In some form or other, the question suffused her mind like tea tinting water,

"I can't help wanting to be me and not a lost flower of youth. There must be something good I can do. I want to be rich in good deeds. Just not the kind that the other sweet women around me do."

"Oh, 'One,'" she asked, hoping that in some clear way, her prayers would be answered, "How can I be good and be me?"

She turned her mind to the incident with Miss Adele and being treated like a child. It occurred to her that even if Miss Adele didn't always 'get' her, she could give understanding to her. It would bring her peace to clean the slate, but if Miss Adele were hurt, not just any words would do.

She pictured different moments in the familiar sunlit classroom dappled by light from the waving branches outside. With her wiry white hair, tiny dark eyes, and jowly cheeks, and pointy nose, Miss Adel was always alive with interest in their questions, in their learning. Though plump and slow-moving, she had endless stores of inner energy. She spoke in small gusts of excitement and gestured her hands as if she were ringing tiny bells. Her delicate, pale hands were her most beautiful feature, and they seemed to dance in the air whenever she became excited over a topic. She was dotty and wise, cheerful, and demanding. She lived and breathed for her small charges.

Miss Adele would often stop a class to share a story of the history of the Treedles and their arrival in Aerizon and the founding of their peaceful Kingdom and civilization. She made the children so proud of their community and their identity.

It was unkind to mock this teacher, a teacher who transmitted goodness. She chided herself, "Where would I be without Miss Adele's love, care and teaching? She has been a second mother to me. Though maybe sometimes an irritating one. But those irritations are like dust that doesn't cling to her true gold. She had learned so many lessons with Miss Adele that helped her understand Treedle culture and how to live the best way possible. "I don't wish for this trouble to be her last memory of me." She decided she would talk to her tomorrow. "This won't be an apology. Those don't change things very much. I will show her my true appreciation."

CHAPTER 3

Wooing Woes

Miss Adele wept copiously when Laela finished her simple but heartfelt tribute to her. She embraced Laela, her body heaving with waves of emotion. "My dear Laela, you have no idea of what your words mean to me. I appreciate them and will never forget them; they show me that you are more than ready to graduate. That you are becoming quite a woman."

She stepped back and looked out the window into the thick green shadow, "I'm sure you think I'm lighthearted and maybe silly sometimes. But I made a vow to be as happy and cheerful as possible for my students. No one wants to be with a sour-faced teacher."

"Maybe you don't know this, but I have had enough losses to keep me sad for the rest of my life. My husband died from a fall after climbing too high on a fragile branch to gather nuts from a tree when Petro was just four. Petro was my only child. Then Petro, who always missed his father, ventured off at age twelve to accompany a scouting team who traveled far to purchase Mergone metal tools. He was a strong and stocky boy and able to carry a lot of weight on his back. However, the team got captured by a military troop of Mergones who were patrolling border towns. I heard tell he has worked as a slave in a mining camp all these years. I have no family left, and you children are my family, my life."

Miss Adele remained strangely silent, with tears dripping onto her plump bosom. Laela didn't move or speak but tried to absorb some of this pain. A loss this great was beyond what she could imagine. After some moments, Miss Adele said, "Thank you. You may go now to your class with Mr. Rorsat. These are your very last days at school, and these are your most advanced and important lessons. I especially want our Treedle youth to know how to protect and defend themselves."

Laela left feeling as if a new pocket of her heart had opened. Sometimes you could be with a person for years and never know the more important things about them. She would carry a part of Miss Adele's pain as a flower pressed between pages in her heart. She exited the main classroom area and walked across the rope bridge to a large log-walled room where they took self-defense and community protection classes.

Treedles were easy prey for raptors and needed to learn to protect themselves from poisonous plants and animals abounded in the forest. Their forms of self-defense must always conform with the Teachings of the 'One.' They weren't killers or hunters, though they might all kill or hunt in prescribed ways and times. The laws took a while to understand, and even the methods of quick and merciful killing took years to master as different methods should be employed with different animals.

Mr. Rorsat, who looked like a kindly tree rat with a thatch of curls on the crown of his head, was their physical education and life-skill teacher. He taught them how to scale trees, jump distances, make ropes and knots, how to swing from tree to tree on a rope, how to lasso and snare an animal who is trying to bite or attack you. He showed them tools and strategies to avoid accidents and falls in the higher branches of the trees. In classes, they would practice using their bodies—bending, stretching, jumping—to escape dangerous situations and avoid hurt.

He told them vivid stories about the habits and habitats of forest predators and how to tell a gentle herbivore from a rapacious flesh-eating or biting animal.

"Remember to be aware of predators, to be ready, and to rehearse in your mind how you will act with each different kind of predator. You must practice, so it becomes a habit—how you will react instantly should a Hookbeak snatch you from behind or a green viper be slithering toward you."

And during this last year of schooling, Mr. Rorsat had especially emphasized their duty to use their skills wisely, "You'll remember that a Treedle isn't a predator but a person who always thinks of the most peaceful solution to violent situations. There's a land where people are predators; they strike, hit, wound, and even kill one another with their hands or weapons. And that land is far below us. In that land, people can be as dangerous and even crueler than animals. They enjoy making their human victims feel pain and hearing them cry and scream, which is an abomination of nature. Even the most rapacious predators in Aerizon make quick meat of their victims when they're hungry. The killing deed is over in seconds.

"Treedles will sometimes be victims of predators, but they must never be a predator. They must never hurt a human or innocent being unless in the last instance of self-defense. And never out of anger and vengeance. Treedles don't kill for fun or sport, only for the small amount of meat needed for the community. Any Treedle who hurts another when it's not a need is worse than a Mergon."

He never lost a chance to remind them of the ultimate enemy, living far below—the most significant potential danger to their civilization. Everyone knew that the Mergon would one day find a way to scale the heights of the forest to procure even more slaves from among them as their cities grew.

Miss Adele would never speak of Mergones as adversaries or compare them to Treedles. She would emphasize that her pupils need to understand their culture and one day be able to 'enlighten' these people who knew so little about peace and goodwill. If Laela's father heard tell of Mr. Rorsat's running commentaries about evil Mergones, he would say this just fans the flame of hatred. And then, how are we different?

Many students, herself included, were interested in how Treedles could avoid becoming victims of Mergones. And still be law-abiding Treedles!

Laela enjoyed hunting the meat that was needed for the community. And this she dare never confess to anyone but Phips. The animals they chose to pursue for food were sacrificed with a prayer. She enjoyed chasing the tree rodents in particular and felt no remorse in capturing and instantly slitting their throats. She associated them as sacrifices for a greater need. She would bag them but let Phips offer them to the community for their basic needs. Though some people suspected or even knew she hunted, she could continue while still a child as long as she didn't announce it. She would be the first to defend innocent life. She knew this. She was the first to protect her community in the face of any kind of threat. Love and care were mixed with a sense of duty to protect herself and others in her heart.

Today, she was the last one to enter Mr. Rorsat's class. He was giving instructions about the finer points of lassoing. She was drawn immediately to Vito's eyes. He was regarding her intently and brazenly—daring her to look away. Vito was one of the taller Treedle youth and by far the most traditionally handsome with his heroic profile, long muscle-twined arms, hair molded artfully with resin-gel, and bold, full-lipped mouth. His posture, confident and alert, he would turn his chiseled cheeks at striking angles that commanded attention and admiration. His sculpted body was the perfect example of prime male physique; sinuous and toned, pectoral muscles well-defined, and even hued, polished lavender skin.

He possessed an uncanny ability to cast a visual moonline and ensnare female attention. To Laela's discomfort, it did its magic on her, and she had reluctantly become one of his many female admirers. However, the more she interacted with him, she felt they were developing a different relationship, and she was his sole genuine interest. His popularity was an obstacle they would overcome. He had moved to Aerizon some three months ago from another nearby tree community. From the beginning, he signaled his interest in Laela.

Laela knew that to captivate such a lovely and bright man, she would have to allow him to chase after her, to woo her, and work to capture her heart. He wasn't only handsome but knowledgeable and talented in almost every way.

Always confident, always with the right answers, constantly gaining admiration. When his female admirers would praise his prowess, he would tilt his head bashfully and defer to his teachers' instructional abilities. "If they weren't so patient with me, I wouldn't be able to hunt a lame squirrel." He appeared to decline compliments while continually eliciting them: an art in and of itself, Laela thought with a mixture of attraction and a bit of nagging doubt.

Despite any vanities, deserved or undeserved, his aura of power was intoxicating to her. He was a match for her—a worthy life partner.

Their flirtation began almost immediately, and Laela played coy when he would brag about hunting exploits or show her how accurately and far he could shoot arrows. One day, Laela commented about her preference for short slings and their accuracy over long slings. Her sling was a natural extension of her arm, and she had learned to hunt small animals with ease and precision using it. She pulled her sling out without thinking and showed her favorite figure-eight throwing technique with a small round pellet. "See that dark spot on the tree over there? Watch!" Whirring the sling behind her, the pellet flew speedily and hit straight on target. Vito observed her with narrowed eyes, and she was unsure if he was admiring her aim or was somewhat annoyed.

"Quite an aim you have. So, is it true you hunt with Phips? Do you hunt the animals, or does he?" Vito's voice was cold.

"Yes." She replied bluntly and defending herself with bravado, "I can hunt and catch any animal you can, Mr. Vito." She saw no reason to apologize for her prowess or lie to him about how she used it, though she immediately felt he might use this information against her—wooing her and all.

Vito's smile was clenched, and his eyes glinted in disapproval. He leaned close to her and whispered, "When you are mine, I will be the man, and you will be the woman. I like how strong and sassy you are, but never forget, you are a woman. Or should I say," he laughed strangely, "Almost a woman."

Soon after that encounter, they were talking after school, and he walked home with her and asked if they could sit in the park. After some stories of his recent hunting and bravery, he leaned in close to her, and she could feel her shoulder tingle, her hair cross her face in the breeze, and a sudden shortness of breath. His presence was magnetic and immobilizing. He tilted her head back gently with the point of his finger and looked deeply into her eyes. He spoke in low musical tones,

"I just want to tell you that there's no one like you. No girl here holds a candle to you. You are full of fire and passion; you are spirit and light. I watch you all the time, lovely Laela, how you speak up in class, how you move, how you laugh. You think differently than other girls. You're smart and also the most beautiful of all the girls in Aerizon in my eyes. You're the queen of my heart."

Laela held on to each word, rendered mute. She felt a trickle of sweat seeping down her neck and her lips parting as if to gulp air. She had no clever or poetic response. No one had ever spoken to her like this. She let his admiration seep through her every pore and stir new passions. In his penetrating dark lavender eyes, she felt seen for the first time, really seen. And also possessed by him, but in a pleasing way. At that moment, she was ready to consider cooking and baby care for the rest of her life if he would quench her thirst for being cherished like this. If he would look at her like this for the rest of her life, tying their souls together, she would never be empty and unmoored again.

Laela spoke at last and was barely able to raise her head, her voice, "Vito, I'm flattered by your words. Let me speak with you later about my feelings. You surprised me right now." She took his hands in hers and said, "Thank you," and she smiled wryly, "Be patient with me, dear Vito. I'm shy about these matters."

She was too overwrought to see the effect of her tepid response. It would become more apparent for her as she looked for clues of what went wrong later.

But not a week had passed, and Laela was surrendering herself in love. She would even wake in the middle of the night thinking of Vito. She was eager for them to create more chapters in their story and for him to transform her heart with warm and alluring words.

After his confession to her, he hadn't been around. She would look for him, and in class, he would avert his eyes from her. She chided herself, "He's waiting for me to make the next move now. But I have to get this right." She debated endlessly with Oti about what she would say.

Oti would gently try to steer her away from Vito. Laela couldn't understand why her friend wouldn't support her and rejoice that she had found her mate to be. Wasn't Oti her best friend? Oti refused to say why, but she could tell that she didn't like Vito. Finally, Laela insisted, "What do you have against Vito? Has he hurt you? Has he hurt anyone? He's excellent at everything he does; maybe that makes him seem too good to be true. Is that it?"

"No, Laela," Oti pursed her lips, reluctant to say the following, "You're such a dear friend, Laela, and I have to say what is in my heart. I want to protect you like a sister. Perhaps, I shouldn't say this because I may be wrong. It is just that I simply don't trust him. I think he has two faces. I can't say why either, but I fear he won't be loyal to you."

Laela cringed at this dream-crushing speculation. It was as if Oti was taking sweet taffy out of her hands, saying it was spoiled, just as she began to enjoy it. "Thanks, Oti," she replied stiffly. "You are my friend, and you should say what you feel. But this makes me really sad, and I just hope you are wrong, very wrong. You usually are so fair in your judgment. But you haven't gotten to know Vito."

"I've never seen you talk to him. This is my chance to experience the love of my life. You have yours; why not be happy for me finding mine?"

Oti shook her head, "I wish I could."

"Who would you rather have me mate? If Vito is the wrong suitor for me, then whom would you recommend?"

Oti's face softened with a warm smile, "There is someone who adores you, always has. He's gentle, intelligent, and responsible. He comes from a great family of Treedle scholars. He would make a wonderful and faithful mate."

"Pray tell?" Laela asked, knowing who it would be. Leon. Everyone from Miss Adele to her, the lady in the grain store, would discuss the merits of Leon in her presence. No one in Aerizon was subtle about matchmaking. It was a major Treedle pastime.

"Leon."

"Now, let me be open and honest with you. Which I always am. Though not on the topic of Leon yet. I never talk to you about Leon as I would rather be an unmarried woman the rest of my life than live with him. He bores me. He's slow: an old man in a young body, an unfit body at that. He's puffy and chubby from lack of exercise. He talks too much about philosophy—also boring. I can't, and I won't mate him. Oti, I can't, WILL NOT be his mate in or out of the mating bed."

Oti gasped, "Laela, that's very unkind of you. You shouldn't speak ill of such a good person. He's one of the finest young men in all of Aerizon."

Laela shrugged. She also doubted how good she was. "Then, I most evidently don't deserve him. And I ask you to please be the first one to stop trying to matchmake me with him. I would appreciate it very much."

So she kept this growing passion to herself. She fantasized all day long about more whispered endearments that would fill her with ecstasy and the world of understanding and intense attraction that would be uniquely theirs. They would feed this love and weave it strong with the secrets of their hearts, with daily stories and encounters. And each day would add richness to the tapestry of 'them,' united, mated forever.

She possessed a heightened sensitivity to his presence and could almost smell where he was or would be. But two weeks had gone by now, and it was time; they hadn't spoken, and she had to make a move.

She feared letting him know how far and fast she was falling. It might cool his ardor to see her as silly and weak as any girl in this field of love. She decided to find him that day after school, determined to be brave enough to show her feelings in just the right amount. She would scout out where he was and then appear to bump into him casually.

After school let out, she began her search walking toward the backside of the primary school building where there was a bench with a lovely view of the forest. Her instincts had led her right to 'him.' She noticed Vito was standing close to someone; they were side to side. It was Lili. Lili was an obvious contender for any young man's heart. She was delicate, and her lips curved up naturally into an inviting smile. She was the epitome of feminine grace and good manners. More beautiful than Laela by those unspoken standards that identified the fairest females of the land.

They were looking intensely at one another and didn't notice her. Laela stepped back close to the side of the wall flanking this balcony. She crouched down, melding into the shadows, peering out between the leaves of a plant that placed strategically at the edge of the wall. She watched as Vito took one of Lili's hands, sidled up close to her, and then tipped her chin back and gazed into her eyes in the same way he had done with her. Lili responded immediately by leaning into his chest and embracing him. She could see Lili radiating joy as if sunbeams were encircling her. Lili was enthralled. In this moment, she was his. His alone.

Laela's stomach contracted, and she all but doubled over with nausea. She couldn't be more surprised. Seeing her magical encounter with Vito played out with Lili instead of her was a bad dream playing out in daylight. If only it were a momentary hallucination or a bad dream, she could melt the panic away with a few reassuring and grounding words. But the truth was clear, absolute, and unbearably harsh. Every emotion she knew was pummeling her inside—shock, shame, anger, sadness. Havoc.

Her first instinct was to walk up to the two of them—disturbing their special moment like casting a stone into a bowl of water. But she would look angry and jealous, hardly a winning move. And why hurt Lili? She was the perfect girl, a delicate and pure maiden who was now looking up at Vito as her lord and savior. It wasn't Lili's fault. Lili had never shown any competitiveness or mean-spiritedness of any kind.

She had to leave quickly now, before Vito, who also had keen instincts, noted her lurking. She took a route home where she would encounter few, if any, people. She headed toward some dark vine-covered paths that Treedles rarely used. Older walkways had been replaced by newer and more visible ones recently. She was running, tears streaming down her cheeks. She didn't want to arrive at home and have to explain why she was so distraught. She had a special alone place for these moments. Halfway home and covered with vines was a tree with a large and deep hollow. She left a straw mat there for times when she wanted to think in calm and quiet.

The old musky tree encompassed her into its time-carved heart. She lay down and listened to the forest sounds, the barely notable swaying of the old tree's branches. She sought desperately for words that might help her through the storm of pain.

If she could understand it, she could bear it, eventually. Her mind swung wildly around different versions of what she had seen. Had she pushed him away with her silence? Was he seeking another woman as if on the rebound from her? But no, she hadn't rejected him. He must have seen how she melted that day. Or had she not shown it? She thought her eyes mustn't have glazed and misted like Lili's, her vulnerability as naked as a newborn baby.

No, the problem wasn't her. Even if she had been so awkward, she had given Vito too many signs of her own growing interest. It was him, and why, why would he do this?

It had to be his nature. She began to re-look at the past, and incidents came flowing back to her in a new light. Times when teachers recognized him for good work or deeds and how he preened with praise. He wouldn't humbly deflect as Phips would or give any credit to those who supported him. He felt fully worthy of that and more. And more. Whenever he helped others, he would make it quite apparent in some way, adding further proof of how wonderful he was. When he spoke his honeyed words to her, it wasn't love then. It was to draw her to him so she would reflect adoration to him. Her swooning loss of self would feed his manhood. He was preparing her to be the woman he wanted her to be. Becoming his mate would depend on how she enhanced him. For now, Vito had seduced her, and she was simply a notable conquest, one that he could dangle on a string along with others. She was his prey and not his Queen. He was as dangerous to her as any raptor.

She simply couldn't be one of many prized coral beads, a form of money in Aerizon. Laela felt rage as great as the swooning love that had taken root so quickly in her. The following ideas firing through her mind were desperately cruel and centered on ways that she could publicly humiliate him. But, if Vito were so competent at conquering women, he would find a way to get even or worse. Revenge wouldn't be sweet for long.

She kept a low profile at dinner. Her parents were thankfully engaged in an enthused discussion on the finer points of cooking a new root that explorers had brought to Tara. She was cultivating different planting systems in the garden.

She left early the next day, telling her mother that she needed to pack breakfast to meet Oti before school. It was a day when school started later, and she would have time to examine strategies with the best of listeners.

Oti didn't say I told you so but held and rocked her. They sat in Oti's comfortable and light-filled living room with its tall ceilings and colorful woven wall hangings. Oti's mother had designed long lace window curtains that left dappled patterns on the smooth oiled floor. Oti's family collected parrots of all kinds. Her totem, Frida, a red cockatoo with sparkly top knots at the crown of its head, was sitting on Oti's shoulder.

Frida looked at her and mewed. Nodding her head as in sympathy with Laela. Oti stroked Laela's hair and asked, "My dear sister, have you really lost anything with Vito? Think with me, what has he given to Lili either? Better, what has he taken from both?"

Oti was the 'thinker.' Excellent at math and science. She observed situations carefully and quickly detected both the details and major lessons that mattered.

Oti's line of reasoning was bringing her a glimmer of hope.

"We are both his victims. We're equally naive."

"Yes, as you should be. Why should you know the ways of a wily mind? Do you think he acts with love, Laela?" Oti looked at her seriously, and she knew this wasn't a question.

"I thought so, but everything points to Vito being in love with himself. Vito, first and foremost. And the worst part is that I'm not over him. I still love him for some crazy reason." Laela confessed. Why not unburden the pendulum that was her heart to her best friend.

"Ah, Laela, passion and desire take strange forms. They hide in the guise of pleasure and joy, and then they rob you of true pleasure and joy. Remember what we learned from your father in our class on preparing for mated life? I think a lot about how tricky passion is. Your Vito is a passion master!"

Laela could say that with just the first taste of it, that passion has its incredible moments. She could easily be swayed, but perhaps not so easily if she remembered her free fall into an abyss of pain. She thought of the words they had studied,

"Material passions lead to disillusionment, and spiritual behavior leads to happiness."

Some of these choices weren't clear, not black and white. Why was passion so enticing? Was her desire for Vito physical or spiritual? Well, for sure, the physical attraction was real. But could it also be a mix of both? How does one tell the sublime from the ordinary when everything about Vito seemed sublime?

"Oti, my feelings tricked me. I was sure this was love, love for all time." Laela's eyes were swollen from the hours of crying.

"I feel sure there will be a right man for you. He may be in another village. You don't have to choose between Leon and Vito. You will have other choices as well."

Laela was resigned, "No, I won't marry. This business of finding a match is showing me; I'm taking the wrong path. I would rather be a spinster. I promise to be a lively one—a great aunt to your children.

I can't bear wanting someone this much again and them not being there for me" Laela was still not ready to think of what she would do next. The pain was fresh and haunting.

After cooling her eyes with tea leave compresses and many assurances that she would recover quickly from this disillusionment, they went to school.

And the first person they saw, the one who hadn't been in sight and tucked himself away somehow even in their shared classes, was standing at the entrance to the school.

"Laela," he smiled effusively. "How are you? We have a conversation to finish. How about we meet on the back balcony after school?"

"I have plans after school, Vito," Laela shot stones at him with her eyes. "However, I'm sure that there are other girls for you to finish conversations with."

The coldness in her voice and gaze should have given him a push to his knees.

She made to move on, linking her arm into Oti's. He came to her side, undaunted, and whispered into her ear, "Jealous, are we?" He winked at her. "There's a cure for that, and you know what it is. I'm an all-or-nothing guy. I take all. Nothing less."

Laela felt the jolting anger pump through her and restrained her hand from slapping him. "Don't bother speaking to me again, ever!" she couldn't help but raise her voice. "You're nothing to me." Oti pulled her along to distract her before she could drive herself into a verbal frenzy. Oti knew her temper.

And then there was Leon. He was watching this scene, puzzled and concerned. He moved as if wanting to be by her side. But she turned her head to interrupt this signal of sympathy.

Right now, in class, thankfully one of their last school classes ever, he was watching her again. Vito and Laela were connecting as they always did when they were in an enclosed space together. Leon, on the sidelines, was watching their dance of daggers and false smiles, not knowing what to do to stop it, aching to move but never moving in—quietly offering his soul to Laela.

Mr. Rorsat was asking for volunteers to demonstrate a long-reaching lasso movement. Vito stepped forward into the middle of the room, "Please allow me to show you my favorite move." He coiled up the strong rope that he was proud to own. He stepped around, holding it to his side, and dancing in a circular pattern, building momentum. Then, he started twirling his lasso powerfully over his head. He kept his eye on Laela, and she braced herself as he was sighting her and seemed to be lunging to trap her in a lasso hold. However, he turned sharply in a snap and veered the lasso toward Lili, encircling her in one fell swoop. He roped her in slowly until she was shivering with giggles in his arms. He released her, and she stood spellbound for a time, snagged into place by the rope of his charm. The students laughed loudly and applauded. Vito passed around to where Laela was standing and tipped his head to her with another luxurious wink.

Infuriating. And she wished she were just feeling hatred. And to find very sweet revenge. If this was a game, she was losing every round.

CHAPTER 4

Engagement

School finished with a simple graduation ceremony held in the school auditorium—a large deck with a thatched roof overlooking their air-born village. It was a solemn event filled with speeches from teachers, students, and community members. Teachers highlighted the special qualities and talents of each student. They talked about Oti's gifts with math and science, her maturity and good citizenship, and praised Phips' manual dexterity and ability to reason. Laela was surprised when they signaled her for her perception, quick wit, and problem-solving skills.

It was harder than Laela thought to say good-bye to what was their second home, every day for four hours since they were three years old. It had prepared them well for community life and work. Her education had been well-rounded and most of the time in class was rich with stories they told or stories they created in their hours of interactions with each other. Learning had been alive, experiential, and meaningful for them. They had acquired many new and needed skills. Only in these last months had schooling begun to seem tiresome. But that was a good sign too. It meant that they were ready to move on.

Laela reflected all that day and into the ceremony how many 'firsts' her cohort of friends had shared. She remembered the time they learned to distinguish leaves and fruits by taste. They took turns blindfolding one another for the taste testing. They had laughed companionably about how hard it was for Phips to recognize herbs. They were in awe of how easy it was for Oti, who could name any leaf by touch or taste. They had learned to tie objects with loops and knots to move and lift them. How many times they had dropped and shattered delicate objects while learning how to handle their different shapes and weights! They had numerous adventures and misadventures, learning to swing from vines, how to use a treetop stove efficiently and not get burned, how to cook meats and roast vegetables. And most often, it was Miss Adel who taught them how to be kind, how to show respect to others, and how to reflect and act upon the words of the 'One.' From learning to write letters, to weave and sew, and their first awkward attempts to use tools and simple implements of self-defense, they learned in an environment of friendship and joy.

The memories sweeping back were so intense, they helped Laela turn her attention from Vito. She willed herself not to look at him during the ceremony. The more they crossed paths, the more it jagged at her wounds. Suffering was dark, splattered ink on a light page. And she was longing to turn the page.

As always in Treedle ceremonies, they read verses of the 'One' and spoke of the tenets of the Treedle Faith. Her father, Alvaro, had been invited to address the gathering. He was often a spokesperson on behalf of the Council. The Pyuva lavender-hued clan had borne a long lineage of leaders of thought, known for purity and vision. He was a merit to his clan and of great support to the Council as he studied their spiritual texts and gave counsel about their interpretation, assisting in translating them into laws. He also served to judge and settle disputes and arguments about the law.

Their clan excelled in the healing arts, poetry, literature, and innovation. They were renowned for promoting beauty and grace in the arts of gardening, poetry, and painting. They were caregivers for everything from butterflies to the elderly. They sought to be in harmony with themselves and others. Their plant symbol was the orchid, and their animal symbol butterflies. Her totem animals included songbirds, toucans, and caw-caws. (Laela's totem, Macecle, was a notable exception) They believed that the power of beauty and transformation are intricately connected. Their poets often wrote of transcendence from the earthly to the heavenly. Through beautiful and melodic verses that could be memorized and repeated often, they urged Treedles to see the extraordinary in the ordinary and scale heights of understanding. If caterpillars confined to creeping and crawling could transform into butterflies that fly wherever they want, so could Treedles learn to fly with their thoughts!

Laela watched her father's humble yet regal posture in genuine gratitude for the family and clan she was born into. He was wearing the shining silver toga used by men of stature on such occasions. And then, despite all her attempts not to, she glimpsed Vito staring at him intensely. And she couldn't help but compare the two. Vito looked like a Pyuva; he was a perfect lavender-hued specimen of one yet had the scheming heart and mind of a Mergon. If their identity were more than skin deep, what of him was really Pyuva? The clan attributes were ideal, and the clan members were all too real, she thought.

She mused to herself, "If not all Pyuva represented their clan's ideals and if clan identity were mainly skin deep, what did it mean to be part of a clan? Our clan, our color, and the history of our descendants are part of who we are. They form a story about what we aspire to be.

"And if I mated with Vito, our children would be beautiful, fully lavender Pyuvas. But not pure Pyuvas."

The community gently discouraged intermarriage among clans to preserve their distinctive diversity. The few children of mixed marriages defied identification and simple belonging to a clan. The

Treedles delighted in tracing their ancestral lineage and remembering the members of their family tree. It was harder to connect mixed children to their ancestors: to say, 'Jojo' is the spitting image of his maternal grandfather, or Susi has the same temperament as her great-grandmother. The range of eye colors, skin, and hair combinations that could result, though usually striking, was unsettling. These children became individual manifestations of a new race of Treedle. That meant that one day Phips and Oti would need to respond to the discomfort others would feel about their children, about how to place them, to connect them to their ancestral history, and to be claimed by two different clans.

So, despite all her happy memories today, a part of her childhood pride in her clan was suddenly chipped away. Vito challenged the simple and comforting belief in the unique worthiness of her clan. No one was expected to be perfect but the thought that some members could be the opposite of all the clan stood for chilled her heart. And why preserve a lineage just to parade one's skin tone proudly?

Her father's calm, strong voice broke through her reverie. His eyes alight; he said, "We're proud of you graduating Treedle youth. This day marks your entrance as adults into community life. You will now be able to participate in community councils, choose your life partners, raise families, and contribute to the growth of Aerizon. You will be the generation leading us into the future. We expect every generation to outshine the last in intelligence, virtues, and action.

"Every day of your life, you should remember and apply the four pillars of your Faith. Your words and actions should reflect Beauty, Wisdom, Truth, and Love. Of these pillars of faith, the greatest is Love. The supreme attribute and power of the 'One' is love.

"We can compare the 'One' to the sun. The sun holds us in orbit around it. It is the most potent force in our world. If our sun ceased to shine—to 'be'—for even a day, our world would drop like a ball into the cold depths of the universe. We would be lost in eternal

night. Our homes, these beautiful trees, would wither away shortly
without the sun.

"What holds us in orbit and gives us strength and power is
our love for the 'One.' His love provides us with the energy and
inspiration to live a happy life, to serve others. Our love for Him
is what connects us to Him. Our love for Him opens our hearts so
that He can fill them with His Love and light. We can't have a full
or meaningful life without the 'One's' love."

Alvaro concluded with specific words of advice on how to live a
loving life in family and community.

In conclusion, all joined hands and chanted one of the traditional
Treedle poems on lessons for the good life:

Lightness and light go hand in hand
On the pathway to the soul's command,
To clear the mind and cleanse the heart
Let go your wishes, and the clouds depart
Ask to be a channel of the 'One'
To serve with joy, life's treasure won,
Beauty is as beauty does,
Lose the self whose cloak is desire and
Whose whispers are embers that stoke a fire
From the cocoon humble in shrouds
Emerges the butterfly whose freedom we aspire

Laela made a silent petition to the 'One,' "Let me be a channel of
light and love in my life." Being of use, of service, had always brought
her joy. Even if her life led her to the most common and typical
routines, she hoped she would be a light to others.

At the end of the ceremony, the students paid homage to their
parents. She was happy to sit before hers—to thank them and ask for
their blessing. Her heart filled with gratitude for being part of such

an honorable family. Alvaro drew her up from her kneeling position and hugged her tightly. He usually was very restrained in displaying affection, especially physically. He whispered to her,

"My beautiful and audacious daughter, I am so pleased with you, and I know a special destiny awaits you. May the 'One' bless you." In his embrace, she could feel him containing a sob and the aging stooping of his shoulders. They were both feeling the intense tug between moving closer together and further apart, that necessary rift before crossing a bridge to a new stage. In more ways than one, she was growing and moving into her own light. Still, she needed her parents with the aching and longing for love and safety they had always given her.

Phips and Oti were waving to her, and she went to join them. They had invited her to their private celebration at Phips' house afterward. Her mother gladly gave her consent as long as Phips accompanied her home not too long after sunset.

They strolled and took time to enjoy the Bouder neighborhood with its distinctive fragrances of freshly cut wood and the thick oniony stews that served to fortify the wood and metal workers. With Phips as their guide, they stopped here and there to admire the many wood-carved objects on display outside of houses conjoined with shops. They could observe the craftsman creating household goods ranging from spoons and bowls to stools and furniture.

Phips' home was large, sturdy, and plain. The door was always open as if to say–nothing to hide and nothing to fear in this home. Phips' mother, Asia, who had hurried home from the ceremony, greeted them with warm hugs and praise for graduating. "Come," she said, "I have packed a special picnic in a basket for each of you. Please keep the basket as it is also a gift made for you. In it, you will find your favorite juices in jars, your favorite cookies, and grain patties. And also a surprise gift."

Phips and Oti entwined hands, and Phips gazed with intense joy at Oti and then Laela, "Laela, we have two surprises to share with you." Oti poked him, "Well, one won't be a surprise, but the other surely will."

Phips led them to a door at the west side of their family cottage. It led to a meandering walkway that was partially camouflaged by lush overhanging flowers and large fern leaves. A spiral staircase wrapped around an expansive tree adjacent to the new home at the end of the walkway. There were no other Treedle homes in the surrounding trees, and the magically inviting home they were ascending to was multi-leveled, built into the arms of strong branches. The first part of the stairway connected them to a wraparound deck jutted out into space. It was enclosed by a fence made of polished wooden bars. Hanging planters, swinging in the breeze, were distributed artfully over the deck. On another side of the patio was a trellis covered with purple firia flowers that grew in thick, brilliant clusters. There were artisanal tables and matching seats with cushions on them. Phips winked at Laela, "This is only the beginning."

A few steps up, there was another smaller, round patio with a woven reed roof. Laela instantly knew this was for babies, future babies to nap in. It was shaded and cozy and surrounded by small pots of flowers.

The house that arose before them next was unlike any other Treedle dwelling. Phips had incorporated combinations of wood shingles, stucco, bark textures, and handcrafted resin windows in artistic, organic shapes. Most Treedle cottages were simple box-like forms or rounded huts. But this house was built around three large tree branches at different angles as if growing out of the tree. Phips had created two floor-to-ceiling stained-glass windows with jewel-like intertwining patterns, flanking the entranceway to the main floor. Light played through them, casting prism reflections on the smoothly sanded outside deck where they stood. The main body of the house was clad in gleaming hardwood panels. Small nook-like rooms jutted out on either side of the entrance, thatched over like intimate bird nests with small, gabled windows and ledges filled with flower boxes. Phips explained that they would view two larger rooms with private balconies that could serve as bedrooms or workspaces when they went inside. On the right side of the house was an imposing tower with a shimmering golden cupula and observation deck. A series of windows alternating from clear to colored in red, yellow, blue, and green formed a band around the tower walls. These looked like the crystals circling the brim of a royal crown. Phips had created a style of architecture that was a mixture of cozy and magnificent, deeply personal yet invitingly charming.

They stopped before the imposing entrance door, and Phips took Oti's hand. Phips' eyes were dancing, but his tone was serious. They both turned to Laela. "We want to share with you that we are officially engaged now. We asked our parents for their blessing, and they have approved. At first, they were too worried about our clan difference. They were hoping we would wait. But we can't put this off any longer. You know as well as we do that there's no other for us."

Oti pulled something silvery and shining out of her pocket and placed it on her head. "I waited until we told you first before I put on my engagement tiara." Her tiara was a simple silver tiara made of resin-coated moonline in spiral patterns. At the crest of the front was a diamond-like jewel surrounded by emerald-colored resin beads.

Laela embraced them both, and they were quiet for a while, letting the natural tears of yet another shared milestone in their lives—one of completion and of crossing over—flow through them. This announcement confirmed what they all knew would happen, but the moment itself was a tender revelation.

Oti circled Laela's waist in a hug and stroked her back lovingly, "You are part of our family. You are our sister, and the home we have made has a special place just for you. We have a present to give you before we enter the house. Reach into your basket."

Laela noticed a packet wrapped in palmetto leaves, tied with a green string. "That's it," Oti nodded. Laela opened it and found a shiny metal key.

"That is your key to this home. You may use it any time. You may stay with us whenever you want, and for however long you wish. Please do us the honor of opening the door!"

Laela paused for a moment to appreciate the thick wooden door stained a rich forest green. It had twelve square panels with sculpted reliefs depicting symbols of Phips and Oti's clans, six for each clan. For Oti's- Texares, Phips chose one of the panels to represent the constellation for Oti's birthday month. The stars also alluded to her clan's passion for astronomy and stargazing. He included a striking panel of an aural spider poised on a giant web, birds weaving a nest, a tree bamboo shoot for good fortune, and in another, an engraved script of the word Wisdom. Texares were primarily associated with the virtue of wisdom and with the skills of weaving.

She was awed at Phips' keen appreciation for Oti: Oti, who gently wove the threads of her their lives together, making connections and capturing ideas into a web that made everything a tapestry, full of meaning, in the end. Delicate and loving, strong and firm, she was a woman to memorialize.

Phips honored his clan with depictions of a Bouder storyteller, famous for the legends he passed on orally, his totem, a high and fast-flying falcon, the strong hands of a builder with three sculpting tools in them, and among others, the engraved word, Truth. The Bouder clan was notoriously forthright, if not at times coarse. Many of their traditional stories were about telling the truth and the consequences of not doing so. Bouders were also known as Sustainers; the community relied on their physical and mental strength and prowess for protection.

On the mantel above the door were reliefs of celestial symbols: Cor and Cora painted in melon and blue enamel flanking a large gold mandala of the sun. Phips had invented a kind of paint from crushed gold scarab beetles, resins, and golden earth pigments to get the shimmery gold effect. As per Treedle custom, they paused for a moment's wait to ask blessings of Cor and Cora, a wink to their good fortune.

Laela was impressed at how smoothly the key turned and how the door opened without a push. The large windows in the living room facing an overhanging tree branch diffused soft light throughout the room. Phips had sculpted and sanded chairs and sofas from gnarled logs and trunks, and Oti had filled their hollows and seats with soft cushions in pale hues of almond white, morning yellow, and sky blue. Laela felt her senses teased with the blend of novelty and harmonious beauty of the rooms at every step.

Oti guided Laela to another door. "Now, open this one. This is your room, and you must stay with us often." Laela felt her throat constrict, outdare, and her hand tremble. Her friends weren't just offering her the gift of a room but a place in their lives.

Laela opened the door to view a pale blue wall that looked like an open sky, painted with a gabori tree, Macecle sitting on a branch, and birds flying joyfully around it. The gabori tree was called the tree of life, and its branches all reached the sky. Her large bed was covered with an inviting, down-filled, pale blue cover. A pair of white shutters opened to a small protruding balcony rimmed with flowerpots. Macecle would play there for hours.

Phips took into account the practical concerns of everyday cooking and washing. He showed her how the kitchen patio was shielded from the wind by a bright blue shutter that they could open or shut. The flooring shined with many coats of red-brown resin. Phips had created a stucco brick stove that needed only small wood chips to cook their meals. All their pans were hanging from hooks on the wall in artful patterns. The cleaning patio was around the corner from the kitchen, sheltered from the smoke.

In Oti and Phips' room, the door opened to a panoramic view of green and blue. The largest fluffiest bed with an arched frame of graceful silu branches. Silvery, smooth, elegant, and signifying abundance and good fortune. Sitting on a white-washed dressing table with a mirror was Oti's sparkling bridal crown. Oti followed Laela's gaze, and Laela nodded with admiration for this fitting and regal headdress. Oti picked it up and smiled, "You helped me have the courage to envision the woman I want to be. I'm not as brave as you, but I hope my union will let me be me. I want to live the life my nana should have lived, with more joy and being able to act on my dreams."

The engagement tiara was a humble precursor to the Bridal crown, which was the important adorning the Treedle bride could wear. Her crown told her story and her female ancestor's story with symbols and hidden messages about the wearer's dreams and values. Often a crown was passed down by generations, but those who wished made their own with the help of family and friends. Laela and Oti had worked together to add Oti's story to her Nana Bisru's crown over the past year.

Oti had asked her grandmother to use her crown-base. It was one of the most elegantly designed in the dominion of Aerizon, a strong, clear resin band with a repeated pattern sequence of ovals in jewel tones of vermilion, ocher, forest green, and azure blue, punctuated by square-cut glass diamonds in between. Though the oblong ovals looked like jewels, they were formed by resins of different brilliant colors and the expert dyeing techniques of Nana Bisru. The upper rim of this band was lined with delicate opal-flower shapes repeated in the same jewel tones.

The base of the crown was strong enough to hold the towering lacey forms that were added a layer at a time. Oti built upon the base of her grandmother's bridal crown with braided silk chords which were dyed in silvery color obtained from processing the scales of the dragon lizard with plant chemicals. In the center of the crown was an oval with the intersecting letters B and E circled with ferns, an emblem of Nana Bisru and her husband Edo's eternal promise.

They had consulted about Oti creating a taller tiara-shaped crown, with strings of diminutive silver beads strung from the peaks of depressed arches around the crown. They worked on it together for several months, with Laela helping to piece and mold the intricate details embedded in the layers of clear resin. The tallest peak in the front was topped with a prism in the shape of a diamond. They also surrounded the bottom rim of the crown with clear beads that looked like droplets of rain. The height needed to be balanced not to topple or wobble and yet flow with the grace of nature's form.

Only two weeks ago, they had spent the afternoon under a gabori tree shaped like an umbrella. Birds of different colors gathered that day to socialize as well, creating a chirping and chattering staccato that filled the lulls of their conversation. Each design detail was used as a story element, symbolizing Oti's life and hopes as a woman, community member, mother, and wife. In her betrothing crown, she hoped that Phips would see and cherish her as a strong and shining woman, a true friend for life.

Laela had already imagined hers and decided to work with metals and stones, something bold, simple, and shiny. However, she wouldn't begin to work on one until a suitable potential mate showed up in her life.

Oti traced her finger over a heart on the crown and letters memorializing her grandparents' union. She sighed wistfully, "I wish I had the chance to meet him, and I hope he'll be present with me on my day. I never told you his story." She lowered her voice. Laela knew he was the victim of the Mergons. It was a source of intense sorrow and shame for a family if one member became a Mergon victim. Treedles who ventured to the outskirts of the Mergon Kingdom to trade Treedle silks, cloth, baskets, paper, and other goods were expected to be shrewd and strategic enough to avoid capture by Mergone militia. Any transaction or trade between a Mergon and Treedle could result in imprisonment for a Mergon and enslavement for a Treedle. Treedles considered themselves far more clever and light-footed than Mergons, who moved with armor and brutal force. Treedles planned carefully how to avoid capture and worked with trusted traders near the Kingdom.

In reality, the Mergons were as eager for Treedle goods and their unique textiles as the Treedles were for tools and implements of metal, glass, and stone. Upper-class Mergon women longed for Treedle silks, bed clothing, and all manner of textiles as these were far superior in quality to the loosely woven and coarser Mergon fabrics. Traders, a special class of Mergon society, sold legal Mergon goods but earned most in illegal market trading of Treedle goods.

Mergons sent mercenaries to outwit and capture Treedles for another economic purpose: increasing slave labor in the mines and fields. The Kingdom maintained a given supply of Treedles and would bring in 'fresh ones' now and again to breed more slaves. Conditions of slaves were so horrific that some Treedles considered that suicide shouldn't be a sin if a Treedle did it to avoid capture and a life of agonizing hard labor.

"If only we could see the mutual benefits of trading. We want each other's goods. I never understood why Mergons couldn't accept that," Oti said, fingering some gold and silver beads. "My nana can't bear to talk of Edo because she knows he may still be alive and working under conditions that are worse than life...."

Phips and Laela circled her in a hug and let her cry softly. Phips wiped Oti's tears, saying, "Time to eat snacks and celebrate now!" They carried their baskets up to the tower deck and sat in colorful hammocks facing the view of the forest and sky. Laela took time to open Asia's present to her—a small and very precious carving knife. Laela's throat knotted in surprised gratitude. This was a gift to give to a dear family member. Asia hadn't given her a rare talent, but one unheard of for a girl. It was Asia's way of affirming Laela's unique sense of womanhood. The knife would serve her well. It had many potential uses—from cutting vines to dissecting, skinning, and peeling.

Oti had brought a large flask with nectar juice, a cocktail of select fruits and flowers mashed into a pulp, boiled in water, and left to ferment into a tangy cider. She poured a cup for each, and they toasted to their friendship, to the end of childhood, and new beginnings.

The deck was lit from without by the changing colors of the sky. Gentle streamers of pale pink, purple, and orange were beginning to waft up from the horizon and cast warm light over them. Over the next hour, they would become bold fluorescent waves filling the sky before being swallowed into the perennial depths of the dark.

After laughing at the most memorable foibles and school stories that only deepened in flavor and texture with retelling, Oti waved her hand as if to make a pronouncement.

"Alvaro moved us all today. He's so wise; he barely seems human."

Laela had the same feeling. Alvaro was mainly unknown to her. He saved speech only for essential communications and to weigh upon matters of import.

"He spoke about our role as the next generation of Treedle leaders and making a positive difference in our community. I was a bit surprised, as our Elders usually emphasize tradition and respect for the wisdom of our Council members and spiritual leaders. They rarely talk about young people leading change! The three of us have often spoken of what we would like to change in our lives, in our community's life. Now our greatest elder has invited us to do it."

The three of them locked gazes with an undercurrent of shared tension, united in the thought that the energy of their dreams would soon disperse from their youthful and idealistic hearts if they didn't act upon them soon.

Oti continued, "I've always been shy, so I tend to want to disappear from sight, to work behind curtains. I don't want to be so gentle that I fear taking new steps. I have thought about this a lot. You and Phips are so much bolder and more courageous than I am. But I also think of your mother, Laela; she has made changes to

Aerizon that affect our community's health and well-being. She has brought so much beauty to our lives through the gardens she tends over. She did this in her way.

"I want to support Phips in making new environments for young Treedle families to live in. How a home is built or even a room in a house changes the way you live and your view of things. I want to partner with Phips in helping people choose textiles and colors that tell a story about them and their families. I want to help decorate interiors with weavings and tapestries. Such a business would employ many Treedle people—women in particular."

Phips looked down at the floor, gauging whether the next idea might be too much too soon. "We've considered whether the traveling traders could bring drawings of some of the home environment goods we could produce to sell to Mergon families. We think that could be a way of building respect for Treedle culture—the beauty and artisanship of our goods. We know that traders bring clothes and other kinds of products we make, but not yet on the level that Oti and I dream of making."

Laela had heard parts of these ideas budding among her friends but not yet expressed with such confidence, with rooted intention. She also dreamed of bringing new and fresh ideas to Treedle's ways of living and changing some of the conventions that the community embraced without thinking.

However, just as Oti and Phips' relationship had grown and matured, and their dreams, too, Laela felt that hers were powerful but still blurred and unedited. She hoped her desire for more freedom of expression for women wasn't mainly selfish. She also wanted to be of service to their community.

Laela nodded her head slowly in affirmation. "I will be your first and biggest supporter. I have to choose a path of service, and I want it to coordinate with yours. We all need support to achieve any dreams we have, especially ones to change some outdated ways of our people. I will always champion you, my friends. We are one!"

Phips and Oti didn't press her to share any plans. They knew Laela needed time but that many seeds were in her mind waiting to be cultivated into life and reality.

Phips stood up, "Time for me to walk the most beautiful women in the tree-land home! And Laela, in two days we will go on our last exploration before our wedding. Be ready!"

If a bit wanly, Oti smiled and said, "I just ask that you two not try to outdo one another. Please just make it an easy outing."

Laela savored her third gift of the evening and headed out with a lift to her step.

CHAPTER 5

Feral Forest Secrets

Laela was packing thoughtfully for what might be her last trip with Phips to the Northeast. The location of these outings was a secret to all but two other people. They had crossed physical frontiers and established community boundaries. And yet, thinking of stopping was impossible, at least for Laela.

Ever since she first held a sling, Laela wanted to experiment with it. She asked Phips if she could learn from him, as he became one of the best hunters in Aerizon by age eight. All Treedles used slingshots in simple self-defense against an animal who attacked them to scare them off—but using them to hunt required finesse and powerful shots. Laela had permission to go out with Phips to collect nuts and leaves while he hunted. But she hunted too and was an avid apprentice with him. Treedles valued small amounts of meat in their diet. Tree mammals were skinned, and their meat hung out to dry in the sun. The meat was cut into strips and distributed to family and friends. They also sought plump birds for soups and savory dishes. They used animal skins to make shoes, flasks, clothing for cool weather, and tent coverings. Hunters were much appreciated as they put themselves at risk in the chase, and some, in the excitement of making the perfect shot, would occasionally tumble to their death. Not all families had providers like Laela and Phips, even though Laela turned her catches over to Phips to ensure her continued opportunity to hunt with him.

Over time, Phips and Laela found that tree game was becoming relatively sparse around their neighborhood. With the town growing, fewer animals nested nearby; hunting could be quite frustrating and unproductive. They knew there was abundant animal life in the Feral Forest lying adjacent to the northeastern borders of their city-state. Only specially trained Aerizon guards, licensed hunters, and traders could go beyond the boundaries for their jobs. This vast and dense forest was off limit for two reasons. The lesser one was due to the significant population of poisonous tree frogs, snakes, and lethal insects. But the main one was that it was the great natural barrier between them and Mergon territory. Aerizon guards were authorized to enter deep into the forest and advance close to the Mergone Kingdom. Guards in camouflage uniforms were sent both to observe and spy on the Kingdom. They took significant risks as they shimmied up and down nearby trees with special telescopes to detect military and other Mergon preparations and activities. Many of these guards and traders were from Phips' clan as they were tougher and more adventurous in general than the men from other clans. It took these specially trained men around five days of vigorous arborist efforts, walking from branch to branch, swinging from vines and ropes to reach the Mergon Kingdom. Traders stopped short of the Kingdom borders and veered farther east to villages outlying it, where mixed breed commoners and anyone the Mergon ruling caste identified as undesirable lived. They had well-marked drop-down spots where they could descend from the trees into the safe harbor and be met by the ground guards from the border towns who were familiar with them. They welcomed the Treedle treats the traders brought and news of their foreign lands. Traders traveled with heavy backpacks and returned with the same weight. Thus, trading products, either way, had its limitations.

The first time Laela and Phips ventured toward the skirt of the Feral Forest, they meandered about as if testing rainwater with their toes. They moved across branches a few meters in, where they could still view the fence demarcating Aerizon's limits. They immediately were rewarded by finding easy prey to capture with nets, lassos, and slings. The only problem was that a few choice animals dropped from the branches before they could reach to catch them. The next time, Phips would bring Ringer, his marsupial totem, who loved catching things with his pouch or a net with a holder they gave him. Phips made many a joke about Ringer as a born catcher and storer! Macecle loved to jump and hang on even by his tail to make catches too. The two totem friends were up for this outing any time.

They made light of their good fortune and hunting place. They were careful not to show all that they brought at one time. However, their ventures weren't lighthearted as the forest was eerily dark, filled with unfamiliar sounds, and they had to coat themselves with lotions to stave off insect bites.

Their explorations soon took on a new focus—how to go deeper into the forest and create a more accessible and safer path of entry and return. Laela had the idea of creating an entry station where they could leave some gear and bagged and gutted animals (tied to the tree). It took two visits to bring planks and build a sturdy platform around one of the tallest and most secure trees some distance from the border fence. They were marking trees with colorful pegs and saving vines to swing from tree to tree when together, the idea of a cable line was born. Laela remarked, "What if we could cut the time it takes to go deeper into the forest? If we could create strong cables with triple-strength moonline ropes, we could move—even glide—from station to station."

Phips was bursting with excitement. "Yes! Great idea. I can imagine how the lines could make the trip not only quicker but easier and safer. The benefits will be awesome. The journey to the Traders' Village could eventually be made in half the time or less. Zipping through the trees, cutting away any obstructing branches, will protect us from predatory animals. And not to mention how much more game we can find.

"But we will need to bring a couple more trusted people into this Laela—our cousins who are traders. This project can't be done by the two of us alone. It will require some mechanics and various people to help secure the lines. We need to bring a couple of interested Treedle men into this."

Laela had one cousin who wasn't attracted to the usual Pyuva intellectual pursuits and became an accomplished trader. He and Phips' cousin often paired to travel together and kept secrets of any shortcuts they found to have a competitive advantage over other traders. So, not even Oti, Tara, or any other families knew of this plan. They would never allow Laela to be a part of it, and Oti always worried about Phips. He was her weak point in calmness.

They would need experienced foresters to identify healthy and strong trees, build small tree stations, cut bramble along the way, and bring the raw materials to the construction sites. It took some convincing for the trader cousins to listen to the ideas of two impassioned and somewhat rebellious youth. However, they had nothing to lose and a lot to gain in supporting the project. Laela was in charge of designing a simple harness to transport them on the cables and Phips and the trader cousins—Evan and Banbo—helped design pulleys and metal rings and clasps (the latter purchased in the trading villages). Over an almost two-year period, they had reduced the time on the trade route from five to two days. The traders had carried the airborne trail more deeply into the forest with Phips as they all decided that Laela shouldn't advance further than three hours into the route. The Treedle male protector role bred into them wouldn't permit any additional risk or danger to her.

Laela hoped they would go as far as possible today, to the third station, short of the halfway point. Traders had to move more slowly through the following four stations as they had to look out and make detours when thieves pursued them. If they left shortly before dawn, they would have plenty of daylight hours to hunt. She dressed in a camouflage jumper with a hoody, leather boots, soft leather gloves, and knee pads for tree climbing. She packed a handful of the round, hardened resin pellets for her sling, a lasso, extra moonline, the knife Asia gave her, and a delicious lunch for them to share with golden berry and nut cakes for dessert. Macecle was nibble-kissing her face with excitement. It had been a long time since they did this outing.

The night was paling and allowing for soft visibility when Laela met Phips at the designated meeting place, on a branch hidden from view hanging over the city fence, which was a kind of mesh net laced through trees. It wouldn't hinder passage, but Treedles, in general, were risk-averse and obedient to community laws.

Phips carried several empty bags on his shoulder, and a large knife, a bow and arrow fastened in a holder at the side of his hunting belt. He had his slings in a pouch tied to a belt around his waist. Phips greeted her with a huge smile, "Let's make this a memorable one, Laela! I hope we can find some choice of meat to dry for the wedding today. I also want to get a few squirrels for making caps and a bori bird for my mother. Oti asked if you could collect some interesting leaves and tree flowers for patterns she wants to make on silk cloth."

Phips lowered his eyes and added in a soft voice, "Oti suspects something. She was anxious today. I'll have to tell her everything after this trip and before we get married. I hope you understand."

Laela stirred uncomfortably, "I have to agree, but my stomach turns in a knot just thinking about it. Let's enjoy today. Then, break this to her as gently as possible. Maybe with a bag of gifts—favorite furs, a new flower specimen." She didn't want to imagine Oti's eyes brimming with tears or her shoulder hunching over as this rather shocking revelation sank in. And it would indeed feel like a betrayal, though it wasn't in any way meant to be.

When they arrived at the first station, they agreed to keep a smooth and unbroken pace from cable line to cable line over the next several hours. Laela took time to savor the views from among the waving sea of emergent treetops, her cable car swooping into and skimming the deeper greens of the forest. She watched the dance of branches casting shadows as the leaves rustled in different sound patterns, from tinkling small bells to strong slapping sounds. The large expanses of sky, clouds, leaves, and strong, welcoming branches and trunks a few feet reach away as they sped toward a cable car station freed her mind of thoughts.

When they arrived at station three, Phips suggested, "How about if I go a little farther north into the trees to hunt, and you find the berries, nuts, and leaves today. Take a rest from hunting and just enjoy the forest and searching for any new plants of interest. We'll meet in two hours. I'm just a call (a throaty bird call they invented) away."

Laela found herself enjoying that idea very much, "You know, Phips, we've been so busy building this route or hunting; I never do stop just to explore and observe the vegetation. Macecle will be in charge of nut gathering, and me, berries, flowers, and leaves for Oti."

Laela quickly lost herself in the wonder of all the plants she hadn't noticed on their hunting trips. She went rummaging through branches, vines, and all manner of flowering and parasitic plants. She and Phips had climbed downward where the foliage was thickest, and there were strong branches to anchor their movements. She put on her gloves to pick a large pink tubular flower she hadn't seen before and bag it for Oti. She also found some new dark purple berries clustered around a tree. She tasted a drop of one, and when it didn't produce any notable side effect, she picked a number of them for her mother to bake tarts.

She and Phips seemed to whistle to each other simultaneously. They met at the station and shared what they had caught or collected. Phips had found his squirrels and two excellent corpulent tree rodents, as well as another small mammal they had never seen but that had the thickest, shiny black hair. Suitable for an evening shoulder wrap.

They descended to some branches below the station to eat their lunch. Phips sat against the tree trunk spreading his legs dangling over the thick slopes of a branch, and Laela sat on a branch below him at a slightly different angle. The limb she sat on was wider, allowing her a comfortable seat with a direct view of the massive umbrella of verdure that crowned the tree overhead. It formed a dark and restful enclosure for them to sit in companionable silence. Laela pulled out some pinkish lupps fruits they collected for their snack. The lupps fruit had a nubby skin that looked like a soft reddish pine cone but was very easily removed. It protected a glistening and delicate inner pulp, full of tiny black seeds. Laela tore open the skin of the first fruit and finished it in a few hungry gulps.

Macecle returned from exploring some of the tree's higher branches and snuggled behind her, pulling a strand of her hair around one of his fingers. He poked her in the way he always did when asking for a treat. Laela gave him two berries. While he was eating his fruit, Laela thought of entertaining him by making a swing fit for him. She anchored her lasso around the neck of the branch and began to fashion a sliding loop that she could fit around Macecle's torso to swing him around but be sure he was anchored securely. They were all on the border of a sweet nap.

However, a shift in the rustling sound of the leaves ever so slight caught their attention. A musk scent. Before their skin could prickle, or they could trade glances and whisper observations, it happened. Stretching around from the back of the tree trunk, where it had been quietly stalking them and now peering above Laela, was the hissing face of a jaguar. She froze in the beam of its menacing honey-green eyes set in an imposing tawny-gold head. There was one extended moment, distorted by extreme fear where she could appreciate its regal bearing, distinctive markings, and glistening muscular presence before it pounced. The jaguar flashed out its paw and dug its four claws into the right side of her chest to grab her. Impaled by the claws, the pain was immediate, searing, and overwhelming. It ripped through her tender skin deep into her chest. She struggled to stay conscious and escape but couldn't move. She felt a scream reverberate through her entire body and lost all control of her limbs, flailing like a floppy doll.

Phips was on his haunches, readying an arrow for what must be a one-shot attempt to stop the jaguar from further mauling Laela. Macecle and Ringer began squalling and throwing pellets and nuts at the jaguar and hit his rump. Phips mustered all his self–control and aimed his arrow at the jaguar's neck. It hit but didn't penetrate it. However, it served to distract the angry jaguar who scratched at the neck wound and, amid the further shrieking jibes of the totems, unceremoniously dropped Laela, who began tumbling into a free fall.

The jaguar looked down and appeared to contemplate its next move. And then, as if shaking its head in disdain, it decided that a Treedle wasn't worth it, with their small frames and so little meat on their bodies. Treedles weren't a preferred food like anteaters and larger mammals, abundant in the Feral Forest. They were even somewhat distasteful in flavor. Satisfied with the mark of its mauling and having signaled its reign over this territory, it casually disappeared into the lower brush beneath the forest top and to the three young cubs it was protecting.

Nonetheless, Laela was in mortal danger, not only from the wound but if she didn't grasp onto a branch. She heard Phips screams to grab one. The forest in motion was a blur of waving lines. She knew she had to use her last shreds of energy to stop her fall. She willed herself to focus through the nauseating fog of pain and move her body toward the outstretched web of arms at the next level of lower branches. She fell into the first strong branch with a slap in the stomach and bent around the branch. She lost consciousness now from the pain and loss of blood.

Phips watched anxiously and sighed with partial relief and began to prepare his own rapid descent. Though momentarily detained, she was precariously positioned and would soon slip off. Phips yelled at Ringer and Macecle to bound down and secure her with moonline. Macecle seemed to fly through the air. He looked at how pale and inert Laela was and instinctively splayed himself over Laela's back to provide her with warmth. She was in shock, and her body was quite cool now. He used his arms to pinion them both on the branch.

Phips put a large hunting bag over his neck and then tied a long rope to the branch. He shimmied down it to reach her branch. He grasped the trunk near the crook of the extended branch and tied the rope around his waist to free both arms. He positioned himself next to Laela, put her feet first into the bag on his neck, and flipped her stomach over his shoulder. He then began to pull them up to the higher branch, arm over arm, surprised at the weight of the two of them.

When they reached the platform of station three, Phips made haste to lay Laela out on the platform and assess whether they could make the trip home now. Well, he thought, it was also a perilous option to wait when all the best treatment was at Laela's home.

Laela seemed lifeless, almost colorless. Phips held back tears at seeing her so fragile and knowing he could lose her if he didn't make sound decisions right away. He thought about the order of things and what was essential to saving her life and getting her home. First, he must protect her from infection, apply a disinfectant, and then quickly restrict the bleeding. He reached into his pouch for a poultice they always carried with them when hunting. Inevitably they would get cut or scratched, though never so severely as this. He rinsed Laela's wound with rainwater that they saved in large gourds at the platform. He dried her a small cloth and applied the poultice to the punctured areas. He ripped a cloth bag used for gathering nuts and wrapped her wounded chest with it. The poultice released a stinging chemical, and this aroused Laela, who began moaning. Phips nodded to Macecle, who was hovering over her that this was a good sign.

In a soft and tender tone, Phips whispered to Laela, "All will be well. I'll get you home safely. You must be patient as we make this trip back. The medicine will take care of your wound, but you must be calm. Just keep thinking you can do this, and we will soon be home."

Macecle and Ringer stroked Laela's head while Phips made a hammock-like sack to carry Laela on his back. He could also move its position to cradle her in front of him as tree scavenging might require. He was determined to arrive back at Aerizon in record time. The cable car rides were about as smooth a way possible to transport an injured person through the forest. But with wind and stopping at stations, Laela frequently moaned and gurgled in pain. Blood was seeping through the bandages.

It was the quickest trip they ever made, and the burden of fear and guilt made it hard for Phips to breathe, but intense panic drove him on. He prayed to the 'One'— "Forgive me, forgive me. Save her, save her." And, as they approached Aerizon, he began formulating how to explain this occurrence without lying to their families. And how to tell Oti the whole story. He owed her that. The consequences of this venture seemed almost as threatening as what was happening to his friend's limp body.

Macecle bound ahead to alert Tara, shrieking and gesticulating danger interspersed with Laela's name. He led her to her infirmary to stand by the small cot, ready to receive her daughter. Tara imagined a broken arm or a cut and readied some healing ointments. However, she was unprepared for the sight of Phips, pale himself, carrying her daughter in a sack from which heart-rendering moans were emerging.

Phips spoke tersely as he laid Laela out on the cot and cut off the bandages from her chest with his hunting knife. "A jaguar attacked Laela. She was sitting on a tree branch, and the jaguar crept around from behind and just pounced on her. She started to fall. Thank the 'One' she fell into another tree branch."

Tara didn't answer but began to examine Laela's wound. She dabbed it with a cleansing lotion first. She smelled for infection and tested for the depth of the gashes made in Laela's chest. Laela groaned and whimpered as Tara rubbed disinfectant into the wounds. She made a fresh dressing to wrap them. She held Lael's head slightly back and poured tiny cups of different liquids into Laela's mouth. After Laela began breathing more regularly, though very lightly, Tara turned to him, her gaze was cool and unreadable, but Phips knew she was at her limit of self-restraint.

"Phips, how could this happen? How can this be? Jaguars rarely come into or even near our neighborhood. They feed and live better in the wild. My daughter could die from this wound, so you have some explaining to do. I will call Alvaro" She gave a cup of water to Phips and bid him be seated across from Laela.

Alvaro flung his hands to his face when he saw Laela's prostrate body and, for one of the few times in his life, became so distraught he couldn't contain his weeping. He traced his fingers tenderly around the pale contours of her face. Alvaro sunk to his knees and began to pray for her for a long time. It was hard for him to even look at Phips, though he would be the first to tell others not to blame and judge immediately—to listen first. He understood the anguish that could make someone lash out as he wanted to do with Phips right then. Tara stood by Laela's feet, massaging them and whispering that she was safe now and must will herself to get better.

When Alvaro mustered the strength to sit up, he directed himself sternly to Phips, "We've always trusted you like a son. How could Laela get into such danger? How could this happen? Please don't spare any details. First, tell us where this happened? We need to secure this vicinity in case others are in danger, like Laela." Alvaro had the presence to ponder whether the jaguar could prey on yet another child and would send a party to search for it.

Phips was so choked up he could barely make his voice be heard. "I'm truly sorry. I never imagined something like this could happen. I have always looked out for Laela. She's like my sister: She is my sister. I would do anything to have traded places with her.

"But, I uh, I must begin with a confession. I don't know how to say this in a way that isn't shocking to you, so I'll just have to say it. We were in the Feral Forest."

Alvaro was speechless. Tara put her arm gently around his shoulders and asked Phips, "Whatever made you go there with Laela?"

Phips asked them to hear him out. "That's a long story. Yet another thing I will need to confess to you is that Laela has become an excellent hunter." Tara averted her eyes from Alvaro. She knew this and had thought it a harmless pursuit, maybe even one that would help Laela in the future if ever her family was hungry or attacked by a raptor. Alvaro had no idea, and his mouth was in a tight line.

"This began some time ago. Laela would accompany me to gather nuts and leaves, but she would also practice with her sling. I would always watch out for her, but he became very skilled little by little on her own. She has a strength and agility in her that few Treedle young men have. She watched me and practiced a lot. As far as sling shooting goes, she's one of the best in the region.

"Then over time, it became harder and harder to find small game and bring back needed meat to our community. One day, it occurred to us to go farther out, to find a place where animals are more abundant. So, we thought of entering the Feral Forest. It's full of game, and it seemed easy and not too dangerous. On this trip, we went further than usual." And here, Phips continued the story, omitting the stations and heading in the direction of Mergon territory. Enough truth for one day. He explained the dramatic jaguar attack in detail and Macecle and Ringer's supporting roles.

Tara and Alvaro were so caught up in the story they didn't know which emotion was greater—surprise, anger, fear, or concern.

Alvaro turned to Phips, "You may go home as your mother must be very worried already about you. Dusk is setting in. I am most disappointed in both you and Laela. We can't blame you for what happened, as Laela is a mature girl and made her own decisions in this situation. It's part of a Treedle man's honor to protect women and children. I hope you will reflect on this and bring yourself to account. Should Laela lose her life, may the 'One' forbid, we will all face an unforgettable burden of guilt. However, we forgive you and hope that you learn from this." Alvaro wanted to say and do the right thing. As a community leader, no matter the personal cost, he would rather die than not do what is wise and good. Yet, he admitted to himself he would punish Alvaro severely were his.

Phips bowed to them and set out for home.

Night had barely fallen when the town lit up with candles, and news began to spread as quickly as a breeze about Laela and her terrifying adventure. Gossip bloomed on porches as thick as the night fragrance of jacithynths, and tongues wagged; "This is what happens to nice families when they give too much freedom to a child. She was trying to be like a man and not a woman—she wouldn't accept her place in society. I hope she gets better but does not forget this lesson. This girl has always been too sassy and impudent for her own good." Parents were admonishing their daughters on the importance of prudence and obedience. Women were meant to be in the home, and this was an honor, not an imposition.

Laela was developing a fever and chills. Tara and Alvaro prepared a vigil to care for her through the night. Tara was putting moistened herb cloths over Laela's forehead when they heard a knock on the door. Alvaro ushered in two most unusual visitors, the town's principal shamans. Ordo, the male shaman, was wearing a beaded and feathered crown with what looked like a snake necklace around his neck. Orla, who attended Treedle females, was wearing a woven crown with dried flowers intertwined through it. Their faces were covered in gray chalk and eyes outlined with coal blue.

Not ones for small talk, Ordo asked, "Is it true that your daughter bears the sign of the jaguar on her chest?" Tara and Alvaro nodded. "May we proceed?"

They stepped aside so the two healing eminences could look over their daughter. They both stood quietly, and Orla lifted Laela's bandages as lightly as possible for both to observe the wound. Then, Orla began to move her hands in circular motions over Laela, creating an almost palpable energy field. Ordo shook a gourd, and the two of them started to chant and hum. Then they each lit incense sticks that gave out lavender smoke and chanted several prayers.

A wave of warmth and comfort enveloped Tara and Alvaro that they were sure Laela could feel even through the veils of unconsciousness.

When they were finished, Ordo rolled his eyes back in a trance-like state. He spoke, "Your daughter will be fully healed in body. Please apply this ointment to the wound daily." Orla took from a pouch a closed vile that she handed to Tara. "There's something more important to tell you. We were meditating today as is the practice of shamans who believe in the 'One'—seeking guidance for the future. We recalled and were discussing the prophecy of the signs of the coming of age of the Treedle people. The time when there will be a renewal of our civilization."

Alvaro's face reddened with a blush of recognition at the prophecy he thought would apply to a man, a fierce male leader. At the same time Ordo spoke, he too recalled, "At the time of the end of one period of Treedle civilization and at the twilight of another, there will appear a fierce leader with the sign of the jaguar. This warrior of the spirit will act as a catalyst for change, questioning the outworn ways of the Treedle people. This leader will be bold and courageous and challenge both Treedle and Mergon traditions leading us to a new stage in our civilization. This warrior is your daughter."

Ordo paused for the couple to ponder this, "Your daughter must be protected until she learns to deal with the forces being released inside her. Visions will move her until she becomes the channel for the 'Will of the 'One.'" She won't be a prophet, a priest, or a healer— she will be a harbinger of intense social transformation. She'll be the first to establish a bridge between Mergon and Treedle cultures. At times, the forces surrounding her will seem greater than she can bear. But she must move forward and fulfill her mission and our destiny."

The shamans bowed to Laela and looked somberly into the eyes of her parents. "Pray to guard this sacred trust with wisdom. Tell no one about the prophecy right now. Some Elders will be aware, but they will hold silent. You mustn't tell Laela about the signs yet. Her awakening to her role must unfold over time."

Orla smiled at Alvaro and Tara's faces, tugged by consternation, "This is a blessing and gift. Your daughter will bring great honor to your family and lineage. Though, for every great blessing, there is a price. Her price will be very great. You must bear this with grace. We'll pray for all of you."

They left as soon as they finished their words. Alvaro and Tara embraced, with every emotion surging between them. Thoughts of disruption to their calm and even blissful existence weren't pleasant. Looking at Laela lying so still and pale, the words of the shamans were strange portents left in the lingering incense and shadows of the room. They would pass the night in vigil with Laela, no less assured of the safety of their girl, bearing a prophecy beyond the limits of her frail frame.

CHAPTER 6

Coming of Age

Laela lay immobilized, her mind struggling to identify the source of the fiery clenching in her chest. She felt impaled. She awakened slowly through waves of nausea—the searing stabs of pain, reminiscent of something. Her hand managed to touch her own sweat-drenched cheek. She was alive, and that seemed important to know. She moaned deeply now.

Tara immediately sat up from the chair, where she had nodded off. Laela could feel the freshness, the tenderness of her mother's hands stroking her. Tara spoke softly, "My darling, you are safe now. You're in pain because a jaguar attacked you. Remember? But you'll be, healing soon; you shall see. Phips brought you home from the forest, and we're treating you with all manner of medicines and poultices."

Musk, amber eyes, and claws that descend—rip through muscle. Falling through a blur of branches. Laela turned her head as if to say no. It was happening again. She started to jolt up and fainted.

"Shush, shss," Tara held her more firmly to the bed. "I'll give you a potent pain reliever now, and you will rest. Try not to think of that moment, but to know the 'One' brought you back to us. Though, you will most certainly have quite the mark on your chest to prove it." She poured a rather sour syrup into Laela's mouth.

Around noon, Laela woke up to creamy, warm yellow sunlight filling the room, and the pain though intense was bearable. She smiled wanly to herself to think she had survived, and that Phips and their totems had undoubtedly saved her. She wanted to call out to Phips to ask him what happened and how he had explained this to her parents? Did he tell the truth? He couldn't possibly reveal their shortcut through the woods, but did he even tell them they were in the Feral Forest? Tentatively she asked Tara if she had spoken with Phips and what he had shared with them.

Tara narrowed her eyes. "What you want to know is how much we know. I know you, my daughter. Well, we know everything, I believe. We know that you were both in the Feral Forest and that you are now quite the hunter."

Tara couldn't resist an ironic jab, "Though you'll need to practice how to save yourself from jaguars in the future. You're extremely fortunate, my dear. Your wound is healing better than expected. I'm using a new ointment that will reduce scarring, and this claw mark may look like just a tattoo with time."

Laela nodded. "Mom, I know the pain could be much worse. Thanks for the great care. I'm truly sorry for the scare I put you and dad through. Am I in big trouble?"

"Right now," Tara answered, stroking her hair, "we want you to rest completely. I'll confess that we're too exhausted to decide what should be done about your reckless behavior. But we're so grateful that you are alive and healing that we want to focus on that. We'll need to have conversations later about your need to explore the forest. Especially the Feral Forest. Just get completely better." A tear dropped from Tara's onto her nose. "One day, you will know what it is like to love a child more than yourself. Then, you'll understand."

Four days later, Laela began to feel energetic enough to walk in the garden and help with some light chores. Her heaviest pain now was thinking about the effects of her jaguar adventure on her mother, father, Phips, and Oti: the invisible web of guilt woven with the strength of moonline over the betrayals this incident exposed.

Total lies, partial lies, and secrets. She still couldn't bring herself to tell her parents the whole Feral Forest story as this involved exposing others. And yet, for a Treedle, the highest value was the truth. She went back and forth, weighing how much it could hurt Phips and others, like the traders, if she divulged everything about their plans and outings. Parents saw things from one perspective, friends from another, and any hurts could last a lifetime in both cases. How to be truthful and how to be protective of others? But, she would have to tell Oti the full and harsh truth. Oh, dear Oti, who only softened her life continually with kindness. It would be the hardest to tell Oti, even if Phips already had.

Tara herself invited Oti to meet Laela in the garden for a visit some days later to celebrate her significant gains in recovery. Laela waited for Oti on a swing that was good for two, hung on a strong branch near the entrance to the garden and with a sweeping view. Oti sidled in next to Laela. At first, she wouldn't look at her directly in the face. She handed Laela a small net bag with her favorite lemon-flavored cookies.

Laela said, "I don't know where to begin," and Oti looked at her in a way she had never seen before without tenderness or warmth. Oti replied, "Begin with the truth."

Anger and accusations were easier for Laela to handle. She wanted to find the words that would make this right and return the ease of unguarded trust in their friendship. "Oti, I love you like a sister and Phips like a brother. Forgive me for not telling you about our plans—the Feral Forest. Oti, I get so tired of everyone telling me not to do things, not to take risks. I was selfish about this. I just wanted to do something I really wanted to do and that could help our community. Not ask permission. Not hear why not to do it. Can you understand? I am different. I'm not as, how shall I say, delicate as you?"

Oti wasn't in the mood to humor her. Laela could feel it, but she could practically hear Oti wondering how to be tactful while her friend was still weak. "Laela, I love you, but I can't always be the one to understand you. I live with more boundaries. It's my way, and I respect yours. But I can't tolerate hiding the truth. I don't hide truths from you like Mergons squirrel away gold (a Treedle expression). I am an open book for you because I trust you. I don't fear telling you things because I think I have to do what you want or expect, or you will stop me. Friends should just give their best advice, but they shouldn't try to control you. Knowing that you and Phips kept so very much information from me hurt me deeply."

Laela allowed for a pause to let Oti know she was reflecting on her words, "You're right about always telling you the truth. But please know that what happened came out of wanting to do something good. We began our adventures into the Feral Forest with a good reason. We were having trouble finding game, and it occurred to us that there would be so many more wild animals in a less uninhabited area. And so it was! Then little by little, we did take more risks; we did venture farther in. And it was my idea to start creating an easier way to travel through the forest and also, better, a safer trade route. It sounds a bit crazy telling you. But the idea took hold of me and then of Phips too. In the end, there were many benefits for our people in this project."

Oti tightened her shoulders and looked ahead. Laela tried to sense how she would feel if she were Oti. The shared dream and adventure, advancing without her, indeed felt like a betrayal. She should have been the first one they both consulted with and early on. But without either she or Phips saying it aloud to one another, the whole idea seemed too wild and speculative to ask for Oti's blessings. And they both knew how she wouldn't only have expressed reservations but begged them not to proceed. Laela hoped that Oti recognized that too.

"Laela, I understand why you didn't tell me, but I don't accept it. You know that Phips is my eternal companion. We simply can't hold any secrets like this from each other. These kinds of deceptions tear apart the fabric of a relationship. You can say it's just one thread, but one line pulls on another and another until real damage is done. I want to protect our union.

"You may not have intended it, but what you did was hurtful to our bond."

Laela contemplated this silently for a while, "You are right. As a friend, I have let you down. I'm truly sorry, as I also want a bond with you for life. Can you forgive me?" She looked pleadingly into Oti's eyes, conveying as much contrition as she could.

"I can, but I need a serious promise from you and Phips that you won't go on any outings together anymore." Oti's tone was stern.

Laela blushed with shame that Oti had to set this condition, though it was certainly fair. "I accept," Laela answered, taking Oti's hands in hers, "I won't go out with Phips like this again. But I won't make promises about myself that I might break. I can't offer you or even my parents to be and think a certain way. Or to never venture out again, ever. But I'll try to show my love for you in new ways. I want us to be able to move on."

Over the next few days, Laela worked to regain strength and move her shoulder more easily gradually. The wound had tugged surrounding skin and muscles. It was a continual reminder of her foray beyond the acceptable boundaries for a Treedle girl and her disrespect for the norms she must embody as she approached womanhood. Alvaro and Tara had long talks with her now about growing out of the selfish and irresponsible ways of children, who can't understand the impact of what they do on others. Children, Alvaro would say, feel and act out; they don't restrain their impulses until they're taught how. Their daughter has been taught how to govern herself and think of the entire network of her community. Alvaro gave examples of the connections with family, friends, neighbors, and the community as a whole and how to respect and cultivate them.

"Collaboration is the key to the progress of Treedle community life. The more we are united, work together, and support one another, the more all will benefit and have our needs met.

"However, our collaboration depends upon how strong our bonds of trust are. And the strength of trust depends on how honest and truthful we are." For once, Laela remained silent. She felt that her father's admonishments were well-founded but that she always—deep down—wanted to help her family and community. She was roused by aspirations that didn't seem to bother her other young friends. She was impassioned with ideas that could help them survive and live better—like more efficient ways to obtain needed meats, furs, and access to speedier and safer travel for the traders. She felt that Treedle's love of tradition and custom meant that her ideas would never have a fair chance if brought to Elders. They were especially threatened by a young girl proposing new ideas. The community's view of her actions with Phips was that they were radical, wrong, and taboo for a girl.

She had even overheard her mother and father talking about a prophecy the shamans told them about during their visit while she was still unconscious. For some reason, the mention of the shamans did conjure up a strong smell of incense. She couldn't make out what the prophecy itself was, but they kept whispering about how they could protect Laela from future dangers. They wondered whether she was ready to use any special powers she had. Laela was intrigued but again thought better than to ask. She would need to confess to snooping to bring up the subject. If she had any real special powers, they didn't save her from being mauled by a jaguar or making all her loved ones so upset with her.

Laela worked in the garden each day. She was becoming particularly moody and thought it best to stay away from friends and talk as little as possible, even with her mother and father. Their attempts to fix her were smoldering any ideas whatsoever. She was moving about but had lost herself. One morning, working in the garden, she felt cramping, and a bright red trickle of blood started streaming down her inner thigh. She knew what it was, yet it still felt surprising and awkward.

She went to Tara, who could immediately see what was happening. Her mother looked at her through glistening eyes and then embraced her, long and hard, "Welcome to womanhood, and may it be well for you. We have much to discuss. But first, do you remember how to care for yourself? Do you have what you need?"

"Yes, mother. A good stock of cloths. Remember, I had more time than most of my friends to prepare for this. I'm the last one in my class to go through 'the change.'" Laela tried to say this with a lilt in her voice, but truth be told, she wasn't feeling prepared for the upcoming days. It wasn't just about the fact of dealing with new bodily fluids trickling down her legs or even the Days of Solitude. It was what lay beyond.

All young Treedle girls anticipated these three quiet and solitary days with pride and fear. Each girl passed through this centuries-old rite of passage, the same rituals, but emerged with a story of her own. Her story would contain elements in common with her family and clan and the delicate details of her own personality and dreams. Laela, like most of her friends, had never spent a night away from home. It would be the first time that she would eat, sleep, and be alone for three days and that her future would be more than her own.

"Good." Her mother motioned her to the kitchen and put a pot of water on the fire-bed to make tea. "Now, I'll make you a calming and strengthening tea. I want to share stories with you about women in our family. It will give you something to think about over the next few days. Tomorrow, we'll wake you up early to begin your time of Solitude. Even though you'll have plenty of time to rest in the Enclosure, I assure you that it is best to prepare for these days with a good rest tonight. Your thinking needs to be clear. The clearer your mind and heart, the more your dreams for the future will be blessed and assured."

All young Treedle girls anticipated these three quiet and solitary days with pride and fear. They would cross into a new role in the community when they emerged. From then on, they would be considered women, real actors in the community. They would be ready and expected to mate soon and attend a family and a home. The Enclosure was a definitive test for any girl. Although a silent guard protected the door, no one could save her from the shadows and the dreams that would surround her. The dreams wouldn't be hers alone but shared with their Elders. The Elders could advise young women toward a more promising future and mate. Laela vowed to herself to make the most of it, even though being confined to one room day and night seemed akin to prison.

The community would never be far from her mind, even in the Enclosure. She would be answering to them in the end. She would become an official member of her clan, of the community at large. Her first menses marked a pivotal turning point. Before, she couldn't mate or become a mother, and now she would be expected to. As a girl, she couldn't pierce her ears or wear a woman's toga. Now she could and should. Young girls played at and then performed most of women's duties as they grew up, but once they had their menses, there was a new weight to all they did and said. A dirty floor, a soggy nut cake, uncombed hair, talking too loudly or too much, fidgeting: Ordinary things reflected differently on a woman than on a girl.

The walls of Laela's stomach sucked in, "It isn't just alone. It's facing—what is the word? Change? My destiny as a woman, when I'm still a confused girl? What if mating isn't my path? What if I 'fail' as a woman?" She laced and unlaced her fingers, knowing that she didn't have the luxury of time to answer these questions. The pressure to assist her in fulfilling her role would intensify. Time would be its trigger. Efforts to matchmake would become anxious and incessant. She had become ripe, but she mustn't become overripe and, most sadly, a spinster. She would be made real, in their eyes, through her union with another—because, naturally, everyone wants that happy outcome for her! Expectations were pressing in on her like juggling spectators observing a trial in the town hall.

Tara regaled her with endearing stories of her female ancestors, all of whom loved home and garden. Her ancestors were gentle specters in this town hall, expectant observers waiting for the right Laela to step up. She awoke multiple times during the night, wrestling to breathe. She wished she could disperse the crowd in this hall of the heart—the ones cheering her on and the ones whispering about the rebellious girl tainted with a jaguar mark. Perhaps clarity would come in the Enclosure.

Tara came early into Laela's room the following day and sat on her bed, opening a bag she had packed for her. "I believe I thought of everything you'll need. There's a nice new silk robe, underclothing, many cloths, a pillow, a blanket, and a sack of your favorite biscuits. You needn't suffer physically through this time," Tara winked.

They went to the Hub where trained doelas, Elders who oversaw the Coming-of-Age rites and helped as midwives for births, would be waiting for her. The head of this group, Elsa, would watch over her cleansing and preparation for entry into the Enclosure. The Hub looked like a light-walled temple surrounded by giant ferns and plants. Before entering the Hub's main room, Tara helped Laela undress and put on a lavender-colored satin robe and slippers.

They knocked on the finely carved doors of the ceremonial room. A group of doelas also dressed in lavender satin robes, symbolic of their Pyuva tribe, and wreaths of flowers in their hair, opened the doors and beckoned Laela to come in. They bade Tara to give a farewell hug to her daughter, which she did, whispering, "All will be well, darling daughter. Open yourself to this passage into womanhood."

The women took her to a large outdoor platform shielded by large caseto leaves. The pattern of the large, ribbed leaves waving in the wind cast a dappled light over the floor mats and the grand bathing tub. Light streams of incense in silvery-hued resin vases blended with the fragrances of lush purple trumpet flowers growing in vines up the wall and over a trellis roof. Miss Elsa appeared from behind an ornate screen on the other side of the platform.

"Laela, we are so pleased you have become a woman, and we're here to welcome you to this new stage of life. Before you enter the purification bath, we will massage you with curico oil, which is the most precious of all oils. It enhances female energy and fertility. As we massage you, we will talk and share with you the guidance of our ancestors. May you bring much pride to your community as a pure and goodly woman!"

They covered a mat with a sheet and gave Laela a smaller sheet to wrap around her chest and private areas. She did this turning her back to them, as she wasn't eager to show her naked body nor the angry tattoo on her chest. When in the sheet, she sat on the mat, looking, hugging herself as if to shield herself from an attack and feeling significant discomfort in her lower belly. She began to wonder why women have to suffer this every month. Miss Elsa's words buzzed meaninglessly around her.

Miss Elsa placed a hand on each arm and looked quizzically into her eyes, "Laela, you seem distracted. Before we continue into this most special ritual of preparing you as a woman in the community, we need for you to be present. What's bothering you, dear?"

"How do you know I'm bothered?" Laela asked, thinking she contained her feelings.

"Well, I've been preparing young women like yourself for many years. There are little clues, shall we say, if the woman is scared or even resisting the changes in her body." She squeezed Laela's shoulders, "See how tight your shoulders are? When I hold them like this," she said, pinching tighter into the muscles, "you feel pain, don't you?" Laela nodded. "Well, your shoulders are telling me how tense you are. "Also," and Miss Elsa laughed softly, "you are making quite the face at me, and I'm surely not an ogre. I've loved you since you were a baby, my dear."

Laela didn't want to offend Miss Elsa, who was every bit as dear as Miss Adel. She ventured, "Can I be honest, and maybe you can help me with what I'm really feeling?"

"Why, of course, please be," Miss Elsa affirmed, patting her arm.

"I find it so inconvenient to think that every month, year after year, I'll bleed like this, and so far, just in this short time, it seems so messy and uncomfortable. It doesn't make me proud like I thought it would. I feel unsafe. Vulnerable. A predator could track me more easily. And what if this all leaks and trickles down my legs when I'm out and about? Also, why do women have to bear this and children too! Why don't men have to suffer something like this regularly? It doesn't seem fair."

Miss Elsa tried to stifle judgment with a bit of a nervous giggle. She paused to think and then answered slowly, "I can't tell you that this isn't a burden in any way. It is a burden in some ways to have the menses and to carry a baby to birth. But let's think of it another way. Women are chosen to gestate and accept the 'One's' most important gift, the gift of life. It's an honor, and honor, in the end, will bring many blessings and joy to you and your family. But there's a price for such bounties. We need to bear the pain and to embrace the responsibility of womanhood with patience. Most of life's most precious gifts come with effort and sacrifice.

"I want to ask you to try to relax. Try not to think so much about these concerns. We're here to guide you to see and feel the beautiful possibilities of womanhood. Let go and just listen for now. Try to find new meaning in being a woman. Try to find your purpose and happiness in being one!"

Three women massaged her slowly and thoroughly from head to toe with the oils. The kneading and stretching of taut muscles did work a kind of magic. The rhythm of hard and soft motions was music calming the body. Laela found herself relaxing, and her belly discomfort considerably eased.

"Now, it is time for your bath. Let the water and our words soothe your soul," Miss Elsa said as the doelas helped her to sit, then stand, and led her to a bathtub made fragrant with flower petals and herbs. The tub was made of resin deep enough for her to lay down in and rest her head on a specially designed sloped side. There were pots of steaming water set over carefully tended fire beds at the platform's four corners. The sauna they created surrounded them all in a cloud of purifying vapor. The leaf walls both cradled the steam and allowed it to ascend into a mist so the young woman could breathe easily. The doelas stood behind her and removed her sheet, and helped her to step in.

When she was immersed, Miss Elsa gently stroked her head. "Close your eyes, and listen to the women of your tribe, and their words will reveal insight for you. The river of red and the river of white are the streams of life that flow through a woman's body. Only a woman can bear them, only a woman. We're strong in a different way than men are."

Then, in came the three other elderly guides, and they carried a fragrant garland of jagapani and more precious floral oils to massage into her skin when she was rinsed and dried. Miss Ali, Goeri, and Bel will sing for you now. Be at peace."

They began to sing as Miss Elsa slowly poured the bathwater over her head;

She is a woman now, a vessel of life;
Her pain in tears and blood is shed,
From the depths of her womb, her fears are bled.

And in her quiet are mysteries unread,
Drop by drop, day by day, her gentle love is spread.
Bringing forth new life after she is wed,
In the joining of man and woman, a seed will grow,
From birth to the breast where mother's milk doth flow,
The river of red and the river of white,
Will ebb and flow when the time is right,
You are a woman now and will learn new ways,
To work and serve and fill your days.
From maiden to mother, from womb to tomb
Rivers of red and rivers of white,
Hidden forces are a woman's might,
Rivers of white and rivers of red
Rivers of red and rivers of white
darkness and loss give way to light
her wisdom calms the red of fight
her calmness stills the rush of white,
She is, to be honest, and wise in word indeed
And the art of peace, she must take the lead.

When they finished, Miss Elsa began to talk to her in a low melodic voice while scooping the milky, fragrant water and pouring it over her head—speaking about the responsibilities and the powerful transformation into womanhood.

"We Pyuva women are known for our gentleness, beauty, and poetic natures. Each clan should preserve its special attributes as together, all the clans contribute to a whole. You can honor your clan by choosing the best Pyuva mate and consecrating your union. As man and woman, you'll become one, blessed by the 'One,' and your entire family will be knit together. Greater. When you birth a child from this love, the child will bring light to you and carry on his ancestors' legacy. So your choice will affect your history and the clan's history."

Miss Elsa leaned closer and spoke in a confidential tone, "I've heard that one of the finest young men in the Kingdom, Leon, has eyes for you. Such a lovely family. So devoted. His father, Dominic, is one of the most studied and pious in the land, like your father. He's a gentleman and very intelligent, they say. I've watched him for years and would gladly claim him as my own son."

Laela suspected that mothers consulted Miss Elsa before the "coming-of-age purification" so that when all softened and buttered up with precious oils, they could be 'guided' to discover the suitable mate for themselves. She gurgled and frowned. Miss Elsa nudged her gently. "Ah, my lively Laela. Listen to me, who watches generations mate. Goodness grows on you, and goodness is a steady companion."

She saw no light in Laela's eyes at the mention of Leon. Hopefully, she wasn't among the gaggle of girls swooning for this new boy, Vito. She didn't trust him from his first smug glance at her at the community devotional. The wave in his hair matched the wave in his smile. Upwardly false. Miss Elsa not only had a keen eye for character herself but also for the lack of it.

Miss Elsa tickled her side playfully and said, "You're surely not dreaming about a certain young man whose name begins with V." Laela pretended to look to the sides at the ferns and blew some suds over her face, to not show color.

She was quiet as they helped her emerge from the bath into a large towel and, after patting her dry, apply yet more fragrant lotions to her skin. She enjoyed smelling like the bath and the garden and hoped the aroma would stay with her for the day to come.

CHAPTER 7

The Enclosure

The Enclosure was bright and welcoming, with a pot of fresh-cut flowers to the right of the entrance, and to the left, a lavender hammock covered with a netted tent strung across it. The room itself was white-washed and cheery—a backdrop for the sky's changing colors as the sun moves from the east to the west, reflected through the flanking windows. There was fresh bedding in the hammock, mats, and pastel pillows in the corner by the eastern window. A low wooden table, surrounded by cushions, sat in the center of the room where she could eat, drink the teas, and sip the dream potions they would bring.

There was also a large bucket of water and smaller ones to soak her menstrual cloths. She could use the window ledge to scrub and rinse them. Each day they would bring her freshwater for drinking and washing. Everything was arranged for her to be still, quiet, to think.

Laela unpacked her few things and sat on the mat, looking out the window at the waving tree branches that cast playful patterns of foliage on the floor. She was breathing lighter after hours of bathing and massages. The room itself was distinct and carried the aura of its history of birthing girls into women. She could see other girls sitting in this exact spot, with the river of red flowing unbidden between their legs, waiting for the potions and dreams that would foretell their future. She could see how the intense beams of the sun during the morning would blanch the room and her mind of frivolous thoughts of girlhood.

She had entered into 'womanhood' at age14, an advanced age for Treedles. She believed that she was prepared for her first mense: it was just natural—part of being female, of growing up. But she was still awed at the brightness of her blood, how it trickled hour after hour—involuntarily, how her body seemingly had a mind of its own. She had heard many tales of first menses. Her friends, Oti especially, had shared every detail of her passage with her. But nothing is the same for everyone, Laela realized as the call to womanhood loomed around her with its own veils of mystery. Each change in her body had budded according to an inner cycle of events that she couldn't perceive or control. The changes were both predictable and unpredictable.

Alone in this cabin, she was held captive to ancient rituals and the tide of blood flowing out of her. She had no control over cramping, blood ebbing and flowing involuntarily round the clock, the brightness of the red that she had only seen from deep cuts on the clean white cloths. She could move a hand where she willed, jump from tree to tree gauging the distance, but she couldn't control one drop of blood over the womanliness developing within her. She felt tenderness in places she had never imagined, and feelings that shouldn't mix, that clashed and yet combined, like joy and sadness twined together like tree and vine.

Laela tried to relax into the silence. She listened to a yellow-bellied songbird tweeting gentle melodies and thrilled at the shrieks of two large caw-caws, with tri-color wings in bold red, blue, and yellow, swooping around the tree in front of her window. Lunch came soon enough, and one of the most ancient doelas stood outside the door while she finished. She could hardly eat as she knew what came next.

After removing the dishes, the doela brought a tray with a pot of steaming tea and a silver cup. She bid Laela sit on a cushion on the floor by the table. Laela's knees felt shaky as she faced yet another liquid that would overtake her mind, just as the inner river had done to her body. She imagined trying to escape through the window and swing out onto the nearby tree. The contrast of tree climbing seemed the very antidote to taking a potion that would put her into a trance-like state.

The doela spoke through a creaking throat as if whispering through a pipe. "Laela, you're now going to take a voyage into yourself. This tea is sacred to our people and made from the rarest white mushrooms and glory blossoms. In moments, your Shaman guide, Orla, will join us. She'll pray for your enlightenment and be present throughout your journey. She'll serve as your dream diviner. You'll dream while awake and will be able to remember your vision."

Laela had heard much about this potion that caused waking dreams, also known as the truth elixir. The trance carried on for the better part of the day, but one dream would be the most vivid, and that was the dream that was a clue to your mission in life.

Orla entered the door in a swirl of incense, wearing a most regal feathered white crown. She sat in front of Laela on the other side of the table. "The sacred waram team must be taken with the utmost respect. It will open the windows of your soul and give you a dream that you must decipher. You must discover in it what your strengths and your weaknesses are. It will reveal clues for your path of service in life."

Laela wondered if most girls dreamed of marriage and babies. The ones she knew returned with visions of a loving family life.

"Let us pray." Orla chanted and led them in a meditation that was both soothing and fierce as she traversed the spirit world through the vessel of prayer. Laela found herself losing the grip of time and place and closed her eyes to listen with care. She did want to respect the shaman.

Orla stopped and looked deeply into Laela's eyes. "Now, you shall partake. Stay quiet until the dream appears, and then when it ends, you shall hold my hands and tell me all." Orla poured the tea with great care into the cup and asked her to sip it slowly but steadily to the last drop.

Laela felt a burning in her throat and notes of musky wood. Nothing like herb tea. Then she felt a tightening of her stomach and nausea. Finally, as if popping through the inconvenience of the body and its uncomfortable sensations, she entered into the dream world.

Oddly, Laela sensed that she was dreaming, but the dream was more encompassing than her consciousness of it. She could observe herself in the dream world, but she couldn't control anything that happened. She was in a forest-top much brighter even than Aerizon's with saturated colors and heightened shapes. Leaves were a shimmering sage green you could taste in the breeze. She was heading toward the edge of town to the Fair held in their land once a year. Villagers from surrounding communities came to sell wares and put on performances. She wanted to buy something she had never tried before, a new game, and plunge into the hours of a challenge it could bring. She looked among the booths for anything that might strike her as strange or different. Near the end of the park, sparkling reflections of colored light caught her eye. She walked up to a booth where a thin vendor with pallid skin and glazed eyes held up shining glass marbles to the sun and then placed them over a dark board marked with many silvery lines and holes. She watched as the vendor drew the onlookers to her, touting the game board as more than a game. "This is a divining board. It holds the keys to the mysteries of your life! If you put all the marbles in the right sequence, the board spins and will leave a coded message that is only for you. A paper with your message appears through a slot hole on the side of the board. However, only you can break the code to decipher this message. It'll be a message that will transform your life!"

The hawker warned that when you break the code, the board will realign again, and if you ever seek another message, the code to unlock it'll be much more difficult. The price of the board was ten times what other games might cost. Laela convinced the expressionless vendor to accept a trade for a magnifying lens she was carrying.

Laela took it home and tried over and over to unlock the code. Curiosity spurred her on. She became more anxious and frustrated with each passing day and attempt. Finally, the alignment occurred, and the marbles and lines vibrated into a geometric pattern! The board seemed to spin brilliantly with a life of its own and deposited her message. To her frustration, she couldn't decipher all the words even though they appeared to clear because her eyes misted over, and she couldn't focus on them. All she remembered was, "Seek, and ye shall find." The board stopped, and the marbles rolled out. It looked like this would be her first and last game with this board. And the paper was now empty as if the words spun out of it too. It was the last day of the week-long Fair. What's the meaning of this? She could start by asking the vendor some questions.

She went to take the board back to the market but couldn't find the stall or the salesperson again. She worked her way through the crowds. Maybe the booth had moved to another place. A child came up to her and pressed a round golden coin into her hand. Bewildered, she examined it. She noticed that it was etched with a bold lotus flower in the shape of a crown. The coin shined like a piece of fine jewelry. The child said to her solemnly, "The salesman who sold you your board says this is the answer to your question. It's the most precious coin in existence, and only one other person possesses the companion coin." The girl disappeared as quickly as she came. Laela understood that she had just received something invaluable.

Laela was shaking her head in confusion and tipping between consciousness and the dream. Orla snapped her fingers and asked

Laela to come out of her reverie. At first, Orla appeared from a distance, but Laela was aware of an increasingly pungent incense and firm voice. Laela came to life, gasping for air and shaking off the dream world. She only had more questions weighing more heavily in her mind than that coin in her hand.

"Laela, you must now tell me everything, every detail of your dream. Trust in me as your mother of the spirit. I'll only be able to interpret your vision to the degree that you tell it completely to me."

Laela found it hard to recount the story as she was entirely baffled about it. She feared it would get her in more trouble as it was hardly the usual stuff of young women's visions. She hadn't imagined her mate heroized in vision or a hearth where she conquered her family with enticing meals. She wasn't in delight about inventing a new nut cookie recipe. She envisioned something that may get her framed as too divergent, or the word some people already used: crazy.

Orla was nothing but kind and respectful, encouraging her to paint the story out, colors, smells, and all. Orla grasped her hands and gazed at her intently, "Now, tell me in words how it made you feel. Just say any words that come to mind."

Laela looked down with shame, "I felt confused, overwhelmed, like this is bigger than me."

Orla was silent for a long time while her eyes flickered in thought. Then, she spoke,

"Laela, you've received a most unusual vision. It's a spiritual vision. It shows that you'll become a leader of some kind. What kind we don't know. It also shows your qualities and your faults. Your curiosity and excitement to learn show no bounds, but you also can be quite impetuous and temperamental.

"The 'One' has chosen you for a path that I can't claim to fully understand. It will be your duty, however lonely or challenging, to seek to understand and fulfill this mission."

Laela had a feeling that Orla was holding back more information, and she was. Orla was planning to consult with Ordo and eventually with representatives of the Council of Elders. Was this yet another sign of the long-awaited leader? Laela was a child of a direct descendant of Asmea. She felt more strongly than ever that it was indeed. She didn't dare discuss all the portents with this girl just passing the threshold to womanhood. Orla felt intuitively that the girl would need to grow into this new position and path. And she also sensed that the course for this quest might be quite perilous. The girl barely survived the jaguar's mauling, though here she was as sparky as ever with the imprint of that claw over her chest, an emblem of her capacity to endure.

It was up to the Shaman to decide whether there were one or two dream ceremonies. Orla caressed Laela's hands lovingly, "Tomorrow, dear Laela, we'll do another tea ceremony like this. We will ask for the second dream to reveal more about the nature of your mission. The second dream helps clarify the mission. Please take this time to meditate more on your dream. The most trustworthy and best guidance comes directly from the 'One.'

"Remember, we can only receive inspiration if our minds and bodies are quiet. You must sit until your mind stills like a mirror, and the 'One' can reflect upon it the knowledge you need." Orla stood and bowed with hands pressed together in the manner of a farewell blessing. She closed the door gently.

Laela decided to dedicate the remainder of the afternoon and evening to enter this meditative state. She was eager to receive any images, words, or revelations intended just for her. Sitting quietly proved to be a most challenging task. Various conversations were going on in her head. The annoying static of others' opinions kept interrupting her stream of thoughts.

She, a leader? Girls weren't leaders in Aerizon. She knew that, and the chattery gossips stationed at the sidelines of her conscious reaffirmed it. They said that the only leadership she should think about is being led to her right soulmate and accepting his leadership in the home.

The pressure from the Treedle community for young women of marriageable age was cheerfully relentless. Laela agreed with not speaking evil of anyone and working on her own perfecting. However, she secretly mulled quite a bit on the irritating characteristics of potential suitors.

She examined Leon and Vito on the candidate chairs.

Leon is non-candidate number one—no fun, kind of dopy—she thought. They have already explored a friendly 'relationship' in talks at the community center, nudged by parents to sit together in homes, taking walks animated by said parents. Leon told her one evening a great deal about his frequent colds and trouble breathing. He asked what teas and foods she eats for congestion. Laela knew Leon was asking about how she would mother him. She was indebted to the high heavens that he couldn't read her mind or hear her thoughts. Even when he showed he would be an equally caring and doting mate, bringing her favorite flowers and sweets, she would shed the flower petals and send them to the wind later on. Nothing could make her mate with him because he didn't deserve her disgust in any measure.

She wondered if Vito could mature and adopt some ounces of Leon's sweetness. He could be her match. She had to admit to herself that his physicality thrilled her. No congestion there. He had shed his awkward early puberty gangliness, and strong, fluid muscles mapped out his body.

When he wanted to, he made her feel like the center of the universe until she realized he made other women feel that way too. It had taken time to see that while she was making him the center of her universe, she was losing her light and was subsumed into his world. She remembered the first times when he would catch her eye every time she said something clever in class and shine a smile—a beam of intense appreciation. His eyes would say, 'there's no one like you.' He would come up and ask her how she felt and what was good about her day. There was something wrong with a day when he didn't see her or ask about her. When he wasn't seeking her out, she desperately sought to engage him. But she knew flirtation had to be subtle. Her laugh would become brighter. She would walk into his sightline while pretending not to see him. She would flatter his best friends to make him jealous. And did he know this? Well, he fed her less and less of this honey. She found herself thinking about and working for it more and more. She had fallen in love—a love trap. Would mating overcome that? Mating would signal the end of interviewing other partners at the very least.

She chided herself. Perhaps, it's not the suitors' lack. If she was so judgmental, then it was she who was the problem. Yes, in all fairness, someone who is not content with any option is the one who is at fault. Or, she may be an aberration—one of the few women born to live a single life.

Now Laela was squiggling and turned on her back to watch the early evening shadows on the ceiling. Her chest opened, and she thought of the gold coin. How fascinating in design. How could she come to possess such a rare and valuable object? The lotus was a noble flower and would float upon a little airborne pond oblivious to heights and depths, fragile yet strong.

She tried again to meditate, but she couldn't befriend the silence or settle into quietness. Maybe someday. She paced the room, and soon, the doela delivered a much-welcomed soup and nut-bread to her table and bade her eat and knock on the door for the guard to remove the dishes later. The doela handed Laela a little prayer book.

"Be sure to read these prayers before you sleep and when you awake. They're just for womankind. They will comfort you. It isn't easy to be alone, but when you ponder these, you will find you're not alone really." She smiled warmly at Laela, like a hug with her eyes. These ladies of the Hub were indeed very dear.

Laela fell into one of the most profound nights of sleep ever and awoke, not remembering any dreams. She looked forward to the next session with Orla because maybe the next dream would be easier to understand, perhaps even an adventure.

The morning and lunchtime passed by, with Laela lost in questions about womanhood and how she would meet the vision's expectations. Orla arrived wearing a lavender headband with a large knot in the front and silvery robes. She was carrying a bowl of incense with the dreamiest smell. Oh, this would be quite the party, Laela thought.

The doela brought the teapot and silver cup. Orla lifted the teapot lid and poured in the contents of two different vials. Her expression was serious and intense. She offered some prayers and then asked Laela to follow her breathing patterns. "Part of meditation is in how we breathe. We must avoid breathing raggedly or hurriedly. We must find a rhythm that is akin to nature and an even back and forth flow. The idea is to calm your breath, and your breath calms you. Again, I'll ask you to share every detail about your dream. Now, sip very slowly."

This tea was bitter, its herbal flavor unfamiliar and incomparable. It wasn't pleasant to drink, but Laela finished it to the last drop.

She didn't feel nausea, but her heart was beating faster, and her body felt flushed. Momentum seemed to be building. She fell into a waking sleep. She found herself in a setting like the Feral Forest. She was walking in a hurry, following a route of swinging bridges and planks like she and Phips had created for their forest stations. Sensing that someone was following her, she began walking even faster as if she were escaping. The forest was thick and cloying with dark, sappy green leaves and wide-lipped, reddish-brown flowers that smelled overripe. Ah, she was in danger. There was more than one creature hunting her. She tried to swing on a vine to make a detour off the path. She hid in the crook of a tree to catch her breath. She could hear them; there was more than one in the party chasing her. She jumped to another tree and another. She was getting so tired.

Then, as she landed back on one of the trail planks, they quickly surrounded her. There were three fearsome military men in uniforms, raising their arched bows and arrows toward her. Worst of all, a monstrously big feline was bounding toward her from an adjacent tree. She knew instantly that the men were protecting this predator and not her. They all wanted her dead. The feline stopped and towered over her, haunched on its back legs, and revealed its massive jaws and saber-like canine teeth. It was a black jaguar, a rare black jaguar. It was preening in the pride of its conquest. It was admiring of its own stance, overshadowing her and how completely she would be overpowered and devoured. Laela screamed from her belly to the 'One,' a two-word prayer, "Save me."

A blast of wind seemed to push her. She began a free fall from the tree, plummeting swiftly down. Before she hit the forest floor where Laela believed she would meet her death, she became tangled in a series of small, outstretched branches. She landed on her feet. She knew two things with certainty. The black jaguar would follow her, but the 'One' would protect her. She felt fear but also hope. She began to walk toward a warmly lit open glade. A kindly voice whispered in her ear, "Not yet, my dear, peace will come, but it will be hard-won. You'll want to give up more than once, but if you persevere, the reward will be greater than stores of gold. You must save your people."

Now, Laela found herself trying to emerge to the surface of this deep well, this world with its strange and cataclysmic events.

Once back to her senses, Laela wondered if she was reliving her traumatic encounter with the jaguar: now in technicolor and not being able to faint and be carried away by Phips and the totem team. Wasn't a jaguar imprint enough for a young girl, barely a woman? She tried to relive the dream. She wanted to bring Orla with her as a witness and a helper to relieve her. She needed to grasp what it was telling her and if she could live up to such a responsibility. She began to cry and shake.

Orla broke traditional protocol and just held Laela in her arms. Her wracking sobs were from realization and denial and realization again. Laela hadn't processed all that already happened with the first jaguar. And now, she was being called to face a fiercer one. How do you meet a future call of epic proportions when you can't solve your everyday problems yet? Orla empathized.

Orla stroked Laela's hair. "Now, try to breathe like I was teaching you. I'm going to sit here and pray for a very long time. When I receive the needed inspiration, I will share some thoughts about your vision. But there, there. How very exciting to be honored by such a unique experience, such a great call!"

Orla prayed for what seemed hours, and evening had arrived. Then she lit the candles set about the room with a small fire starter she carried. She asked Laela to sit in front of her.

Orla closed her eyes, and as she was talking, her voice became huskier and more assertive. She said, "The 'One' has spoken to me. I see the magnificent tapestry of your life: you will be a woman of the trees, strong and flexible. You'll outgrow this girlish selfishness. You will be a wise and renowned leader who will promote justice and compassion. But your tests will be longer and harder than those of the other women. You'll need to make a great effort to overcome every test.

"You must remain steadfast in your reliance on the 'One.' For every test, the 'One' will give you the powers to overcome it. You must arise to do this for your people."

That night Orla and Ordo consulted with the Elders of the community in a secret Council meeting. The men raised their eyebrows and stroked their patriarchal beards in amazement. They didn't want to offend Alvaro and his lineage but simply couldn't imagine how Laela could become the protagonist of such extraordinary circumstances. A girl known to be more opinionated than demure, more adventurous, and even rebellious than quiet and virtuous. How could a 'Calling' flow through such an unworthy vessel?

Tandor, the oldest of them, waited for the ebb in the heated debate, "Esteemed Councilmen, we must be humble in examining this most unusual situation. The 'One' doesn't work in the ways of people but in the ways of His-self. Should He choose a girl to be a herald of the new age, who are we to question Him?"

Sidhe, one of the youngest Councilmen, who thought Tandor was becoming dotty with age, countered, "We have no evidence that these signs are anything more than a coincidence. The girl got mauled by a jaguar because she ventured outside the town limits. Then, of course, she became terrified of jaguars and dreamed of an even bigger one. The hero who will really be this leader will surely be a strong, courageous, and virtuous man. Has it ever been otherwise?"

Tandor looked at Sidhe kindly, "For centuries, men have ruled over our Kingdom. But, in our Holy Scriptures, the 'One' promises that this new age will be a turbulent one with unexpected changes. There will be transformations in our way of life. The 'One' can make a vessel of any being he chooses. I say that these are real signs and that we must pray over this young woman. No one should oppose her or arise to shame or hurt her in any way. I believe we will offend the 'One' if we don't recognize the signs, even if they occur in a way that we didn't expect. For two signs have been fulfilled, and only one more is needed, though it's the greatest." Tandor vowed in his heart to be Laela's well-wisher and protector. She would need it as all the forces of good and evil were amassing to challenge her. He prayed for her daily from that night on as she might be the key to their people's future security.

The men didn't discuss the mysteries and promises of the New Age as they were frightened by such abstract concepts as the end of times. They had imagined an end to an era to be a myth more than a reality. Something they would never witness! The Council would need to meet many more times to read and reread their holy texts and pray for guidance. All left, sharing the very same unease that Laela was experiencing that night.

Orla left Laela with a small pill to help her sleep. She understood that Laela would need many months and even years to grow into the woman she needed to be. For now, she needed to rest and unpack this vision little by little over time. Laela slept very late.

During the afternoon of the third and last day, her entourage from the Hub, Elsa, Orla, and her mother, Tara, prepared her to leave the Enclosure, the final step in becoming a woman. Tara rubbed Laela's ears with a numbing agent, and Elsa heated up a needle to pierce them. All Treedle women wore earrings to signify their coming of age. Tara and Alvaro had purchased an excellent set of earrings fashioned from gold and silver filigree—shaped into delicate flower buds.

They brushed her hair and styled it with a woven lavender and silver headband. They were excited to show her a matching lavender silk tunic stamped with a floral pattern. It was all the craze for such occasions. The tunic was longer than a girl's, and flounces were sewn in around the hips to make her look more expansive and more womanly. Laela felt encumbered by the outfit but thrilled for the beautiful earrings made from precious metals.

The women made a circle around her and sang again:

You are a woman now, a vessel of life.
The river of red and the river of white,
Will ebb and flow when the time is right,
You are a woman now and will learn new ways.
To work and serve and fill your days.
Your heart has grown stronger and more tender.

To all in need, you are a protector and defender.
When a woman's menses cease to flow, so the seed of new life
will grow.
From the womb to the breast where mother's milk doth flow,
The inner sea doth ebb and flow, but love is the answer to your
journey.
Be honest and wise in word and in deed.
And in the art of peace, you must take the lead.

When she emerged from the Enclosure, Oti was there smiling. She handed Laela a basket of flowers and gave her a long hug. Oti whispered joyfully to her, "We are both women now. We're going to always be there for each other. Dear, dear friend." Laela wanted to linger in this sweet embrace. However, she did not want to tell Oti or even her mother about the dream visions until the volcanic heat of them settled more in her mind. She could barely wait to be in her room again and play with Macecle, who had not been permitted to visit her. She wanted to plump her nose in her fragrant bedroom pillows and be a girl again. At least for a while.

CHAPTER 8

Soulmates Wed

The weeks leading up to Oti and Phips' wedding involved the whole neighborhood in preparations. Laela was a member of the production team, making floral garlands and keeping them freshly sprinkled with water and hanging them in nets. Oti and Phips insisted on a simple celebration, but no one seemed to hear or understand the request. Tara had helped Oti's family create a delicate wedding canopy for the couple to make their vows. They wove the shiniest threads and the most achingly lush-petaled pink flowers through the billowing nets.

On the day of the wedding, the weather was neither too breezy nor too hot. Laela began by surveying the outlying tables around the park. Everywhere she walked, the smells were joyful reminders of this union day. There were tables set out along the park's border, with fruits and herbs cut into small mosaic pieces forming floral and other patterns on platters, spicy nut cakes, and cured meats with dipping sauces. Only a few children were sneaking small bites and laughing.

Laela went to the dressing room by the park to help Oti into her shimmering silver wedding gown. It hugged her waist tightly, enhanced the curve of her bosom but only revealed the suggestion of shadow between her breasts. Little crystal stars woven into the delicate netting and lace covering the dress twinkled, capturing light in winking glints. With the crown on her head, blush on her cheeks, and eyes ablaze, Oti held Laela's hands and thanked her, "Dear sister, you have been and will continue to be my other soulmate. You will always be a part of our lives, our home. Don't be sad. Enjoy this day with us."

Oti wanted to die of shame in that moment as she was hoping she had hidden her pain. She hugged Oti without words and went to explore the park. Guests were gathering and beginning to sit on the small, polished benches set around the wedding canopy, from which the garlands of flowers extended out like rays of the sun.

She walked up behind Phips to congratulate him. His most ribald friend, Koehn, was in front of her. He sidled up to Phips and opened his palm, placing some pellets in his hand, "Here, brother, this is a guarantee for a 'full' night of happiness with your bride. It only takes one for the 'fun' to last for hours."

Phips looked at Koehn with disappointment and firmly returned them in Koehn's pocket. "Brother, I don't need help. Save them for yourself one day." Phips turned away, and he looked with serene dreaminess at Oti, laughing with her friends and distributing one flower each from her flower-chain necklace. He started walking toward her, and Laela followed him from behind at a distance.

As the guests focused on the little gazebo where musicians were beginning to play, Oti and Phips moved as if magnetically drawn together, heading quietly to their predetermined point of encounter. The private one where they could repeat their vows and promise themselves to each other fully in the moment. Laela felt her gaze shamelessly drawn to them. Fluid energy was streaming around them, like fragrant rainwater, as they held hands and joined together in a very long embrace under the canopy of their favorite Windlapping tree. Its long fern-like leaves cascaded a semi-transparent curtain over them. There they stood entwined, caressing slowly with their hands sliding up and down each other's backs and around their necks. Kissing, languid motions of them rocking together, tugging each others' lips with teeth nips, laughing, and holding in sweet silence with only their eyes locked, for the longest time. Laela, watched them from a lower vantage point, behind the twiggy crook of a thick tree branch nearby. She saw the closest two people to her, the ones who knew her secrets and shared her every day with her, moving away.

She felt a new emotion, in addition to the guilt of sneaking up on her friends. She wasn't sure of the name of this feeling, but it wasn't rejoicing for her friends. It was as if the wafting power of their union had taken them up and away. The gentle rushing, thirst-quenching waters of their long friendship with her had moved on in their wake. They were leaving Laela alone and dry.

She was so entranced; she jumped with a shriek when Leon tapped her on the shoulder. He looked at her with solemn pity or worse, a higher level of understanding-compassion. She felt nauseous to have him catch her in such an intimate and vulnerable moment. He invited her to sit with him at the ceremony. She accepted numbly.

Laela and Leon sat in the front row with the closest family members. Her father Alvaro would officiate the ceremony, ending in the Treedle vows to formalize a union between man and woman. However, the two mates were welcome to create their program. Oti and Phips chose sacred verses and texts for different family members to read. They invited the younger children to sing a song in rounds. Laela read the opening prayer about love standing to the side of their wedding canopy while Oti and Phips held hands and locked eyes.

Nana Bisru had asked to read a poem in honor of the couple, reminding them to be of service to their people:

Awake your mind, open your eyes,
Don't let dry leaves litter its skies,
Greet the sun, gaze on the trees
Hear birds songs harmonize with the breeze,
The light in your heart is as bright as the love for your brother,

Nothing surpasses the joy of serving one another,
Whether dark as the pupil of the eye or white as a cloud without
a trace
Every face you behold is born from a cradle of grace,
Many a day undreamed, unsung passes as a widow grieves,
Forgetting the chances that drift away like leaves,
The moons wax and the moons wane,
And we will find healing for every pain.
Listen, don't lose the moment, the time of now,
To see, to feel, to learn, to lift your brow.
Plant seeds of love, of life, of hope. Live your vow.

Then came the time to seal the vow. Oti and Phips took turns looking deeply into each other's eyes and repeating, "We come from the 'One' and return to the 'One.' We do the will of the 'One.' We will be faithful to the 'One' and each other in word and deeds." Then they each kissed each other's hands with reverence.

Quiet turned into loud and boisterous cheers and whistles. A group of boys, in charge of festive sound-making, banged pots, rang bells, popped pellets, and hooted. Musicians who had been in the audience joined the Joy band on the gazebo. The instruments in a Treedle band or orchestra all began with 'J' sounds associated with joy, rhythm, and graceful movement: jambo, jambor, jahnjoh, jorkoh, juepi, jejejo with wooden keys attached to taught slim chords on a board in a carefully measured increase of the shortest to the most extended lines varying the tone and pitch of these marvelous instruments. Musicians were often called "Js," too. The music chosen for this occasion would stir body and spirit and raucously celebrate for hours to come.

Oti and Phips left to drink some water and get ready for their triumphal entrance as life-mates entering the center of the dancing circle. They would choreograph their dance and steps and invite others to join them. Of course, the new mates would have a significant advantage in dancing the dance of their creation, and all others would pale in their efforts to follow their lead. As the band played a well-loved, Treedle tune, Oti entered, waving a glittering green streamer and Phips behind her with one hand on her hip and the other waving a red streamer. A call out to their clans. They soon had the crowd weaving, spiraling, collapsing in laughter in a line dance, and then reorganizing for dancing in pairs.

Leon asked her for the first couple's dance. His face was sweating heavily, and some beads of sweat fell on her lips. He squinted his eyes as if in pain, and she felt his hand on her back, clasping her to him with a clinging pressure. She suddenly understood that he was desperately in love with her. He was barely able to steer her among the growing number of Treedles on the dance floor.

Was it her lonely state, but for once, she wished she could love him back. What a promising young man he was. Extremely intelligent and caring too. She hugged him to her and spoke softly into his ear,

"You're such a dear man. Like a brother to me," she told him. She had to be honest and remove a hope that would only hurt him more over time. "I could never see us together as mates. But I hope that your mate will be one of the most beautiful young women in Aerizon. One who can match you, if this is possible, in kindness and goodness. A woman who will give you her whole heart and life to you and your family—which I hope will grow very big."

Tears welled in Leon's eyes, and she saw the male bone in his neck throbbing." Laela, thank you for telling me the truth. I want your happiness. I just fear that you will seek love in the wrong place, in the wrong man. If I thought there was any hope of having you, I would wait for you forever."

"Don't—you, mustn't. The 'One' will provide you with someone better for you than me. I can promise you that." Laela was very sure that neither would be happy in the end if obliged to mate. The first set of songs ended, and they excused themselves. They both needed to break away and walk to a quieter spot in the party for now.

Laela was ready to eat an entire mammal of any size. Macecle found her and led her to the food table so they could eat their treats together. Eating and breathing calmed her considerably. It was time to mingle now and greet friends and family. She would surprise teacher Adele with a hug and then compliment Nana Bisru on the poem reading.

Someone tapped her on the shoulder. Someone she had almost forgotten but who was always lurking in some shadow of her mind. Vito. She noted that he had probably sought her out as she and Macecle had all but hidden behind bushes so they could eat in peace.

Vito turned her around and cradled her lower back with one hand. He looked steadily in her eyes without speaking, and he slowly traced a line from her chin down to her belly button with his fingertip. His eyes seemed dark and intense, belying his unhurried liquid touch. Laela felt goosebumps and a challenge; she drew taut and pulled away.

"Now that is hardly a proper greeting, do you think?" she admonished him. Here he barged into her space, her reality in such an immediate and urgent way. It threw her off guard, which is where he always seemed to land her.

"You know we have an unfinished conversation. And you have a choice to make. I saw you with that house pet who moons over you. You can't stand him, can you? What do you want? Or should I say, who do you want?"

"Please don't insult Leon. He's too good for me. About a mate, I can't answer that yet. So, I ask you: Vito, do you want me?" she asked, her voice shaking slightly, "or do you just want to 'have' me?"

He narrowed his eyes slyly and smiled. "Both, my dear. And I believe you want that too."

Laela hesitated, wrestling with the emotions boiling inside. He was stroking her forearm, and she felt entirely unsafe even with a touch as light as this.

"I believe I'm not ready to make a big life decision right now. As you have probably heard, I've been through a lot lately."

"You've wrestled a jaguar and survived. You've entered the Enclosure and become a woman," he said, fondling an earlobe with her shiny new earrings. He stepped back to appraise her.

"Hmm," he mused. He let his eyes run from Laela's head to her toes this time, lingering on her breasts and hips. "I would say you are certainly ready. Maybe more than ready. You know fruit can get overly ripe, and then who would eat it?"

Laela wanted to slap him. Anything less than humbling herself before him would be a rejection to him. She snarled and tried to turn away, but he caught her wrist and twisted it awkwardly. "My dear, I'm a real man, and a real man doesn't let women play with him. Not in this way. If I 'have' you, be sure that I will teach you to be a real woman. And you will like it. I will provide better than any man around, the best house, the best clothes, the best mate. But I'll expect my woman to appreciate that."

However lewd or rude Vito could be, he was right about her options. Unfortunately, not much awaited her outside of a good mating match. Maybe they could tame each other in the bonds of daily commitment this union would impose. Always together, supported by family and friends. She was ashamed of wanting him only in an impure way. Her instincts were'nt virginal, and that could lead her astray.

"I need time to think, to be sure of what I want," Laela reaffirmed.

"Well, time is running very short for me. I'll take you as my mate and care for you in every way, but you must come to me before the month ends and be ready to give yourself to me."

Laela was tempted just to give herself away right then and there. She could melt into his arms, and all other decisions, the mind-wracking dreams, the doubts would fade away. She would have a safe place in society. And there was one way that he would surely please her.

"I'll think and pray about this. And if I say yes, you will also be blessed because I won't enter a union half-heartedly."

Laela watched the dance floor, declining most invitations to dance and sipping nectar drinks. As the evening progressed, she noticed that some men had red-flushed faces from drinking forbidden alcohol and not dancing too much. Vito was among the group of men passing a flask around, supposedly out of sight. Vito didn't so much as glance her way.

She was watching him, but in the side-eye unmated women learned to do with potential mates. He went up and bowed with a self-mocking flourish and offered a hand to Lili to accompany him to the dance floor. He whirled and twirled her and then held her tight, aligning their swaying movements. She could see him whispering what must be endearments in Lili's ear as she blushed a furious red. Vito's eye finally met hers from across the room. His expression was unapologetic, and he nodded to her as if to say, the ball is in your court.

She turned to Nol, a former classmate, and asked him to spin her around for a good long time. She prayed that her sentiments, the whole unruly lot of them, would get lost in the stomping and foot-beats.

Laela had little heart for the rest of the party, and she was already full when others sat down for dinner. She tried to concentrate on her love for her friends so she could tell their story at dinner. She had chosen an ode to her best friends for dinner. "May you be shining lines in the web of life. May you be joined in the closest of ties strengthening yourselves in a lasting union. May your family be the pride of Aerizon! I love you."

It was night. Oti and Phips stood up in silhouette before the full twin moons, Cor and Cora, and twining their right arms together, toasted with nectar for lovers. They couldn't ignore the tradition to seek the moons' blessings of protection before inaugurating their new home in the trees with the consummation of the marriage.

CHAPTER 9

Month of Signs

Laela waited to visit her newly wedded friends for over a week, the customary time for them to be alone to set up their new home or space in the man's family home. She could imagine Oti and Phipps cooking together, enjoying the treetop views on the surrounding patios, and sipping drinks, and watching sunsets in the tower room. On the eighth day after the wedding, they invited Laela for afternoon snacks. She had had little time to talk with them after the period in the Enclosure as they were advancing wedding plans and consumed with the details of a party involving the better part of Aerizon.

Things had changed. Oti met her dreamily at the door, looking over her shoulder at Phips. Her eyes lingered on him adoringly every time he spoke. Phips would touch her to ask for more of that fantastic gorberi juice she makes, and his hand would continue to trace some contour or other of her feminine figure. They made attempts to include her and listened attentively to her story of the Enclosure. She shared the two dreams. But they were so immersed in the captivating madness of love as a married couple; they were immune to hot and cold, wet and dry. They still needed more hours alone to bask in the life that emerges when two people merge into one.

Laela was determined not to let their happiness make hers less. She had to find her own. The days ahead would be for making her own first decisions as a woman.

As Laela walked home, she meandered through the different Treedle neighborhoods to look through the windows of life of the Bouder and Texare tribes. She stopped to admire a carving that a craftsman, one of Phips' cousins, made of thick-tailed blue-bird. Sitting surrounded by sawdust and wood chips, his chubby face radiated with pride. Laela admired his ingenuity in making such a standing bird, beginning to lift its wings, from a piece of wood. He would polish and paint it later, to the point that it would look real from a distance. She passed by the row of houses where Oti used to live and admired the colorful weavings women were making on the patios. Rugs, curtains, wall hangings, soft bed covers. One of the older women stayed young in spirit by weaving hangings with patterns of waving red, yellow, and fluorescent green and blue stripes. These bright textiles added cheer to a child's room or served as material for clothing and jackets for them.

She admired her friends for uniting their two cultures. She felt that many young Treedles would be watching their lifestyle evolve and how they would stretch the limits of cultural mores, ever so gently but with meaningful intent.

That night, Laela sat on her window ledge and convened with the moons Cor and Cora for inspiration. The 'One' would guide her life, but He was so exalted that she sometimes felt more comfortable meditating through nature and the wonderful signs He deposited in it. It was the beginning of the month of Signs. What more auspicious time to reflect on next steps? She asked the forces that be, "Should I mate? With Leon? With Vito? Vito can't wait much longer for an answer. But my throat clenches up every time I think of him. I know he's not safe for me in some ways, but maybe he would be if tied to me with the eternal moonline?" Women in the community often joked that they had to educate their mates like another child to become real men over time. Men were always more of a work in process than women, who settled and gained enough wisdom for them both.

And the bouts of restlessness. "Why do I want to return to the Feral Forest like an itch that won't stop? I can hunt again nearby. I'm afraid and yet longing to go deeper into it. I feel a job was left undone there. I want to try to overcome my fear of another encounter with a jaguar. I would be armed this time if I did. And the black jaguar. If it's my destiny to meet this beast, I would rather it be sooner than later. What should I do, keep working in the garden, safe at home, until I become a lonely spinster? Or worse—homebound forever."

More than love, more than desire, more than wanting a haven, Laela confessed to herself the truth. She wanted to explore and discover what lay beyond Aerizon and the Treedle universe. But who could hear this and understand? It had to be kept secret and how to deal with it as well. She thought of strange Orla, the Shaman, the only one who looked at her and saw her soul's yearnings. But even Orla wouldn't encourage her to do anything without consulting her parents. Parental authority was sacred.

How could she make good of this insistent drive? She didn't want to hurt or upset her loved ones anymore, but she had to go out one more time, to venture far out before she could resign herself forever into domesticated life.

She made up her mind. She shouted inside, "I'll do it. Yes, do it." And it felt correct; well, fear, excitement, and confusion too. She whispered a prayer to the 'One' for confirmation and forgiveness. She wouldn't lie, but she would disobey. Or not? Her parents hadn't spoken anymore about the Feral Forest incident.

Little did she know that they were utterly confounded, for once, about how to handle their daughter. They had heard from Orla directly about her visions, and Alvaro shared with Tara that the Council was far from united in concluding the significance of Laela's dreams and the connections to ancient Treedle spiritual prophecies. They had decided not to give her any more advice or admonitions for the time being. They wanted to be sure what to say next. To

Laela, the silence was so unlike them. They were always teaching her lessons or prodding her to examine her life and actions through the Writings. She had been relieved about the respite, but still, she did value their guidance.

Laela spent the next day in the garden tending to Tan and Gibble's feeding rituals. She wanted them to make an ultra-strong moonline rope for this trip. Once decided, she wasn't going to venture out just for a picnic. It would take no less than four full days to explore where she wanted to go and then get back home. She needed to be well provisioned to carry tools and weapons of defense. She would also need to prepare her mind. Treedles were inherently fragile little creatures. Explorers and soldiers achieved victories using their wits and senses. What brute force they lacked, they made up with creative strategies and quick exits.

She questioned an old hunter about protecting against jaguars. He looked at the round-eyed, lavender waif before him, and after laughing until he toppled over, he advised her to find the jaguar before he saw her. If the jaguar saw her— "back away slowly, don't make eye contact with one as they don't like a challenge. Move away slowly, but if it decides to attack, start screaming and flailing your arms. They hate a fuss. Protect the back of your head. They often strike there."

Laela would make a leather cap for this purpose with a flap over the back of her neck. She started training Macecle how to screech even more and to jump about should an animal attack them. She enacted scenes with him using Lucas's wooden toys to represent the animals. Macecle also became deranged with mirth. She scolded him. "This is serious, Macecle; you must learn to protect us better."

In a week, she would be ready enough. She sharpened her hunting knife, purchased a new leather flask to carry drinking water, and created a backpack to carry slings and store camping supplies and dried foods. Macecle would help her gather edible tree food, and there was a small stove at site three where they could stew some meat if no one were nearby. Traders didn't travel every month and had just returned from a trip before the wedding. Since she and Phips had never sighted any Treedle soldier or spies, which were very few anyway, she imagined they had the interest to remain incognito. She would need to be ready to get off the trail at a moment's notice and not be spotted by anyone, be they innocent or dangerous. Secrecy concerning her whereabouts was essential to her mission!

The biggest challenge would be to go to station seven. It was the farthest outpost and the closest to the Trading Village. Laela had never gone beyond station three, nor did she have a map that showed how to get to it. But she was confident about picking up such a concrete trail as this one marked by cables and making it to the last station. During one of the expeditions to build the route, Phips had asked if he could take Macecle to accompany him and Ringer. He and the two traders, the three men that would go, could use some nimble hands for casting and securing lines. Macecle and Ringer were in their element on such outings and would be most helpful. She hadn't debriefed Macecle, but this meant he was familiar with the entire route. Even if he weren't with her, Laela could quickly figure out how to hop onto the following connecting zip line. She just had no idea how far apart the stations might be or how long it would take to get to the end, but nor did she have a fixed time she needed to arrive near the village.

Laela barely slept the night before her departure. She had decided to take Tan and Gibble with her to continue working on the new moonline rope. She had a comfortable pouch for them in a large pocket on her tunic. Her last duty was to write a note to her parents about the alone time she needed. She inscribed on parchment:

Dearly Beloved Parents,
I am writing to thank you for all the loving care you have given
me and to assure you that I sincerely appreciate you and all you
have taught me.

I have decided to spend some time alone to reflect. I will be gone for several days. I beg of you to understand, so please don't send someone after me. I will take excellent care of myself and return home soon.
Love,
Laela

Laela got up two hours before dawn and left the note on the dining room table. She shushed Macecle, who was excited about the outing. They could easily skirt the town and even get to station one in the Feral Forest before dawn. The moons provided enough light to find their way and hide in shadows where no one would see them. This head start was essential so that no one could find them at the crack of dawn to dissuade them from setting out.

They made it to station two before mid-morning. They stopped for a late breakfast, and Macecle gathered fresh nuts and berries in his pouch to last them two days. After this brief rest, Laela kept them at a steady pace, moving, moving, zipping from line to line, tree to tree. They stopped to rest briefly at station three. She didn't know how far distant station four would be but needed to find it before nightfall. The moonline cables led straight from tree to distant tree, and though the pattern varied overall and zigzagged among clusters of thick forest, one led to the next. And then it was time to move forward without distraction to a station she hadn't seen before.

Macecle understood the plan and was eager to lead the way. Laela saw how well Phips and his team had constructed the cables and admired the whirring speed as they moved across and through treetops. The men had done an excellent job of clearing branches and obstacles that might slow the trip. Fortune was with them as Laela and Macecle saw no one and didn't stop long enough anywhere for a predator to catch their scent and attack them.

When they arrived at station four, the first hints of approaching sunset—crisper breezes, and tinges of yellow and pink—Laela needed to catch her breath to celebrate this victory. She squealed with excitement and thanked the 'One.' She always asked for His blessings even when she knew she wasn't in a position to attract them.

A plump tree gerber was just in sight when they laid down their gear. Laela nodded to Macecle to catch its attention and quickly downed it with one shot from her small sling. They would risk making a stew as they all needed more protein for the energy they were expending. She would keep the embers low on the stove and fan off any smoke. They were miles from possible settlements, but precautions were still advisable. She was grateful for this station's comforts and the two bowls, spoons, and cups the traders had left. As the stew was brewing with some of the herbs she brought, she looked at a new hole carved into the tree and found a wooden box tucked into it. There were some vials, a few empty sheets of writing parchment, a stylus, and a leather sack. She reached into the bag and pulled out a folded parchment. It was a map with annotations from the traders. She was thrilled at the level of detail she was seeing. What a gift. She planned to go as far as the Trading Village and then do some of her snooping and spying. She would find Mergons there and could observe their habits. She could use her cap and a cloak to look like a boy, possibly a trader's son.

Sunset was coming soon, and even though there were a few small candles at the site, she needed to study the map thoroughly in a good light. She noticed that the map indicated the traders' drop-off point to enter the border village and delineated key Mergon territory. It was evident that the three stations away, station seven was close enough to the drop-down point to enter the Trader's Village. She gauged that it would be a day out compared to the distance she had come. However, the border of Mergonland was distinctly southeast, and no cable lines were leading to it, probably for security reasons. Laela thought about how they might glint in the sun. The border town, where traders headed, also appeared to lay around a day northeast of the Kingdom's flatlands. Thus, both locations—the village and the entrance to the Mergon Kingdom—were roughly the same distance from their current outpost. Like a triangle.

They had never seen or studied such a map in school, and it was the first time she had ever visualized where the heart of the Mergon Kingdom lay in relation to the Feral Forest. A thrilling thought came to mind. How many of these trips could she make? They would most probably ground her for life upon return to Aerizon. What if, just what if she scouted out around actual Mergon land. She could enter where it wasn't densely populated, observe, and return to the high forest within hours. She was good at scouting. The idea of glimpsing briefly into Mergon life—the lands, the houses, some of its people, the actual citizens of the land—all were intoxicating to her.

She brushed away, fears flying around the edges like a dark cloud of parasitic flies. She needed to shoo away from this new vision. There was danger in every choice she might make. She was just a young girl (though now technically a woman) straying over a border to look at some farms. What harm could happen if she were careful? She was clever, determined, and everything in her life had prepared her to explore a village.

She noticed a large flat expanse, annotated as fields for crops at the Kingdom's northern border, flanked by what they called hills and much farther even from the fortified area—the King's castle. She would head for the farming area where there would be many fields and fewer people than in the heart of the Kingdom. Here would be the closest and probably safest entry point.

She would need to chart out a different route and look for forest landmarks to find a safe way to pass across the Mergon's top border. She and Macecle would remain in the forest's perimeter until they could safely move into an open area. She would use Macecle for backup and ask him only to follow her when signaled once it was time to advance into open spaces. Notes on the map indicated that traps were laid out in hidden places and showed that border guards regularly patrolled the periphery of the forest. She would need to look for a large tree to descend and not be seen by guards. There were also patrol animals; a note reminded Treedles to camouflage smells to avoid being detected by trained four-legged conchos. Conchos had sets of teeth almost as formidable as jaguars. They were vicious and persistent hunters. Laela noted that several pomade vials were also stored in the tree. These would indeed contain ointments to mask Treedle scents. She was familiar with them, and they aided Treedle hunters in surprising prey. This was quite a shower of gifts.

The forest between this station and Mergonland would bring them into uncharted territory. They would need to move slowly and cautiously. It might take more than a day to get there. Though Treedle spies visited there with some regularity, they would take care not to cross paths with traders after this juncture and would certainly try not to leave easily identifiable trails. She imagined; however, they would need quick and reliable entry and escape routes and would leave subtle clues for easier tree-trailing that she hoped to detect. She would have to think of ways spies might have made the path easier for themselves, leaving clues only other very experienced Treedles could figure out. Just as there were dangers in the Feral Forest, there might be new and unexpected ones around the borders of the Kingdom, especially approaching the flatlands that farmers would populate.

As she explored the possible scenarios and risks of visiting Mergonland, Laela knew her mind was made up. She hoped that this was inspiration from the 'One' and not just a spirit for adventure, filling her with excitement and confidence. The voices of tradition, community, and fear were always whispering when not actively intervening to stop her from exploring different realities. But today, far from home and faced with a once-in-a-lifetime opportunity, they were beckoning her to reckon with them to pass through them and be led forward by the vision of seeing Mergons for herself. She had to be willing to face dangers and be forged through tests to develop new understandings. Her short life had taught her that this was true and that though there was a price to pay for pushing beyond traditional boundaries, the learning and knowledge were worth it.

The Mergons were people too, and she wanted to see them with her own eyes and not through what she was told. She wondered how different they were from Treedles and why Treedles believed there was no hope of friendship or reconciliation with them. Treedles didn't want to inhabit their lands, and Mergons most certainly wouldn't choose to live in the treetops. It seemed that collaboration between the ground and air people should far outweigh the benefits of hatred and mistrust between them. She was eager to see the possibilities, even if from short-lived glimpses of the culture.

Laela and Macecle bathed themselves using the full tank of rainwater at the station. They brushed the leaves off the lid of the tank filter and left it to collect water for the next visitors. Laela opened the two vials and discovered they were scented skin ointments. She detected the heavy musky scent that serious hunters used to disguise their Treedle smell. They would apply some to sleep well tonight and even more to cover their scent at the crack of dawn before they departed. Laela planned to use her small compass to get them heading south but in a more easterly direction than the border village's location. From thereon, they had to hope for some clues here and there to shorten their trip. However, they would arrive sooner or later, and the map in her backpack was an assurance of that.

Laela slept in a tightly woven netted, moonline hammock with Macecle huddled over her for mutual warmth. They slept and woke up the following day easily. Dawn on the treetops was heralded by all manner of bird chatter and tweets. Avian friends moved about the skies and trees, singing, cooing, and calling. The caw-caws usually flew in pairs, the raptors alone, the smaller birds that nature dipped in the saturated colors of the rainbow flew in flocks or alone but in proximity to their family. The sky brought quieter but just as powerful reminders of the morning as warm pink, orange, and yellow light began to stream through the leafy canopy above them.

After a hearty breakfast of leftover stew and nuts, Laela took the compass and plotted her first move. Looking at the trees' pattern in the compass's direction, she now had to surmise which ones would lead her to the next and then the next without going off course and without jumping and swinging on to weak branches that might crack under their weight, causing them to fall. As they moved and swung from one tree to another, Laela could sense that they were descending a kind of slope and that some of the jungle landscape below was more full of bramble and leaves. They found two markers, gourds swinging on moonlines. Nearby were some moonline cords that acted like the ziplines she, Phips, and the traders had created. They indicated a trail shortening the distance and helping them move more securely from one point to the next. Laela had brought the little harness and clip belted below her tunic. About five hours into their journey, they stopped to rest in a particularly tall tree that stood out from the rest. Out of curiosity, Laela climbed to its highest possible safe branch. She put her hand to her mouth in shock to realize that the whole plan had worked. They were within two hours of the rim where the forest ended and a colorful, plotted treeless region began. She could see only fragments of the countryside. With this slice of reality, she could amend their direction slightly to come down near empty fields and not right by houses bordering the forest. She had heard that some crops were as high or higher than Treedles, especially to come close to the cottages.

Their route was now heading downward. There were fewer towering, ancient trees, and they began to see more of the leaf-shedding trees that also changed colors that Laela had seen in drawings in classes about Mergon culture. Now, she would need to camouflage better as a keen observer might detect her in these trees. Gratefully, Macecle, if he stayed quiet, was a known species of animal. However, Mergons didn't breed marsupials like him for totems. They used animals as they did Treedles, for service, and as slave labor. Laela wove a wreath of trees over her cap and hung monster leaves over her front and back, tied by some string.

As they approached closer to the fields of Mergonland, she stopped and planned the next steps. They could be sure there were Mergon guards nearby, but 'where' was the question.

"Macecle, you must scout, hiding behind trees, and see if you see people. They will be Mergons and tan or brownish men. Let me know where they are." Laela spoke to Macecle with urgent undertones.

Macecle returned an hour later. Through simple language runts and pantomime, he indicated that he had searched around the nearby perimeter of the forest. He stretched his hands every which way to convey that there were big fields ahead. Around a half-mile to the west of them, were five men and as many conchos. However, the men were drinking a lot and falling over each other.

It occurred to her that maybe the men were celebrating some kind of festival or event. They had to find their entry point before the guards dispersed into directions that could intersect with them. Laela moved from tree to tree, followed by Macecle, and then had to descend to walk. Laela had never walked on the ground before. She stooped to touch the earth and was awed at the millions of crushed stones and debris that went into creating it. It was gritty but smelled foamy and was unyielding under her feet. She would need to learn how to navigate the forest floor that held the very trees where Treedles lived. She was used to calculating distance and movement from above—not from below.

They headed toward the perimeter of the forest at sunset, the purple and pink evening sky beckoning them onwards. Laela realized that she wasn't prepared to make the next decisions. She had focused intensely on arriving safely, but how could they stay safe now? How could they avoid Mergons and yet spy on them? And where would they begin tomorrow?

They found a pile of rocks, rubble from construction, by the edge of the field and arranged them to look haphazard and form a hollow for them to sleep and store their gear. They ate dried food for dinner, chewing slowly and quietly inside. Laela looked out through a peephole in their little tunnel and preened to see Cor and Cora from a belly position. She could contrast the orbs against the horizon line. She imagined folks sitting on their porches moon-gazing just as Treedles do.

With this first expansive view of the world, from the bottom, she felt humbled. Small. What was her purpose here? Should she turn back? They could be hunted, enslaved, or killed. She doubted herself and the cocky confidence that led her here. She prayed contritely to the 'One,' "Please forgive me for all I do that is wrong. May this trip not be in vain. May I do something of service to my people through this venture? Protect me, please."

CHAPTER 10

At The Edge of Mergonland

A predawn chill and the smells of soil, grain, and dew aroused Laela. She sensed that the climate here was neither very hot nor cold. Most probably, all species of animals, plants, and fauna live well in this land, except, Laela mused, Treedles, whom Mergons held less respect for than most animals. She peeped out of the hole of the tunnel and saw a fringed-top wall of shining wheat but a few yards away under the cupola of serene, cloudless blue sky above.

Laela emerged from the tunnel and instinctively shimmied close to the ground to enter the field, trying to camouflage herself in the shadows of waving golden stalks that rimmed the lower half of the clearing. Laela had seen small patches of this grain in Treedle gardens but never such a field, stretching over more than a mile in the distance. Peeping through the stalks, she could see that this valley rolled into small hills covered in patchwork fashion with rows of crops intermixed with trapezoid fields of herbs and flowers. In the distance, mountains loomed up like hulking shadows in tones of hushed purple with mists passing over them. She had heard of these and was awed at what seemed a breeze traveling from afar toward them and ruffling through these golden locks covering the earth.

Macecle was snuggling closest to her, but he was restless. He might pop up inadvertently and call attention to them. Anyway, she needed him to be on the lookout until they found a safe hideaway.

A place that Mergon guards or dwellers wouldn't find suspicious or search.

"Macecle, I need you to cover me. Go back to the forest. Move quickly and quietly and scout out where those guards are now. Then go up on a tree in this sightline." She directed her hand like an arrow to where she would be moving. "I'll stay low to the ground and can't be detected. Look for me to raise my fist to motion you to follow me from a distance when the time looks right." Macecle started to sulk and cling to her, and she had to give him a firm push, "Go." To make sure that Tan and Gibble wouldn' be grumpy also, she found some extra bundi leaves for them to lie on and for Gibble to munch in her pocket.

She surveyed what she could of the area, trying to peer out from under cover of wheat grains. Her eyes traveled to the nearest farms and fields. Some farmers cultivated large flowers: deep red-cup-shaped flowers, stalky ones with sheaves of yellow and white flowers, green leafy patches of food crops, and trellises with climbing vines and hanging fruits closer to the cottages. It was a cacophony of color and light: a patterned garden spilled out over vast spaces. One field of any crop stretched more vastly than an expanse of hundreds of trees. It would take hours to run through and wind up and down through each row of crops and plants. On the right side of the wheat field, small houses with thatched roofs created a semi-circle, and to the west of them was the forest, whose towering trees formed a dark silhouette at the foot of the village.

Laela pushed gently through the waving grasses, sturdy yet graceful, sweet but earthy in smell. As she approached a break in the field leading to the next, a large shadow appeared suddenly from her right. It was too late to run and call attention to herself or to escape if it detected her. How could she not have heard it? Had she seen a flash or spot of 'it' and been too distracted to pick it up? Perhaps the unfamiliar smells, colors, and shapes of this foreign land had thrown off her sharp sense of presence. She squatted quickly and curled into a tight ball close to the ground. Then, just as quiet as it was quick, it was standing by her, like the flash of a well-wielded machete cutting a stalk.

Using her defense of appearing small and helpless, of being no threat, she breathed into her fear. She knew that if 'it' were here to fell her in one swoop, it would have happened already. She instinctively felt the threat of this 'it' was somehow neutral. It didn't release the peculiar smell of one on the hunt. Glancing up ever so slowly, she peered the dark golden-toned ankle of a youth set firmly into a leather moccasin. Laela let her eyes continue to sweep up shyly at the view of sculptured legs and the firm outline of a muscular torso, broad shoulders, apparent through the thin white cotton garments he was wearing. His large hands were holding aside the brush as if to create a path of light. The sun was casting a coppery halo around the tousled hair of a young man. Why was she feeling more excitement than dread at this moment?

She began to unfold her arms and legs and push herself up to meet the stranger. She shifted her position to raise herself to his side, obliging him to turn so that neither would stare directly into the sun but be facing each other. She stood and appraised the figure; his sinewy feline frame and firm, sculpted chest—his arms revealing honey-colored skin—like a smooth golden jaguar, glistening and poised. Yet, gentle in presence. So, this was a Mergon. Not fearsome whatsoever, though very unlike a Treedle in gesture and stance. She noticed an odd object with two lenses swinging from his hips. She knew then that this was how he had found her.

She was much smaller and lighter than him. To assert her presence, she stretched up, feeling the length of her frame, and took a confident stride toward him. She opened her eyes fully to meet his, a challenge in the animal world. Wide almond-shaped eyes that were unguardedly curious met hers. They were brown with flecks of light gold and grassy colors circled with tawny eyelashes.

He stared. How rude of him. She could see that he was taken aback and was trying to make sense of the new discovery dawning on him. Laela wasn't a misplaced Treedle slave or an escapee: she was an alert young woman who had uncoiled herself as if about to pounce with the taut energy of a fierce margay. He had never seen a Treedle like her, with such a vibrant hue of lavender skin, round shining eyes, and graceful arching, petal-shaped eyelids. She wore the pierced earrings that Mergone girls also used to signify their change into women. He immediately felt a stab of fear for the girl and responsibility for finding her. He would need to assess the situation and take swift, appropriate action.

"Welcome. I'm Mateo." He outstretched his hand in a somewhat stiff manner. She put out her hand to reach his, observing her first Mergon greeting with interest. Treedles greeted with raised hands, often slapping them together on their palms or a hug. Mateo spoke the same language as Treedles but with a more resounding cadence. She responded. "I'm Laela. A Treedle from the Pyuva tribe. I come in peace," She signaled Macecle, who had already lost patience and was on his way to her. "My friend, my totem Macecle is just about to join us." Macecle reached them and gave such an odd look to Mateo that Mateo had to stifle a laugh not to offend the girl or her totem.

"Why are you here, and how did you get here? I mean, who brought you here?" A Treedle so evidently a young female, so free in movement, was an absolute anomaly in Mergonland. But no female in either Mergonland or Aerizon would travel far without a male escort.

"I'm from the community of Aerizon in the very top layer of the forest. I'm alone. This visit," she hesitated shyly, "wasn't planned. I like to explore. For reasons that would take a long time to explain, I've learned how to hunt and make my way through the forest. I wanted more than anything to experience a new land, to visit here one or two days and then return home." A tug of unexpected pleasure ran through her body. She wanted to explain more. However, there was information that could get others in trouble or disclose their locations on the travel routes.

She looked at his shocked face, "Most unusual, I know. A girl arriving like this. But Macecle is a better partner on this kind of trip than many men would be." She was trying to assuage the worried grimace on Mateo's face. "I mean no harm. I'm and, as you see, will go to great lengths to satisfy my curiosity. I just wanted to see a glimpse of Mergon life."

Curiosity also began wrestling away at Mateo's better senses.

"Listen, we can talk further, but not standing out in the open." Mateo looked at her with a genuine concern that didn't require cultural interpretation. He spoke as if out of breath, "I don't want to be rude or ungracious in welcoming you to our land, but you are in grave danger—more than you can possibly imagine. No one can see you. You have to return to the forest. Head back home as soon as possible."

"Follow me to my horse." He pointed to a sizable furry brown mammal tied to a nearby post who had baskets hanging on both sides of his plump midsection. "I'll carry you and Macecle to a safe enough entry point." She had heard of these large furry animals who were typically gentle and transported people and products on their backs. Mateo bade her follow him, staying low in the grasses until they arrived. He took charge and quickly bundled her in a soft cotton blanket, all but covering her face, and set her into one of the large baskets strapped over the horse's back and hanging to its side. She was pleased about hiding in plain sight and where she could observe the countryside as the horse walked along. This was the safest she had felt in two days. She realized she hadn't stopped worrying for a minute about being seen or tracked by dark forces.

Mateo sat still atop the horse for a while—thinking—and took up his glasses to survey the surrounding fields and cottages a short distance away.

Laela realized he was probably looking for the best route to escort them back to the forest. She looked up at him imploringly from inside her basket seat, "Isn't there anywhere you can suggest for us to hide and to spend the day at least. We're too tired to make a long journey back right now. I can disguise myself in a cloak to walk around some."

Mateo's eyes darkened. "Maybe, but if anyone discovers you, you are in danger of your life. I'm sorry to tell you this, but your people are treated like slaves here. At times, worse than animals." He couldn't bring himself to tell this wide-eyed, vivacious girl about the slave-breeding mills and the deplorable conditions of the Treedles there. They became drained of color, hope, and looked like varying kinds of grayish zombies. The original Treedles, ones from Aerizon, were so brilliant in color. They only occasionally captured traders or Treedle spies to continue the breeding process and upgrade Treedles' quality to become physically more productive. It was all but unheard of to capture a woman as Treedle women didn't travel to the Kingdom under any circumstances.

Mateo sat, thinking. He opened his leather bag and passed around some wheat buns spread with red berry jam in the middle. Stopping to eat gave him an excuse to delay and strategize what to do next, and Laela and Macecle appreciated the mid-morning snack.

"Laela, I must introduce myself better. I'm a crown Prince, second son of King Malcolm, King of Mergonland. I live and work here in the agricultural region of Mergonland. Even though my home is somewhat distant from the royal Court, there are those tracking my every move. So, you see, to not upset the King or break his laws, and to guard your freedom, we must be cautious. I have to escort you to safety."

Mateo watched her disappointed reaction as if he were stealing a dream from her. He also wanted to know more about this fascinating woman, and so in an uncharacteristically impulsive move, he took a risk.

"Well, I too would very much like to know more about your land and people. If we make our moves with caution, I can offer you to stay in my home for a day or two, as I really can't think of anywhere else safer to recommend you to shelter. I'm not sure how else to protect you in this situation. But I have two trusted servants who live with me, and you could stay on a separate floor with Ana, a Treedle woman."

It was the same rule in both Treedle and Mergon cultures that a young woman shouldn't be alone with a member of the opposite sex, at mating age, for any length of time, let alone accept lodging in his home. But Laela sensed this was both a generous and courageous offer from Mateo, as her presence could get both of them in trouble. She understood that he was probably a most uncommon Mergon. Thus, other offers of hospitality wouldn't be forthcoming!

"Thank you!" She beamed. "We're exhausted from days of travel and need to rest. We'll follow all your instructions. We certainly want to stay out of trouble. And, Mateo, I believe you'll enjoy hearing some stories of the true Treedle people, not the slaves. Our customs are beautiful."

"Then let's go," Mateo smiled at her for the first time, and it inspired her to cultivate more of these smiles later. His face lit up, and his eyes crinkled in an endearing way. Where was the Mergon rudeness and cruelty Treedles warned about so much?

Mateo scouted the area as he spoke, "We need to move quickly. We'll head far to the right of those cottages. When we're closer to my home, I'll leave Sasha here in a field to eat and rest. Then we'll walk the rest of the way. You'll need to stay covered from head to toe. I'll lend you a cloak from my bag."

And, Laela thought, Macecle can ride in my backpack and not jump about while I do the walking.

"You'll need to stay close behind me and let me know if my pace is too quick by tapping me on the shoulder. We'll speak no more until we arrive at my home. It's some distance from the cottages you see."

Treedles, who read ancient literature, knew of the word cottage. Laela was eager to hear other words only Mergons use. She was brimming with questions to ask Mateo and could only hope to stay long enough to satisfy her yearning to explore a world different than her own. She was too intrigued to contemplate the magnitude of her arrival, alone and as a female Treedle in Mergonland.

After they left Sasha off in a fenced field, they began a winding climb around a hill. Laela easily kept pace with Mateo, focusing on following and mirroring his gait. They wove in and out of grassy areas, crouched behind rocks, and took pauses to listen for any people sounds. They then entered a very thick part of the forest that rimmed the open fields. Laela felt from the tension in Mateo's back and his frequent surveyall of the area that he was now on high alert and that they were approaching his house—perhaps the last but most danger-fraught stage of their trek. Mateo moved slowly and tried to clear branches that might scrape Laela. She began to sense a freshness in the air and hear the sound of rain on the ground, becoming more notable, a powerful, whooshing sound. They approached the sound of the pounding downfall into a refreshing mist that didn't cloud the cerulean sky beyond the forest bramble.

There was no time to stop and appreciate something she had only read about, a small river. Bubbly water swept over rocks and branches softening the earth to form a moving path and playful reflection of light. Mateo tugged Laela's cloak. They began to crouch as low as possible around the riverbank and behind its thickest vegetation. They approached a small clearing, and Mateo whispered, "We'll go under a waterfall to get to my home. It's the safest way, and it will lead us to a tunnel that goes to my workroom and greenhouse. I'll need to hold your hand to steady you, so you won't slip on the rocks."

Laela and her friends made miniature waterfalls for their gardens. But the idea of slipping below one made no sense. She suppressed a giggle of excitement. The sound of the water became louder and more compelling, like a storm localized in a shaft of space. They headed up the path and rounded a large boulder. Then she saw it. Laela had to pause to keep this in her mind, forever. What was greater? The roaring power of water as it fell from a great height? The freshness of sparkling droplets that swirled up through your nose and tickled your pores? The majestic structure—the massive movement of water emerging from the shoulders of the mountain?

Mateo urged Laela on toward a rocky, narrow path, a branch off the main one, that would lead them directly to the edge of the widest part of the now deafening waterfall. There, the path connected with a flat slate ledge underneath the waterfall. Mateo entered first, grasping Laela's hand and wrist tightly. They traversed the dark, glassy ridge underneath the middle of this pouring giant with their backs to the mountain wall. The sparkling spray coming from the heaving curtain of water covered them with droplets but didn't soak them, as they stayed close to the mountain wall. She did fear slipping, though. No ropes, no lines to secure or lead them. The ledge was extremely slippery, and they needed to take slow and cautious steps not to slide off it.

They emerged on the other side into a small tree arbor that Mateo had crafted over a smooth flat boulder. It was a place to rest and for cover to watch his beloved waterfall alone and unobserved. There was a handcrafted wooden bench and round table inside. They were both dripping, and she did as he did, shaking off water still clinging to them and wringing the bottom of her cloak.

From the arbor, there were two paths. One led to a steep, rock-strewn meadow area and the other to a cave-like opening between two rocks. Mateo pointed to the latter, signaling her to be completely quiet, and mimicking that she must tiptoe upon entry. A tiny older man from a tribe unknown to her sat hunched, shriveled like dried fruit guarding two massive wooden doors. Mateo made some hand motions for her to keep her face down and hidden in her cloak. Mateo spoke three words she couldn't decipher, and the guard opened the door. She moved behind Mateo in synchrony with him. They gradually descended into a dark, calm, and moist tunnel. It was built to go around the small hill and lead them to the lowest level of Mateo's multi-storied home. They weren't long in darkness before they saw an aperture of light and another wooden door. There was no guard at this door. Mateo signaled to her to stand directly beside him on what appeared to be a semi-circular wooden platform. He did five staccato stomping movements with his feet. The door swung open slowly into the vestibule of a very large, airy, and brightly lit garden. The door swung shut behind them and became a wall of hanging plants. Above them were arching rafters of delicate metal, covered by glass.

Mateo smiled broadly at her. "Well done, Treedle friend. For now, we're in a safe place. No one except those I authorize may enter this workspace, and today is a day of rest in Mergonland. My two most trusted servants usually stay at home, even on their day of rest, but they'll leave us to ourselves.

"Later, I'll take you to an upstairs room where you can rest for the night. You will be next to dear Ana, and she take you to a room in the women's wing and provide you with all the bedding you need. Are you hungry?"

"Very, and I would appreciate some water." Laela answered frankly, "I wanted to stop to drink at the waterfall. What a wonder of nature it is. I hope to see it again."

"I'll bring us some lunch. I had requested large portions for myself as it would be a busy day in the field. And it was. The servants know I like to work long hours without being disturbed, so they leave me plenty of food to last throughout the day on rest days. Then, I can eat when I wish."

"Are your servants slaves?" Laela blurted this out from concern and curiosity but then repented as soon as the words slid out. She didn't want to offend her host and protector in any way. However, she couldn't reconcile this kindly, radiant man as the master of slaves. Treedle slaves.

She had studied history lessons of how the wealthy and powerful Mergon classes all possessed slaves. Treedles were captured by Mergon mercenaries when they ventured out on annual expeditions to trade with outlying ground tribes. The Treedles who descended into the border areas of Mergonland were aware of the life and death risks of this commerce. Once enslaved, they were treated with abject cruelty. Laela had heard they used them to breed more Treedle slaves with the few and rare Treedle women captured in the past (perhaps rebellious adventurers like herself) and the women of non-Mergon tribes captured in border wars. What Laela didn't know was the extent of the slave's degradation.

There were several reasons that Mergones hadn't until this time invaded Treedle territory to enslave them all. One was that there had been enough slaves to fuel their economy until now, an economy in which only the ruling class could possess slaves. The other was a great fear of heights bred into Mergons. Why would they scale these heights and take any risks to procure goods that aren't valuable or hold dominion over worthless lizard-like people in the sky? They were called sky lizards and pigeon people, among other spleen-crushing names. (Yes, these words were passed to Treedles, close to maturity, to prepare them to encounter enemies). However, rumors had even reached the treetops that this would be changing and that the Mergons had plans that required increasing the slave population three-fold.

Mateo frowned slightly. "As a son of King Malcolm, the King of Mergonland, and in my role as a Prince, I must observe the customs and rules of the Royal Family. I have had to make some difficult choices. I have Treedle servants working in my home and shops. I do pay the Treedles who work for us, but they aren't free. If I 'free' our servants and they leave my compound to live elsewhere, they'll be captured and enslaved. But I can assure you that all of our 'servants' are all very well fed, clothed, and live comfortable lives."

Mateo turned around to hang up their cloaks, and she could see he didn't want to continue this conversation.

His answer wasn't entirely satisfying to her, as Laela felt impassioned about the fate of her people here. It struck her how real this slavery was, and that Mateo believed he was powerless to change the Mergon system. Laela couldn't bear to think about this now, though. She needed to be a better guest and not put her host on the spot.

"I'm sorry, Mateo. One of my faults is speaking too bluntly. I can't thank you enough for such a warm and, well, exciting welcome. I've been in your land for only a few hours, and I'm in awe."

They were sitting on comfortable cushioned chairs at the entrance to the garden encased with magnificent glass walls. She had yet to look at this sanctuary and was eager to examine Mergon plants.

Laela continued, "I've just come of age' as the Treedles say. I was feeling a strong desire to leave 'home' to explore. I didn't know where this feeling was coming from or even why. But now that I am here, I know I had to take this risk. I have to learn more about other peoples and lands and to investigate for myself about the Mergon way of life."

"Ahh, Laela, a risk so much greater than you can imagine. But let's enjoy a brief time to know about each other's worlds. We must make every minute count before you leave. Your return home must be carefully planned."

Mateo paused and gazed at her in silence. She could tell this was his first encounter with a fully-educated Treedle. Long conversations with slaves were forbidden so as not to encourage proximity. She could feel how he tried not to stare but drank in her eyes. The heavy lavender lids might remind him of one of the tropical flowers he grew.

They sustained this silence longer while a penetrating empathy passed between them. They were two seekers compelled by their inexplicable questions and passions to break out of traditional boundaries to see and know more. The intense energy that two such mutually curious people could convey was inviting them to explore their different worlds. She had already entered the threshold of his fertile mind. She admired how a war-born Prince of Mergon could be communing with her in a fragrant garden like this.

Mateo grinned in complicity. They had read each other. "Please enjoy the gardens and dry off as you do. I hope you will enjoy Mergon food. I'll bring various kinds for you to try." Mateo directed her toward the plant nurseries that led to more extensive orchards of fruit trees and slipped away. "Enjoy the indoor nursery for now, and later we can explore the orchards together. The orchards are outdoors and are walled in by a giant cliff."

The nursery was paved with a brick path and lined by small flower and herb beds and a variety of graceful trees. Pots of flowers hung from the larger trees and orchids gracefully embraced their trunks, similar to their airborne garden. However, except for orchids, almost all the plants were different. Laela was heady with the fragrances wafting from the heavy petaled flower bushes in lush melon-pink, white cream, and blood-red colors. She wandered through the nursery, admiring each new flower and fruit. She cupped her hands around a flower that was yellowish-green with a heavy bulbous bottom and thinner top. She admired the gleaming skin of bright red fruit and the tickle of the fuzzy skinned ones that were tinged with swirls of orange and pink, like a sunset. She could only begin to admire the various sections of this seemingly endless internal garden.

Some plant beds were organized like crops in rows, and she assumed they were probably sold or traded in the market. Laela couldn't resist trying one of the jewel-colored, red berries growing up a trellis. It tasted as tangy as it looked.

She began to organize a list of questions for Mateo in her head. There were so many, and he had reminded her that time wasn't their ally. Her consciousness of being a Treedle in a hostile land was growing as fast as her interest to explore it.

CHAPTER 11

Minds Meet

"Let's have lunch," Mateo offered when all were yawning with signs of hunger. "The dining room and main living areas are upstairs, and on the third floor, there are two wings with separate quarters for men and women where we sleep. Follow me, please."

He led them up a small flight of stairs to a door leading to the second floor, and it opened to a wide corridor. They walked down a hall of tiled floors in blue, grey, and brown mosaic patterns past walls filled with paintings framed with gilded edges. From ground to ceiling, everything gleamed—freshly polished. They entered the dining room off the hall, and Mateo motioned them to be seated around a long wooden table set with silver plates and utensils. Laela was especially intrigued with the chandelier over the table with eight candle cups holding tapered dove-white candles. Dangling prisms hung from its outstretched arms, twinkling in the light from the nearby window whose brocade curtains were drawn and tied with gold cords. There were trays of savory-looking food in the middle of the table. The massive chairs squeaked as they pulled them out.

Laela noted that objects occupied space here as if they were entitled personalities. She had never seen Treedles' houses and furniture as being so light. Compared to Mateo's mansion, they seemed organic to the forest setting, like outgrowths of branches and vines. Breezes always flowed through Treedle houses: here, even the air seemed formal. Nonetheless, the picture window with its entirely transparent glass allowed them to enjoy a garden view with birds flitting about a stone fountain and charming colors of the flowers, bushes, and trees basking in the ever-changing light. All in all, the dining room made eating a banquet-like occasion.

Macecle jumped into Laela's lap as she sat at the table, blissfully unaware that animals of any kind weren't allowed near Mergons' food. Laela first tried the heavy-fatty meat of an animal grown on a farm. Mateo explained it was from a tannish-white, four-legged creature five times bigger than a tree rat. Laela recognized the stringy green vegetable that Treedles grew in their gardens, but plants that extend deep into the soil were unknown or rare. Laela hesitated about eating two that looked like white and orange squash that had been boiled and buttered. She wasn't sure what they were.

Mateo was watching her pick at them and said, "Those are yuko and dango roots. We also call them tubers. You can cut these into smaller pieces and eat them with your fork. When we serve them mashed, we eat them with a spoon. We grow a lot of root foods deep in the earth. I'll show you what the plants look like before they're cooked." So as Laela and Macecle tasted the roots that were pleasantly bland and easy to chew, Mateo showed them the coarse, leather outsides of two gnarled root plants. He cut into one and sliced it for her to see the brilliant orange color and smooth, hard texture inside.

Mateo explained that some people like the roots or tubers roasted and others softer or chewier. Laela nodded, "We also vary how we prepare our vegetables—either crunchy or soft. Some of our most colorful and delicious fruits look like your roots—all knobby or brown on the outside."

Laela took a mental note that Mateo, a Prince, had served her, a Treedle, as warmly as a Treedle friend would. She wanted to ask him more about every facet of his life but decided to begin with his garden, "Your garden is enchanting! There are so many plant varieties. Do all these grow in Mergonland, or do explorers bring some of these to you? There appears to be a purpose in the organization of the garden beds, too." She didn't want to pry but felt there was something very strategic as well as beautiful about his garden.

Mateo nodded to her with his eye-crinkling smile, "Clever of you to notice. My mother and I have been working for years to create a garden to collect and study every plant species we can find in the Kingdom and neighboring ones. I'm a doctor, and my mother is my assistant who specializes in making tonics and remedies from flowers and herbs. We meet with shamans and Elders, Treedle and Mergon Elders, to glean knowledge about all the curative properties of plants. We're always learning something new."

Laela said, "I was hoping I could take some plant cuttings and drawings to show my mother what an extraordinary garden you have. Some Mergone fruits might grow in Aerizon, and we would welcome the new textures and flavors. My mother would be most interested in the medicinal uses of plants. She's a healer and sought after by Treedles all over Aerizon.

But she works mainly with herb and nut oil potions for healing."

"Who do you treat?" she asked, "You live far away from the Court, and your house isn't in the village."

"We mainly serve people from the countryside. However, members of the Court come to me secretly! A cottage in the village serves as our dispensary where we attend people twice a week. If someone is very ill, the road on the other side of our home leads quickly to the village. A family member can advise us by ringing a large bell by the wall which surrounds the house—and they can and do ring it any time of day or night!"

Laela imagined that there were many more doctors and shamans in the Kingdom of Mergon but wondered if they all practiced healing like Mateo did. She asked, "Do others practice healing as you do—do they use the same remedies?"

"Not really," Mateo seemed glad to delve more into his favorite subject. "Thanks for asking. We use several traditional and well-known remedies; however, we experiment with new ones and new approaches.

"Our friend Davi is an inventor and helps us make tools and little machines to produce our medicines and instruments for treating patients. We experiment on sick animals—to heal them, and even ourselves. Most doctors just use herbs, but we've found that flowers have many medicinal qualities. My mother makes both floral essences and extracts and bottles them."

"You must see our lab, and" he blushed a bit, "I'd like you to meet my mother and Davi."

Once again, he surprised himself as that would mean committing to another day of harboring a Treedle fugitive. And it would be unprecedented to introduce a Treedle as a friend to his mother. Not that she looked down on them, but she had never met a free-woman Treedle. Yet, he felt that they had to meet.

From there on in, the two barely took breaths between their back-and-forth banter. One question led to another, and they were feasting on the novelty of their two cultures. Their conversation took on a life of its own: exhilarating, like they were creating a dance with new steps.

After lunch, Mateo invited Laela to their library, and Macecle wandered off to the indoor garden to play. On their way, he stopped to give her a tour of the living room, the central, formal reception area of the house. He showed her the two carved wooden doors that served as the main entrance for visitors to the house. The doors opened to steps leading down a stone pathway lined with sculpted bushes to the main entrance gateway. The bell Mateo had mentioned hung by the gate on the steep rock wall protecting their property's front border.

She could see how fitting the living room was for entertaining distinguished guests, nobles, and Royal Court members. There were large sofas with curved backs and plump cushions. The two most imposing sofas were covered in twilight-blue leather and various chairs were in shiny gray brocade material. The room's centerpiece was a gray-stone fireplace with a thick wooden mantle, on top of which sat several large white porcelain vases, painted in feathery blue strokes with scenes of forests, skies, farmlands, and animals. In front of the sofas were marble tables with ornate feet. Other small tables crafted from dark elaborate metal frames had marble tops and held lamps or smaller flower vases full of blue, white, purple, and yellow blooms.

Mateo explained to her that his mother was involved in designing the furniture and the room. "As you can see, she loves the color blue," he said, motioning his hand around the room. "She had this fresco commissioned and painted on porcelain tiles,"

The gleaming fresco covered the whole back wall like a tapestry painted in hues of indigo and bird egg blue, depicting different scenes of the Kingdom and its people. There were large mirrors on each sidewall wider than a Treedle is long and framed in burnished gold. A person could stand in front of them and admire a full-length portrait of themselves.

The sheer size of the room discouraged intimate conversation, but it was beautiful by any definition of the word. Laela imagined that few Mergons lived like this, probably only the upper classes. There was little distinction among Treedles in class—maybe because they didn't have as many things to compete for or envy. She had never seen so many precious commodities like glass, metal, and stone objects in one room. She wished her friends and parents could be here with her to share the tour of this house and its possessions.

She was glad to enter the library, which though ample, looked warm, cozy, and inviting. It contained a vast collection, with shelves filled with documents and books, which were rare objects in Aerizon. The spines of the books revealed different colored coverings—most in dark earth colors and greens. Some of the books had gold lettering and bands to indicate their status and quality. Mateo lit a fire in the fireplace, and it gave a warm glow to their faces and the room. They sat on either side of an ample, chocolate brown sofa. To the right, red and gold curtains were drawn to reveal another glass window and view outside of fruit trees and beds of flowers. Beneath their feet was the skin of an animal that Laela didn't recognize, but its earthy tone added warmth to the tile floors, which were reddish-brown in this room.

Mateo offered her a soft blue cloak to use inside the house to keep her warm, as dwellings by the forest could be humid and cold. He had changed into an oversized white tunic shirt and heavier pants and shoes when he disappeared to find them lunch. Laela felt under-dressed in her tunic. She used a homespun wrap at night that was simple compared to this cloak, so velvety in texture and with a hood that rippled around her shoulders.

The library was a place Laela could explore for days. But Mateo wanted to hear about her life in Aerizon. He listened raptly, asking in detail about Laela's family, her father Alvaro's honored role in the community, her friends and their new home, Joy Park, and how all Treedle young ones learned survival skills at school. Mateo couldn't hide his absolute shock in hearing about Phips and Laela's outings, her learning to hunt, and finally, their ventures into the Feral Forest. He admired her courage and audacity—not only to hunt there but to invent the idea of a faster and safer trade route between Aerizon and the outlying trader villages near Mergonland. It was simply unheard of for a girl to hunt, let alone for one to ideate what could be the beginnings of a crossroad between civilizations. This Laela was a phenomenon! And each of her close relations sounded like a person he would love to meet.

"Speaking of these marvelous Treedles, who light up your eyes, Laela, aren't they worried about you? Did they know that you were planning this visit to Mergonland? I mean, if you told them, I can only imagine they would have tried to dissuade you. It's not clear how you found our fields. I choke to think of all the possible dangers you could have encountered; an evil-minded trader, a spy who would bring you back for punishment, a raptor, a snake. Laela, the list goes on. And the worst of all would have been a Mergon soldier to greet you upon your arrival! The 'One' indeed sent you a guardian angel. But pray tell how you made this journey and landed in that wheat field."

Laela had been putting off the part of why, the dreams, the real, and the envisioned jaguar—the elements of her journey which didn't seem like coincidences but a catalyst of Divine guidance provoking her search. How could she explain this to a person she just met, from a culture foreign to hers? Sitting in such a comfortable and well-appointed home, talking to a Prince and a doctor by profession, she would seem like a wildly fool-hearted girl, albeit a lucky one! Her actions would be inexplicable to a Treedle Elder, the Council, Ms. Adele, or any mature Treedle. Laela didn't want to display the depths of her heart to be laughed at or share a quest that might make no sense to such a young man, a Mergon, however noble and kindly.

"We've just met Mateo," Laela said, looking solemnly into his avidly curious eyes. "I don't know how to explain this in a brief way that will make sense to you. I realize that to any serious soul, be they Mergon or Treedle, what I've done seems crazy, risky, and even wrong for a girl like me to do. I could have gotten hurt or killed. I think my friend Phips understands my love of exploring as my longtime buddy for outings. Even I can't put into words what brought me here, to be sitting here with you!

"I left a note to my family that I would be gone for some days. They know I like to explore, and I promised to be careful. However, they're surely not happy about me leaving. I didn't have a set 'plan' when I wrote that. But I must return soon, so they don't become overcome with worry. I believe if I return home within the week, all will be well."

"How did you find Mergonland, though?" Mateo asked, "I've never run into a trader or spy on the ground, especially one that just showed up so casually in a field." He was poking fun at her but in a friendly way.

"I've told you about the trader's route. I was familiar with most of it, and my trip went smoothly. Before I left, I planned to go as far as the Trader's Village bordering on the frontier with Mergonland. Maybe just observe it from high up in the trees. I just wanted to see another part of the world! It also occurred to me to try to enter the village without being detected.

"Now, I'm trusting you with my life and the lives of our Treedle traders with such information. When we arrived at the last station built, station five, we found a map stored inside a box in a tree's hollow. It showed the terrain, the fortress of Mergonland, and the countryside with the low-lying fields where you found me. When I realized I had accurate directions and a compass with me, I thought about how much more exciting it would be to peek into Mergonland itself. We chose an entry point where the fields border with the forest, and Macecle and I could run and climb any number of trees to escape quickly."

She reached into her the pouch around her neck below her tunic and pulled out a long rope of moonline and her treasured compass. "Macecle can escape detection and move between trees, helping me tie the moonline from one tree or another to move quickly and out of reach from one tree to another. It makes it possible to cut great distances when there are hills involved or if someone below is tracking you."

It was night already, and Mateo beckoned Laela to sit on a cushioned bench by the window in the library. This garden took on a new form where the tips of the grassy lawn and leaves of the bushes picked up glints of the moonlight. Cor and Cora were two waxing crescents—half bright, half shrouded. Turning around together in tandem.

Laela and Mateo looked at each other, and neither could talk for a long time: the synchrony of the two moons and their minds in silent communion. So much to say and so much beyond words.

Mateo broke the silence and said quietly. "Let's have our dinner in the library. There's a whole tray of food for us to pick from in the kitchen. I'll just bring it here. Would you like a cup of wine?"

Laela shook her head no, "Water or juice would be fine."

Mateo sensed her discomfort at the mention of wine and asked, "Do Treedles not drink wine?"

"Some do," Laela answered, "But Treedles believe that the 'One' forbids it. So I've never tried it. I try to follow our laws, though heaven knows my people don't consider me to be a very obedient Treedle woman."

"No worries. We have juices, but I'll bring wine for myself. We have a lot of fruit wines in our pantry. My mother distills the fruit alcohol as the base of many of the tonics she makes."

Laela nodded, "My mother also makes alcohol for the very same purpose. Some remedies are best preserved that way. So I'm familiar with the smell and the taste in medicines."

"I must appeal now to my servant Didor to help us with some dinner. I don't know my way around a kitchen. He always serves me dinner at this time. He'll be surprised as to the nature of my visitor tonight."

Mateo rang a bell to call his servant, Didor, to ask him to bring dinner to the library. Laela saw an aging, pale-faced Treedle man, perhaps of the Bouder tribe, dressed in dark cotton pants and a matching jacket approach them. Didor was dismayed at the sight of Laela and stepped back with a gasp but then quickly composed himself. She could see that he wasn't a sad 'slave' as he smiled warmly at Mateo. She imagined that Didor was as shocked as a Mergon would be to see a Prince entertaining a Treedle girl.

Mateo instructed Didor about what foods to bring. He also told him that he and Ana, his wife, must maintain the strictest vigilance and confidence about this visitor. They must protect Laela at all costs for the few days she would spend in Mergonland. Mateo reminded Didor that he trusted him like family and to guard any friend of his as if he were Mateo himself. Didor nodded, and she could see him arching an eyebrow as if to contain questions brimming up. Mateo noticed and said, "I'll explain more to you and Ana later about how we will take care of our guests. I'll also share with you a bit about the unusual circumstances of her arrival as we must plan for her to leave safely."

There was a pause in the flow of conversation as they both thought of the following topics to explore. Mateo's skin radiated golden tones from the firelight. He brushed the wheat color strands of hair from his eyes, which were keen and somewhat unsettling to Laela. He seemed to both listen and see with those deep brown, honey-flecked eyes. He wasn't striking poses like a certain someone, but he projected a strong masculine fluidity from any angle: comfortable in his body, exuding gentle power.

Mateo walked over to the library shelves and pulled out a large, leather-covered tome with gold bands. He brought it over for them to open together.

"I thought you might enjoy looking at this illuminated volume of our 'Holy Book' that contains all the Words of the 'One.' The pages of the book are made of animal skins to last longer. Our best scribes in the land write out the texts with quills and black ink. Artists embellish the pages with borders and pictures of flowers and woodland scenes."

Mateo was familiar with some of the history of Treedles and knew that they often wrote on scrolls. Mateo opened to a page with delicate script, but a depiction of a tree with broad branches and stylized emerald-green leaves filling the page's center. Above and below the tree were short verses from the 'One' about how every part of a tree is used for service and good, from the roots that hold the earth to the leaves that give us fresh air, to the fruits we eat, the shade we enjoy, and the homes trees give to people and animals. It concludes, "to give your all without thought of self, is to be truly alive, to be good." A dark gold border with looping edges framed the page.

Laela gazed for quite a while on this page. She thought of the tireless labors of Treedle scribes to produce texts on parchment in ways that could be stored and protected within pouches. Treedles didn't have many books, especially heavy ones: perhaps more could be brought to their land. The Elders possessed such books but only brought them out as most precious treasures guarding them against touch. Laela hadn't seen one so fine, even in her father's extensive library. She thought this a possession worth seeking for every home. It honored the 'One's words—each page provoked awe and reverence.

Mateo let Laela look through the pages and sat watching her as she drank in the jewel-colored illustrations of the sun, stars, the two moons, and the flowers, trees, and birds of Mergonland. Each is a symbol of spiritual teachings that guided the tribe on earth and those above.

Laela commented, "We worship the same 'One,' and we live and share the same earth, here or higher up. We practice the same teaching, with just a few differences. What a shame our people can't be friends."

"I think the only main differences in our practices are that Mergons can drink and divorce," Mateo said grinning. "It seems to me that that shouldn't cause division. Because if someone doesn't believe in drinking or divorcing, he shouldn't do it. If a person from a different sect has been taught this is legal, why judge him and fight about it? I believe the important thing is always to do what you believe is right but try to understand and appreciate others' beliefs."

"Then we agree," Laela answered, relieved. "I don't like to argue about doctrine and interpretations of the Writings as even our Elders do. Everyone thinks it is important to be 'right' and the holder of the torch of justice. The leader of the light and the right! I think religion is about us living a happy life and doing good to others." Laela had a fleeting vision of Mateo and her holding the traditional 'torch of justice' together, the one used in ceremonies where the Council made critical decisions about breaking Treedle laws—laws derived from the Writings of the 'One.'

Didor brought them hot soup made with tubers and meats and some buttered buns by the side. He wasn't very subtle about sneaking glances at Laela or lingering too long at the door. Laela thought she must find a way to spend time with him and for them to share life stories. She could only imagine how eager Didor would be to hear about free Treedle brethren and their life in the trees.

Eating the soup relaxed Laela to the point of sleepiness, and a short time later, Mateo rang the bell for Didor to retrieve the plates. He said, "Time for a good night's rest. I will ask Didor to have Ana escort you to a room. Ana has been a part of my family since before I was born. She's like a second mother and will take care of you well while you are here." Laela was relieved to talk about sleep. Typically energetic, she felt overwhelmed by all the newness and needed a respite in the dark and quiet to let events begin to settle in her mind.

Ana, Didor's wife, looked as old as Nana Bisru. Her wrinkled skin was a drab gray color, slightly tinged with the reddish-brown undertones of the Bouder tribe. However, her dark eyes shined brightly. They were the keen eyes of a woman who doesn't miss a thing. Ana was wearing a long, floor-length robe, and Laela wondered how women dressed here. Mateo had been wearing pants and shoes and no shirt when he met them in the field. But at home, he had changed into a loose white shirt with enough material for two Treedle dress-up shirts. She noticed that Ana was trying not to register shock at her tunic and that she kept assessing Laela as if something were missing. Laela surmised that Mergons must cover themselves more, a supposition that would be confirmed the next day.

"It's very late, my dear, and you must be exhausted," Ana said gently, nudging Laela to sit on the fluffy bed where she kneeled to remove Laela's shoes. "I must confess that I have never seen a girl from Aerizon. If you please, I would like to ask you to tell me something about your Kingdom. I was born a slave, and seeing a free Treedle like yourself, well," she tried to control tears, but they streamed down her face, "I could never imagine the day.

"Tomorrow, I'll bathe you in that metal tub over there, with fresh warm water. Then, if you allow, we will dress you properly in some Mergone clothes. They'll keep you warm as it gets chilly here."

Laela was cold. She sunk into layers of heavy blue covers, one layer in Mergon cotton and another in wool, like the one Mateo had wrapped around her shoulders from a kind of furry farm animal. As she was drifting asleep, she heard fragments of Ana talking to Mateo, "Master may we use... she needs clothes... cold... Amelia... old... of course."

Laela cuddled Macecle, who joined her on a pillow. Grateful for his familiar smell and warm presence. They fell asleep quickly, snoring lightly in unison.

CHAPTER 12

Family Secrets

She woke up way past dawn with Ana pulling open the curtains and turning the room from dark and cozy to fully lit. Ana opened the bedroom door, and a small, drab Treedle man with a respectfully downcast look came in with a large jug of steaming water to fill the tub.

"Now out with you," Ana said, shooing the male servant, "And up with you!" to Laela. She pulled Laela to a sitting position and took off her tunic before Laela could protest and cover herself in shocked modesty. "I've seen all kinds of girls, my dear—Mergon and Treedles. Just not one from Aerizon, but I assume you have the same body parts we all do. Now, here let me bathe you."

She helped Laela out of bed and bade her drop her underdrawers as well. "I'll wash your things later, and we will try to shine up those battered shoes of yours too. Now soak and scrub yourself with this soap all over. They'll bring a few more jugs for rinsing, but I'll receive those and help you rinse off."

Both the soap and the steamy water were scented with lavender and what she thought might be the crushed petals of the lush many-petaled flower with the intoxicating smell she had seen in the garden. Laela was happy to bask, glide the soap over her body, and put her face in the water.

Ana left the room and returned in short order with her arms full of clothing and carrying two pairs of shoes that looked to be dainty women's boots with strings to tie them up the ankle. Ana hung these in a carved wooden armoire in the room. She took a large white cloth out of the armoire and said, "We'll choose a dress when you are dry. But first, let me wash your hair, rinse and dry you."

The same Treedle had returned and left a refilled jug at the door. Ana fetched it and, not waiting for Laela to protest, finished bathing her as a mother does a young child. "And," Ana added, "Your Macecle is quite filthy too. We'll bathe him outside. I shudder to think of the journey you took. Master said you came all alone. Should we be expecting other Treedle girls to show up here?" Ana said in a teasing voice.

"No, Ana, rest assured. I believe I'm one of a kind. I'm strange in Aerizon and now even odder here. Treedle girls are homebodies and never venture out very far. But I wanted to learn about a new culture, and now I hope that I may do something for my Treedles in Mergonland."

Ana's face immediately turned dark, "Dear Laela, I want you to enjoy this special invitation to spend a day or two with Master Mateo. But he knows, and any Treedle here surely knows that you aren't safe. Not even in this refuge—not for long. You can't do anything for us, not for Mergon Treedles. And you won't be able to do anything for yourself should they catch you. Heaven forbid. It would be most unfortunate for a beautiful girl like yourself to get captured."

Ana was drying Laela. Laela looked at her quizzically, "I don't understand why Treedles are slaves. What have Treedles done to deserve such treatment? Why do they accept it? Why don't they just arise to change their lot, to escape? And why does Mateo make you call him, Master? We are all equal. If he loves you, he knows that."

"You know why we call all Mergons Master Laela?" Ana's tone was cold now, "Because if I or any Treedle were to talk to a Mergon as if they were equals, they could be tortured or beaten to death. I would risk my very life if I acted like a Mergon's equal.

"We don't call Prince Mateo, Master, by his request or command. He forgets and talks to us like we're family; I'm like his second mother. Nonetheless, we call him Master, never to make a mistake when we come in contact with any other Mergon except for Mateo's mother or Davi. Should they see us speaking or acting freely, they would report us. It's a criminal offense for a Treedle to directly look a Mergon in the eye, talk without being bidden, and ask personal questions or favors. I am most frank and direct with you because I'm a Treedle and have heard how freely spoken the people of Aerizon are. Sometimes when Aerizon traders or spies are captured, we hear of their outspoken natures. That doesn't last long. Not even for days. You can believe me when I say most Mergons delight in breaking such a Treedle. I can't bear to repeat the stories about Treedles who have tried to free themselves.

"I thank the 'One' that I'm one of the most fortunate Treedles in the land, as Master Mateo would never hurt or chastise me. He often seeks my advice, which makes me as happy as a Mergon with a sack of gold.

"But enough now on this topic. Haven't you come to find delights here? There's much beauty indeed in this land that I can't help but call my own too. Never set foot in those trees up there!"

For once, Laela was speechless.

Ana felt it was necessary to warn this talkative, even cheeky young girl. She liked her fiery spirit, but it could doom her and maybe even others in Mergonland.

She had noticed how Mateo's eyes lit up when he said her name. He was too interested, already. Ana thought he might enjoy a few days of frolicking with this unique young woman. They must stay in the compound, of course. And he had approved of Laela wearing what would be a Mergon girl's clothing. There was no harm as they wouldn't be meeting anyone who wasn't strictly 'family.' Ana wanted Mateo to see how charming a Treedle could be. And she wanted Laela to feel as confident and comfortable as possible in this setting so she would be willing to tell them stories of Aerizon.

Laela stood with the large white cloth wrapped around her body and looked at the three dresses in the closet. Only one was practical and made of pale blue wool. However, Ana chose a different one for her.

"Here, let's put you in this green dress," Ana said, pressing her hands warmly on her shoulders like Elsa or the doelas might do, "My favorite. These belonged to Mateo's cousin, Princess Ellie, who used to wear them during visits. She's now Prince Marl's wife, but before she got married, she came here for extended stays with her mother and aunts, who all love the countryside—to walk in the gardens, get tonics and relax. Ellie is somewhat delicate, but Prince Marl disapproves of her visiting here anymore."

The dress that Ana held up would land midcalf on Laela. It had a white scalloped collar embroidered with pink flowers and was lightly gathered at the waist and covered with a silver sash as the waistband. When Laela put on the leather boots over silk stockings, the hem of the dress would touch the top of the boots. Looking at the soft, sage green dress with its delicate folds and graceful shape, Laela realized that she must have seemed quite scantily clothed to Mateo out in that wheat field. Mateo must have been slightly shocked to see a girl with so little clothing. She was nervous to think of how he would react to her in a proper young lady's dress.

But before Ana let her dress, she decided there was one more order of duty. She pulled out a pair of sharp scissors from an apron pocket and asked Laela to sit in a chair. "Laela dear, we simply must arrange your hair a bit. I'm going to fix it to make it more flattering to you. Highlight your eyes! You have been traveling, and you haven't had a mirror. Let's just say that your hair could use a bit of trimming here and there, and just like a plant needs some shaping and sculpting to stand out in the garden, your hair would benefit from some care."

Laela had never really arranged her hair. She combed through it or pulled it back with lines or ribbons when it was in her face. Ana had neither solicited nor asked her opinion about this change in her hairdo or lack of one. Laela started to feel disgruntled but then thought about how even Treedle friends had hinted how her hair looked unruly and that she didn't always tie it up fashionably when she pulled it out of her face with moonline. Well, she surmised, why not do something the Mergon way. She had asked for a Mergon experience.

Ana put some light oil into her hands, rubbing it through Laela's damp hair. Then, she took out a pair of fine pair of scissors and said, "I'll trim your hair so the waves will fall nicely around your face and frame it better."

Ana helped her into some cotton underclothes, stockings and pulled the dress over her head. She even put on the boots for Laela. She brushed Laela's hair once more and tied a thin ribbon around her head to sweep her hair off her face. Ana led her to a full-length mirror, and Laela became entranced with the image. She had never envisioned herself presented this way. It made her think of being a bride, and she became so flustered that Ana soothed her with clucking noises, "Now, now. What a shock to see it! But remember, you are most certainly NOT a young man, and it won't hurt to explore this side of yourself. Here you are dressed like a Mergon now!" And, she said, confirming Laela's assumption, "You must know, the tunic you were wearing looks like underclothing to an uneducated Mergon!"

Laela frowned, and Ana continued more reassuringly,

"Though the minute I set eyes on you, you looked like Treedle royalty to me. You're so poised and well-spoken; you could be a princess of any tribe. So, I just couldn't dress you as a household servant." Ana had heard about the Pyuvas being artists and thinkers.

Her heart went out to Laela, who, in a Treedle slave's eyes, was a noblewoman of their common ancestry.

Laela thought Ana was a fiercely protective mother for any culture and hugged her with gratitude and affection. Ana had also mentioned to Laela that she had never seen such a 'lavender' Treedle. Most slaves had descended from Bouder traders and explorers as they were the more adventurous tribe and thus accounted for most of those enslaved. She would be sure to share as many stories of their ancestors as possible so that Ana could be proud of her true heritage.

Ana escorted Laela to the dining room for breakfast, where the smell of a bowl of steamed grains and fruits met her nose. Mateo stood to greet her and blinked his eyes as if not sure of what he was seeing. His eyes lingered too long, traveling up and down the length of her petite figure. Laela was unsure what emotion he was feeling and thought he might be conflicted seeing her in his cousin's old dress. He nodded for her to sit, and then he smiled his gentle crinkly-eyed smile.

"My friend, for a minute, I was taken off guard and thought a new woman had entered my house, another Treedle. But then your face is unmistakable. And you light up a room no matter how you are dressed. Though, I must confess that this dress quite becomes you."

Laela was aware of the aura of her allure—the mist of lavender emanating from her skin, the way the dress accentuated her waist, the swirl of the skirt. It was impossible not to play Lili for a moment. She even tilted her head demurely and then almost laughed at herself. But she couldn't stay in character for long and was soon engaged in concentrated conversation with Mateo—with each of them beginning to ask more profound questions.

Mateo said they could take a long walk on the compound's grounds so he could show her more of the natural beauty of Mergonland. He asked Didor to pack them a basket with a picnic lunch. Mateo shuffled his feet a bit and seemed uncomfortable, "This might seem like an odd request, but I am curious to see how you use your slingshot. You spoke so fondly of the outings with your friend Phips. Would it be too much to ask you to show me how you use it?"

Laela grinned with relief. She welcomed an invitation to be herself. "Of course. I will bring one and some rope too and share some lasso moves."

"We can put your things in the basket that I will carry." Laela's dress had no pockets and hanging an apron to hold tools over it just wouldn't do.

"Before we leave, I have something else to show you." Laela had stealthily hung a light pouch under her dress with Tan and Gibble. "I want to ask if I can leave my little friends Tan and Gibble under the bundi tree in your downstairs garden so they can munch on the leaves."

Mateo's eyes widened, and he understood immediately, "You mean the spider-worm couple who weave moonline? I've heard about how Treedle moonline is produced but have never seen it for myself. Can I watch them?"

Laela opened the pouch for Mateo to peak in. Tan and Gibble were glaring at him, but only Laela noticed it.

"Tan and Gibble are a bit temperamental, but once they get started and aren't hungry, you can watch them. They understand basic commands. Can we go down and get them started?" Mateo nodded enthusiastically and led them to the garden where she had entered just yesterday.

Laela placed the duo in a mound of bundi leaves that hadn't been swept and put them into a box for safekeeping. Mateo promised that no one would be entering the garden today and the spider wouldn't be interrupted. Laela gave them instructions to continue producing the strong moonline needed with a return trip coming up. They both bleeped in discontent at her for the lack of care and consideration during this heavy trip. She explained to Mateo, who tried to hide his amusement at the situation.

Mateo opened a door on the left of the indoor garden. They walked toward a glade covered by a canopy of lime green, yellow and russet broad-leaved trees. The air was crisp, and leaves fluttered down as a carpeted entrance to a deeper forest. Mateo said their walk would lead them to their family pond, where they swim and catch fish for meals.

They padded through the forest until it opened the way to the shimmering body of water, named so simply—a pond. They stood under the shade trees near the pond, and Laela was mesmerized by the many brilliantly colored aquatic birds she saw. Turquoise, pink, orange, and vermilion with an iridescent sheen. Some with long necks, others short, some with head combs, and others smooth, but all regal in their manner. They were gliding gracefully, probably by paddling feet or underwater wings, over this liquid mirror reflecting the sun, clouds, and silhouettes of trees. Each bird made a series of circular ripples as it moved silently over the surface.

They drew closer to the edge of the pond, where the water lapped clear over the light brown sand. Fish, also in a rainbow variety of colors, moved in random currents through the waters.

"We collect and study water animals as we do plants," Mateo said as he pointed to a long, gold-orange fish with silky fins. "Some we eat, and some we just watch and put into streams by the gardens to liven up the waters with their colors and movements." Mateo threw a small piece of bread he pinched off a loaf in the basket over the water. Three glistening fish jumped up, angling to snatch it. This could serve for a whole morning's entertainment, Laela thought and asked if she could also pitch a few bites to the fish.

"Good throwing arm you've got," Mateo commented, "Do you want to show me your sling now?" Laela got the sling from the basket and looked at a metal cup as a target. She saw Macecle running up to them. He had trailed them even though Laela had told him to spend his time in the garden for now. Since he was here, he could help her set up the target.

"If you don't mind, I'll use the cup or any object you wish as a target." Mateo handed her the cup, and Laela told Macecle, "Place the cup on the table over there Macecle," she pointed to a forlorn table a few meters away." Macecle did as told and stepped away. He would retrieve the pellet for her.

Laela aimed, took the shot, and hit the cup hard with a crack. The impact tossed it into the air and onto the ground. As if luck were on her side, a small flock of startled birds flew out of the forest. Laela tracked them quickly and shot, bringing down a plump, medium-size brown bird that Treedles also hunted and put into stews. She'd wrap it in leaves, and they could bring it home in the basket. Ana would know what to do with it.

Mateo made a slight bow to her and said, "Any Mergon man would now be in a state of shame or fury at your prowess. Your speed, your grace, your aim." Then he couldn't resist teasing, "I guess this Prince is only good for healing the wounded you leave in a trail behind you."

"Oh, I would never shoot to kill a person," Laela vowed, lest he think her a potential murderess out in the woods with a gentleman. "I'm a hunter, not a warrior. Though to be honest, I would attack someone who tried to hurt a loved one."

"Of course you would, and you should!" Mateo agreed. "Whether you plan to be one or not, you do have the skills of a warrior. I admire strength used for just and good purposes. I admire you, Laela." He smiled so approvingly that Laela was warmly reassured. In turn, she respected him for how reserved he was about his power and privileges as a Prince. He hadn't asserted his station and had even deferred to Laela so far. Everything indicated that he had the musculature and deft movements of a skilled potential fighter, but instead of becoming a Mergon warlord, he used his strength to serve others. He didn't feel less of a man showing tenderness.

"So Laela, could you show me some of your lasso work too," he asked, pointing to the basket, "This is a nice open area for it."

Laela took out the moonline rope that had come with her on her trek to Mergonland—seeing this familiar item she had brought from home tugged at her consciousness—her sense of responsibility on this visit. As she held it and ran it through her hands, she remembered the connection to her family and people. Images of her parents huddled together waiting for her, staying up late with candles lit, of Oti and Phips wondering where she was for sure. She sensed how worried they must be by now, after just two nights' absence. There were no genuine absences for a Treedle girl. They were always accompanied or close to home.

An idea flashed into her mind to send Macecle to the forest this afternoon to leave word of their whereabouts at station five. He could deposit notes in the tree hollow for her family, Phips, and Oti. Any Treedle trader passing through on the way back to Aerizon from the trading town would deliver them and would probably have heard news of the missing Treedle girl recently turned woman. Macecle could move faster without her and be back in time to accompany her on her return trip to Aerizon.

Mateo, watching her musing to herself, asked, "Have I upset you with these requests? I understand if you don't want to show more. Would you like to sit?"

Laela realized how strained her expression must be, "No, I'm not upset about showing you how I use the lasso. It's just that it reminded me so clearly of home and family. I was so thoughtless in not having sent a message when I arrived. I realized that Macecle could serve as a reliable messenger to leave notes at the last outpost, and traders passing through will hopefully deliver them before my arrival. Every day counts to those who fret and worry!" In her mind, Laela felt she needed three more days at the least to gather memories to remember and recount over a lifetime. Her family should be pleased to know how well taken care of she was.

"But for now, I must live in the moment," she chided herself.

She decided to use Macecle as her object to lasso. She told Macecle that they would play a lasso game, one they had played before, and she would try to catch him. Macecle delighted to be the center of attention, screeched, ran, and jumped about, pirouetting with joy. He waved his hands to challenge Laela to get him. Laela forgot her ladylike attire and ran full speed after him, waving her lasso high, and he slipped away on her first attempt. But she managed, after a continued and spirited chase, to get him on the second try. She pulled him in and removed the lasso from his belly. He wrapped his arms around her neck and nuzzled her affectionately, thanking her for remembering his need to play. She tried to keep him from dirtying the dress as best she could and hoped Ana wouldn't scold her. Mateo went over and scratched Macecle behind the ears to thank him for the fun and patted Laela gently on the back, "Laela, I could watch the two of you all day. What fun. And I don't know which impresses me more, your lasso or your slingshot skills."

Mateo paused and held up his looking glasses to scan the area. She knew he was checking for their safety. He said they should move on, and they reentered the forest on another path, with Laela stopping to admire luminescent, waxy-orange fungi on a tree log. Certain colors were associated with poison, and Mateo indicated that this was highly poisonous to eat but that Danie used extracts for certain medicines.

Mateo took her off the path, deeper into the forest, and they came to a tree with a massive circumference, covered with thick clawing vines. Its dense foliage rippled within. The other trees surrounding it seemed to be its courtiers nodding to it in deference. He whistled, and dozens of shimmering pale blue butterflies fluttered out and encircled them as gently as baby's breath.

"This is a tree of hope. The vines and darkness surrounding it represent suffering and hardship, and the butterflies are the hope of the good times that follow the bad. Our people come to such trees to make wishes and ask that the burdens of their hearts be lifted." Mateo looked at the tree with such affection that Laela knew he had come to make pilgrimages to it. The butterflies surrounded them with such sweet lightness that she imagined they deposited all the sadness in the dark, rumbling tree.

Laela watched a butterfly on her finger, and she made a wish and a prayer for the 'One' to protect her and her new friend Mateo from the darkness she knew was lurking in this land.

They returned to the path and arrived at another small meadow. There was a shrine to the correct entrance, the height of a tall Mergon. It was finely carved out of limestone (Laela had seen tiny pieces of this stone) and polished smooth. A bowl-like feature was carved into the shrine's base. People deposited stones of different colors and some metal coins into it as petitions to the deity. This base supported its central part: a sun with striking geometric beams radiating from it, painted in gold. It was a shrine to Razi, Laela noted with keen interest. She had never seen one before but had heard of them.

Mateo answered an unspoken question, "As you know, Mergons worship the 'One,' but many pay homage to Razi, the sun. We can't see colors in the darkness, so there's a custom among many people to make petitions to Razi, leaving colored stones and coins. Razi is associated with life, health, and prosperity.

"But this shrine was a gift from family members who visit here, and they're the ones who strongly believe in Razi's blessings. Our immediate family believes only the 'One' can protect and guide us. The celestial bodies He created remind us of his immense powers. But it's best to never argue over such matters. We never criticize what other members of the family believe or how they worship."

The glade was also a place for picnics, and there was an ample stone table and benches, a perfect place for lunch. They both set out the tablecloth, plates, and cutlery. The basket was full of savory and sweetbreads, two small pots of jams, some cheese, and slabs of pinkish meat. Laela and Macecle mainly ate slices of bread from the small loaves and some nuts that Macecle had gathered and kept in his pouch. The cheese from a braying animal that eats grass was creamy and tasty, though heavy for Laela to digest in any quantity. After lunch, they packed up what remained in the basket. Mateo suggested they lie out another cloth under a shade tree in a grassy part of the glade to rest.

They sat for a while in silence, watching clouds billow up beyond the trees. Mateo looked at her as if drinking her in and then turned his head away as if frustrated, "You know I shouldn't befriend you." He blurted out tersely. He was clenching his hands, and she could sense turmoil, jarringly out of place on this balmy day.

Laela was taken aback and insulted for the first time since they met, which now seemed an age and not a day ago. Her eyes flared at him when he returned his gaze to her, "And," he acknowledged, "And you shouldn't befriend me. But here we are. I can tell you that I'm torn. I can't forgive myself if any harm befalls you on this visit."

He looked at her for a moment like Vito used to, "And, I must confess, I don't see you as just a friend. I see you as a woman. So, Laela, there's now an added danger- to the one, I'm already putting you in by hosting you in my home. I'm loath to let you go, but that is the only right thing to do in this situation."

For the first time, Laela sank into the feeling she was fighting off. She let a warm yearning overtake her. She had trusted this young man from the second she met him, and she had always seen him as a man. Now she saw him as a desirable man. She found herself admiring the outline of his hands as he grasped a cup—every contour of him in sunlight, firelight, and moonlight. She wanted to touch him, explore his face, chest, and hair with her hands. But worse for her was that with his every word, she was more drawn to him. An inadmissible admission was clutching her throat. She was falling in love. For the first time, she understood how different this was from the powerful forces of mating animals, the smells, the entanglement that looked like fighting, and then the withdrawal. It was by far more powerful than male-female sexual attraction. And it was utterly forbidden between a Meron man and Treedle woman.

How could she be so drawn to someone who should remain a stranger, albeit a friendly one, and now be in this situation where she didn't want to leave him? She knew she was looking at Mateo in a way reserved for mating. Maybe it was the proximity. She had talked to him more than in all the months of acquaintance with Vito. There was a matching curiosity and an intense desire to learn and expand their world views. They weren't opposites, nor the same: they were discovering that they were complementary. But a Treedle girl meant for slavery could hardly be linked in a real relationship to a Mergon Prince. Not even with a Mergon pauper in the countryside. And she shuddered to think of her family's opinion, so she did not.

"Mateo, as a 'woman,' I'm responsible for myself and my actions now. Anything that happens to me is my responsibility. It's in my nature to act on what stirs my soul. In my heart, I don't believe I'm here on a whim. If it's not too bold to say so, I also think that the 'One' guided me to you. I'll probably never see you again when I leave, but I'll cherish your friendship forever. I will pray to the 'One' to guard and keep you safe and happy." She still didn't want to speak more about urgings and dreams bringing her here. She concluded, "But I'll leave today if my presence puts you in danger."

Mateo responded, "No, it's you who are in the most danger, and I'm conflicted because I don't want you to leave yet. A Mergon has to turn in a Treedle that they find entering our territory. But I'm not afraid of my potential punishment—I just fear what could happen to you. I'm thinking of how to keep you safe if you extend your stay a little longer. I want you to meet my mother and visit her in the adjoining compound tomorrow. Our compounds are guarded by men and the best trained and fiercest conchos. I'd like you to spend several more days here. And, together, we shall study a way for me to visit you in Aerizon. Devil beats me (Mergon expression) if you can be so daring and bold and I can't. What kind of Prince would I be, a real plucked chicken (another Mergon expression), if I can't engage in such a quest for friendship and understanding among our people and us?"

That was the first time Mateo hinted at the idea of a connection between their people. It thrilled Laela, and she cuddled Macecle harder not to bound over and hug Mateo.

Laela wondered, "Why are you so different from other Mergons, especially your Royal Family? Do they accept you as you are?"

I haven't spoken of our relations with the palace and my extended family. I'm a Prince but live like an exile in my land. My half-brother Marl is a primogenitor and will inherit the Kingship when my father passes. He would rather see me dead even though he knows that I don't desire the throne and would never compete with him for power. Yet, the people in our land have come to love my mother and me because we serve them. That can seem like a threat to those who want complete submission from the subjects."

Laela was intrigued by Mateo's lack of interest in royal privilege and pomp. "What brought you and your mother to live here in the countryside? It seems that for either better or worse, you are left to yourselves and can live and work as you please."

"Yes, we've been blessed by both misfortune and fortune. What I shall tell you is quite confidential, but I want our friendship to be founded on truth and openness." They stopped by a brook and sat on a boulder while Mateo told her his family history.

"My father, the King, sought his first wife from among the families of nobles in the land. He wanted to marry the most beautiful young woman and one from a family that would provide a powerful alliance and help protect the palace and our Kingdom's borders. He chose a young maiden from the Nagasha family. All spoke of her shiny raven hair that she often wove into a large bun over her head. She was considered a bit temperamental, but it was seen as a positive quality in a family known for the art of war and feuding. However, over time, she was despised by all in the Court; I'm sorry to say. I ask not to hear the stories, but they seem to pour from people's lips. She regularly beat servants and twisted someone's arm more than once until it was dislocated or broken. It took her three years to get pregnant with Marl, and she berated many doctors until she did. His birth didn't calm her, and she became especially dark in her moods after Marls' arrival. She left him to the wet nurse and couldn't bear to hear him cry or fuss, which supposedly he did a lot. The baby, without a doubt, had the same dark hair and temperament as his mother. They still talk about how it took a small army of nurses and maids to care for and control Marl.

"Nila, his mother, wanted to finish all childbearing tasks and ensure her family's line for the Kingship. She decided to try for another son. It took her three more years. She tolerated Marl, but even she could find little joy in such a demanding child. She always commented to the staff that she would talk to him when he was older. As she became more and more short-tempered and abusive, the list of her enemies grew. She went into childbirth in the seventh month with what would have been her second son. She had become pale and given to terrible stomach cramps and vomiting during this pregnancy. Tongues wagged that she had been gradually poisoned. She died during the premature birth, and the son born, who was deformed, was stillborn.

"Thus, my half-brother had a tremendously difficult family life as my father was too busy with Court affairs to pay him much attention. An older aunt then raised him.

"Soon after, my father sought a woman from a different kind of family. His advisers urged him to take a consort from a religious philosopher's family, from among the wisest Counselor-Scribes in the Kingdom. He chose my mother Danie's family. When he laid eyes on her, it was no sacrifice to unite the Kingship with religious authorities through another of the Kingdom's fairest maidens. My mother's father, my only living grandfather, is a scholar of renown. He expounds upon the Writings of the 'One,' interprets dreams, and gives the King counsel as requested on matters of state.

"She married my father by arrangement to be of service to her people. She hoped to serve as a tempering voice, to influence the King's decisions for the good of our people. She wanted him to tax the farmers less and provide more care to the poor. She wanted for the two of them to study the Writings each day together. However, her personality was highly irritating to the King. He found her to be too talkative, out of place, and he put his foot down about giving him any kind of advice on his affairs.

"He did let her visit the compound nearby frequently because it belonged to her father. My mother grew up on this lovely estate, and by my grandfather Asme's good graces, I was able to build my own country home on these lands. The King was happiest when my mother was far away from the palace as he worried about her influencing Court members. She realized too that she wasn't the best match for him either and felt she should respect her King and people by offering services—like bringing him a plentiful stock of the fruits, flowers, and fine meats that grow so well in our gardens on our farm. She had been studying since she was a girl about how to make tonics and beauty potions. All of the Court, including the King, asked for hair and skin lotions and oils. The King wouldn't start a day without her energy tonic. He liked to spend free time with ladies to entertain him and look and feel his best. His lack of faithfulness didn't hurt my mother, as it relieved her of the burden of his company. She didn't tell of her sufferings, but I know they were both physical and mental. She preferred to stay as far and as long away from the palace as he permitted. And he gladly allowed this. After I was born, he never received her in his chambers again.

"There was a horrible rumor circulating that my father had his first wife poisoned. He wanted to marry again to a consort that pleased him more. He also wanted to ensure that my mother need not visit the palace except for grand occasions. So, when I was three, he divorced her and gave her permission to remarry. She could spend time on what brings her joy.

"A philosopher and scientist who worked with Grandfather, Ivan, had always adored my mother but never showed any intentions toward her. He was from a lower social class and believed he couldn't support my mother as she deserved. My mother began to work with him as he helped her understand the science of alchemy and mixtures of plant essences and substances. Their admiration turned out to be mutual, and it became stronger over time. Grandfather noticed and gave his complete blessing to their union. So, I have a loving stepfather, Ivan, who has raised me. In my heart, he is my real father.

"My mother and Ivan live in a new wing added to Grandfather Asme's mansion. They share a common area, like my living room, where all can gather together. My mother's workshop and the studios to study religious and scientific texts occupy large rooms adjacent to the house. I have a brother, Gabe, four years old, the real Prince in our home. We're devoted to him and his every whim!"

"That's my story." Mateo grinned. They both came from honorable and loving families, even if a wily King was a somewhat menacing shadow figure in Mateo's life.

Laela wanted to share more of her story, though it seemed so simple compared to his. But what she was treasuring was his gift of vulnerability, and he might be braver than her in revealing himself.

Mateo looked at the sky and the thicker clouds associated with late afternoon. He lightly brushed her shoulder with his hand and told her that he must go to the village for some hours to tend patients. Laela welcomed the time to spend the rest of the afternoon writing messages and dispatching Macecle. Then, she would really be alone in the Prince's house. And the evening would be theirs.

CHAPTER 13

Messages and Revelations

Laela waved to Macecle, watching him from the second-floor window, as he climbed up a tree outside the compound. His first duty was to scout and scout some more before advancing. She had repeated instructions to him several times about staying out of sight of guards, conchos, and hunters. For the first time, she could feel in the pit of her stomach what her parents must feel. She would be imagining every step of his trip, gulping down fears, and was already feeling remorse for sending him on this mission. She would pray on her knees and with a fervor that the whole heaven would watch over this close as a sibling companion.

Ana came to the room and wasn't pleased to see the state of the dress Laela was wearing. She clucked her tongue, "Miss Ellie wouldn't have dirtied such a fine dress like this even if she wore it for a week! But no mind, I'm a wonder at washing out stains." Ana helped Laela into a warm blue dress and told her she would meet Mateo in the library for their evening meal. She accompanied her and left the door wide open. Ana was reluctant to leave them alone, but it wasn't her duty to supervise the Prince. A fire was crackling and had spread a cozy haze of warmth around the room. The night was especially chilly, and distant flashes of light along with sudden gusts of wind that seeped through the window cracks promised a storm. The window that let the outside world in and inside world out seemed an incredibly fragile barrier between worlds. Laela would need to look away, as she feared lightning bolts, as most Treedles do.

Mateo stood by the shelves and picked out a thick leather-bound book. He brought it to the table in front of the couch for them to look at together. "This is a book written by several generations of Mergon scholars. I thought you might enjoy this history of our people," he said, opening to the first page where a jewel-tone illustration and lilting black text transcribed in perfect, measured flow jumped from the parchment page. "Mergons, even educated ones, prefer to look at the pictures while someone reads aloud to them."

The first chapter depicted the beginning of time. The four tribes, less distinctly colored, lived and worked in different occupations under thatched structures by an ocean—a shining, waving body of serene blue water that she had heard about but never seen. Boats were bobbing in a nearby cove by a grassy hill. The following series of pictures showed the waters rolled back as if sucked into the horizon and then returning in the form of an ominous wave growing more prominent until it soared up, replacing the sky. Chaos ensued. Tossed, roiled, and pounded, their world was engulfed and broken apart into the roaring jaw of the wave. Trees were upended, hands flailed up from within the water, bits, and pieces of huts, and objects floated randomly in the flood it left. The next picture showed a group of people fleeing, holding hands, and running toward a hill—higher ground.

Mateo read parts, starting with, "Thousands of years ago, there was one land and one people, the inhabitants of Araneae who were mainly weavers and fishers by trade. They made nets for fishing, hammocks for sleeping, and cultivated spiders who could weave stronger and stronger, steel-like threads to honor their planet's name. Four tribes lived together as brothers. They worshipped their same Creator, the 'One,' and were illumined by the Teachings that the Prophet Asmea had revealed to them a century before. They based all of their most important personal and societal decisions on the study of the Sacred Writings. Asmea was from the tribe of what we now call Pyuva, and his wife, Denai, was from the tribe that is now Mergon. These were the two most different tribes in physical aspects and tribal customs. The people referred to the blessed marriage as a symbol of peace: the couple was like two birds of different feathers sharing the same nest and trilling the same song.

Araneae was the fourth planet from the sun. They saw the sun—Razi—as a symbol of the 'One,' uniting and drawing them in His hold as He did with the planets suspending them in space, maintaining their orbit through the invisible web of His attraction and power. Cor and Cora's twin moons guarded the night sky, and the people were protected from darkness by day and night. The web of unity between man and the 'One,' man and nature, was perfect.

Over time the tribes began calling attention to and priding themselves on their differences and competing for primacy over their seashore dominion. They debated over different interpretations of the Writings of the 'One' brought by the Prophet Asmea a century before. Asmea foretold a great calamity that would come upon the people if they didn't follow the laws of unity. He also promised that the people would be redeemed in the distant future, and a golden age would begin when the lines of the Pyuva and Mergon were reunited. He left a series of signs that the most learned must guard and study. They would need to watch for and discern when the prophecies were met to support their peoples' transformation and reunification. He promised that the catalyst for this change would come from an unsuspected source. The change would be initiated by one with the sign of the jaguar—descended from the prophet's family line."

This passage struck Laela, who clutched the table as if not to fall. Mateo stopped to ask if she was okay. He gave her space while she tried to calm her thoughts. She felt like this prophecy might have something to do with her—she then choked in shame to think such a thing. Her father was descended from the prophet's family but rarely mentioned it due to his modesty. The sign of the jaguar, the imprint on her chest. A strange coincidence. Weren't prophecies always about men and the way they would lead? How could a girl, often scolded for unworthy deeds, be part of something divine in nature? She must seek counsel on this later. She told Mateo that she would explain later and asked him to continue reading, which he did in his melodic voice.

"Leading up to the time of the great calamity, the tribes argued over which descendants among them would be the holders of the true faith. They disagreed about governance and whether there should be a king and, if so, from which tribal line. As their population increased, questions arose about the locations of dwellings and sharing resources. Growing discord and division spawned fights and feuds. That was when the 'One' sent the Wave as a punishment upon them. The tribes could no longer hold onto their traditions— gone were the seas, corals, and sands—the frothy palms and creeping crabs. They had clung to the shoreline and then, in one fell tide, were unmoored from all they had known and held dear. Those who survived escaped with few possessions.

"The days of exile began. There was only one way to survive in the wilderness they headed toward; the new terrains, animals, and plants they would encounter. The tribes needed to unite. The Mergon tribe deliberated and decided it would be easier to survive in a small group than a large one. They walked southwest for days, exploring a place to settle in the lowlands by the great forest. The Pyuvas, Texares, and Bouders made a pact to respect each of their tribes as equal partners in building a new and more peaceful society. They headed in a parallel direction to the Mergons but entered the vast tropical forest where the abundance of nuts, fruits, plants, and birds would easily sustain them. Scouts searched through various wooded areas for a place with the sturdiest trees and most abundant wildlife. Over time they built their civilization in the arms of a colony of ancient, home-like trees whose branches could cradle dwellings and that remained firmly rooted in storms. They gradually move upward to the top layer of the forest, making net paths at first and later building structures in and around the trees. They didn't have to struggle to exist, and each tribe could specialize in services to enrich their community life.

"The Mergons, rooted on the ground, founded a more advanced civilization in which they developed agriculture, metallurgy, and governance systems. They developed housing structures, machines, tools, and weapons, while the Tree Dwellers—Treedles—subsisted through foraging, hunting small animals, and primitive methods of cultural development."

Laela winced at the comparison the Mergon scholars made with the Treedles as they continued on about their civilization's superiority. There were pages with pictures highlighting one accomplishment after the other, from building the fortified palace complex to the invention of farming machines. Mateo stopped reading and blushed. They both realized simultaneously that this account placed Mergons as the real civilization builders and makers of history. Mateo had never noticed the bent in history until meeting Laela. He read history books as if they were second to the Writings. The scholars had given the nod to the peacefulness of Aerizon. But Laela burned for how her people were exposed in these accounts and the shadow of their disregard. In comparison, Treedles were collectively shamed. If civilization were summed up in gold, the weight of houses, farm animals, and things, theirs was the inferior society. How sad. She couldn't stack up her people's true beauty and power like gold coins to compete in measure.

Mateo closed the book with a thump, "That's enough of Mergon history. I want to hear more about yours. You come from an illustrious family. Everything about you shows the influence of a highly educated family. And in the end, such a family is a product of its culture and traditions."

Laela smiled at his diplomacy. He spoke such solemn words, but he looked flustered. She didn't know how deeply embarrassed he was to have read this passage and that it was getting harder to look her in the eyes for so many reasons.

"You've been honest and open with me, Mateo. Thanks for sharing so much of your life story with me! The lives of Mergons are so eventful. Treedle dramas seem to happen more in our heads. We're risk-averse people, and we protect one another fiercely, continually. We live in the open, surrounded by dangers, so we do all we can to avoid them. I can assure you that I'm atypical in my culture!"

Laela meandered around stories of Phips and Oti's union—mating for Treedles and marriage for Mergons. Then she decided to jump in and tell him about the gist of her discomfort, what propelled her beyond all boundaries: the jaguar mauling, the black jaguar, her dreams in the Enclosure. As she spoke, the sky was streaking with lightning veins casting an eerie light on the gardens.

She explained how she and Phips were instrumental in making the streamlined travel route through the Feral Forest and how the temptation to hunt there was overwhelming. Within hours they could track and bag plenty of wild game to fill their family's and neighbors' needs. She carefully described the attack setting and could almost taste the pulpy fruits in her mouth that she had just eaten, her state of joyful relaxation. Then the lantern eyes, musk, and mauling. Tears were streaming down her cheek. She opened the top of her dress and showed Mateo the jaguar's imprint over the right side of her chest. It seemed a deeper purple in the flickering firelight.

He reached out to trace the part of the marking with his fingertips. His touch was delicate and respectful, as if he were examining a patient. He looked like he wanted to ask questions, but she had to get all of the inexplicable incidents out at once. Her heart was pounding insistently. She proceeded to tell him about the Shamans, Ordo and Orla, her time in the Enclosure, and the dreams of the marketplace, the gold coin with the lotus design, and the terrifying force of the black jaguar. As if one jaguar weren't enough for her to fathom.

"Orla interpreted my dreams, and she told me I'd have a mission to promote justice and compassion." Laela couldn't repeat the parts about being a leader, overcoming tests or the buzz of concern—the fragments of conversation—she heard about herself before she left. For now, she was only a leader of a temperamental duo—Tan and Gibble and Macecle—when they weren't being willful and forgetting her commands.

Mateo walked over by the window and began pacing. Rain was hitting the windows like pellets. He paced for a while. His jaw was set as if he were frowning, and he held up his hand as if to say, wait, give me a moment. His silence was maddening as opening her story meant reliving the encounters and dreams that created an inner storm, and his response was critical. He could push her further into the vortex just by not understanding. She had never wanted to be seen and heard as she did now.

Then lightning and thunder, like clashing and flashing swords, overtook the room. Laela began shaking and noticed that tears were streaming down her cheeks. Mateo snapped out of his reverie and rushed over to her. Without thinking, he drew her up to him and held her close. He began stroking her hair and murmuring— "there, there"—and let her cry into his chest until she drenched his shirt with tears. He gently tilted her chin up, and she saw that his eyes were also welling with tears but intensely focused, two shining orbs tugging at her with magnetic force. Looking into his gaze felt unbearably pleasurable and painful at the same time. She lowered her head again and willed him to wrap his arms around her even tighter.

He whispered to her, "When you look at me with those eyes, I get lost, enchanted. So, please don't look up until I finish, or I won't be able to complete a thought." He began slowly, trying to choose his words carefully.

"First, thank you for sharing your remarkable story. I'm touched beyond words. I know something of the prophecies. That is why I was trying to quiet and calm myself. There's so much to tell you. I believe our meeting isn't by chance and that you aren' just a headstrong girl seeking adventure. Your encounter with the jaguar is a sign. Your dreams are powerful, Laela—full of meaning, of portent. I believe the 'One' has sent you here, directly to me. I'm to be your protector and you the protector of your people. That is what my heart is telling me. I feel confident as a doctor and healer, but this is unexplored territory. I'm not sure how to support your mission yet.

"There are some images in your dreams that are clues about the nature of your calling. My mother, Ivan, and my grandfather can help you with some missing pieces of information and history. I don't want to overwhelm you, but your quest is both delicate and extremely dangerous. It seems that your parents haven't shared much about future prophecies with you, nor should they. Mergon Elders are similar to Treedle Elders and have guarded such discussions to the wisest and most studious scholars. I just had the privilege to hear many of their conversations. I can assure you that my mother's family will help you. If you agree, we will visit them tomorrow and spend the day."

Laela beamed. She could only nod—her hungry soul trying to digest the sudden banquet of kind support.

Mateo now looked into her eyes again, lighting another hunger. "I think you've been through too much tonight—remembering. We can continue to discuss this more tomorrow." His gaze lingered, and he tenderly kissed her forehead. Then tilting his head slightly as if asking her permission with his eyes, he ever so gently kissed her lips. She wished they could replay this moment over and over. One little kiss created an ardent bloom, and she was standing helpless, like a love-struck Lili. Mateo wasn't condescending about her dazed state. He led her by the hand and deposited her by her bedroom door.

Then with a husky voice, half laughing, he said, "Lock the door. There might be a jaguar in the house that is after you. Help me control him!"

Laela's voice had returned, and she was up to the challenge. "Well, this girl can put up quite the fight!" She shut the door, thinking of her struggle not to 'attack' him. She discovered a 'girl' could have some passionate feelings about this too!

CHAPTER 14

Maternal Family

Mateo and Laela walked across a small stone bridge over a bubbling stream marking the border between his grounds and his family's compound. They stopped for a moment to sit on benches under a tree filled with thick-petaled, creamy white flowers. Laela had to pick one and dive into its intoxicating fragrance. She thought it would suit Oti in her hair—pure loveliness. Laela looked up at the panoramic view of the estate where Mateo's maternal family lived. He pointed out the main stone house and workshops, vastly larger than his own, set on the plateau-like top of a small hill. The manor, protected by stone walls, was surrounded by a smaller version of the patchwork crop lands below in the village. A meandering path flanked by velvety green grass and varied flower gardens lead to the iron gates at the inner compound entrance. In the distance, a wooded area covered a gentle slope. She could see the reflections of a pond glinting through the trees.

Laela was impressed with the sheer openness of the fields, the impenetrable and mysterious nature of living areas walled by stone, and the amount of land—of nature that belonged to one family. They had left Macecle behind, and she wanted to dig her fingers through his tufted hair, the fuzziest parts around his ears, and find her footing in this strange land. He had come bounding up to the window early in the morning and told her that he safely deposited her messages in the tree at station five. So, at least she had left word with her family about her safety and warm welcome in Mergonland. Mateo's home seemed familiar already, and she was hoping to spend more days there. How could a few more days matter if her family knew that a Prince was protecting her? But she was reluctant to climb the hill to meet new Mergons. Even if they were Mateo's family, she was beginning to feel that Mateo was one of a kind in so many ways. How would his mother and stepfather view a free Treedle? A girl who just became a woman two months ago. Would they be discomfited for Mateo to present her as a friend—an equal? Would they see her as an odd lavender being that carries little physical or other weight? Laela was already learning that there was a world of people who didn't value her or her people. They worshiped the 'One.' It made no sense.

Mateo watched her, drooping into herself, and brushed a strand of hair from her eyes. He intuited what was on her mind. "Laela, I sent a message last night to my mother and Ivan and this morning received one back. They're waiting to welcome you with open arms and are very excited to hear about you and Aerizon." He hugged her, "So cheer up. We're the 'good' Mergons, I assure you."

After passing through the iron gates and climbing stone stairs, doors opened to a vestibule, a quiet hall entrance to the main house. It looked like a sandy tunnel with its cornsilk-colored floors and walls. Large tapestries of pastoral scenes in blues and bone white hung on either side. An aged Treedle servant, dressed in dark cotton pants and shirt like Didor, greeted them, opening a thick wooden carved door with symbols that she had no time to cipher. She wondered fleetingly if he lived a shadow existence around the family. She would never get used to seeing Treedles without a life of their own.

The servant ushered them into the main living area. It was laid out like Mateo's reception room with large leather sofas in earthy browns, blues, and golden-tan colors. Three different sitting areas with tables, chairs, and small benches made for gathering places in the same room. Thick patterned rugs in muted shades of dark red, dusk blue, and ombre gold were placed in front of the sofas, and one long rug ran down the adjacent hall. These helped soften the echo of the various stones and tiles used to craft the floors and walls. Facing them were framed picture windows of an intricate garden, where cobblestone paths diverged from a large fountain shaped like a palm tree. The fountain sprayed water out of the top, over the stone leaves, and into a wide stone basin with smooth ledges. The variety of plants in the garden could serve as a full-day exploration for her and Macecle. Someone, she suspected Danie, had quite the decorative eye, as they had also brought elements of the garden inside and placed various small trees and bushes in ceramic pots matching tones of the room in gold, blue, and earth colors. Phips and Oti would be delighted with this room.

She turned her gaze to the large room adjacent, where a fire was crackling in a large hearth with a pot hanging on an iron lever—letting off the steam of silverweed leaves that Laela's mother used to clear up chest ailments. To the side, a woman in dark blue was leaning over a cradle to pick up a wailing child. This must be Mateo's brother Gabe whom he had spoken so much about to her. The woman handed the baby to an elderly Treedle woman, who could be Ana's sister and rushed over to them.

Danie was a regal figure from head to toe, even dressed in a modest cinched-waist indigo tunic that villagers might wear. She was tall and slim with golden-tanned skin. Her brown eyes, flecked with honey and hints of green, seemed to light up from inside. Danie didn't look like a mother of two and had kept her slender finger. Her thick chestnut hair was swept into a soft bun and pinned with two butterfly clips.

She smiled at Laela with the open innocence of a girl, immediately soothing her anxious heart, "Welcome, dear Laela! You must forgive me for not meeting you at the door. Baby Gabe has terrible chest congestion, and we're working day and night to soothe him."

Danie reached inside her tunic and pulled out a gold necklace with a medallion, patting it on her chest as if to say, all ready to greet guests now. She held out her arms to embrace Laela. Laela approached, entranced with this new woman in her life. Her nose knocked into the edge of the gold medallion, encased in a frame. She wanted to look at it later, as gold was a rare treasure, especially Treedle jewelry. She felt this necklace must be very important to Danie as she dressed simply enough. She didn't have time to look at it closely as Dani stepped back and laughed, "Did I frighten you, poor girl, with such a big hug? Where are my manners? It looks like I knocked the wind out of you. What I want you to know is that any dear friend of Mateo's is ours too." She spoke of her husband Ivan, who was still outside in their orchard and heading toward them. This room had a charming view as well, and she could see Ivan, who had sandy-hair, light skin and was tall and thin, carrying a pail of fruits as he approached.

Ivan came in, and she could tell he was both kindly and shy by the way he shuffled up, looked at her warmly, but seemed to grasp for words to greet her. Mateo had told her that Ivan could talk for hours on matters of import, but they laughed at him at the Court for his lack of social graces and polish. That had won him to Laela's heart before meeting him.

Mateo suggested they tour some of the workplaces on the compound so that Laela could see the range of activities going on. He asked where Davi was. Ivan told him that they would see him in the invention room, where he spent long days, barely pausing to eat.

Danie led them across a covered walkway with a purplish-colored tiled roof. Her studio expanded from an indoor to an outdoor garden and was similar to Mateo's in layout. However, she had an additional workshop full of wooden tables and herbs and plants drying in bunches, hanging from a trellis suspended from the ceiling beams. Laela could identify some of the plants and the smells reminiscent of Tara's herb garden. Rows of shelves with box-like dividers lined an entire wall. In each cubby, there were different bottles of tinctures, oils, medicines, and tonics. Danie showed her an outside hearth where they boiled and prepared essences of flowers and a hutch with empty vials to bottle them. She pointed out a metal-ribbed vat of pure alcohol they used to mix the medicines.

Danie picked two amber-colored bottles with different markings on them. She gave them to Laela and said, "When you return, please give these as a gift to your mother. Mateo tells me she's a healer. The one with the blue x is my miracle cure for the fading away disease, the one that depletes people from the inside. This one with the red x is a tonic that brings joy and relief and is for her anytime she becomes too sad. We all do at one time or another."

Laela was touched that Danie was treating her like Mateo did, instantly befriending her. That was the greatest gift possible.

Ivan seemed to stand straighter and become more alert as he opened the door to his studio. Laela was familiar with a scholar's studio—the many scrolls and tablets laid out on tables and the tiny tendrils of dust gleaming through the rays of the sun from so much opening and closing of parchments. New, were books organized by themes in the library. But the wall in front of her was what captured her attention and dazzled her eyes. The entire wall was painted in shades of cerulean and dusk blue, and the whole universe, all the constellations of stars from season to season, was depicted as if they were looking at the night sky over time. The stars shined in silvery tones, some tinged by orange, blue, or red. Ivan explained that they had various telescopes and found that no star, no sun, was the exact same color as another. On the adjacent wall opposite the library area, Ivan and his team had painted a map of their solar system. It showed the planets in relation to the others—the elliptical trails of their orbits around Razi, the sun. The sun was a fiery ball, brilliant gold with undertones of orange and wisps of flames around it. Araneae was the fourth planet that stood out as the most impressive. It was the second largest, and they had painted indications of the ocean and land masses, showing it to be a diverse, life-filled planet. The perfect melon and pale blue globes of Cor and Cora accompanied it in their own orbit.

Laela had never seen her sky world depicted in this manner: it was as if the jeweled paintings in Mateo's books became larger than life. His family's knowledge and artistry humbled her. She felt apologetic for her own people who had the brilliance but not the means to reveal secrets of the universe in this way.

"Next, you need to visit my friend Davi's shop." Mateo winked at Laela, "Don't ask Davi in detail about any of his inventions, or he'll go on and on. He talks in terms that none of us understand very well, no matter how much he explains. We just admire, and we certainly do need his marvelous machines."

Seeing Davi with his large protective eyeglasses, soldering wires with sparks flying around, brought a moment of comic relief. His shop looked chaotic, and he a bit wild with his untamed curly blond hair and overly big brown eyes. He took off his gloves and extended a hand, greeting her with a friendly grin. He nodded approvingly to his best friend, "Happy to meet you, Laela. Welcome to our land. It was nice of Mateo to bring you over." He raised his eyebrows teasingly. "Usually, we get daily visits, but Mateo has been quite occupied as of late!" Davi patted Mateo on the back and said to her, "Mateo is like my brother from another mother. So, you will have me as a friend too. I look forward to hearing about Aerizon and dream about visiting there one day. So much information about nature that I could get from being on the treetops!"

Davi gave her a tour of his studio and his most recent invention to harness and transform energy. He was working to create panels that capture and store the sun's power and turn this into another form of energy that produces light. As Davi talked about the process, he picked up a large glass globe with a helix-shaped filament in it, then pressed a button on a small apparatus on the table, and the globe lit up from within. Laela had gotten lost in the train of concepts he explained, but she could certainly understand that Davi was producing a miracle of sorts. His invention would allow a whole home or village to have light, to dispel the darkness that hid dangers for both Treedles and Mergons.

"Davi, this is marvelous. You have taken sunlight from the day into these globes, which must look like small moons at night. I hope one day that Aerizon can benefit from this discovery!"

"Well, Laela, I'm also working with a team of scientists to invent a new method of communication over a distance. If it works, we will find ways to communicate later anywhere in the known world." She could tell that Davi wasn't boasting, just sharing the excitement of his work."

Laela felt she would need to spend months, not days here, to access the books and studios filled with knowledge. She had reached a saturation point for today and was relieved when Danie beckoned them to move into the dining room for lunch. Laela saw that three more family members were waiting. Gabe was sitting in a high wooden chair, and a Treedle girl, a few years older than her, was feeding him. He had half his food on his face and a goofy grin. He looked endearingly familiar, but Laela winced at the girl her age with a wan complexion. The petal-shaped color that clearly identifies a Treedle's tribal origin was a muddied shade of gray. Thus, most of the Treedles here, she had to admit to herself, looked somewhat drained of life and beauty compared to their treetop ancestors. The Treedle girl couldn't stop gaping at Laela, and Danie seemed uncomfortable for the first time. She said, "Grazi, my dear, I'll take over from here. You go have your lunch now." Laela imagined the servants must eat in separate quarters. When Treedles had servants, which was rare, they ate with the family. But Laela stopped herself from further comparisons that might be unflattering to this kindly Mergon family.

Laela then noticed the two elderly Mergons sitting at the far end of the table from baby Gabe. They both had wizened faces like round dried fruits, capped by soft white hair. Despite their advanced age, both of them had twinkly eyes and a gentle demeanor. She knew immediately that these were Danie's parents, though they looked like fraternal twins. Later she would find out that they were actually distant cousins who had a remarkable resemblance. Meeting Mateo's esteemed grandfather, the wisest Mergon in the land and a descendant of the Prophet through his wife's family line, was more daunting than visiting all the workshops. Though Grandfather Asme looked easily approachable, Mateo had told her that any mortal was a galaxy away from him in knowledge and recognized that as soon as he spoke.

Danie had two Treedle servants, the man who opened the door for them and the older woman, pass around steaming dishes of meats, tubers, and vegetables. They served from elegant silver platters, offering two kinds of meat, which Laela distinguished only as darker and paler in color, taking a bit of both. They also served the tuber dishes she had had at Mateo's house. Laela was relieved to be familiar with most of the foods—one less new challenge. She found herself eating more of this fragrant meal than usual to calm and fill an anxious void.

She had hoped to avoid being the center of attention at this table, but Danie artfully engaged her in conversation. And it was all about Aerizon. Danie asked her to describe her home, Joy Park, and her mother's work in the gardens. She moved gradually to questions about her father. Laela tried to explain how honorable and wise her father was without appearing to brag, a sin among Treedles. Everyone laughed when she said how rarely they saw him as he spent long hours in his studio and in consultations. They were as pleased as she was to find common connections. In the end, she was also from a scholarly family too.

Danie pushed a little further to ask about her hunting outings, and though a bit surprised, the men didn't express any disapproval on their faces but instead curiosity and eagerness to hear more. After lunch, Danie asked to spend some more time with Laela alone in the sitting room. The female servant brought them hot chocolate in ceramic cups and a plate of sugary biscuits. And Laela followed suit from Danie in dipping a hard biscuit into the chocolate and taking small bites.

Sitting close to Danie, her eyes wandered to the gold medallion she was wearing, and she was aghast to see the lotus crown pattern— the same as the coin in the dream. Danie asked her what was wrong and took her hand to soothe her. Laela responded in as calm a voice as she could muster, "I have seen this medallion before."

Now it was Danie's turn to receive sudden, shocking news. She sputtered, "I only wear this out where it is visible around family and special friends. How have you seen this before? There is an extraordinary significance to this medallion. Do you have any idea what it is?" She could tell Danie was feeling protective of the medallion and its story. She was clutching it nervously.

Laela realized she must have blurted out words that needed softening, a more thoughtful introduction. She responded ruefully to Danie, "Please forgive me for the shock I just caused you. I had no idea I would ever see this medallion outside of a dream. My story doesn't make sense to me yet, but I'd like to share it with you as Mateo says you will be able to guide me. I have trouble sharing what is deepest in my heart and fear that no one will understand, or worse, people I care about will judge me harshly."

Danie had composed herself and spoke warmly again, "Please do. Take all the time you need. Your visit is a matter of utmost importance to my family. I want to know you much better, not just because of this medallion but also because Mateo can't take his eyes off you. I've never seen my son like this before. I need to know the woman he is falling in love with." She nodded with an inviting crinkle to her eye, a familiar crinkle.

Laela thought it best to start from the beginning and highlight the critical turning points in her life, when she started to hunt, when questions about womanhood and her role in Treedle society started to afflict her, when the restlessness grew. Danie asked many questions about the final outing with Phips to the Feral Forest, trying to hold back emotions that Laela could read in her eyes. Laela trusted her animal instincts, and people revealed so much in their body posture-their eyes. Danie asked her in great detail about the encounter with the jaguar. She could tell that Danie was struggling not to be impolite, but she was looking at Laela's upper chest as she spoke.

Laela asked Danie if she would like to see the imprint, and Danie responded that if it wasn't too much to ask, yes. No one else was in the room at this time, though she thought she saw Mateo peering around the corner. Laela opened her dress for Danie to examine the entire wound, which Danie did with respect bordering on reverence. A few tears welled in Danie's eyes, and she brushed them away.

"Thank the 'One' for saving you. I don't know of anyone who has survived a jaguar mauling, but I'm sure there's an excellent explanation why you have. Please continue." Danie said, sitting back again.

She proceeded to share in detail her days in the Enclosure, reliving yet again the intense emotions and sharing as a daughter would with a mother. No holds barred. Danie appeared visibly shaken again when Laela told her about the dream of the medallion. When Laela was done, Danie told her, "The signs in your story are so powerful, my dear, that if you allow me, I'll seek consultation with my father. But first, let's take a little walk to the pond, get some fresh air, and

I'll share with you some history and information that will help you understand your mission."

Laela thought, again—the word 'mission.' She wondered why her father hadn't commented on her dreams, on the religious history that this family knew so well. But she did know the answer. In Aerizon, these explorations were for the initiated, those who would dedicate their life to holy scripture. And she felt her father didn't see her as mature enough to handle religious mysteries or sacred missives.

They walked toward the wooded area. Laela could see floating flowers on the pond from a distance. Trees bent over the pond, making a waving green border around its perimeter. Danie pointed out the lotus flowers to her. They were different from the tiny lotus flowers they cultivated over puddles of water in the trees. They drifted lightly over the waters' surface, growing up from flat round leaf trays. They were like delicate pink and white ladies, carried by the lightest boats imaginable.

"The lotus is a symbol of peace for both our people. These don't grow up in the trees, but still, they represent a shared symbol." Danie began, "The lotus seeds stay potent for years, and these very lotuses are descended from the lotus pond that Asmae visited some centuries ago."

In the time of the Prophet Asmea, before his union with Denai, Asmae spent some months in a cave meditating, fasting, and dictating many of the Writings of the 'One' that we read today. Next to the cave, near a hill, was a small pond. Asmea saw water lotuses floating upon it, but brilliant rays of light surrounded them. He sat raptly meditating on the scene, and the 'One' spoke to him in a vision that the lotus flower would be the symbol of genuinely uniting the tribes, especially the two that were most distinctly different. As black is to white, so were the differences between Mergons and Pyuvas. There was distrust between them as the Pyuva seemed so in the air to Mergons, and Mergons seemed stuck on the ground to Pyuvas. Of course, I'm greatly simplifying here.

The 'One' bade Asmea go in the cave with a disciple, a trusted craftsman, to make two gold medallions according to the pattern that Asmea would see in his dream that night. Asmea was perplexed as to where to find the gold and how to work a design into it. When he slept, he dreamt of a lotus crown and designed this immediately on tree bark when he awoke. He and the craftsman searched deeper in the cave and found shining malleable gold in what looked like an oven. The craftsman prayed for inspiration, and using a few tools, he crafted a mold into stone in the design Asmae showed him. He poured in the molten gold and made two gold medallions from the cache of gold, which he carefully polished.

The two of them then heard the voice of the 'One' saying their work was good but that they must destroy the mold. Only one other person could know about the gold medallions, and that was Danae. These were symbols of Asmea and Danae's union and the union of their peoples. They told their followers that these sacred objects must be passed down through both of their family lines. At any time, a Mergon and Pyuva would each be a keeper of one medallion. Through prayer and meditation, the family member would choose a son or daughter devoted to the 'One' to keep the medallion. The medallion would bring special blessings to their family and the obligation to protect it with their lives.

The 'One' said that this day and age wasn't the time for the great union of the tribes. At a later time, one of the descendants shall arise, in the sign of the jaguar, to start a new epoch in history. This future unity will result in a time of great prosperity and progress. However, it will come about through sacrifice and pain. The dawn of this era will be blessed by exchanging the lotus medallions between the two families holding them. Not even the wisest and holiest of scholars are sure of the meaning hidden in His pronouncements about the jaguar and lotus and the events that will begin to change our worlds.

Danie, put her fingers to her lips and cautioned, "You mustn't speak of this to anyone. I believe your father, who is from the holiest

of your lineage, may well know where the other medallion is. I wear
this trust at all times but rarely show it. A Mergon woman wears
underclothes, and when I go out, I put it inside my dress over my
underslip. For whatever reason, today, I kept wanting to draw it out.
But if people do see it, few would know its meaning. They would
think it was just a piece of family jewelry. Wealthy and prominent
women here drape themselves in gold every day! My father gave me
this, and I will bequeath it to Mateo. He knows about the immense
responsibility it carries."

"Laela, I know you are chosen for a role in this exciting turning
of the times. I will ask Papa to bless you and keep you in his prayers."

Laela sighed, "I'm just a curious girl and surely not ready for
any 'big' responsibilities. But I wish for protection if I'm to serve the
'One' in any way."

Grandfather Asme was sitting on the porch in a cushioned chair,
looking out over the flower garden. He asked her to sit beside him,
and she pulled up a bench. He closed his eyes, and she waited for
him to formulate his thoughts, which practically hummed through
him. He glowed, radiating a sense of safe presence. She could sit by
his side just to bask in his light.

He opened his eyes, and she saw hope and concern. "My dear, we
must live our lives as servants of the 'One.' We each have a mission,
and none is too humble. However, yours is, how can I say—unique.
The 'One' works in mysterious ways. I dare say he has a sense of
humor. He doesn't choose the mightiest or the strongest to carry out
His plans. He selects a being to become a vessel, an instrument to do
His Will. This chosen one to outward seeming might look like an
unlikely candidate for bearing a message or leading the way to change.

"You're a girl, and you are just beginning to understand yourself
and the world. But the signs point to you as the one chosen to face
the black jaguar. You come from the line of the prophets' family,

and you fulfill the prophecies of the jaguar and the lotus. Few will suspect or believe that a young, inexperienced girl could ever be the repository of such trust."

Laela began to cry. She felt it to be true and didn't demur or protest. She didn't see how this would work and thought she was most unworthy and unready for such a calling.

Grandpa Asme stroked her head. "Blessings upon blessings be upon you, dear one. I must tell you that your dreams were only a shadow of the reality to come. Whatever befalls you, trust in the 'One.' Trust even more during the darkest times. Dark iron will become steel in the heat of the fire. Your path of service will require courage. So, your courage will be tested. You'll think that you can't bear it.

"Sometimes, there is only a fine line between the dangers of the sky and the earth, like the silvery thread the spider weaves. We must hold this line with faith but move with courage and confidence. We must know when to hold on to the line for our very lives. You'll need to hold on to believe as you would to moonline over the forest treetops. It is all that will save and comfort you."

Laela wanted to ask about the details, but Grandpa Asme dismissed her with a brilliant smile and made the motion of his hands, blessing her as if he were pouring water gently over her head. She felt parts of herself rattling loose inside and was unsure where these pieces would fall and what she would be afterward. She knew only that whatever came next, she surely would need to make herself a worthy vessel, as she had no way of filling her own heart with courage.

Later in the evening, Laela chose to be quiet and went to her room early to think and sleep. Sleep brought mixed dreams. She woke to recall that she had tried to visit the lotus pond on her own again, but dark forces were pursuing her, and she ran through wheat fields trying to hide and couldn't stop to take refuge.

CHAPTER 15

Promise

Ana looked at Laela's face in the morning and came in with what she called the solution for every girl's pain—an even more lovely dress than the ones in her closet already. Ana narrowed her eyes mischievously, "Noone will be the wiser about this dress. I'm dressing you for a celebration today, as Mateo told me he's planning a special day with you. He'll be taking you on his horse, and you will need to cover yourself with a robe and hood for this outing."

Laela had never seen silk as fine, with tones of lavender and pale blue. It glimmered like the pond and swished like soft waters. It was light, and she appreciated how it let her move freely. There were only a few tucks at the waist and a draped scarf-like neckline. Oti would adore this dress!

She felt like the lady of the manor as Mateo greeted her in the dining room. He looked at her as if drinking her in and smiled with such delight that she was willing to commit to more 'feminine' efforts for him. Especially if a dress was comfortable like this one.

They spoke at leisure over cups of steaming tea, and Laela felt ready to share her emerging story with him. Meeting his family had brought so many missing pieces together. It had also added new ones that needed to be carefully examined to absorb fully.

All of a sudden, she felt achingly sad, thinking about the need to leave soon. She looked at the last remnants of the buttery biscuit on her plate. "I wish this could last. This meal. These talks. There's so much more I want to know about you and your people. But I feel I should be leaving soon. My family is distraught, I'm sure."

Mateo reached out for her hand, "I've planned a great day for us together, and we will talk more about this. I agree that I mustn't keep you here much longer, maybe a few days more at most. But I simply can't let this go as a chance encounter. A wonderful one. A friendship, a special kind of friendship has already been born."

"But the distance, the two worlds we live in are so far apart." Laela choked back tears. She couldn't start now, and this might ruin a perfectly lovely day that she would cherish for years to come.

"I've thought of nothing but that distance. But as we say—where there's a will, there's a way. I'm not tied to this land, and I can visit you. It might stir concern and even opposition, but I plan to do it. Why not? I can justify it on so many accounts. My father and half-brother Marl know deep down that I don't want power and won't interfere with their affairs. I'm not after the palace wealth or the King's power. I can convince them of a benefit to them—bringing more medicines and increasing trade with the people of Aerizon. Slaves can't make the same quality of products because life gets sapped out of them."

Laela nodded, and his words were sparking fresh hope, answering her greatest unspoken wish. Mateo meeting her family, Phips, Oti and making the first links of friendship between their people. Seeing him again. Hearing his voice. The honey eyes she wished she could look into for the rest of her life and that would fade or morph over time into a fantasy-memory.

She couldn't quite imagine Mateo climbing trees or navigating the Feral Forest. Though, she could see him spending whole days with her father reading, her mother making remedies, or talking shop with Phips. There was a 'groundedness' to Mergons. They didn't think about each step, balancing on branches or falling between them. Treedles climbed, but they rarely ran. Treedles looked up at clouds, Mergons at mountains. Every aspect of the Mergons' daily life was in harmony with earth and soil. She couldn't imagine a Mergon preferring Aerizon to their fields and stone-walled homes.

Mateo said, "My mother feels sure that we were fated to meet and that you are to be in my life. She believes that you are a messenger of change we need here. I say let's do this together. I want to join you. Misery awaits me if I live for the Court, and worse misery awaits me if I let you go. The only choice for me is us."

"Us? How? How can that be?" Laela wasn't sure if he was implying what she thought. What she most wanted. She didn't want to swoon over a well-intentioned promise made out of the novelty and excitement—spinning their wishes on a fast spool.

"Let's get out of here to talk. I want to take you into the forest to a place that calms the mind. We must be careful as it is outside our compound, and you must be covered in a cloak. You can ride with me on the horse."

Mateo pulled her up onto the saddle and engulfed her in his arm while taking the reins. He adjusted her hood so no one could detect who he was carrying. She could be a family member or a villager.

The morning was still hazy as they skirted the shadowy gold wheat fields to enter a dark patch of forest. They came to a 'pine' forest. These trees were smaller in comparison to the towering heights of the trees in Aerizon. Yet, once they stepped on the ground and looked up, the tips of the trees soared far into the skies.

"I want to show you what we call an outdoor cathedral. It is a place to ask for the confirmation of the 'One.' I'm sure you'll prefer it to a stone church." Mateo loved how she breathed in and flowed with each of the natural environments they visited. Her lavender arched eyes would widen, and he could see the delight of discovery as she tilted her head.

Mateo held her hand as they walked down a crunchy trail of browned needles among the tall, stately, and triangular-shaped giant pines. They ducked occasional pinecones falling from the thick, spiky boughs of the pines. The path led them to a grassy knoll, surrounded by a circle of spired pine trees. The pines were forest green, fringed with emerald highlights where the sun glinted on the needles. The rays of the sun split through the pines to light up the middle of the knoll. The air glistened with sparkling freshness and a keen, pungent fragrance. A breeze like an invisible imp flowed through their hair and rustled their clothes, cooling and teasing them. Mateo pulled her to stand onto a flat moss-covered rock. As clouds passed over, a soft green haloed light surrounded them.

Mateo drew her close and gently guided her head to his heart. "What do you hear?" he whispered. She rubbed her cheek against the cool texture of his white cotton tunic, and under it she could feel the intense warmth of his skin and the thunderous pounding of his heart.

Laela teased him, "I think I hear a drum beating very loudly." She was afraid to name this feeling out loud, one she wanted to hear with all her heart.

Mateo took her chin into his hands and looked into her eyes, his own eyes darkening with intensity, "That drum is beating. I love you, I love you, I love you. Laela." Each repetition made her ache with longing to draw herself closer and to merge into its rhythm. He seemed to hear her thoughts and pulled her to him much tighter. Laela opened her mouth to respond and was drawn into a kiss like a question. First inquisitive, then probing. Their lips and mouths were exploring a new language. One that would belong to them. They tasted one another hesitantly and then more urgently. And it was Mateo who nudged them apart. "Laela, look at me, and I want your answer. What do you feel for me?"

Laela blushed, "I'm showing you. I love you too."

"The Elders would say it is too soon to call this love," Mateo mused while running his fingers through her hair.

"I'd say it is too late now," Laela quipped, and they both laughed.

"Yes, it happened. Time is logic, and our love isn't logical." The doctor in Mateo spoke, "Yet like in medicine, illnesses and cures are full of surprises. Sometimes you are sure someone will die, and they're quickly restored to full health. So, our love has its mystery."

The laughter dissolved in the next moment as her thoughts turned to the future. She leaned into Mateo, needing him to hold her up. She felt weakened with desire and the thought of unrequited love and separation from him, the real difference in their world and realities, too much to bear. Why were they here tormenting themselves with the impossible? Laela cried softly, wetting Mateo's shirt. "But where does this lead? Where can it lead?"

Mateo motioned to the pine trees as if they were dignified witnesses, "As these trees are evergreen, so will be my love and loyalty to you. Love will sustain us through every test."

Laela thought Mateo was more romantic than herself. Anything seemed possible in the gentle atmosphere of his compound. But outside of its walls?

"I don't need more time to know that you are the love of my life. The 'One' sent you to me. And I'll devote myself to you, to our family. This pledge I'm making to you is part of how we will do this."

Mateo reaching into his pocket and held up a ring—a brilliantly faceted emerald cupped into a gold setting. It seemed to contain the essence of the forest, such a deep green and perfectly polished. Laela had seen a small emerald once but nothing so regal and awe-inspiring. A jewel of the greatest value for Treedles and Mergons.

"I'll do whatever it takes, make any sacrifice to have you as my wife. Laela, will you be my life's mate?" Mateo offered her the ring.

Laela slipped her finger into the ring without thinking. It seemed to have been made for her. It fit perfectly. Mesmerized, she held it up to the light. Her surge of joy was tempered when she remembered Treedle law and custom. Treedles must ask and receive permission to mate. She shouldn't receive such a significant symbol from Mateo without her parents' blessing and approval. Laela now looked anxiously at the ring she had just eagerly accepted. She didn't want to let go of the ring or Mateo, but she was in no position to make this life-changing decision without her family behind her. She slipped it off, held it in the palm of her hand, and offered it back to him.

"This is the most beautiful gift I have ever received, but I can't keep it," Laela sighed woefully. "I must honor my parents by discussing all of this with them first. They will have a hard time believing what has happened in such a short time. Not to mention what this would mean for both our peoples." She explained Treedle tradition.

Mateo wasn't taken aback, "Please keep it. Take it with you as a promise of my intentions until such time I can ask your parents in person for their blessing. Just keep it very secure. It is one of a kind. My grandmother gave it to me to gift to my true love." Saying this, Mateo's whole face lit up. "Mergons also seek their parents' blessings, but it's not a strict law. However, I can't approach my father, the King, on the subject for reasons you well know. But my mother, Ivan, Davi, and grandparents have given their full blessings to 'us.' They did warn that the next steps wouldn't be easy, but let's not think of that right now. My real family supports our union."

Laela put the ring in the inner pouch she used to house Tan and Gibble, drawing it closed tightly.

"I will guard this with my life," she vowed, "as this will be all I will have of you till heaven knows when. I will mate with you or live alone for the rest of my life. No one could ever compare to you. I never met a man, besides my father, with so few faults."

Mateo threw his head back and roared with laughter, kissing her playfully on the neck. "So, my darling, is this the most endearing thing you can say to me? You also have very few faults, but one of them might be how free you are with romantic words. Never mind, those lavender-gray moons you have for eyes that tell me all I need to know!"

Laela continued with her practical concerns, "I admire you with all my heart. My mother told me only to let my heart go to someone I could admire for the rest of my life. You are the one. I'm sure you are the only one for me. But how on earth can we be mated? Ah, my darling Prince, I fear we have created a dream that can never come true."

Mateo smiled confidently. "No. It can come true, but we must both use our wits and pray for the 'One's confirmations. Right now, it is impossibly dangerous for us to live together here. My brother wants me gone and resents my popularity with our people. And he'll have his way should I do something taboo in our land.

"If you have me, I'll come with you to Aerizon. We could marry there if your family accepts me. I would find a way to move between both worlds over time. I can practice medicine anywhere and be content if I'm with you."

They walked a bit along a trail, taking time to let their intentions settle a bit, just as the pond after a big fish jumped out of it. They walked swinging hands, smiling, and flirting with their eyes in absolute delight to have shared the same confession. They found a grassy knoll and spread out a blanket under the shade of a wide-skirted tree. Mateo brought their lunch basket with them, and they pulled out small loaves of bread and an assortment of salty cheeses and garnishes.

When they finished, they lay down, looking at each other side to side. Mateo tickled Laela's nose with a wildflower that he snatched from the grass.

"Davi is our most avid supporter. He told me he wants to visit Aerizon with me and find a Treedle girl half as beautiful as you. Then we can be brothers with the same cause."

Laela decided to surprise him with a romantic move of her own. Little did he know he was awakening sentiments in her that they both assumed were the domain of the male animal. She loved him for his princely manners and restraint with her and trusted he wouldn't make any attempts to damage her purity. However, she needed to return home soon as she couldn't trust her instincts. Her sentiments were hardly virginal, and she was shocked at herself. Oti would laugh at her, or maybe not, wanting to ravish a man! But they must wait for the all-important blessings of family and the 'One.'

She sat up and straddled him tickling him with her hair and whispering endearments, "My honey jaguar. My handsome Prince," Mateo basked in the little kisses that ensued. She was eager to improve in this area of lacking, and Mateo would testify now to her growing capacity to please him.

Laela gently moved and sat by him to look at the results of her caressing endeavors. It was the most relaxed and playful moment she had experienced in months. Mateo was humming with contentment. Later, she would wonder what it was about her and relaxing in the best of company after a delicious lunch. She saw the distinct flash from behind a tree slightly to the right of where they were sitting. She knew instantly the flash was from the kind of glasses Mateo used to survey from a distance. There was a rustle she could hear as the person using them began to flee—assuring her that the person didn't want to be detected. Mateo couldn't hear the telltale crackling of the pine needles unless he was keenly focused on listening—which he wasn't. Laela could.

Mateo felt Laela go rigid and opened his eyes to see that hers were wild with fear. Laela jolted up and barked tersely, "We need to get out of here right away, find Sasha, and get back to the compound."

She extended her hand for Mateo to get up. She hurriedly packed the blanket and the remains of their lunch in the basket without looking at him.

"What happened? Why this sudden change? Where did lovely Laela go?" He said, watching her with a mixture of bemusement and concern.

"Mateo, someone was spying on us. I don't know for how long. I saw the glint of the glasses you used to observe from a distance. I heard the person flee. It happened in a few instants. Just now."

She could see Mateo start to demure and catch himself. He knew he was with a huntress, and she could better evaluate such a presence than he could. Wasn't he just lolling and dreaming about more kisses? She could see the truth sinking into his conscious and draining his color pallid with it.

She tugged at him, "We must move quickly and not just wait out in the open here. Where there is one spy, there could be others." Laela urged Mateo to take them galloping home. She was assessing the situation and what to do next as they entered the gates of the compound. She felt a temporary relief. These walls weren't impenetrable, and Mateo didn't have any guards of value. Why were his guards so old? He wasn't a very strategic Prince about these matters.

They sat in the library to discuss what to do next. They both knew what that was, but it was a question in Laela's mind, only if she could leave by night or just before dawn. She could navigate a better escape from an unknown region and entry point to the forest, with more light. However, it was time to return to Aerizon and quickly.

Mateo shared her urgency now. "I apologize, Laela. I'm so ashamed that I brought you to an area where someone might discover us. I was carried away with finding the most romantic spot for a proposal and thought it was enough to cover you with a cloak to arrive there.

"But I want you to leave safely. We can go on Sasha before dawn to get to the area of forest where you arrived. I know how to skirt around the villages and fields quietly with her. I will ask Ana to pack light food provisions for you.

"I plan to follow after you soon. I'm going to copy the map you used. Davi and I can find a way to the Trader's Village and from there, use your trade route. You will need to warn people about our arrival. We would hopefully travel with a Treedle to guide us."

Laela spent the late afternoon preparing her small backpack, getting Tan and Gibble ready to travel, accepting the emerald ring in the pouch, and giving copious instructions to Macecle. Ana brought her a plain, comfortable brown travel tunic that would keep her warm and camouflage her. Ana kept hugging her and whispering advice like a concerned grandmother, "Be careful, be careful."

They would depart two hours before dawn when the first shade of dark blue appeared in the sky. Laela and Mateo just picked at the food brought to them that evening. Neither wanted to try to sleep. They sat with the curtains drawn, conversing and cuddling, both nodding off here and there and both awakening in the discomfort of sitting positions. For a journey like this, Laela needed to steel herself, and she picked away at the fears popping up like gray mushrooms to focus on the immediate objective. Being present in this departure, or was it escape now, would be vital to success.

CHAPTER 16

Capture

Didor reminded them that it was time, and that Sasha was saddled and tied to a post by the side door. Mateo planned a route that would take them over a rustic path parallel to the road, skirting around the village. They would initially need to leave through the front gate and cross over the road quickly, scouting to see that no one was there. The route from the first floor leading under the waterfall was too dangerous when it was still dark.

Laela put on her backpack, and Mateo covered her with an additional dark cloak. They walked with Didor to the service entrance. Didor went to open the door for them, and the first clue that something wasn't right hit Laela standing behind Mateo. She could smell the conchos and even the fumes of the heavy drink that nighttime Mergon guards liked to guzzle to keep themselves warm. There were moving shadows in the slice of night revealed through the half-open door. She snapped into high alert. What should she do? They had Mateo and Didor in their sights.

Her first instinct was to protect Macecle, who they would harm if he jumped about and screeched. Directing her most severe, commanding look and using hand motions they used in hunting to signal hide and extreme danger, she told him to hide. She dropped the backpack and passed it over it to him with her foot, motioning him to run and hide with it in a tree. She needed to look innocent, and the less she carried and showed, the better. How did she know this? She was praying. Macecle obeyed and scurried off.

A burly guard with the signature blue cap with an ornate M embroidered on it restrained both Mateo's hands behind his back and had his neck in the crook of his other arm for added precaution. There appeared to be four other guards with him, and as they pushed through the door, Laela saw that more reinforcements had swarmed in from within the house. Another five guards were coming up through the hall adjacent to the entryway. They must have entered through the main door.

An equally gruff guard, dressed in a coarse blue uniform with a wide belt from which dangled an array of weapons, lunged toward Laela. He had an unpleasant, meaty body odor and large splayed hands. He grabbed Laela's two wrists in one hand and mimicked the other guard by wrapping his left forearm around her neck. Laela felt fear and an unexpected reaction to laugh. She was afraid the guard would squeeze too hard even without meaning to and crack her neck or wrists, and at the same time, using such brute force on two besotted teenagers seemed utterly ridiculous. She had to bite her lips not to emit a cackle of nervous laughter. They weren't criminals, and the guards hadn't captured them through bravery, warding off a real threat. Their bravado seemed downright silly in these circumstances.

One of the best-dressed guards stood in front of Mateo and held up a parchment scroll tied with red tassels. Mateo's guard barked in explanation, "We are here on the orders of King Malcolm to detain the Treedle intruder for questioning and trial. She's charged with spying, and you, Prince Mateo, with aiding and offering sanctuary to a Treedle trespassing on Kingdom territory. We have a message from the King for the Prince to read and respond to in three days. The trial is set for the morning of the sixth day of Jarman."

The guard's grip on her neck made it hard for Laela to speak up, but she projected her voice as best she could, "Please let Prince Mateo go. He has done nothing wrong. He was going to escort me out of Mergonland to return to my people. There should be no problem with this. If you let me go, I will show you that I'm leaving through the forest as I came."

Mateo looked at her in shock, shaking his head no. She assumed that meant not to talk or try to defend him.

The guard holding her neck helped her better understand. He began choking her. The guard holding Mateo looked at her, his face red and contorted, "Who do you think you are talking to, Treedle scum? Shut up and do as your told, or things will be even worse for you and the Prince."

He said to Mateo as if whispering in his ear but almost shouted, "You got a mouthy one. We should beat her properly on the spot. You have been bamboozled, but we're going to help you, Prince. Stay calm."

He was the commander and spoke to the guards, "Don't listen to anything the tree lizard has to say. She must have used witchcraft to cast a spell on the Prince. No one in their right mind would bring one of these into the house as a friend."

And less gruffly, "See here, Prince, no lack of respect meant, but we're here to protect you and your property. Once we get this little harpy in the pit where she belongs, you will surely return to your senses. We have heard that you are a good Prince, so cooperate with us fully, and all will go well with you. The King will only allow for one response, and that is your complete cooperation."

Laela's ears perked at the mention of a pit. What pit? Where? And she held her tongue as any words could be used against Mateo. She wanted him safe. He could only help himself and her if he cooperated with the authorities for now. She had never heard such a grotesque insult about Treedles, but at the moment, it was the least of her worries. They were itching for a reason to hurt her.

Laela's guard threw her down on the floor, and with the help of another guard, firmly tied her hands and feet together to make her into a bundle for easier transport. The rope cut into her soft skin, but she tried not to wince. Mateo was looking at her in abject horror. He was letting out pathetic moans without even realizing it.

The gruff chief guard reminded him that resistance would only incur more punishment and pain for Laela, "Let the lizard go. No sounds, no protest, and we will tell the King that you obeyed his wishes. That will make things go better for her, as you care for her."

Her guard took her outside and hung her over the back of a saddled horse, tying her more so that she wouldn't slip off. She willed herself to ignore the discomfort and to listen and watch for any information that could be of use. For the first time, it occurred to her that her life was worthless to all outside Mateo's compound family. They could kill her.

Think! Think, she told herself. She remained still and quiet. Observing would be crucial to survival.

The road felt bumpy, and every step of the horse jolted her stomach, which was the main contact point with the saddle, and reverberated through her body. For whatever reason, the guards didn't seem to know that her ears weren't tied shut. Or that she had excellent hearing. She was grateful she could control her desire to scream and moan as it would call more attention to herself. The idea crossed her mind that the more she could act as a nonentity, the safer she would be. Weak animals played dead, and it was a better defense than trying to counter-attack if outnumbered and overwhelmed by strong predators.

The guards, tongues also loosened by abundant fermented drink, began discussing among themselves, "Should we give her a golden shower when we get to the pit? What fun, how about a game of stone tossing, more fun. A few shots at the head should keep her quiet."

A burly guard who sounded more serious countered, "This isn't any common thief or criminal. Remember that the Prince has his contacts inside and outside the palace. I say we don't touch this one. We could get ourselves in trouble. The King wants her ready for trial. It promises to be a show. I wouldn't mess with her."

Laela began what would become an endless prayer: Protect me. Save me. Help me.

She was close behind as they had loosely roped her horse to the one in front carrying the most thoughtful and one of the aggressive guards on it. They must assume that Treedles don't pick up very much. Their main interactions with Treedles were as slaves or beasts of burden.

The mean one said, "Reckon you have a point there. The Treedle slave that ratted her out belonged to Lady Danie. She said the whole family acted like she was a Mergon, an important Mergon. She thinks the girl might have bewitched them all. But we couldn't let that slave go back to the family. We had her send word to Lady Danie that she visited a cousin in the Traders' Village. Then we took her on a trip she wouldn't return from. Ever. Best we don't look at or touch this Treedle. Heaven forbid one of us gets bewitched!"

Laela held in the gut-wrenching reaction: she started to vomit but swallowed it. No distracting noises. She had learned more than she wanted to in the first hour of her capture. She was already responsible for someone's death in Mergonland. A Treedle, no less. If she hadn't ventured here, the Treedle girl would still be alive. Never mind that the girl wasn't loyal to the family. Maybe she really didn't know how to handle the shock of seeing a Treedle treated like an honored guest at the table of Mergons. And Mateo? what would be the consequences to him for welcoming and sheltering her? At this point, she felt she might deserve this discomfort and more.

The sun was rising when they arrived at the pits, a whole field of them, which had their own peculiar stench of sweat, blood, feces, and urine. As her guard untied her, he informed her that this was where they brought Treedle agitators, prisoners of war, and the very worst criminals. "The King says that anyone who dies here won't be missed, and he can save the bother with one less trial. Welcome to the home of the worthless."

He pulled her to a pit cell near a tree and unlocked the iron grate that covered it with a key on his belt. He untied her. He then picked her up by the hands and swung her in and down into the dank shaft.

The pit was deep in the ground. In the dawning light, Laela observed the different shades of red-brown bloodstains running down over the uneven stone surfaces—the last vestiges of both guilty and condemned prisoners who were tortured through the process leading to their death. An impenetrable cold and clamminess surrounded her, seeping through her every breath. She could lie down in it with her head touching one wall and her feet another because of her petite frame. But the dampness would be close to unbearable, and she would rest upon layers of body waste.

The guards had chosen a pit for Laela under a tree. She heard them discussing how a special detail would be on duty just to watch her by day and night. The guards preferred shade for themselves. The tree would give her some respite from the implacable sun during the day. But it was scant comfort all in all.

Laela found a small metal cup on the ground and passed some hours making a division in her cell. She scraped layers of dirt from the area where she would sit, lie down, and sleep and made a little mound to the side of the wall with an indentation in the bank. She could take care of personal duties within that mound. Scant comfort, but arranging it gave her an immediate purpose.

As she worked, she was often stopped by cramps of hunger and nausea. Each wave came with a cascade of worries. Torrents of dark thoughts swept from her mind to every part of her body. Where was Mateo? How was he? What might they say to her at her trial, and how should she answer—to be freed and never return? How would her family know if something happened to her, and if they knew, how would they recover from the pain?

She heard the guards above talking about the change of guards who would be on the night detail. Shadows indicated that it was late afternoon. The new guards looked in at her through the grates with impassive expressions. The thinner one, and my, but they all looked so similar, told her that she would be given one meal a day in the evening.

How would she face a night alone here? She was trying to imagine how she could soothe herself and rest for an even greater test to come. Suddenly she heard a familiar voice. It was Mateo, and for an instant, she panicked that they may be putting him in a pit as well. However, his voice sounded reasonably confident as he addressed the guards, "I've come to bring some simple provisions for the prisoner. She hasn't been put on trial yet, and we don't know what the Court will decide. As you can see, she's a young girl. I wish to give her these blankets and a few food items."

Then in a less cajoling tone, Mateo added, "Igor, I'll be attending to your father tomorrow and also your aunt, who is quite ill. I will continue to serve them and all other family members without charge but ask for this simple favor toward my friend. I've also brought you a basket of Ana's most delicious, sweet buns."

"Prince Mateo, in honor of the family members you have saved, I will authorize a short visit with the prisoner. Stand back, and we will inspect what you have brought. If approved, we will give it to the Treedle." She could hear them discussing what Mateo brought. The other guard said to Igor, "It is just some bread, nuts, a cup, and a plate. I checked, and nothing is hidden in the blankets."

She heard the plodding feet of someone approaching, and the thin guard, Igor, opened the grate and threw in the provisions, glaring at her and then locking it soundly again.

Mateo said coolly, "Now if you don't mind, I would like to speak with the girl through the grate. I will keep my hands where you can see them. Please allow us to talk." She could feel the sullen agreement in Igor's voice, "Okay. Don't return again. Just this once."

Laela tried to muster a semblance of dignity. She patted her hair down and brushed the dirt off her tunic. Not much to work with in the pit. This might be the last time she would see Mateo ever. He shouldn't return before the trial, and after the trial was another dark question. It would surely involve some kind of no return to the best days of her life.

Mateo just looked at her in silence for some moments. Each gauging the sadness and strain on the other's face and grasping for some way to comfort and provide each other hope.

"My darling, there are no words for the remorse I'm feeling. It is my fault that you are in this pit. Can you ever forgive me? I couldn't even imagine something like this happening to you. I fell in love with you so quickly. I lost my mind." He spoke in as low a voice as possible so the guards wouldn't hear.

"It's I that owe you an apology. I've trespassed on your father's lands, and I was told how Mergon's detest Treedles. When I met you and your family, I thought there were more like you. I didn't realize the danger I was putting you in by staying in your house. I'm truly sorry."

Laela also hung her head, telling him about how Danie's young servant was gone—because of her.

Mateo shook his head, "Her disloyalty could get either or both of us killed. I don't mourn her loss. We must concentrate now on what to do to get you home safely.

"First, know that I love you. I will be at the trial, and my family and I are committed to ensuring your safe exit from Mergonland. We will do whatever it takes. But here, you have to combat an enemy with clever strategies, my dear. They have a lot of physical power and might, as you have seen. We must use this encounter to discuss strategies for getting you released. And we don't have a lot of time to plan."

Laela wondered, "Is there any way as a son that you can just talk to your father? Maybe you can convince him in person that neither of us meant any harm. I can be on my way as soon as I am released."

Mateo shook his head, "I'm not allowed to visit the Palace and must be present at the trial. The King will only hear me there. I've sent a message, but I believe it will fall on deaf ears.

"I've tried to be a faithful and loyal son. But I ask myself if it's a divine joke that I'm the scion of the royal throne and tribe whose most remarkable attribute is justice. And my father leads with hate. He scorns the poor and the weak. He lives to amass gold, jewels, and fortunes for the Court. He's the leader of war and slavery. He stands for everything I abhor. Yet, I must obey him."

"What can I say at the trial that would help our cause?" Laela looked at him, studying every blink of his troubled eyes. He brushed tawny hair from them and replied,

"What I most fear, Laela, is for you to say the wrong thing. He has a terrible temper. You must try to soothe him with your words. You mustn't speak back, and you must act innocent and very meek. Very meek, do you understand? That means talking to him like he's all-powerful and wise, and you are as nothing."

Mateo sounded like her father. Peeved, Laela turned her eyes away from him. She did know what he was asking; but acting differently than herself under enormous pressure might not bode well for her or him.

"Laela, we don't have time to become irritated with one another. I have to ask you to do just as I say, to save your own life. Laela, if you thought the guards were a bit rough, you have no idea how cruel my father and Prince Marl can be. They enjoy seeing subjects who cross them tortured. Their tortures are worse than death. I have to warn you, darling. Please look at me."

"I'll answer truthfully to your father. I'd rather die than tell a lie. I'd rather be enslaved than betray my people." Laela hissed at him.

"Laela, for the love of the 'One' then, please listen. You must be very humble."

She interrupted him coldly, "No, what you are really saying is that I must allow myself to be shamed and accept being humiliated."

"Laela, it will save your life if you don't answer back and just plead for mercy and forgiveness for trespassing. I'll offer some tribute and gifts to the Palace on your behalf to save you."

Laela looked at him with tears of frustration. "What is wrong with your people? Why do they hate us so much? They have twice as many things and possessions as we do. What more do they want?"

"It's not time now to think about that. Yes, many at the Palace are cruel. Now please help me to protect you. Your parents want to see you alive. I'm going to send you messages in the form of edible paper. Macecle can quickly drop such a message at night for you. You can read it under your blanket and then eat it as soon as you do. Other than that, this is our last meeting for now."

Mateo looked at her with such love and concern that she remembered her passion, and her anger turned to gratitude. "No matter what happens, Mateo, know that I love you with all my heart. You've brought me so much joy, opened a new world to me. If anything happens to me, just know that it was worth it to meet you."

"Thank you, Laela. Your words are the greatest gift I could receive. I'll pray and work with my family behind the scenes here. We'll do all that is possible for us to do. I love you, my precious one. You're the light of my life. Keep praying, and the 'One' will protect you even when things seem the worst. Grandpa Asme promised that would be the case."

When the guards called and motioned for Mateo to go, Laela forced herself to send him off with the kindliest expression she could—a slight smile. But the minute he was out of hearing distance, she sobbed inconsolably. She looked at her own lavender-tinted hands, so tiny and pale against the somber stones. She was fragile. How could a single Treedle girl face such an ordeal?

Even with the generous number of blankets, the metal cups and plate, and food to nourish her, nothing diminished the nature of the pit. When the nighttime came casting misty shadows around the entrance of the hole, she looked beyond the two moons and then closed her eyes to implore the presence of the 'One.' There was no sweetness in this communion but a sense flowing through her body to gird up her energy. It was telling her from within to be strong to act strong. She must find the strength the 'One' was depositing in her as needed. Her inner defense and weapon for good. She knew she had already entered into the lair of the black jaguar. There was a time to show all meekness and a time to bellow and charge against predators. She repeatedly prayed that the 'One' would guide her, prompt her to lay low, and stand tall as any confrontation with the enemy might merit.

Every time she awoke, stirring in the cold soup of anxious sweat and musty air, she tried to find refuge in the innermost part of herself. All she could sense was aloneness and abandonment. She needed to create an invisible moonline connecting her with the 'One.' She needed a bridge to carry her safely between worlds and not drown in the cruelty of Mergon condemnation.

CHAPTER 17

The Trial

The trial was set for mid-morning on the fourth day of her imprisonment. Ana showed up at dawn with food and fresh clothing for Laela. She had known the two guards in charge of the pits this day: they had grown up with Mateo. She offered sweet buns to them and an admonition to respect the Prince's wishes and allow her to prepare Laela to enter the palace cleaned up and dressed in fresh clothing. She reminded them how much the King likes cleanliness and tidiness and that it would be a lack of respect to send Laela wreaking of the pit. Ana was one of the few Treedles who might talk to Mergons like this. She had helped to serve and mother all who surrounded Mateo. The guards grunted unhappily but gave their consent. They opened the grate and allowed Ana to stand over and bathe Laela.

Ana brought over two buckets of water from a nearby well. She shooed away the guards and first had Laela pass her up the blankets and remove her clothes. She gave Laela lavender soap, poured water on her to lather up, and then more to rinse her until her body and hair looked glistening clean. Then she sent down a drying sheet and asked Laela to stand on top of it when dry. Finally, she handed down a modest gray tunic, stockings, and boots for her to clothe herself.

Laela had never been so grateful for a bath in her life, even one in the pit. The last three days had seemed to pass within a haze of dread and discomfort. Listening to moans echoing from within the nearby stone pits, imagining the suffering of fellow prisoners, and reliving the last year of her life in the judging eyes of both Mergons and Treedles. On the second day, a guard, who was Mateo's friend and who, evidently, had many from all walks of life, let Didor bring her some food and a message from Mateo. Didor had hidden Macecle inside his cloak. They both shushed him to be quiet, and he handed her little fruits through the grates. Laela sent him air kisses and received what he dropped into her hands with smiles and nods of gratitude. Didor leaned over and whispered, "Now Macecle is going to give you a message from Mateo and a tiny sack with pills that he's carrying in his pouch. Please read and then eat the message. Mateo has written it on an edible parchment that Davi invented." Macecle gave her the small parcel, and they were off.

She quickly read the message, "My love, my only and true love. I have sent you some small pills from Danie. Take one each day after breakfast. They will help calm you and may make you a bit sleepy. They're made from the essence of lotus flowers. You're not alone. I am with you always. The 'One' is watching over you. I'll see you again at the Palace. Then, you should be on the way back home. Love and more love, Yours, Mateo."

Laela read the message again and then ate it. It had a pleasant, sweet flavor. Her only comfort was to remember that Mateo was thinking about her kindly. Being restrained in a small place that smelled wretchedly wasn't conducive to positive thinking. Yet to win any battle, she must focus on the invisible moonline that would help her see over and above the nagging discomforts of her prison cell. This must be her practice. Little did she know how much she would still need this practice.

In her mind, there was only one plausible ending to the trial today, and that was to depart for Aerizon—even if dragged by guards and conchos to the edge of the Kingdom. They would see what a young, innocent, and admittedly foolhardy girl she was. She was barely a woman and certainly not fully mature yet. They would see that too. Mateo would never allow her to be a slave, so she must go through one more test before leaving. She would ask Mateo for her backpack at the trial. It would be tough without a few implements for climbing and safety.

The guards hauled her up, and she could tell by looking into their quizzical eyes that she must look strangely presentable for a Treedle. She had given a name to each of her prison guards, such Mean-gon, Dumb-gon, Long-gon, and Duhduh-gon. The one holding her arm and directly in charge of her was Unhuhgon. He had a puffy, nondescript look about him and never looked pleased or unpleased. He was neither helpful nor harmful. The guards looked over at Ana and told her that she must leave immediately. She could tell they didn't want to handle a possible fuss as they prepared to take her to the palace. Ana couldn't help herself and wiped away a flurry of tears, hugging her, saying, "I already love you like a daughter. I will be praying for you. Till we meet again!"

'Unhuhgon,' who had been holding her hands from behind, tied them tightly with a cord. Then he threw her over the horse's saddle on her stomach, seating himself behind her and adjusting like he would a sack so she wouldn't slip off. They circled the wooded region and eventually arrived at the foot of a large hill designed with gardens in jewel-like colors, vermilion, brilliant yellow, and greens. She could better appraise it if her head weren't hanging upside down and she weren't feeling so nauseous again. They began a slow ascent and arrived at towering iron gates, elaborated in repeated patterns of intricate scrolls and crowns with KM lettering above them.

Unhuhgon stopped at the entrance and unloaded Laela, who had to take a minute to adjust her whirling head and vision. A royal guard opened this gate. A pathway paved in gold and silver coated stones, probably painted, led to the marble steps at the foot of the palace.

From the ground up, the castle projected a somber and majestic presence. She could now take in the soaring marble columns that created a facade with depth and mysterious shadows in front of the Great Hall's main entrance. They had overheard them refer to this as the Great Hall and the Hall of Joy and Horror at the prison.

Unhuhgon looked at Laela's quizzical face and commented, "We are going to leave you in the vestibule of the Great Hall where the King receives visitors and conducts trials. Members of the Court are invited on the day of judgment on the last day of the week. I will be handing you over to two Court guards. You will wait in an inner chamber until the King summons you. When you go in, you must bow and curtsy to him."

Two royal guards flanked the thick wood doors to the hall's vestibule. The doors were carved with elaborate friezes in ode to the King. The royal palace guards were dressed with more pomp than Laela would expect of the King himself. They wore well-fitted dark blue jackets with gold buttons and gold braiding draped on the shoulders. Their pants were dark red, and their boots shiny black. They held large, partially encased silver sabers and a baton at their hips. She could barely see their eyes under the shade of their large white fur caps. Their posture echoed the marble columns lining the vast corridor before the great hall.

As they climbed the last step, she glanced at Unhuhgon who looked pale and tried to avert his eyes and shield her from seeing the scene before them. This made her curious, and she peered around him to see two palace guards exiting the Hall carrying a large silver platter with a severed head on it. There were globs of blood and gore in its matted hair and spattered over its face. She could instantly identify this as a Treedle of Puyva descent. She knew this was the head of a slave and a message for her. She felt a tug in her chest and lost the capacity to breathe, tumbling and losing consciousness.

Unhuhgon caught her before she hit the ground. He eased her down and began patting her face and wetting it with water from his flask until she sputtered and came to. Leaning in close to her, he whispered, "If you want to live Treedle girl, do as I say. The King will want you to beg for mercy. Humble yourself before him. I can see there is something special about you. I wish you well." She felt oddly comforted that this Mergon captor was showing some heart. But now it was 'time,' and he was turning her over to yet another pair of well-dressed palace guards with smaller caps. There was no way to flee, no way to buffer herself from the omnipresence of the King's power. Danger was set into the marble veins at the heart of the Kingdom.

They led her into the vestibule, where a wooden wall that didn't reach half the grand ceiling's height blocked the view of the Hall. She could hear the King's booming voice, echoing in the marble cavern beyond, sending out a petitioner and announcing that they could bring in the prisoner.

Her senses fluctuated between sharp and blurred as waves of anxiety flowed through her. Surely, she had done nothing so great as to merit her head on a platter. But, in hate-filled Mergons' minds, random outbursts could come at lightning speed, burning reason and anyone in the way of their will.

Her heart was already so attuned to Mateo that the first person she saw as they moved forward across the multicolored marble floors was him. Armed palace guards were stationed on either side of him. Mateo looked distraught but restrained. She could feel him choking back a scream as if he were somehow surprised at her presence.

Along the walls of the hall, noble spectators in lavish clothing, wearing silks, brocades, and thick golden necklaces and chest pieces flaunted their position, wealth, and power: fans waving, feathers bobbing, men adjusting their wide belts with enormous gold buckles. She could feel them preening and also sense the mounting excitement flowing in currents around the room. They were entitled onlookers and participants who jeered and cheered at the Kings' urging. They savored the anticipation of an upcoming condemnation or spectacle of torment. And Laela was the case of the season. Would this cocky Treedle live or die, be imprisoned or released, or be the object of some new torture?

The palace guards brought Laela to stand on a slightly raised circular platform set to the left of the raised stage where the King and Queen could view the entire hall from their thrones. King Malcolm and Queen Mali sat on a gleaming black onyx platform crisscrossed with gold lines. Their thrones were embossed with gold and behind them was a giant depiction of Razi the sun god, his beams striking out like golden lances. Long silk tapestries with symbols and shields she couldn't decipher hung from the ceiling to the floor.

The King was the animating force of the stage. Smaller than Mateo in height, he was corpulent, had sour yellowish skin, and a long black beard that ringed his reddish lips and grew to point at his chest. However, his rank and stature were trumpeted loudly in the gold, gems, and other royal accouterments that bedecked his person. He was cloaked in floor-length vermilion robes trimmed with a jaguar skin attached to the back—its paws forming lapels. His gold crown had arches and spire-like peaks that were encrusted with dozens of precious gems: rubies, emeralds, sapphires that glinted and seemed to revolve around the audience's faces when he paced the stage. Skylights were specially staged in the rafters to assist in this show of divine radiance. He wore several large gold rings that showcased large jewels.

In his right hand, he held the Royal Scepter, the Arm to the Throne, called the 'piece of resistance.' It was covered in gold engraved with cryptic code and its hood shaped in an arching cobra head. The cobra's mouth was open but dark. Each day, they placed a specially bred fluorescent green viper into the scepter's hollow cavity. Its head was rested and ready to emerge from the golden roof of the cobra's metal mouth. The King had only to point the scepter directly at one condemned to death and pull the trigger that was carefully rigged within to open the cover to the mouth in an instant. The fast-striking vipers seemed to cause as much impact on his subjects as beheading, hanging, and other forms of execution. And this is one that he could do to perfection. He was the ultimate executor and could kill with one flourishing gesture. Just a press of his fingertips, and all could watch the most potent man drop immediately in agony. More pit vipers could be brought in to work their way through the body. They would dig in their fangs, mulching into the flesh until they chewed down to the bone. The crowds also appreciated the lesson in that.

From the peak of his crown to the tips of his leopard-skinned shoes, the King mesmerized Mergon society from peasant to the Grand Vizier. The Queen by his side, who could be as young as Laela, was chosen for her beauty. She had perfect creamy skin, doe eyes, and luxurious long hair braided to the side. However, she looked lost and vacant under her heavy crown.

Laela, stationed on her round perch, was unaware that she was standing at the center of the pedestal over the viper pit. She made an awkward bow and curtsy directed toward the throne. Murmurs, laughter, and finger-pointing rippled through the crowd. She imagined that her bewildered attempt toward protocol had been less than effective.

An assistant to the King announced that the next case to be brought before his lordship concerned the Treedle Intruder, who calls herself Laela.

The King was now beaming his menacing black eyes her way. She drew a breath, and as she exhaled, she asked for courage. Courage to face the black jaguar and protection to escape alive.

"So, Treedle, what has caused you to trespass on Mergon land?"

Laela had prepared for this question and answered, "Your Majesty, there has been a misunderstanding. I never meant to trespass on your beautiful land. I thought only about visiting it briefly."

"You are the first Treedle girl in history who has thought to visit Mergonland. Briefly?" The King arched his black-winged eyebrows into a puzzled v-form. A few nervous titters erupted.

"Yes, I'm probably the first girl to do this because I always liked to play in the forest and was adventurous. As I grew older, I was curious and wanted to go farther into the woods, to explore. When I left my home, I didn't plan to go so far. It just happened. When I arrived in Mergonland, I wanted only to see it. Again, I was curious but meant to return home quickly so my family wouldn't worry about me. I certainly didn't want to cause trouble to anyone in your Kingdom or my parents.

"From what little I have seen, you have such a beautiful Kingdom. Again, I meant no harm to anyone, and I will return to my home right away and not cause any more trouble to you or your family. These guards can escort me and see that I disappear back to where I belong."

Now, the crowd shifted uncomfortably, trying to adjust their perceptions of this Treedle who spoke eloquently, with the inflections of a highly educated person, and who could muster a reasonable argument in front of a great crowd. Treedles brought there always murmured, groveled, and emitted more sounds than words as they knew they would likely not leave the Hall alive. None had ever spoken in reasoned self-defense or impassioned self-righteousness at the injustice of their plight.

The King's neck vein pulsed as he listened to Laela's direct and confident appeal. Was the child stupidly fearless, or did shen't know the station of whom she addressed.

"Listen carefully, impudent, bird-brained Treedle girl. Who do you think you are talking to? You don't tell me what I 'can' do.

I am the supreme authority of Mergonland, the Master of the known Universe. I rule over all you can see far and wide. When my people worship, they worship me.

"Your curiosity is called spying. Your adventure into our territory is called illegal entry. You trespassed into the King's private fields. There's a penalty for this in our land."

The King paused to puff up, lifting his chin and chest to a 'preposterously' commanding presence, addressing his 'subjects' on lessons he expected them to pass on for generations. "We're a land of law, order, and progress. We aren't a place for a spy disguised in the form of a silly girl."

"Please forgive me; I truly didn't know I was breaking the law to visit here," Laela replied. "I respect your law, and now that I know, I wouldn't break this law by visiting again."

"Visit? Again? You can be sure that there will be no second visit," the King said scornfully. "Not from you or the ones who sent you here. So, who did orchestrate your arrival here?" The King tapped his chin and mused. "Humm? Now, who would that be? Your people are so cowardly that they will allow a girl to come in a man's place to scout our Kingdom. You were sent to bring back information to your people."

"No one sent me. I swear before the 'One.' I wasn't supposed to leave Aerizon. I had no plan." Laela felt it necessary to repeat her plea, "I am the only girl I know of who likes to explore the woods. One day I went too far. I just kept going and arrived at your lands. Then, I was curious to see Mergons and Mergonland—just for a short time. I descended to see your land and planned to return quickly."

"Curious? Or used as a decoy? How can a dim-witted girl travel so far on her own and then suddenly come down out of the forest near where the Prince lives?

"Your people are after something. And what do your pigeon-brained people want now? Are they envious of our gold, our well-built homes, our jewels, our beautiful women, our weapons? Do you think you will ever advance? Never! You are fit only to be slaves, our slaves, and always shall be." The Kings' eyes glittered with excitement.

Mateo couldn't contain himself. Mateo pulled against the restraining arms of the guards flanking him, "Your Majesty, a word please, I beg of you. This is my fault. I should have oriented this innocent girl to return immediately to where she came from. This is all my responsibility."

The King turned coldly to his son, "Prince Mateo, you are out of order. If you interrupt this trial again, I'll immediately dispose of this Treedle. I will presume that she has bewitched you. We can't have that. We can't allow such a creature to cause disorder in our Court or our lives. You will be called to account for your actions after we have judged the Treedle. Shame on you, Prince, shame on you."

The King turned to Laela, "Show the Treedle the instrument of justice that will be applied to her if she doesn't speak the truth to the King."

Around the circumference of the platform on which Laela stood, the floorboards cut into eight sectors of burnished wood opened like hatches simultaneously. Glass encasements in the form of an octagon were windows to an underground pit beneath the floor. The pit was filled with brilliant green and orange-yellow viper snakes. She glimpsed snakes digging into the headless Treedle's body. There were latches on the glass to open a space large enough to push the condemned one and then close it again so that all could watch the vipers crunching and feasting on the corpse below. The best hope was that death would come quickly after the first bite of venom, so the victim's suffering might not be prolonged.

Most Treedle's greatest fear was of vipers and cobras. They could strike quicker than a Treedle could move and then eat them, allowing no proper burial. In the presence of one, Laela would freeze in panic while uncontrollable nausea coursed in waves through her body. This was happening now. But an inner voice like a moonline anchoring her to a tree warned Laela not to let this fear overwhelm her. If ever there were a time she needed to think, defend her people, and alert the Mergons that a different way existed, it was now. In a flash, she knew she mustn't 'see' the snakes. That was her only recourse. She prayed with the entirety of her being, one supplication, one word. ONE. She willed herself to be one with the 'One.' She didn't stop to ask, doubt, or wonder if He would be there. She was utterly powerless but empowered now.

"King, with all due respect, the Treedle people live in peace. We worship the 'One.' He guides us and illuminates our lives. Everyone in Aurizon has plenty to eat. There are no slaves. All of us learn to read, write, weave, and grow and hunt foods. We're educated equally, and all are treated with respect. Men and women are partners who work side by side, in harmony together like the wings of a bird that makes it fly. We are all a family. We don't need or want what you have. We'll never try to take anything from another person or tribe. That is stealing. We're a good and happy people!" Laela saw numerous eyes widen with shocked awe. No one had ever witnessed such a speech from a Treedle, let alone a female of any race. The chords of many hearts were being touched and vibrating, even against the wall of their hatred.

The King raised his scepter. His rage had mounted to a new height with it. His face was turning purple-red, and his eyes looked like they were painfully squeezed, "You are an abomination—the devil's spawn. And you're a liar! Your birdhouse kingdom is a joke. What's up there? The sky. Nuts on trees? Every Treedle secretly envies our wealth and way of life. Treedles don't have anything. And now they send a woman to speak for them.

"Treedles equal to Mergons? Is the day equal to the night? Is a twig equal to a tree? Treedles aren't evolved. And you yapp more than parrots with nothing to say!" He looked for approval, and though men applauded enthusiastically, many women's smiles were forced lines. But they nodded their heads submissively. The King heard all silence and all cheers as conformity to his views and will. No one in the room, except for Mateo, would question him. They must note that he was arguing quite a lot with someone he considered worthless—not even a person.

The King looked over at Mateo, who was hanging his head and recoiling like a wounded animal. It further infuriated the King to see his flesh and blood commiserating with a Treedle trying to mock and outsmart him in front of his people.

"Enough!" he bellowed. "I want answers. I must protect our people from the plots of all outsiders. We all know that the Mergons have built the best and the only real civilization on Araneae. Outsiders and non-Mergons may only visit by invitation or special permission. I smell a plot from your people. We know that a Mergon girl couldn't venture out like you did without a male protector and survive. We don't believe you came alone. Confess now about who sent and accompanied you."

The King's voice was overwrought with rage, and his face looked like a bag instrument ready to emit a full wail if touched.

Laela had considered mentioning she hadn't come alone but discarded the idea of bringing up a talking marsupial who helped her navigate the forest. That would be almost incomprehensible to the Court and add to the theory that she might be a witch.

She responded, "Your Majesty, I can only tell you the truth. I came alone. I disobeyed my parents by leaving the limits of Aerizon, and they will surely punish me when I return. But I came alone."

The King now became redder than the tater fruit, pounded his fist on the throne, and as he screeched, "It's impossible. You can't have come alone; you can't fool me. I want an answer to my question. I give you one last chance to confess, or you will be no more!" He barely finished his words, and his face turned an acrid yellow. It appeared as if he were choking on his abundant spittle. He sputtered, then he held his hand to his heart and collapsed.

All action froze; time seemed to disappear like the King's breath for a few moments. She could see Mateo struggling to push the guards away to get to the King. He yelled out in the firm, clear voice she loved to the crowd, "I can save the King. Allow me. I must act now! Guards, bring me the medical bag you took from me." The guards, confused about who was in control and seeing their King inert on the floor, released Mateo. All were familiar with the bag as Mateo often brought it with him to Court. Even this day, several family members asked him to give them medications and treatments after the trial.

He ran over and positioned the King face up, tilting his head back slightly. Servants brought a small pillow to ease his head. Mateo tested the King's throat with his fingers and began to administer a series of compressions to his chest. Some in the audience were shouting out not to hurt the King. They wondered how it could help him to press so hard on his chest when the pain came from there. Mateo yelled, "Faster with my medical bag. He needs a remedy right away." The guards appeared shortly with it, and he opened it, searching for a particular vial. He held up the small brown glass flask as if to measure how much to pour in the King's mouth. He carefully poured in the liquid to not choke the King. Shortly afterward, the King emitted his first moan and then stirred in movement. A collective gasp of relief circled the room.

Mateo held up his hand, "Stand back: he's still struggling to breathe. He needs air to circulate. I will continue to treat and revive him. In the presence of all in the Court, I ask His Majesty to graciously spare this Treedle's life." He said with conviction, "Father, if you hear me, just nod. I have saved your life. By the most sacred law of Mergonland, which states a life for a life or a death for a death, I ask you to pardon this girl in return. Let this Treedle go and return to her home." The King nodded ever so slightly, but enough so that those standing over him witnessed it.

Mateo continued to minister to his father, taking his pulse, massaging his legs, applying refreshing herb-scented cloths to his face. Mateo gave the order to empty the Hall. Only the most essential guards and those who directly cared for the King could remain. Gradually, the King's coloring returned to its everyday sallow shade.

Mateo gave orders to cover the King with a light blanket and let him rest around a half-hour more before trying to sit him up or move him back to his chambers. Mateo came to Laela, standing over the inner ring of flooring surrounded by fluorescent serpents under the glass cover. Laela had looked anywhere but down and was captivated as all were by the scene of the prostrate King.

Mateo ordered the guards to take her to a nearby seat and to bring her water. One guard stayed nearby, and Mateo told him to step back so he could converse briefly with the "Treedle."

"My darling," he whispered in a hoarse, emotionally drained voice, "The King almost died from this heart crisis. I saved his life with a tonic that my mother and I have perfected over the years. He owes me a life in return. Noone could ask that it be my own because, by law, I did not commit a crime warranting a death sentence. He promised me to spare your life. I could tell from what I saw that he was planning to execute you. Now, it is essential to get you out of here as quickly as possible.

"Davi and I are working on getting messages to you through the traders when they make trips to the trading villages. You must prepare the ones that you trust to bring us along with them to visit you. Soon. Macecle is outside. I gave him orders to follow you from a distance when you leave so they do not question why you are so attached to an animal. Let's make haste now."

Mateo turned to a guard, "Escort the Treedle out of the palace. Take her to the forest where she'll return to her family." Mateo was interrupted by the King, whose hearing was not minimally affected by his heart problem. He asked his servant to prop his head up and said loudly enough to be heard, "The Treedle stays. I granted her life but not her freedom. Her conduct has been grievous. We must see who or what is behind her entry into Mergon lands. She'll remain in the palace as a house slave to the women so we can watch her and wait to see who will come for her. My son is to be put under house arrest until further notice. He must also pay for his indiscretions. The story isn't finished, and we will have the whole truth in the end."

The few present were startled at the King's recovery, which was nothing short of miraculous. He was back to giving orders, and he had enough energy to project his voice.

Laela felt her world, her hopes, and the safety of her person shifting precipitously in the winds of fate, like the up and down movements of a child's boing-boing toy on a string. Mateo, by her side, gasped but didn't answer his father. He squinted his eyes as if willing himself to concentrate on something. Then, he whispered to her more urgently now, "This isn't a moment to argue with my father. I'll send a message to the Court about him keeping his promise. I'll find a way for Macecle and others to send you messages, the edible kind. If it's safe to do so, I'll send you with pen and parchment to answer me as well. Please be patient. I'll find a way to get you out of the palace. I promise."

The King was tired and now mumbling, but his courtiers heard his last instruction, "Put the Treedle in foot chains so she can't run and take her to the room in the women's wing as a house slave. Frida will be in charge of her." The King was drowsy. Mateo gave instructions on how to put him onto a stretcher to carry him to his chambers.

The King said to Mateo, "Your Treedle won't be executed because of how you served your King today. But her deed cannot go unpunished. My councilors believe we must watch to see if others come after her. We are on the alert for some kind of Treedle incursion.

"I have authorized that she be a household servant, where we'll watch her movements, and she can begin to pay for the trouble she has caused. She'll not be harmed."

A guard brought the heavy foot chains for Laela. As he locked them in place, Laela tried out how it would be to walk in them. The chains wouldn't only weigh a lot, they would chafe her skin, and she couldn't really walk well but would need to shuffle. She fought back tears as they would make her look even more pathetic. Fury and rage as powerful as Mergon steel and as deep as their pits and mines could go all but blinded her vision.

In the back and forth between his father and his loved one, Mateo came over and asked the guards for one last minute with Laela. He looked at her and the chains with such palpable grief; she could feel he meant it sincerely when he said, "Oh, that I could wear these and not you. Oh, my darling. Stay strong, please. I know you can. You'll be released. I'll be thinking of you day and night and how to make that day come soon. But don't try to go on your own now. You have seen how dangerous it is here."

Laela poured her heart out to Mateo: "This is a place of fear and danger. Your father's eyes are like glass covers to the empty pit of his soul. Oh no, not empty but also filled with vipers. He enjoys killing Treedles, even hope in his people. He wants people to worship him. He wants to be the 'One.' How can this man be your father?"

"Hush," Mateo looked at her severely, "You must never say words like this out loud again. You'll be killed immediately. Your words are true. That's why I am dedicating my life not to be like my father. But Laela, you mustn't these release feelings right now. They'll put you in danger. Please, darling, you must pretend to obey them and do as they say for you to stay alive. If you don't, they will hurt you badly. Tell me that you'll do this, for now. You need to be clever, and we need to use our best strategies to get you out. The 'One' will help us."

Guards now came to escort Mateo one way and Laela another. They led Laela down an inner corridor, a stone tunnel with torches for light, into the innermost center of Royal Family life.

CHAPTER 18

Enslaved

At the end of the tunnel were two doors. The guards opened the door to the left with a silver key. They dragged and jerked Laela into a large kitchen filled with several hearths and cooking areas. Clouds of fragrant steam wafted through the room with aromatic notes of herbs that Laela could now recognize, and that signaled intense hunger to her empty stomach. She saw a Treedle woman with a blue kerchief on her head, looking like a plumper version of Ana standing over a copper pot. She felt a momentary sense of relief. The woman glanced at her with discreet curiosity. The guards directed her out of the kitchen and through another door into an indoor courtyard.

All the comfort of the warm kitchen immediately evaporated as they entered the women's wing. She saw column upon column of white and gray marble in stoic procession down the corridor of the wing and endless polished floors. And as far as she could see, all the wooden doors to the heavy-walled chambers within were closed. To the other side of the hall was a central gathering place for the women. This social area was somewhat more inviting. The centerpiece of the room was a blue-tiled pool with multicolored stone ledges. It was surrounded by fluted pillars crowned at the top with scrolls and ornate leaves. Marble pots with palm trees and other plants created hints of charm and life but did little to soften the palace's echoing hardness. While some might see it as grandeur, Laela sensed the palace's inner chambers were about as welcoming as the Great Hall. The family, she later found out, was in a meeting room, following up on the crisis to the King's health. All was eerily quiet.

The guards led her down a narrow hallway to a room where Frida, the head of household services, met them. Frida had the nondescript but brutal look of a prison guard. She was one of the sour yellow versus honey-skinned Mergons. Mergon skin tones ranged from pale yellow to tannish and darker brown. Frida's forehead was compressed by the three deep lines formed by continual frowning. Her eyes were dull lightless brown, shaded by thick brows. She was of average build, but her hands looked thick and powerful like she could twist a chicken's neck with one snap, which she could indeed.

She surveyed Laela for a moment and then practically barked, "So, this is what all the fuss is about. I hear this girl almost killed our King. We shall see if she continues to make trouble under my guard." Frida's voice sounded rough and hardened from years of treating others harshly. She told the guards they could leave, but not before mentioning, "The King is too merciful. He should not have spared this one after what she put him through. Long live the King!"

The guards repeated in unison, "Long live the King!"

"Well, Treedle girl, you have made this a most unfortunate day. You look attractive enough, but what a little devil you must be on the inside—upsetting so many people like this! You will be a reminder of our King's unnecessary suffering. Know that you are most unwelcome here and that all will despise you in the Court. The King said to keep you alive. Now, I have the burden of making a plan to keep you out of sight as much as possible. It will be hard to protect you from the family's anger.

"Tomorrow, a guard will fetch you. You will work in the gardens and help care for the smaller animals. You will also have cleaning duties and will clear the bird cages. We will show you later how to do that. The King has graciously conceded to put you in a room that we used as a storage closet. Come with me."

It was difficult for Laela to keep up. Frida walked at a fast clip. They came to a bird sanctuary under an open skylight. It was an aviary garden with an array of the rarest birds in the Kingdom, flying flowers in brilliant reds, golds, blues, and greens. They moved within spacious cages, built like gilded metal palaces, surrounded by slender trees with delicate fluttering leaves. The floors were decorated with a swirling mosaic of dark and light stones, inviting one to walk in and among the cages.

Frida commented over her shoulder, "You will collect the droppings from the trays at the bottom of the cages for the herb room. We turn them into skin beauty products." And she smirked at Laela, "For those with golden, not purple skin." Laela tried to register a moment of gratitude that she would see flashes of color and life as she passed by there each day.

Beyond the sanctuary was a half wall, and behind it, some doors that Frida said were for storage rooms. She took her to a small room at the very end of the women's wing. Her room was located at the end of this dark and isolated hall. Frida opened the corner room door with a key and showed Laela into the room. As with all rooms elegant or humble in the palace, the internal walls were thick, and the outer walls even wider as a barrier against unwanted entry. Never mind, Mateo had told her that no Mergon or outsider had ever tried to break into or attack the palace up until now. The room was big enough to sleep in. There was a thin mat for her to use to cover the concrete floor so she would not show up to work smudged in dirt. Mergons loved cleanliness. There was a barred window high up, too high for her reach. Laela noted the branch of a large tree practically poking into the window. She imagined Macecle on that branch and withheld a smile.

Frida pointed out a chamber pot and a hole leading to a drain on the floor to empty water and bodily wastes. There was a bucket of water and a cup for her to drink and use for bathing, but only using a bit at a time as she could not flood the room. She noticed the door had a little window that opened from the outside. Others could peer in at her or pass her food should she be locked in her room for some reason.

"At dawn tomorrow, Tomas, the head of gardening, will send for you. You will be locked in promptly after dusk—when your duties are done. Always look down when spoken to and just nod your head and say yes sir or yes mam to show you understand. If you don't obey orders immediately and make haste in all tasks, you will be punished. You may not answer back or ask questions of me, but only the Treedles, Tomas, or Nena, the head of the kitchen. If any Mergon in the palace gives you an order, you must follow it immediately." Frida waited for Laela to answer by nodding her head. Laela looked up into Frida's lightless eyes with a dazed expression. She wanted to ask for food and realized she shouldn't ask for things.

Frida's face was reddening, "What did I tell you, stupid girl. Take your eyes off of me." Frida slapped Laela so hard in the face that she fell to the ground. Frida asked her again, "Do you understand?" Laela bowed her head and nodded. Then Frida left, locking the door with no further explanations or instructions.

Laela paced the room, her cell, and tried to begin praying. She wasn't able to concentrate. She tried to calm herself, drinking two cups of water. She kept reliving the trial, trying to understand how the King could be so outraged when she had done no actual harm to him or his Kingdom. The pain of hearing such grievous insults to Treedles, the slap on her face, grew worse the more she thought about them. She realized the threats were real and present. The jaguar was stalking and swiping at her: it was ready to pounce and snap her jugular at any moment. The hateful words repeating in her head warned her of the growling intentions of the predators around her.

She tried to focus on practicalities and search the room for possibilities of escape and hiding things such as moonline that would help her scale walls and trees. Such a thought was relieving and stirred up an ember of hope. She noticed there was a rectangular outline near the corner of the wall by the door. If the door were opened, no one could see it. It might be a cover for a niche or shelves inside the wall. Indeed, it was. It had been created to hide a cache of gold if need be. She carefully pulled out the piece of wall fitted to slip in and out fairly easily. Inside was a cavity and a shelf on top of the empty area, perhaps intended for lighter items. When the Mergon guards would open the door to take her out each day, they would close it outside and not be aware of this hidden space. She could use it for storage should she have something to store. A small comfort.

She waited for footsteps and someone to bring her something to eat. But no one came with food in the afternoon or evening. Hours passed. Laela had never felt so hungry in her life. It was more than hunger—it was abject fear. It was a screaming ache for comforting arms, to feel Macecle's fur, to look at Mateo's honey eyes, which it seemed she hadn't seen in days rather than hours ago. If Macecle and Mateo were out of reach, she couldn't imagine her parents and friends at all. Her memories seemed to be locked out of this room. The room did what the pit only pretended to do: it created a solid void of non-humanity. It isolated her from all connections to others, to the hour of the day, to interactions with nature. She couldn't even listen to the banter of the guards or the everyday sounds of other prisoners. The room was pitiless and bare. She was worried she would get lost in its unyielding silence.

As night fell, Laela looked at the shadow of Cor frosting the thick leaves of the tree outside her window in tinges of blue. She felt the forest beyond moan achingly as if in sympathy with her.

If she could have any wish in the world now, it would be to be safe. Safety was something she loved to risk in Aerizon because it was so abundant. She could take it for granted at home, in school, and almost everywhere in her community. Treedles learned to weave safety habits into everything they do and to protect one another as a second reflex. Just as someone would greet another in passing, so would someone quickly catch and save another, quickly care for them if hurt. Safety and protection were such givens in her life. She would never think to be grateful or happy for the network of security cradling her life. What she would do to cuddle in her soft, fragrant comforter at night or smell the porridge cooking in the morning, or visit Phips or Oti without a care.

As the night deepened into impenetrable ink, darkness began to fold away time and place, and memories of Aerizon started to return.

Of all people, Laela thought of her grandparents and a sweet prayer that Emau, her long-gone maternal grandmother, had taught her as a young child. Ah, the darkness could be soothing.

She had lost all four grandparents before she was seven. Her fathers' parents—Lola and Enu—fell prey to a raptor. Enu loved to go to the edge of town where nature's call was more open, and he could reflect on its immensity and the beauty of sacred Writings, undistracted by people and daily business. Sometimes Lola accompanied him, and they sat close together studying, praying, and meditating. One day they were absorbed in their devotions, and a dear friend saw an enormous purple raptor dive in from a distance and capture them entwined together in its talons. Before the friend could act to call out or save them, the raptor flew off with them. No traces of them were ever found. Laela liked to think that the raptor hastened their flight into the real heaven. She was one when they were gone and had only the vaguest memory of their sweet lavender faces. Some years later, when she was seven, her maternal grandparents, Emau and Edvin, succumbed to a lung illness. There were two main seasons in Aerizon—wet and dry. The dry season was extremely parched that year, and diseases spread by breathing. Coughing took many of the elderly. Lola and Edvin died the same day despite her mother's shamans' best efforts to cure them of the malady.

She remembered when Emau held her in her arms and told her to keep her inner thoughts pure so the 'One' could work through her. Emau would ask her to recite this prayer: 'Oh 'One,' I am small, my heart is pure. No one can live in it but You alone.' Laela whispered this to herself over and over until tired. Undeterred by the hard floor, she finally fell asleep.

Frida unlocked the door at dawn, looking Laela up and down with disgust, and then bid her follow behind. Frida commented that they were heading to the kitchen, where she would introduce her to Tomas. Most of the palace was still asleep, but some were now arising to get dressed, and there were murmuring sounds behind closed doors.

Tomas, a wiry man, probably around thirty years old, was dressed in black and directed his gaze down as Frida told him what was expected of Laela. She admonished Tomas, "We do not have Mergon guards to spare to watch this rebel raiser, but you and your entire family will pay if she causes any trouble in the palace or tries to escape. The girl is to be quiet, do her duties as told, and you may beat her if she doesn't comply. Or let me know. She can do garden work, help cleaning out of sight of the Royal Family, and she should be taught to gather the bird droppings."

When Frida left the kitchen, Laela noticed other Treedles appearing as if out of the shadows. All seemed to breathe a sigh of relief when she stomped out of the room. Tomas lifted his head, and she noticed that he had twinkly eyes with uptilted petal eyelids that made him look happy and good-humored. Later he told her that he rarely let a Mergon see his face, as it was better not to engage but to appear as close to invisible as possible.

Tomas and the primary cook she had seen yesterday led her outside the kitchen to the food gardens stretching out like a small farm, with orchids, a whole plot just for herbs and vegetables, and a nursery for plants and trees. They directed her to a shelter with a ceramic-tiled roof, where gardeners could sit in the shade and sort fruits and vegetables. There was a little tower of baskets, and they showed her a makeshift bathing place with two stalls with wooden walls and stone floors next to it. Inside were barrels with rainwater, cups to bathe, and soaps in a metal basket hanging on the wall. Those working outside needed to come in clean and not leave any trails of telltale dirt.

After this brief tour, Tomas introduced Nena, the head cook, "Laela, this is Nena, the head cook but also our leader here. She keeps our spirits up and gives us the best advice."

Nena took Laela's two hands gently within her strong, weathered ones, her eyes shining with both tenderness and the light of keen intelligence, "On behalf of the Treedle slaves in the King's household, we welcome you. Your bravery and your defense of the Treedle people have brought us the most hope in our lifetimes. Never could we imagine a young and such a beautiful Treedle girl speaking out in front of the Royal Family and the nobles of the land. You are the talk of the Kingdom, and you are the pride of every Treedle slave.

"You must be from the most blessed lineage. We believe you have a mission here, or the 'One' wouldn't have let you get so far. We'll all be doing everything in our power to protect you. But now, please, dear Laela, listen carefully to our counsel so that all will go well until you are released.

"The Royal Family mustn't know how much we care for you, or it will be worse for you—and us too. Don't show any affection or familiarity to us in front of a Mergon. You have to keep your head down, and no matter what a Mergon does to you—taunt, strike or hurt you in any way—you must stay silent. If you answer back or try to defend yourself, they will become more violent and accuse you of disobedience and disrespect. You must even obey the children if they call on you. The members of this household must always feel that they're right. It's dangerous to speak the truth out loud. It could cost you your life."

She saw the horror on Laela's face. "Yes, our dear Treedle Princess, it is true." She pulled out two wheat buns and put them in Laela's hands. They were still warm and smelled of sweet jelly and nuts. "Eat these quickly, lest Ms. Frida returns to check on you." Laela noshed into one with the full force of hunger and ravished the bun. Laela, cleaning nut paste on her lips, apologized, "Excuse my manners. It's been a while since I have eaten. Thank you for such delicious food."

Nena nodded, smiling, "These are a favorite of the Royal Family, and I have found a way to ensure that our Treedles in the kitchen and gardens may try them upon occasion. Tomas and I will show you all that you can eat in the garden while you work. They allow us only subsistence meals as they think being a bit hungry keeps slaves in control. But you have the best job and the safest, so please, my dear, do as you are told to keep it."

It was hard to get around the garden in the chains, but Laela was an eager learner. Tomas started her on weeding with a spade and basket. He showed her two weeds, one with bright tufted yellow flowers, excellent for a Treedle's diet.

"Lucky for us in the gardens, the Mergons aren't aware of all the parts of plants that are good for eating and medicines. Prince Mateo often visits to learn from elder Treedles about herbs' healing uses and how to plant them. We can all stay healthy by eating from the garden and catching the occasional tree animals we roast."

As Laela finished the last of weeding in one plot, she heard a loud swarming sound. A raucous group of Mergon children was approaching her. They were led by some loud, chubby Mergon boys screaming, "There she is!" They encircled her and began commenting upon her like they had sited a rat. The tallest one, their apparent leader, looked like a definite, round-cheeked, sour-faced descendant of King Malcolm. He swiped strands of black hair from his eyes, "We found her. Look at the Treedle devil girl. Working in the dirt where she belongs."

Other kids pressed up close, jockeying with each other to be close to the scene of action. Whoever had the most proximity to her now would have some kind of advantage. Laela gripped her fingernails into her hands to fight off the shock of being helpless prey to a group of children. Given the rules she just received, she couldn't think of a strategy to escape: she shouldn't talk or show her face, and she must defer even to children. Her mind went blank.

"So you think you are important? You think you can tell Mergons something? You wanna tell us something?" This came from the second tallest child, taunting her and looking at her with squinty-eyed contempt. "Go ahead, Treedle. Tell us something. What do you think of us? Of Mergons?"

Laela looked down and tried to adopt a humble posture, curving her shoulders in.

"Tell us why you think you can be friends with a Prince? A lizard and a Prince?" They all yelped with derision and laughter. One of the kids was trying to lift her skirts with a stick. But the second tallest one sidled up to her, "Answer me, idiot Treedle!" Laela was silent.

A quick upward glance showed her that the two biggest boys were rearing up to push her down, "Then eat dirt lizard," he yelled as he and others pushed her to the ground. Laela stumbled over her chains and barely braced her fall but, behind her, other children shoved her harder, and her head hit a rock. She lost consciousness briefly and came to with the smell of urine mixed with blood flowing over her lips.

The boys were chanting, "Give her a golden shower. Filthy lizard. Eat dirt and drink pee!" They were roaring with laughter and jostling to finish off their work.

Nena appeared and firmly asked the boys to move on. She couldn't exactly scold them, but she looked as stern as her slightly enhanced slave position allowed her to be. "This is no way to treat anyone. You don't make something right this way." A few of the more calm-tempered ones looked down.

Laela felt the egg forming on the side of her forehead, but the throbbing pain was nothing in comparison to the shame and degradation she felt. How could she survive here, let alone keep her dignity? She sat dazed and confused until Nena and Tomas gathered her up.

"Nothing that a shower can't wash off. Shame on them, not on you," Nena said, looking after the group swarmed back in the palace as quickly as they had come out. "Be patient. After a while, you will no longer be of interest to them." Nena led her to the shower and told her to put all of her clothing over the wall, bathe herself, and she would fetch a change of clothing. The cool water and soap did help. Nena provided her with a simple gray dress much like the one she arrived in. It smelled clean, fit, and was comfortably soft. Probably from frequent washings.

Laela welcomed the end of the day and saved some tasty weeds and small fruits in her pockets to eat when she was closed into her room. Tomas was entrusted to lock her in, and he brought an extra straw mat, a cotton cover, and a pillow for her. He assumed they would not be checking her room. He just told her to fold these things up and set them behind the door at dawn.

The cell was still as lonely as the night before, but she saw that the walls that kept her in kept others out. There should be no surprise attacks at night. Laela's ankles ached, and the skin was inflamed. She would find herbs for that tomorrow.

Laela had had a notion of slavery in her head, but until she wore chains for just one day, got beat upon, and saw the mirror of hatred and disgust staring back in everyone's eyes, she didn't know what it meant. If she survived, and she must, how would she ever describe this to her family and friends? In one day, she was learning to hang her head, not look up, cast her eyes on the ground, and not meet the eyes of another who would stab her with hatred, shuffle, not walk, be silent, and act submissively in every possible way. She had to act like animals who play dead to a predator to save their lives. She had to learn this well and quickly. She had to die to herself around Mergons to save herself. Living in this well of hatred and rejection was the venture she felt least prepared to handle. She looked up at the window for its brush of light, its reminder of infinite skies. She knew where the only answers, the only hope lies.

CHAPTER 19

Growing Resilient

A month passed, and a certain routine defined her life. Laela worked harder physically than she had ever thought possible. Between the energy of completing demanding tasks to avoid punishment or burdening other Treedles to pick up her work and the drain of avoiding Mergon gazes, she was whittling herself down into a waning moon. She didn't dare to contemplate how the impassioned girl had turned so quickly into a subdued and compliant slave. Laela narrowed her sights to the task at hand: delving into the present moment of uprooting a tuber for lunch or planting another was the only thread of light leading her through the moments of the day. Everything else was lost in a dense fog with feelings, memories, and even days of the week blurred together shrouded in murky gray clouds.

Tending the royal birds was one of Laela's most pleasurable duties, causing actual moments of delight. Three days a week, she would feed them and clean their cages. Orfi, a very silent Treedle slave, except for when training the birds, was in charge of caring for the regal rainbow birds, which Treedles called caw-caws. These were the largest and loudest birds in the Mergon Kingdom. Tree raptors were larger in Aerizon, but caw-caws were attention grabbers.

The rainbow birds had bodies of scarlet red, cerulean blue, and bright yellow. From their arched beak to the tips of their trailing tails, they were larger than any Treedle. When they spread their wings, they opened a feathered rainbow in all the primary colors. They were housed in the most elegant of the avian palaces and perched on white branches gilded with gold. Their wings were clipped, so they couldn't go far if they escaped the cages. Orfi fed them favorite treats to train them to shout familiar Mergon greetings and words. Orfi wore a broad leather hat, wristband, and shoulder pad. He would regularly take the birds to and fro to entertain courtiers, children, and the Royal Family. They were also brought to add charm to garden areas for tea times. They always began their repertoire, "May it be well with you," considered the more educated Mergon greeting.

Prince Marl had also insisted that Orli teach the birds to say shut up when the children were too noisy. Impolite bird chatter never ceased to get the young children's attention or make others giggle.

Laela brought a pail of seeds and one with water and rag-cloths to shine the granite ledge surrounding the birdcages when she was done. She placed two metal jars she was carrying in her pockets on the floor. When she was done distributing the seeds to the many feeder trays, her next task was to find and collect their droppings into the little metal jars. She would take these prized ingredients to the King's apothecary to be made into facial creams. She chuckled to herself to think of the vain ladies of the Court covering their faces in tweety poo. However, there were so many uses for all types of natural elements, even excrement.

She heard the padding of plump baby feet and saw Princess Merli's three-year-old son approaching her. She had watched Timi with his mother from afar. He reminded her of Lucas.

Princess Merli and her cousin Princess Ellie were inseparable, spending most of their days tending their children together. Ellie with her two-year-old son Azer and Merli with Timi. They had not approached Laela, nor she them. They seemed happily absorbed in the world they had created. They could be Oti and her. Another reason for their intense and exclusive bond became evident over time: both women were trying to escape news and gossip about their husbands. Ellie had everything to fear about Prince Marl, and Merli was often disappointed with Prince Roy. They were creating a haven with each other.

Laela had admired the ethereal beauty that radiated from both of them. Ellie was petite and had long thick, light brown hair that the sun highlighted with golden threads. Her skin was an even creamy tan, like milk mixed well into dark tea. Her warm cocoa-colored eyes seemed curious and expectant. Though whenever Prince Marl, her husband, entered the room, she looked downcast and unnaturally still. Merli had blonde curly hair that begged to be touched and played with and an infectious laugh. She was a naturally easy-going young woman, always looking for the positive in others. Laela noticed how much Merli instigated walks into the palace's wooded areas or took the children into the garden to play with tamed animals they kept as pets. She could see Danie's family line, the life spirit shared by her two sisters in the women. Mateo must love his aunts and these cousins dearly.

Laela had been relieved of any potential services to Merli, Ellie, and other women as she did not meet the Mergon standards of grace and excellence, especially when serving tea or hot chocolate. On her third day at the Palace, three of King Malcolm's sisters called her to accompany the servants bringing the afternoon tea. They shared a common lounging area connected to their chambers and thought to liven up their daily teatime with a look at the Treedle girl who rocked the Kingdom. They were curious about all the clamor surrounding the audacious girl who had stricken the King with her outlandish assertions. Thus, Laela was sent to assist a Mergon food service attendant. Laela trailed behind the Mergon servant carrying a vase of freshly cut flowers to set on the tea table.

The three sisters were sitting around the hearth. They looked like a trio of pale-yellow hags hunched over their knitting. The finery of their clothing was incongruent with their congested and disgruntled faces, which were topped by shiny black buns, curled in the fashion of the day. They had an air of Frida about them. Other Treedle servants said that the sisters complained the day away, competing to find fault in the maid services above all. The servants never relieved their ailments or satisfied their endless needs. The aunties suffered from the inclement weather—always too hot, too cold, too dry, or too humid. The food was always too salty or not salty enough, and the service too slow or too hasty and sloppy. They savored the wrongdoings of the women in the household. Only one spinster cousin met their high standards of virtue. They never ceased to criticize Princesses Ellie and Merli for the way they raised their boys. "The poor Princes will never grow into real men, molly-coddled, breast-feeding like wet nurses—why that Ellie is still nursing Aser. He's a boy, not a baby. And the two of them reading so many books and talking about so many ideas. No wonder their husbands can't bear to spend time with them."

Three pairs of avid eyes watched Laela's every move as she came in their room. They began commenting immediately about her as if she weren't there, "Bug-eyed creature, not much to her, how can such a wee thing cause such a stir!"

Laela set the flowers down gently enough on the tea table, but as she attempted to back away, bowing self-effacingly toward them, she stumbled on her chains. She ignominiously tripped over a small stand with their favorite piece of china. It shattered and pieces scattered all across the floor. One of the more energetic sisters began to curse her and slap her soundly, screeching, "Clumsy idiot. Stinking tree rat. Good for nothing. May you be sent to the vipers!" The sister wasn't able to strike hard physically but insults about Treedles always pained

Laela. The Mergon servant girl, who seemed sympathetic to her, grabbed Laela and pushed her out the door, telling her to disappear quickly. She added, "I will fetch a broom and try to calm down the sisters, though the 'One' knows that is close to impossible. Away with you, it was hard for you to balance yourself in chains, let alone handle a vase with care."

The sisters would lament the loss of the china vase down to the tiniest blue and white fragment. But Laela's clumsiness temporarily enhanced the stature of Mergon servants. Frida thrashed her, and for once, she felt the punishment wasn't so far off from the crime. Frida locked her in her room for a day without food. However, Tomas and Neena found a way to drop food through the slot in her door with more than she could eat in two days. This incident marked the end of any possible plan that might require Laela to interact with the Royal Family members.

Princess Merli and Princess Ellie had the fortune, or misfortune in Laela's opinion, to be married into the former Queen's family. Merli's husband, Roy, was Marl's cousin, his maternal aunt's son. Roy and Marl were cut from the same cloth though Marl was tougher and crueler than his cousin. When they weren't competing at fencing, they were one-upping each other with stories about their voluptuous Mergon mistresses. It was beneath them to put a Treedle woman in the mistress category, though occasionally they accosted young Treedle female servants.

Laela gradually put names, faces, and family connections together as she watched the Royal Family come and go from the dining and social halls and trays of food and drink delivered to their chambers throughout the day. Treedle servants prepared the foods and trays, Mergons delivered them. The Mergon servants also attended the large pools below where men and women could bathe separately, which Laela never saw.

Sometimes Laela worked until well after dusk and witnessed the nighttime visits of the husbands and wives to each others' chambers. Occasionally, the men summoned their wives to their chambers, but they often preferred to go to their wives' rooms. It took her a while to realize why. There was another corridor adjacent to the men's where the Court entertainers and suppliers of personal services were housed. She couldn't help but notice the courtesans and mistresses, dressed in sensual silks, with feathers and baubles and faces painted in almost ludicrous colors, as male servants escorted them to rooms in the men's quarters. Once, she even saw a woman painted in lavender with a grayish-lavender wig in a grotesque imitation of a Treedle. Given the number of 'painted' women, she began to wonder if any men were lifelong mates and faithful to their wives.

Though well-dressed, well-fed, and spared from hard labor, the women in the palace had about as much freedom as the servants. If she were mated to Mateo and bore him children, she would rather die than have him disrespect her in this way. If two people loved each other, faithfulness was as essential to their union as breathing is to life, why even most animal species mated for life and defended their families with their lives.

She felt deeply for the young and lovely princesses, who had only a slight notion of the full indignities their husbands were reaping on them. They didn't really have husbands. She saw no sign of the friendship, trust, and complicity she shared with Mateo. How on earth had he escaped the Mergon royal male mentality? He, Danie, Ivan, and Davi were so very different. She imagined that pastoral effects of the countryside far from the Court influenced their less worldly ways, but they had courageously chosen to live life on a higher plane than their 'noble' compatriots.

Neena and Tomas tried to shield Laela from palace gossip in the kitchen and at mealtimes. But even she heard the story about the time one of Prince Marl's mistresses challenged him about wanting and deserving land for her family in return for her services. She was from a humble but well-respected carpenter's family and was extraordinarily beautiful and clever. The Prince got drunk and became more and more enraged about her demands. She was one of the few strong-minded women he had that had spoken back to him, or in his eyes, fought and attacked him. It is rumored that she threatened him with the knowledge she had of him siphoning off some gold from the King. He tied her up, carried her through the palace screaming, and entered the Great Hall with a few trusted servants following. Then, he threw her into the viper pit in the Great Hall. He warned all future mistresses of what would happen if they made false accusations or unwarranted demands upon him. His mistress's family was well-respected and had many sympathizers. Her death wasn't forgotten. Her last screams for mercy reverberated in their hearts. Mergons savored revenge, and one day her family planned to get it. The mistress's family felt she had been forced into these duties and that fellow Mergons shouldn't be used as slaves but rather compensated in some way for their services.

Laela had also learned more about surviving in her role as a slave. She didn't want to be in the sights of any of the Princes, the most dangerous palace predators. She was thankful to the 'One' for her garden duties, where she could mingle with plants, earthworms, butterflies, and wild birds. Around Mergons, she had been practicing how to become a shadow, how to shut down. Every step she took, every person she spoke with, put her in danger in this castle prison. Silence was her best guard. The less she 'was,' the safer she was. She spent her days now learning to be quieter in her movements, diminishing her presence, and diverting attention from herself. It was quite an art, learning to camouflage her real self.

So, as an observer from afar, Laela hadn't talked to or interacted with any Royal Family member. Timi must also have had few personal interactions with Treedles. Nonetheless, he waddled right up to her and smiled an uneven smile. He had dimples in his peachy-round cheeks like her brother, Lucas, and an abundant crown of his mother's pale-gold hair. His eyes were round as large berries. Laela had to withhold herself from scooping his plump body into her arms and squeezing him into giggles. Timi stretched out a finger in front of her nose to show her something proudly. He was carrying a seed.

Laela didn' ask herself why the child wandered off or if he was lost and just dove into the moment of joy. "Why, Timi, how wonderful. Do you want to feed the birds?" Laela asked in the gentle tones she used for the very young, those who still inhabited a semi-conscious world where a Treedle was a person and a Mergon too.

Timi was eager to tell her, "Yes. I found a special seed. Can I give it to them?" Timi was very expressive for one so young, but he lisped endearingly.

"Yes, of course, you can," Laela replied, motioning to Orfi, "Orfi, lend us some sugar- syrup, please. It will help Timi here attract one of the hummingbirds. They love sweet tastes, and Timi, if you are patient, one of them will stop on your finger for the seed." Laela put some drops of sugar syrup on Timi's finger, and they positioned the seed. Timi let her guide his hand into the hummingbird's cage, and one of the iridescent turquoise ones hovered over his uplifted hand and dipped onto his fingertip. Timi shrieked with joy. He reached over to Laela and hugged her. Laela unconsciously hugged him back as if he were her baby brother. His belly was deliciously round, and she almost tickled him but stopped herself.

"What's your name?" He asked, and she responded, "Laela." He studied her face for a minute and proclaimed solemnly, "Laela, you're so beautiful. You have purple on your eyelids. I like your eyes." He leaned over to trace her eyelids with his sugary fingertip.

Laela closed her eyes and tried to memorize the gentle touch of his fingertips. Like the fragrance of a flower.

She wiped Timi's hand with a fresh cloth just as she started to realize that someone must be missing the child and that he was with the Kingdom's most unauthorized servant. She turned to see Merli beaming at them from a short distance away. She had stepped behind a pillar, not wanting to disturb a magical moment for her son. She always thought of ways to fill him with innocent joy to stave off the need for dark pastimes later.

Merli looked at Laela as if seeing her for the first time, intrigued and interested in her. Merli's gaze wasn't as innocent as Timi's, but nor was it judgmental or harsh.

"Why, Laela, how kind of you to entertain my son this way. I hid behind a pillar to watch where my son's curiosity would lead him. Then, I saw how he was drawn to you and the birds. You certainly have a way with the wee ones. Thank you. He'll surely talk my ear off about the seed and the birds feeding on his fingertip!"

Merli swept up Timi, who made bye-bye with his chubby hand. Laela lumped in her throat as they disappeared down the corridor. The sweetness of the moment made her especially sad.

That night Laela curled in a ball, trying to comfort herself. The contact with Timi opened the door to feeling, to wanting. She wanted Mateo: Mateo's honey eyes, his kind voice, his heart filled with inner paths of beauty to be explored. She wondered if and when they would ease up on Mateo's house arrest restrictions. She understood how careful Mateo must be, and this is why he hadn't sent even one message. They both had to draw attention away from themselves. Being patient, which was especially agonizing for her.

At some point, Mateo should be able to find a way to send Macecle to visit her—maybe even through her window at night or the end of the garden. She had tried hard not to think of either of them, let alone pine for them. Pining for Mateo, Macecle, and her loved ones in Aerizon caused close to unbearable pain. It was like tearing off the first growth of skin on an open wound. Laela had to distract and numb her mind. Working hard—concentrating on doing a task well helped maintain a slight shield from the pain.

She was praying in a new way to the 'One.' It wasn't so much to ask for specific things. Even with so little time and experience in chains, she found that wanting too much led to despair. She could no longer cling to wants as a child clings to toys. She was stripped daily of the most important ones. Over time, she found herself asking for inner peace and spiritual closeness that no Mergon could touch or take away from her. She asked if she could be an instrument of light where so many hearts were disheartened. There were even restrictions to giving, but she asked to give love, to plant a seed of hope in this elegant but monstrous pit—the palace.

Why ask for things that couldn't be given or be taken away? Her vivid desire to be with Mateo tonight and the painful longing it awakened were reminders to keep these feelings in storage, hidden for now.

The only thing that she willed for herself in prayer was an escape plan. Escape wasn'a 'want' but her only hope of survival. She instinctively knew it was becoming a choice of life and death to remain there. Mergons, in general, did not seem to forgive or forget. She would always be suspect to the powers that be. She was only alive by the King's grace—for however long that would last. And though Laela never saw the King, she saw his best reflection—Marl. Marl lived and breathed to avenge his and the Kingdom's honor. At some point, she would be to blame for something else. Not a broken china vase. But they didn't need to seek many more errors than enraging the King into almost dying from a heart attack. They would eventually condemn her. And, she had a responsibility to her loved ones to try to avoid a wretched demise.

Every day she thought about escape routes. The plan mustn't be improvised, especially with her lack of knowledge of the palace layout and surroundings. The most viable way she could envision would be to leave from a well-known access point—over the garden's back wall where she worked every day. She would need to find a way to scale the wall, which was quite high. When she asked Thomas what lay beyond the wall, he had told her there was a barrier of thick and rampant underbrush and then an open space leading to the edge of the forest on a nearby hill. Guards with conchos regularly patrolled the area.

Fortunately, there was one tree right next to the wall inside that Laela hadn't climbed because of her chains—and on the other side, two apparent relatives of the same tree stood close enough to the wall. She could use the inside tree for strategic positioning to reach the outside ones. However, she would need a moonline and hopefully Macecle's help on the other side to tie it to a branch. Then she could climb the wall using it for leverage and rappel down the other side. She would practice secretly, but of course, that would require the chains to come off. Getting rid of them would require a minor miracle of some kind. She would need to leave her room before anyone was awake on the chosen day for departure. That required the keys to her room. However, if she took the keys from Tomas to unlock her door, he might be tortured when she escaped. She might be able to give Frida a sleeping potion and take hers, but then events had to line up for her to have access to Frida the evening before the escape and a pretext for getting her to drink what was sent to her.

The details went on and on. Her plan would require Macecle to become familiar with the garden location and meet her at the rendezvous point at an appointed time. She couldn't dream of leaving without Tan and Gibble—they were like family. Right now, they were safe in Mateo's Garden. To be ready to face the many challenges of a rapid escape journey and the dangers of the forest beyond, she would also need her compass, a supply of moonline, and her backpack or some kind of apron to store small tools, her sling. How to smuggle Tan and Gibble and her backpack or its contents into the palace?

Her entry point into Mergonland had been so distant from the palace. Ideally, she should have more information about the terrain beyond the wall and skirt the thickest underbrush to arrive at the forest behind the palace. A key step would be contacting Mateo for more information about movements in the region and to let him know when and how she would try to escape.

Once out of the palace complex, there was no place to hide in Mergonland. If she went to Mateo's compound, it would put him into trouble for harboring a fugitive. He would want to elevate her from slave to betrothed. But now, it was clear as a bell that such a radical move would endanger both of their lives. It wasn't a reality that any but a handful of inspired Mergons could contemplate, let alone accept.

The sweetness of the hummingbird alighting on Timi's finger and the bright day heightened the contrast between her ultimate dreams and the current obstacle course toward survival. Tumbling through a cascade of worries, she sought a ledge or branch of hope in the recesses of her mind. An image appeared of a moonline, a silvery thread connecting from one tree to another over a large chasm. Faith was like this thin but powerful line leading across the dangers of the sky and the earth. Only the 'One' could give her the balance, grip— the capacity to brave through clinging to this filament of hope.

Before she slept, she asked the 'One' for assistance with the tests and dangers surrounding her. That night she dreamt that she was by a lake with lotuses: pure cups of floating beauty and expectant grace. A being veiled in a glimmering mist of white light stood beside her. She knew without seeing details of her face, but through the power of her presence that it was Denai, wife of Asmae. Denai repeated to Laela in a melodic and kindly voice, "Be patient, be patient, be patient." Laela bowing her head, answered, "Beloved Denai, you are a saint. I am a girl who struggles to live out teachings. How can I do this?" And Denai answered as if the light around her were a welcoming smile, yet again and more firmly, "Be patient!"

CHAPTER 20

Emerging from Chains

There was a pleasant breeze in the garden, and dappled light fell on her tunic from the trellis where she was picking blue-red pilo berries off of vines climbing up around it. She placed them in a basket, thanking the 'One' for the abundant harvest. She couldn't resist tasting them— surprisingly tangy-sweet and refreshing. She realized her lips must be as blue as her fingers were and that she needed to wash before entering the kitchen where others would see her. The most minor of privileges and pleasures caused gossip and jealousy among the Treedle slaves. It would spark ire in a household member should they perceive a Treedle as delighting herself, which meant she felt entitled to a privilege and wasn't working hard enough.

Among Treedle slaves, there were many degrees of hierarchy, and it was expected of all to pay due respect to them. Nena and Tomas were at the top of the Treedle slave pyramid for their expertise in cooking and gardening exotic plant foods, respectively. They worked in the household, and by filling bellies and finding or making treats for all, they were hugely popular among all but the most mean-hearted. The other Treedles in the household lived on the border of hunger, fed only once a day—foods that the Mergons found worthless, such as stems of plants and low-grade tubers. Treedles who cleaned bedrooms felt superior to those who cleaned bathrooms. Treedles who cleaned Mergon bathrooms in the palace outranked

Treedles who shoveled animal excrement in the barns. And these Treedles were thankful for the job, and the smell of the manure, which they quickly became accustomed to, as they weren't working in the open fields all day. Finally, the field workers praised the 'One' and the sun, Razi, that they weren't in the bowels of the mines where death came the quickest through beatings, caving tunnel walls, and exhaustion.

Laela felt a twinge of guilt about her selfishness, helping herself to a treat other Treedles couldn't enjoy. She thanked and apologized to the 'One' simultaneously as the berries were a zesty and luxurious, though short-lived adventure, in her mouth: a wee taste of hope and joy. She would never want to cause envy that sprung from other Treedle's nagging hunger or irrepressible desire to enjoy a bit of life's abundant pleasures. She hoped it didn't mean she felt a notch above other Treedles to allow herself some berries.

Lost in ruminations about berry-eating guilt, she was a bit startled when Timi ran up and grabbed her around her waist, followed by his mother Merli looking out of place in a swishing blue frock, her cheeks flushed deep pink from running to catch her son. Laela smiled warmly at Timi while trying to wipe her face quickly with the edge of the cloth covering the basket of berries. Any of these details: the berry stains, personal use of the covering cloth, and hugging Timi in the crook of her arm without thinking were out of the order.

Laela bowed her head, "Excuse me, Princess, for the berry stains and Timi. Just so happy to see him. Your Timi must be the most charming lad in the land, and he has captured my heart." Laela realized she had blurted out what she was thinking and was talking too much to a princess. Yet, she felt that no mother could rebuke someone for seeing the beauty in her child.

Merli also blushed and looked around uncomfortably. "Excuse my son; he shouldn't be interrupting you while you work. He ran away from me." She tried to pry Timi away from Laela, and he protested, "Mama, please let me play with Laela. I wanna play here in the garden and pick berries. I wanna see the birds again too. Laela and I can feed them—we can give them these berries."

Timi broke loose from his mother and spontaneously wrapped his arms around Laela's neck, tracing his fingertips once again over Laela's lavender eyelids. He looked pleadingly at his mother, "I want to play with Laela."

Merli looked perplexed, and Laela could see her trying to bite her lip not to smile and humor her son. Laela took another gamble and shyly asked, "Could Timi watch me for a few minutes. Could he pick some berries with me? I could hold him, so he doesn't stain his clothes and then wash his hands right away."

Merli's expression opened up, and she all but snorted with laughter, "I wish my biggest problem were him not getting dirty. We must change his clothes two or three times a day for all the ways he manages to get food and dirt on them. My problem is how curious he is. I turn my back, and he's climbing up a wall or crawling down into a hole." She grimaced, thinking about it, "People will talk for days if he gets scratched by bramble or cuts himself with something. I can't even bear to think of the trouble if he gets injured—breaks his arm falling from a tree. If I even turn to talk to a friend, he can run away from me, far from me, in seconds. He's running me needle-thin" (a Mergon saying, as a woman needed some curves to be comely) "with his adventures." Merli stopped and blushed harder as she realized how much she had just exposed herself before a Treedle slave.

Laela grinned inadvertently as she thought how much like attracts like in life. However, she dare not compare herself to the little Prince.

"Okay, Timi," his mother answered him, "You may play a few minutes here, but you must follow Laela's instructions, and you may not eat any berries until we wash them." Timi had already slithered out of Laela's arms, plucked a berry, and popped it into his mouth. His mother sighed with ragged weariness.

Timi was happily immersed in berry picking for quite a while, and Merli was able to rest on a bench under the tree for the very purpose of a Mergon visiting this garden. Laela showed him how to pick the berries, not to squeeze and squirt their juice away. When they were done, she brought a bowl of water and carefully washed his hands and mouth (he had cheated on the berry rule), drying them with a clean cloth.

Merli thanked Laela warmly. She looked like she wanted to say something more and held herself back. But Laela was sure that the berry-picking time had been satisfying to all three of them for different reasons.

After the evening meal, Nena had said in a loud voice for others to hear, "Tomas and Laela come in the storage room with me and help me move some boxes, please." Nena asked them to follow her and Laela wondered why they were standing in a room full of jams and jugs of ale as the sunset began tinting the sky in orange and purple outside the little window, casting an eerie light on the room which was collecting shadows now.

Nena spoke in nervous and urgent tones Laela had never heard from her before. "Laela, I was watching you today in the garden with Timi. I need to warn you. I feel this won't be the last time you have encounters with Princess Merli and Timi. She'll do anything to make him happy. He's the only real light in her life."

Laela nodded as she felt that Timi would be back in her arms very soon, and the thought filled her with cheer. It gave her something to look forward to, though it created new conflicts in her. Being present for moments with Timi made her as vulnerable as a recently hatched birdling- waiting for the warm wormy feedings of smiles and hugs. She was becoming practiced already at shrinking away from others and into a smaller and smaller safe place, revealed to no one. This, when not praying, was the closest semblance of safety she had.

Nena looked at her imploringly, "She may seek you out again, but you, our dear Treedle princess, must take care. Closeness to royals means danger to a Treedle. Merli's husband, Prince Roy, is a right hand to Prince Marl, and where Merli goes, so goes Princess Ellie. When you are close to one of them, the others are nearby watching and telling stories. Their husbands have spies who help them keep tight control over the women. I worry about your association with them.

"There's no one more cruel or dangerous than Prince Marl. Just yesterday, he had a Treedle servant tortured for spilling hot soup on him and burning his hand. The Treedle, Jon, came back with his hands so mangled and with so many bones broken that he took a knife from the kitchen and ended his own life. Our masters have ways to punish and torture slaves with beating and hanging, and ones that don't show physical effects—with water or putting Treedles in closed black boxes—but also of equal damage.

"Tomas and I have been spared from severe punishments as we have very little direct contact with the family, and they aren't aware of the mistakes or errors we make. I always cook extra dishes if a Royal Family member, especially a Prince, doesn't like the day's meal. Tomas and I work day and night for this privilege, this measure of safety for ourselves and our families.

"Laela, be careful what you say, what you reveal, and stay out of the sights of Prince Marl however you can. The more invisible, the less he hears your name, the better for you. And well, the better for us too as we are connected to you." Nena hung her head and said in a tone tinged with sadness, "If you're in their sights, we may be too, or they may find us guilty by association for anything you say or do. We have families. Please be mindful of what you tell them."

Laela's throat constricted, and she felt an internal shiver, a sudden understanding that her life and fortune were tied to theirs. There was no free 'joy' for a Treedle.

"Nena, thank you for telling me this. I'll ask the 'One' to protect us and speak as little as possible with the Princess. If she calls upon me, I'll find a way to play with Timi to help get out his boyish energy so his mother is relieved when she takes him back. I'll do anything to shield you and Tomas from harm."

Nena hugged her, almost crying with relief. She was starting to become attached to Laela. Laela spent the next day pondering the preciousness of silence and why it was such a shield of protection. She had never been aware of how much she loved to talk until now, how her excesses were like winds that blew away or even obliviated delicate things. She thought of the many hurts and exposures her wagging tongue had brought to herself and others. Being mindful of what she said wouldn't be easy, but it would be lifesaving.

Two days passed, and early on the morning of the third day, Frida, not Tomas, opened her door a little later than dawn, later than usual. She entered with a small storm of furious energy, jangling her key belt, and shoved Laela to the floor, saying, "Put your feet up, girl, so I can unlock your chains. Yes, your chains are coming off at the behest of Princess Merli. She needs help looking after Timi. His nursemaid has taken ill. She has asked for you to replace the maid, but heaven knows why she chose you."

Frida's eyes were black pinpoints shining fiercely," I am sure you have bewitched her in some way, you wicked girl. It is sheer nonsense placing you close to that child. But I will be watching after our beloved Princess. You do anything wrong, and I will ensure the most severe punishment for you, one you will never forget if you survive. I will tell Prince Marl and be sure it will happen even if the Princess comes to favor you.

Now, wash well and report to the social court in a half-hour, where Merli will be waiting with the Prince."

Laela responded meekly, "Thank you. I will act in a way fitting to honor service to the Princess and Prince."

"You couldn't do that even with your best efforts," Frida hissed back at her. "You are what you are and always will be; a worthless Treedle not fit to kiss the feet of these masters."

As soon as Frida left, Laela sat massaging her bruised ankles telling herself not to think of any unsightly or possibly permanent scarring. A door had opened, and for now, she let herself delight in the gift of being freed from chains. She could walk more easily; she could climb and pick fruits; she could feel like a regular person—at least for moments. The symbol of shame and degradation was off her body, even if never out of Mergon eyes.

When she arrived at the courtyard, Timi was waiting for her and ran, leaping into her arms. He gave her cheek a wet kiss and clung to her. She had to hold him a while until he got his fill of loving hugs and was wiggling to get moving again.

Princess Merli had been watching quietly and nodded her approval. She took Timi's hand and encouraged Laela to take the other, "Now, let's go somewhere where you can play, my darling. Laela will care for you. She's coming with us."

Merli led them to a section of the palace that she imagined was closer to the King's special wing. They entered a white-walled corridor illuminated by a series of tall, arched stained glass windows set at evenly placed intervals. They cast images of brilliant color on the flanking wall and white marble floors. She wished to lag behind to admire the geometric tracery, the intricate designs woven in glass pieces as brilliant as rubies, emeralds, and sapphires. One central panel was of King Malcolm in his finery and purple robes lined with jaguar skins. The King's pale, impassive face framed by a pointed black beard and capped with a shining gold crown evoked menacing royal grandeur.

At the end of the hallway, they arrived at an adjacent corridor to the left. Merli led them up a broad marble staircase leading to the women and children's quarters of family members closest to the King. Merli mentioned to her that the next stairway led to the towers for Prince Marl and Prince Roy, and the very last and greatest tower was for King Malcolm and Queen Mali. That tower was situated in the innermost heart of the royal compound.

Timi took her hand as they arrived at the second floor and piped up excitedly, "Now I will show you my room. We can play there too." He turned the brass knob on a blue wooden door with both his hands. As it swung open, fresh piney air tingled her nose, and they entered the room. Stately window doors opened to the balcony, and swathes of light beamed across the silvery, white wooden floors. The room seemed to open its arms and invite one to skip around it. An extensive collection of painted wooden toys took on a life of its own, recreating a realistic scenario of both rural and palace life. There was a blue and white cottage with flower boxes under the windows and a mock thatched roof. It was surrounded by a woven green carpet, representing a pasture occupied by a brown and white spotted rocking horse with a full bristling mane and tail and other country animals. On the other side, a painted backdrop of the castle was guarded by handsome wooden soldiers holding silver spears. Replicas of Merli, Ellie, and the two great Princes dressed in finery stood on bases. She admired the flaxen hair on the Merli doll, woven into a bun draped with beads. The personages, set on stands to keep them from tumbling over, were light enough that Timi could move them about to play-act with them. There was also an altar for Razi, and below it was shiny colored pebbles to represent wishes and petitions.

Timi ran over to his bed shaped like a castle with four turrets covered with thick brocaded quilts. A few smaller day beds upholstered in velvet flanked the surrounding walls. She assumed that a servant, and sometimes Merli herself, might spend the night with Timi. Timi patted the bed and motioned for her to sit with him. He gently nudged her to lie back among the pillows, and then he sat on top of her playing a game of tickle, streaming his little fingers irresistibly up and down her neck. He obviously felt free to play with his servants, which was the best duty Laela could imagine. She giggled with abandon, then snapped to remembering Princess Merli was in the room. To her relief, Princess Merli acted like she was distracted and was looking out over the balcony.

Timi ran to where she was standing, and Laela followed. She held back a small gasp at the unexpected panorama before her. To her left was a monumental, sculpted fountain, spouting cascades of water in rippling patterns descending to a basin that looked like a pond rimmed in golden stone. Pathways lined with flowerbeds spoked out from around the fountain, leading to a variety of garden areas connected by fanciful bridges and cooled by swaying trees.

An avenue led to the edge of a pond surrounded by woodlands blueish green in the distance to her right. Merli mentioned to Timi that the King and Queen must be out for a ride. They saw the royal pleasure boat moving dreamily over the surface. She imagined small thrones set in the middle under the canopy of delicate white curtains fluttering gently in the breeze. Standing boatmen, holding large oars, guided the boat with expert dipping and pulling movements.

Laela stepped back, realizing that this was the garden where the King, the Princes, and their direct family members sported themselves. She must not be seen. She felt Merli read her thoughts when she turned around and said to Laela, "We shall be picnicking today but not in the formal gardens. Princess Ellie and I like to take the children near a wooded stream where they can sit in a small natural pool and bathe. They love to splash and find colorful pebbles there."

Merli leaned down to look into Timi's eyes, "Do you want to go with Auntie Ellie and Prince Aser for an outing?" Timi shrieked with excitement, "Yes!"

"Well then, we shall pack our things. A bathing outfit for you, dry clothes for later, your shovel, and pail." And Merli stopped to smile as Timi was already packing a small sack with said belongings.

CHAPTER 21

The Outing

They set out from the Palace in a small procession with five sandy-colored horses decked in royal heraldry from the bold-colored saddles cloths to the small, bejeweled crowns on their heads. A mounted guard led the way on his horse, and another guard followed in the rear of the royals. Merli and Ellie sat on comfortable double saddle seats with their children in front of them. Laela followed last as the guards were there to protect the Royal Family members—not her. Her horse moved slowly and seemed to be so familiar with the route that she needn't manage the reigns or do anything more than cling to it with her legs.

They were heading down a well-worn path through a valley of wild yellow flowers that looked like dancing daystars lighting up the dark green fields rolling into the distance. Laela basked in the late morning sun. Nena had found her a bathing tunic to wear under her dress so she could care for the children in the stream. Laela was as excited as Timi for their very first outing together. The Palace was built on a plateau, so they needed to gradually descend to a thickly wooded area, dotted with grassy knolls here and there. They finally stopped by a cottage with a fenced yard, surrounded by woods, and a caretaker came out to help the guards lift the children and ladies off the horses and carry the large picnic baskets to a table under a tree. Timi immediately ran to a stone stairway winding through bushes and trees leading to the steam. Merli, a guard, and Laela followed in suit. Ellie waved after them and promised to catch up soon. Laela could quickly hear the inviting gurgling of the brook and was enchanted when she saw how the trees seemed to bow toward it as if lifting their rustling skirts to keep all safe below. They provided cooling shadows that mingled with the refreshing breeze.

Timi was already ripping off his day clothing and dropping them on a large flat boulder. The boulder could not have been more perfectly placed by a sandy pool, a shallow bathing spot in the brook protected by an underwater ridge. If they walked further upstream, there was a small beach coated with colorful pebbles. Laela envisioned rightly that the children would be lost in play for hours between the pool and the pebbles.

Merli nodded that she should follow Timi into the water and confided, "Aser will play in the water too. But we've noticed he's more of an observer. He will not just jump in, and he clings to his mother. However, Ellie would appreciate it if you could get him to play more too."

Laela removed her gray tunic and folded it neatly, placing it in the basket of Timi's toys as Merli indicated. She had not bathed in a stream but would certainly not want to reveal any intimidation or lack of knowledge now. She had to be an asset at all times to Merli. She was unsure how to ground herself in the squishing mud and whether any creatures were hidden in these waters that might bite her. She was always conscious of predators big and small. However, the most significant danger right now was Timi slipping away. She had to pull Timi back continually from trying to move inward and explore the small rapids and eddies beyond the pool.

She loved the cool, soothing flow of water around her legs and even sat with Timi in her lap in the middle of the pool, letting the water embrace them. Ellie placed Aser with them at the shallow edge. Aser watched them with serious big honey-brown eyes. He was a strikingly beautiful little boy, reminiscent of Mateo. His skin was a creamy tan, and his hair was streaked with flaxen highlights. He had balanced features and a look of unusually keen intelligence. She wondered how such a small boy could look so serious as if burdened with knowing too much already. She reached out to Aser, too, and gave him the pail to fill and empty as he pleased.

Both Aser and Timi sat with her to make groups of similar colored pebbles and build a miniature house with larger stones. Aser, though a year younger than Timi, could speak in sentences. Aser began to sit by her side and looked up at her earnestly, and asked, "Why are your eyes so different?"

Laela let him touch her eyelids as Timi had. She knew that the lavender-petal-like shape was an ornament with which nature graced her and healthy Treedles. She understood that most of the Treedles he and other Mergons had seen must appear as gray and undistinguished. They had somehow lost outer color and inner vitality, too, through the slave-breeding.

"I'm different, Aser, but we all are. No two humans look just the same. But inside," she pointed to her head and then her heart, "we can all think good thoughts and love one another, no matter what our colors." Though ever so young, she could tell that Aser got the gist of her message, and his face lit up with a fleeting grin of joy.

The children were distracted and remained so for quite a time, gathering stones, examining them, and trying to pile them up in ways that they would not topple over. Laela could not help but overhear Merli and Ellie engaged in rapt conversation. She could also not restrain herself from listening with care as she busied her hands in buttressing the little castle they were building. It occurred to her that the princesses did not have a safe place to empty their hearts' secrets as the walls did listen in the Palace.

They talked about themes so intimate that not even their closest family members should hear, let alone a Treedle slave girl. However, she felt instinctively that their stories and destinies were tied together now. Whether as a slave or a princess, there was a common fear and threat that Mergon culture imposed on women. They were all expected to mold their speech and movements in ways to demonstrate their submission to power. They had to teach their daughters to not only bend to this oppression but defend it. They had to encourage their sons to wield their lordly powers over women and all other 'inferior' creatures—not to be outsmarted, overspoken, or outwitted. It was particularly dangerous for the women in the Court to think and act freely on any ideas that diverged even slightly from prescribed and limited roles. Women must perform roles as mothers, wives, daughters, and even friends that were all but written for them word by word.

Ellie was beginning to sob softly, "I'm trying not to despair. You know how much I do to support Prince Marl. I attend to all his needs; I massage his feet and make sure he is served his favorite foods at all times and that the food is just the right temperature. I don't contradict him or interrupt him ever. I keep Aser quiet in his presence, which is easy to do, as my boy cowers in his father's presence. I don't ask him for anything. Yet, he finds me continually lacking. He sees no end of faults in me and now Aser."

Laela couldn't glance behind her but imagined Princess Merli raising her eyebrows when she said, "Oh, Ellie, sister of my heart. I dare not say what I think of your husband as I might be executed for it. Prince Marl has always had a mercurial temperament and can strike out like a pit viper. You mustn't repeat this, but we have all noticed his foul moods have been getting worse. I believe he has a mind-illness and should take calming potions. Though heaven knows you can't be the one to recommend this course of treatment." She paused, "Maybe Prince Roy can. He might find a way to tell Prince Marl that doesn't offend him."

They were quiet for a moment while Ellie sobbed louder. "I wonder," Merli continued, "if he's not becoming sick with frustration and rage. My Roy tells me that Marl obsesses day and night with increasing mine operations, expanding the Kingdom, producing more gold, and above all, about how Mergons must increase the number of slaves. Roy tells me he thinks that Mergons are becoming willy-wishers and forgetting that the source of our wealth is based on war and conquest.

"I've also thought, and this is even more dangerous for me to say, but I will, you know me, as your best friend, that he sees you and Aser as a reflection of Mateo and your maternal family. He hates Mateo more than any other person in the realm. Have you noticed that Aser looks very much like Mateo?"

Laela could tell that Princess Merli was trespassing a boundary that even the closest of friends in the palace might not dare to vocalize.

Now, Ellie sounded like a wounded animal, moaning and whimpering, and it was eerie to listen to. Laela had let the boys wander off, but they remained in her sight, and she could bound quickly to them if needed. Aser had followed his cousin up a small slope by the bank to collect a few sticks. In particular, she was relieved that Aser couldn't hear his mother's agonizing grief, as the sounds were a universal language, and he would understand and never forget.

Ellie eventually calmed herself and said, "Look at this." Laela snatched a glance as Ellie lowered her dress off her shoulders, and Merli peered down at her back.

Merli shrieked, "Oh no. That animal! That ogre with a crown! I'm not worried about being executed now; I'm worried that I'll kill your husband with my bare hands."

Ellie answered in a lifeless voice, "He suspects that I side with my family, with my mother (Danie's sister), and with Mateo. And he's right. He's right. I dream of escaping him. He wants my total loyalty, but how? I can't help being me, being born to a loving family whom

I adore. I can't help not being like him, not adoring him, and well, not even liking him.

"I feel he knows deep down, and it enrages him further," she paused. "It gets worse, he can't stand the sight of Aser, and he has come to beat him too. I do all in my power to keep him from his father. He told me that if I raise another Mateo, we shall both be put to death.

"Merli, I had to tell someone. I am going crazy with fear. If I tell my family, he will punish them and me. Merli, I couldn't keep it in any longer. I'm so sorry I have put you in this position. To bear my confidences and stay silent on the matter. But no matter what, you can't, you mustn't tell anyone. It could put their lives, mine, and Aser's in danger."

Merli let Ellie cry for what seemed a long time, and then said, "I'll pray about this. I understand how dangerous the situation is. But we must believe that the 'One' will help us deliver you from this evil beast. We mustn't give up hope. And the two of us together are clever. We'll think of something."

"Merli, for the love of the 'One,' you must keep this a secret, even from Roy. First and foremost, from Roy. He isn't violent, and he would want to protect me, as he has told me that he cares for me like a sister. I am thinking of finding an excuse to spend time in the countryside at my parents' manor and spend time with Danie and Mateo. My dream is that he tires of me and divorces me. There are so many beautiful women who would be eager to take my place. I see them compete for him. I wish them well when they do.

"It is relieving to confess this to you. And I do apologize for the burden I have put on you. Forgive me." Ellie once again collapsed in Merli's arms.

When Aser and Timi returned, after searching for and collecting sticks, then watching a giant lizard and poking it with some of the sticks, she pulled Aser to her, who sidled trustingly into her lap. She looked at him for telltale signs of abuse. She noticed a few unusual scars on his wrists and upper arms. Why had she not seen them before? She played like she was smoothing his shirt, tugging it outward slightly, and surreptitiously peered down at his back. There were some old scars and then some fresh purple welts, with the fine blue-black lines of dried blood from the crack of a belt or wiry object on his back. She bit her lip not to cry out or draw attention to her discovery. She wanted to take Aser with her and escape into the woods right then and there.

Lunch was somber and quiet as each of the three women recoiled into themselves to mull over these revelations and adjust to the weight of a secret burden they couldn't release but that would unite them in bonds that only suffering can create.

Laela couldn't taste the food. She stared absently at the fruit orchards that rimmed the northern edge of pasture by the cottage. She had heard the guards discussing the fences around all the royal properties and could catch a glimpse of them beyond the orchards. An idea came to her that might allow her to be alone, tree climb— and even survey this area as escape was also on her mind—and collect fruit for them all. She went over various versions of acting for permission. Still, she noted Merli so distracted that she simply asked, "While Timi and Aser take their afternoon naps, may I go to the orchard to gather us some fresh-picked fruits for afternoon dessert?"

Merli mumbled un huh. So first, Laela rocked Timi in a hammock strung between two shade trees until he was deep asleep and snoring lightly. A guard sat under one of the trees by him and had heard Merli assent to her visiting the orchard.

The largest trees in the orchard were those near the large, white-washed wooden fence at the end of the rows of trees. She left a large empty basket below the largest tree, climbed it, and began to fill the satchel she had over her neck with fragrant golden-pink-tinged fruits called royal nectars. She filled one satchel, emptied it into the basket, and then scooted up the tree to better visualize what lay beyond the fence. She saw fields of cotton plants and Treedles moving over them to pick the cotton balls. The slaves all moved as if in coordinated motion, and Mergon slave driver walked among the rows slapping a whip to the ground as if to pace them and occasionally cracking the whip over one of their backs. Near the edge of the fence, she saw the reddish-brown face, the distinctive and healthy color of a Bouder from Aerizon.

She quickly finished filling the satchel and deposited the fruits, then ran to the fence. She went to the section where the possible Bouder slave worked and found a fair size gap between two vertical boards. She was two arms lengths distance from Banbo, and she needed only a whisper to draw his attention. She threw a light stone on the ground before him, and he looked up, his keen hunter's vision spotting her immediately through the crack.

She whispered, shhh, in a low sound that mimicked a bird. "Banbo," and he almost raised his voice, "Laela?"

"Yes, it's me. Banbo, I can only stay a few minutes as the Princess will be suspicious if I am out of view for long. How did you get here?"

"I was captured landing in the Trader's Villages. They brought me here for questioning." Banbo looked down, his shoulders drooping. He glanced up shamefully at Laela, "They questioned me a lot about you. Did I know you? Who sent you to Mergonland and why? Who is coming to find you? They inflicted pain on me, but I promise, I kept saying that I was from another tribe and didn't frequent your home or come close to you and your family. I told them even though everyone knows each other by name, they don't know personal details about other clans and families. I told them I hadn't seen you in a long while. I asked them how you got here, whether you were captured, and of course, they beat me for asking questions."

Banbo looked over his shoulder, and he turned his back partially to her; she saw the crisscrossed flesh wounds of the deep-cutting whip they used on him.

Laela realized that Banbo, if not enslaved because of her, was undoubtedly interrogated and severely beaten on her behalf. There were far-reaching consequences of her venturing out of Aerizon on her own that would continue to reveal themselves. She must do all in her power to set what she could right.

"Banbo, I didn't plan to visit Mergonland at first. I entered the Forest to explore and wanted to go as far as the Trading Village. I came on my own, and when I found a Trader's Map and saw how close Mergonland was, I wanted to see for myself what it was like, hoping to return quickly. But there's no time to tell you my story. I'm a slave for now but will escape if the 'One' so wills. I have the support of Prince Mateo, and we are committed to each other," she blushed.

"All the Treedles in Mergonland down to the last slave has heard your story, dear Laela. It fills us with hope and pride. You must take good care."

She continued, "If by the Grace of the 'One,' I get out, I promise to do my best to find a way to free you or to ease your conditions. Stay low, stay quiet, dear Banbo. I will pray for you. I must go. If over time you aren't released, you must attempt to cross this fence, there's a stream nearby, and you can follow it out of the vicinity and keep away the conchos."

Banbo looked furtively over his shoulder to be sure no one was listening, "Before you go, one last thing. Edo, Nana Bisru's husband, still lives. He's so wise and capable that the slave masters at the mine have him care for the books. He lives relatively well as our lives go in this land. About escaping, we all have to think twice about saving ourselves. The Mergon Master torments those left behind."

"Thanks for the news of Edo. Let's pray and wait for inspiration from the 'One.' May you be blessed and protected." Laela was pleased to know that, at the very least, Edo's life wasn't fraught with physical and mental pain to the degree other Treedles experienced it. She was determined to help Banbo, somehow, some way.

Laela scurried back through the trees, carrying her basket of sunset-colored fruits. As she was heading to the tree where Timi was napping in his hammock, she noticed the sun glinting off the waving sides of a fluorescent green creature. Rapidly focusing, it could only be a serpent. She approached more carefully and spied an emerald-green boa constrictor heading down the tree and beginning to arch its head in anticipation of a meal. She dropped her basket of fruits and thought about what to do next. She picked up a large stick that had fallen on the ground. She tried to move soundlessly, smoothly, and quickly, holding out the stick to lure off the snake before it further arched its head and chomped its fangs into Timi and began to strangle him in its coils. She moved with such a rush of energy; it was as if she was flying. She put the stick under the boa's open jaw, jolting it away while prodding to engage the snake's body to twirl it around the stick. Then she flung its full force away from them down the field to the side. She scooped up Timi from the hammock, still feeling like the snake was after them, and ran with him over to his screaming mother.

Merli had been watching Laela arrive with the basket and was briefly annoyed and suspicious about her delay when she observed Laela picking up the stick like a sword and charging toward the tree where her son was napping. At the same time, the guard who was supposed to be guarding Timi and who had fallen asleep propped against the tree awoke startled, confused, and then grunting as he realized what the commotion was about—the green snake could still be seen slithering a few yards away.

Timi, brought rudely out of his nap, was taken aback by the three red-faced, adrenaline-pumped adults surrounding him, and began to cry fiercely. Laela handed him to Merli, who cursed at the guard as she cradled Timi, "How dare you fall asleep while guarding the Prince. You will be lucky if the Prince does not cut off your head!"

Timi was now shrieking—emitting unpleasant volleys of high-pitched screams mama-mama, snake, snake. Ellie stood back looking panicked. Her shoulders were heaving while Aser was crying and clutching at his mother's neck.

As the din subsided, Merli, cradling Timi, turned to Laela, her eyes softer blue through the mist of tears, "By my life, you saved my son. You saved a Prince, my dear. How can I thank you? We shall think of a reward, but for now, we must return to the palace, rest, and bring in the doctor to treat us all for nervous exhaustion."

That evening, the two Princesses, their sons, and Laela took the evening meal in Timi's room. Servants brought in tables and chairs from another room. Merli asked them to bring up a simple meal from the kitchen, and they were content with soup, bread, and some dried fruits. Merli announced at the end, "The palace doctor is coming to give us all a relaxation and sleeping potion so we will not dwell on the snake. We all need to sleep well." She looked at Ellie, "Tomorrow, we will put on our happy faces. Sometimes if we are too dramatic or tell too many stories, people here ask too many questions. We must not bring that kind of attention to ourselves." Ellie nodded gratefully, and Laela, in her mind, did too."

Merli asked the servants to make up the day beds for the night and bring comfortable silk quilts so that all could sleep in the same bedroom. "We shall tell the family about how we ended our lovely picnic with a slumber party. Everyone drink your remedy to the last drop; we will light a fire in the hearth. Just as this fire will keep us warm, be sure that the 'One' is looking over us, especially blessing our children, our pure darlings. The 'One' loves you, Timi and Azer. Be sure He is always near to you and will make all things right."

Timi and Azer looked like glowing pink angels standing in their nightgowns and waiting for the doctor to give them the remedy. Ellie took hers reposed from her bed. Laela was the last to get some of the potion, and Merli invited her to stay with them that night. She led her to a cozy bed next to Timi's, where he could see her and she him as they drifted off to sleep.

CHAPTER 22

New Friendships

It happened slowly, a dawn beginning as an inkling—a hesitant wave of light turning into a soft hue and then the new day appearing, bold and bright. Undeniable. So, the new friendships with the Princesses grew.

After the outing, Merli began to talk to Laela more as a collaborator than a slave—a partner in Timi's care. Laela knew she had earned Merli's trust. She felt sure that Merli and Ellie had either assumed she heard part or all of the heart-to-heart they had shared by the stream. When they were in the palace, they spent most time together in Timi's room, which was unusually spacious and conducive to socializing. It also meant they were located in a different tower than that of the Princes. When they wanted to talk, they sent the servants out and sat on the balcony drawing out the awning so no one could see them from below. Privacy was a benefit they all cherished. The princesses never asked her about what she heard nor warned her about keeping secrets. They both began to speak freely and openly in her presence. And before long, they trusted her as a confidant.

The walls prohibiting friendship came tumbling down, and there was no way for Laela to keep her distance from the women who were becoming her sisters. She worked as a servant but caring for Timi and Azer was no different from caring for her brother Lucas. The mothers didn't boss her, and if anything, over time, she advised them on how to handle Timi's willfulness on the one hand and Azer's shrinking introversion on the other. The princesses never tired of hearing stories about their children and having Laela bring to their attention the delightful moments when the children made discoveries or funny comments. They all laughed together at Timi's impudence, the way he rebuffed the palace ladies who pinched his cheeks—telling one of them she looked like a scary clown. He was always hiding treats in his pockets and would reach in to give crumbled cookies to Azer when he looked sad, which was any time after he had seen his father. Azer showed his underlying intelligence as he played doctor and tried to give herbs he had picked to cure a sick household dog. They all enjoyed watching and savoring the boys' play and rampant curiosity. The Princesses found more pretexts to leave the palace walls and spend days picnicking in the gardens and forest as the days passed. They always took Laela with them as the nanny for both boys. But now, when Laela walked behind them, hanging her head, and casting her gaze away from any Mergon they met on their escapades to fake subservience and the fog of gray selflessness that made slaves shadow people. All three were complicit in carrying out this ruse of deception and took care to project traditional roles and appearances to protect one another. If others were near them, they immediately assumed typical roles as mistresses and servants. Merli occasionally pretended to berate Laela to throw off any sense that she was favored, let alone a friend and confidant. She would give Laela a conspiratorial wink as she did.

The five of them: the two Princesses, young Princes, and Laela began to go everywhere together, shying away from palace events and gatherings as much as possible. The Princesses rarely brought along other family members, women friends, or even female servants on the walks and outings, preferring the accompaniment of the quietest male guards who remained at a distance. Most of the Princesses' social circle included women relatives of either the King or Queen whose many hours of leisure became too dull without the addition of salacious gossip, drama, and making judgments about the real and imagined wrongdoings of others in the Court. Tongues wagged that the Princesses had become haughtier and more exclusive than ever—that they felt above even the highest placed royals. Speculations were arising that they were hiding something and outside for clandestine meetings of a questionable nature.

The truth was something had happened the day of the outing to the stream that changed everything. Too much had been said, too much heard and overheard. After that, the three women became complicit in sharing their secrets, the forbidden longings of their hearts. What they each most desired was greater freedom to be themselves. However, their escapades were escapes from a reality that was pressing in on them, nonetheless. Deep down, they knew how very limited their self-expression could be.

Laela tried to avoid meeting Frida's glare of hate and disapproval and Nena's glances of fear and displeasure as they were the only two people not fooled in the least. Frida was infuriated that Laela slept in Timi's room regularly. When she had the opportunity to pass close to Laela, and no one else was close, she snarled at Laela, making her eyes into triangular darts and commenting in a sly hissing voice, "This won't last for long." Nena didn't acknowledge her presence or speak to her again—offering no more motherly advice or sweet biscuits. Laela believed that her friendships with Merli and Ellie were innocent enough, and the things they shared should in no way endanger other Treedles. However, she didn't stop to think that her very presence with them was a daring challenge to the unwritten rules and taboos that permeated the entire Kingdom.

One day as the boys took an exceptionally long nap, the three women sat on the balcony in Timi's room, and the princesses began to ask Laela about life in Aerizon. It was the first time they had asked about her as a Treedle, about something not related to the boys or their duties as mothers. Laela felt honored, and it occurred to her that she was about to reveal information regarding Treedle culture that no Mergon in the palace, let alone the Kingdom, had ever heard. Mergon masters exchanged few words with household servants, and these were mainly requests for them to do services. Servants nodded and assented in humble grunts. Unless freshly abducted from the forest, a slave would have had little or no hands-on knowledge of life in Aerizon, and if they did, they would know better than to speak of their lives as anything special.

Laela wasn't sure where to begin. Then she thought about their perspectives—how they were ardent mothers who adored their parents and how these connections were of the highest value to them—so that she would describe Tara and Alvaro, her family, in detail, to them. She prefaced her personal story first by saying, "My people live in the treetops of Aerizon, and though we have fewer possessions than Mergons, we are happy and highly educated in a way that is different from Mergons."

As she began to talk, a power flowed through her, and she felt the 'One' was with her, opening a door and causing words to flow out that she had never uttered before, "Treedles value family, service, and making their daily lives beautiful. Living for us is like making a prayer or a poem come alive. There must be meaning in what we do and say, and there must always be love holding us together. We learn that the bonds of love are a strong but delicate web connecting us and all living things around us."

It occurred to Laela as she spoke that this was happening here and now. The three women were weaving a web of bonds so unique and powerful that they were creating a new reality: one she hoped would last their lifetimes.

Ellie looked at her thoughtfully and questioned her, "Do you believe in the Prophet Asmea?" Ellie, like Azer, was more intellectually curious than Merli. But Laela could see that Merli was profoundly touched and meditating on what she had just heard. Merli understood with her heart.

"Yes, we believe in the Prophet Asmea, and we study his life. However, most of our home and community observances center on studying the "Words of the 'One' that Asmea brought to us.

"We worship the 'One' by praying and reflecting on his Words to give us peace and guide our decisions. The Elders and the Council members consult about the significant issues in light of what the Writings say. They urge us to align our souls with the spirit of the 'One,' to do His Will—to act in accord with His teachings in our daily work and lives. We believe the 'One' created the plants and creatures, the skies and heavenly bodies—all of nature—as a mirror of the spiritual world to teach us lessons about the significance of life and relationships. Life for us is not about having many things, but rather peace of heart and mind. And many loving friends and family!"

There was a moment of silence. Then, Merli shifted on her velvet cushioned seat and asked if they could also know more about her, "Laela, I am eager to hear about your family. Do tell us all about them."

Tears streamed down Laela's cheeks as she opened the lid to the memories she trapped tightly to survive in the palace. Her throat was constricted, and she had to almost force the words out from the pain of remembering.

"My father, Alvaro, is an honored scholar and member of the Council that governs our community. He spends hours in his study and does not speak lightly. My mother, Tara, is a healer and oversees a grand garden. A large section of the garden is open to the community. Joy Park, we call it, and it is located at the center of our town. The gardens are protected by a raised iron wire structure shaped like a cathedral in the air and covered with netting to keep in the butterflies and small birds. There are little paths with benches, and Treedles come to sit, relax, and enjoy various flowers and small flying creatures in one place. But my mother also grows many medicinal herbs and plants and makes medicines."

When she paused after describing her family, baby Lucas, and even Macecle, Ellie responded as if thinking out loud, "Your father sounds like our grandfather Asme, and your mother like my Aunt Danie. Your family must also be descendants of the Prophet Asmea." Ellie twined her hands nervously, realizing that there were Treedles who had the same distinguished bloodline and spiritual heritage as she did.

Laela nodded, "And so they are. But this is something I dare not mention, except to the closest of Mergon friends."

Laela continued to tell them about Oti and Phips. She took them on a minds-eye tour of their home and described their personalities and talents. She also told them about the wise advice Oti often gave her.

Merli brushed away tears and said humbly, "I must confess, Laela, that I had never thought of Treedles as people, at least not people like us, before now. I am ashamed to say that even the most highly educated Mergons know nothing of your people or culture. And," she looked down, "I didn't realize how much alike we are, how much I would want to meet your family and friends."

Laela knew what she meant. Mergons saw the Treedle culture as primitive and almost nonexistent on the human scale.

Ellie looked at Laela thoughtfully, "Tell us how a girl with such a kind and loving community runs away. I don't say this to criticize. I just don't understand. What made you venture into the Feral Forest alone? To leave all that is safe and your good life?" At that point, the boys awakened hungry for a snack and wanted to go outside again before night. Laela was relieved to have more time to think of how she would answer.

Should she share the dreams and signs that disrupted her life and all but drove her on this quest? Might this be confusing or overwhelming to her friends? She felt they would hold her in their circle of kindness, but it would be so difficult to tell people with such a different history and background, who know so little about Treedle culture in a way they would understand. Mergons didn't seem to talk much about visions, and their shamans interpreted dreams to find what fortune awaited them or whether to say yes or no to a business venture or a marriage proposal. Treedle Shamans wove a more complex narrative and gave a spiritual interpretation to dreams. She would need to think about whether to tell her whole story—her explorations in the forest, her dreams. If their husbands questioned them more, she decided not to divulge anything about the cable lines and stations.

Over the next two days while the boys were napping, Laela finished telling her life story. She decided to tell them about the jaguar mauling. She showed them the purple imprint over her chest. She spoke in vague and elusive terms about the Shamans' signs and warnings and the stories Danie told her about. The princesses gasped at this story, and Merli tentatively touched the imprint Laela bore as if it were still a live wound.

"Most assuredly, this is a sign that only the oldest and the wisest sages would be able to decipher," Merli said in hushed and awed tones. "I simply can't imagine how you would venture into the Feral Forest with your friend Phips and, after this terrible scare, go out again alone. Some angelic force is guiding you. Though, certainly, no Mergon could dream of a woman going on a quest alone like you did."

"No Treedle in Aerizon could either," Laela grinned, trying to make light of it. "I am inquisitive and willful, as you can see." She didn't talk about the route she, Phips, and the traders created to advance the connections between their two lands and peoples. But she tried to explain better how everything she had learned since early childhood had prepared her to explore the natural world.

Once she crossed a certain threshold in opening up, intimacy became as intense as with Treedle friends. They spent a whole afternoon sharing stories of their entrance into womanhood.

Merli was particularly entranced by Laela's coming-of-age story, the ritual bath, singing doelas, and Miss Ellie's advice about mating. Merli doubled over with laughter about Laela's impertinent retorts about the honor of bleeding monthly and her comments to the entourage preparing her to enter the Enclosure. Various women in the palace also engaged in blatant matchmaking attempts like those of Miss Ellie, but none helped women through their passage to womanhood with such poetic ministrations. The whole Treedle ritual seemed very charming and quaint to the Mergon women.

Ellie mused, "Our coming of age is different. We're not alone for a minute but spend most of the day in a room with other menstruating women who are in foul moods. The palace women don't need to hide during their menses unless they're in pain or grumpy. These are the women who guide us through our first menses. The complainers call the menses the devil's curse on women because we're inferior. They say we are meant to feel pain inside out to remember our lowly state before men, who never experience this pain or give birth.

"But I and many others believe this is because we're stronger and fiercer than men deep inside. I see how the men can barely withstand cold or sniffle and take to bed. Would they be able to birth their sons? Most surely not. Women have learned to withstand and to protect life through any kind of pain," she said proudly. Laela felt for a moment that if Ellie were a shaman or priestess, her teaching would center around the goodness of women: their power to create and care for others.

On the last story-telling day, they heard a loud voice outside the door, and Ellie immediately turned pale, "It is Prince Marl. He never visits me here. He must have gone to my chambers, and they told him I was here." She pulled Merli into the room with her and told Laela to stay out on the balcony. She waved to the outdoor curtain where Laela could stand against the wall and hide in its folds. She need not tell Laela why it was best not to be seen.

She could hear him stomp in and talk in curt tones to Ellie, "Woman, why are you and my son always in this room? Don't tell me the boys are sleeping like babies, and the afternoon is ripe."

"Your lordship, the boys like to nap in the same room, and it easier to take care of them together. Every day we take them to walk, hike, and run outside. Look at your son's rosy cheeks. He's growing bigger and stronger every day, just as you please." Laela could tell the boys were wide awake now.

Timi piped up, "Why is Uncle Marl mad? Why is he yelling?"

"I will tell you why Timi," the Prince responded in an unmodulated booming voice, "because you and your cousin are Princes of Mergonland. Princes don't lie around and sleep all day and play with dolls and houses. They don't go on picnics every day either. They should be learning to hunt, use a sword, fight, and give orders to our slaves. Princes lead their country and bring it more gold and honor. Princes are the greatest warriors of the land!"

"I am strong, Uncle," Timi protested, "And everyone says I am brave too. I didn't get bit by a big green snake, and..." She could tell Merli was clamping his mouth shut with her hand. He might have said next, "Laela and I ran away from the snake." Merli had thought quickly.

"Well, Timi, you are doing better than my son. His mother needs to stop treating him like a girl—or he will grow up to be half a man. A King must be ALL man." Not caring to protect their marital privacy, the Prince began to attack Ellie, "You are neglecting your duties as a Princess. You haven't visited my aunts or family members for tea in weeks. I've been very busy with state affairs and new projects, but I've just found out that you are acting very strangely. And that you are letting the worthless, stinking Treedle into our lives to care for our son. Speaking of which, where is she, where is the Treedle rat who is always with you?"

Merli spoke up in the firmest tone Laela ever heard her use, "She's not here at the moment, Prince Marl. I'm using the Treedle servant's service, and Prince Roy has allowed me to do this because our nanny is quite ill and won't be back for at least another month. Ellie always takes great care of Prince Azer. He's so intelligent and robust in the body for his age. He'll be a great man and Prince one day."

Laela felt that Prince Marl was slightly mollified by the lower grumbling noise he made, "Nonetheless, Ellie, you may not let that tree rat take over our Azer. The last thing we will raise is another Mateo. Mark my words." And, as if it were proof of his concerns, he said to Azer, "Stop whimpering, boy, or I will give you something to cry about."

"Ellie, you are to be in my chambers tonight. There's more to discuss and adjust in your attitudes, and I know just the treatment for it," he said chillingly.

Merli sent the two boys out with the servants bringing in their afternoon snack. "Take the boys to the courtyard and take very good care of them," she admonished sternly. "Don't bring them back until they're ready for bed tonight. And did I say to take excellent care of the Princes!"

Merli sat on the bed talking to Ellie's heaving back, "Listen to me. You need to get ready. You must have a plan for tonight, dear friend. You must seduce the Prince before he gets into a rage. I've seen him, and once he gets going, the anger grows like a spitting fire with endless fuel to feed it. He all but promised to beat you tonight. Ellie, you must be clever and carry out the plan I am telling you. There's only one way you or any woman can get the upper hand."

Laela came out from the fold of the curtain, beads of nervous sweat dripping over her lips. Ellie lay on the bed enfolded into herself as a snail pulled out of its shell, wanting to hide. Laela stood to the side, watching quietly.

Merli had made quips about how she and Roy enjoyed their marital bed and how such 'good' relations were the solution to almost all their problems. Ellie never countered back with anything of the kind. But now Merli was telling Ellie,

"Ellie, I'm going to dress you in the most alluring outfit I have. One that never fails to enchant. I'm also going to put makeup on you in a way that will make him see you differently.

"You will come to his room dressed in a large, velvet green cape, looking mysterious. When you drop the cloak covering you, I promise he'll swoon with desire. However, the first thing you must do is stand near wherever he has his canter of beer or wine. I'll give you a vial with double the sleeping potion we occasionally use for Timi when he can't sleep. It will, at the very least, make him very relaxed and drowsy. He won't have the energy to fight or be physically active and will want to rest if not sleep. You must find a way to put it into his wine or beer. He's constantly guzzling something. Do this either before or as you take off your cloak.

"You must close your eyes then and look relaxed and welcoming like a true Prince is coming to sweep you off your feet. Well, you'll need to use a lot of imagination, but you must do it."

It wasn't safe to spend the night in Timi's room, and Laela excused herself quietly without fuss and made way to the room she hadn't seen in days. That night she prayed for Ellie as she would for a member of her family. Her closet-like room seemed chillier and more inhospitable now compared to the days of beaming sunshine and billowing clouds that cheerfully filled the skies from the large windows in Timi's room. She wished Mateo would come to rescue her or that she had a more secure plan of departure for herself. But she felt that first she must warn or say goodbye to the love of her life. If she escaped without seeing him, there might not be a way to ever get a message to him. She felt they both deserved some form of closure, however simple. Even so, he would be more emblazoned in her heart than the jaguar pawprint on her chest, and the claws of this love would burn deeper and longer.

Laela knew another change was coming, some form of reprisal and repression from Prince Marl. He would command multiple punishments on his wife for her acts of self-assertion, her walks and talks outside of the palace routines, and for blithely ignoring the rules. Women should bear themselves like light-stepping, prancing palace horses, who wear visors to shield their eyes from straying and bend to the reigns guiding them in measured steps on paths mapped out for them. Ellie had hinted that Marl relished focusing his creative energies on revenge for every imaginable slight or infraction of his subjects' abject and complete servitude to him. His wife was his greatest servant, and it was his marital right to command her, no matter how noble or lofty her background was. She was his consort and property to do with however he pleased.

It would now be dangerous to be around Ellie's son, and she and Azer spent whole days with Merli and Tim. Laela tried to imagine how they could continue the friendship and lighthearted camaraderie they had enjoyed for this short period.

She realized that every attempt at seizing joy or letting love blossom with other Mergons only put her and them in more danger. No wonder adults in both Aerizon and Mergonland were always prescribing boundary after boundary to protect young people. Adulthood was learning about staying in line, in boxes—neatly grouped and contained. Rooms everywhere, in the trees and on the ground, had four walls and a door to close you in and keep others out. Your people could best protect you if you adhered quietly and stayed neatly within the cultural perimeters. A web of mental moonlines bound the Treedles, and stone walls locked in the Mergons. The more mindless and compliant one was, the less pain and danger they would suffer. The price of security was the caging of every aspect of your life.

Laela was angry and realized she was ranting to the 'One.' Why? Why did she have to see and feel like this? Should she just make herself die and live like an ant. A worker following orders. A woman raising the next generation—cooking, cleaning, and sweeping herself away at the hearth of her home. It was as if the essence of life— knowing and loving her inner self and others, exploring being, were the most rebellious and threatening of all acts. Like Laela, her new friends were pushing boundaries that their culture held sacred. They were expected to follow traditions that defined good womanness, a cult where spirit itself was snuffed out, and the forms that hold the light were worshipped. A woman who expanded her mind and heart was at best flighty and confused, needing to be subdued, and at worst, a revolutionary or a witch to be hunted down.

Being angry wasn't helping. She tossed and turned. Finally, tears of exhaustion. She whispered the last prayer, "Help me. I am lost. Help me."

That night the Shaman Orla appeared to her in a dream. She seemed to tower in the darkroom, silhouetted by the radiant melon-colored light of Cora, her hands working madly through a tangle of moonline. Her movements varied from awkward jerking motions and streaming flowing ones, hands weaving in and out to unknot the lines. Finally, she held her hands up triumphantly with the moonline whirring in orbit around the tips of her fingers. Light streamed within this circle and lit up Orla's face radiating with a confident smile. She looked upon Laela and said, "There are more tests to come. Let the 'One' guide you. Rely on Him and Him alone. Look to the end of things. Persevere. He will not abandon you no matter how fierce the tests are. Believe, and the solutions will appear. Great tests yield gifts of great value, but you must face them in fortitude and faith."

Laela understood that she was to seek protection above and beyond the narrow limits of what any friend or person could offer her. She must face even the harshest reality for herself and know that a Divine presence was surrounding her. She instinctively knew she was chosen and had chosen a path untraveled—a journey no woman of her generation had ever taken. She could be overwhelmed at every turn, bitter for each pain, and terrified of each threat and attack, or she could hold on to powerful hope that Orla was showing her soul. The ways of the spirit were mysterious, and perhaps each person who ventures on such a path must find their secrets and powers in their own way—the key to the deep trust that brings them through.

Frida appeared early at her door the following day, eyes glittering with mirth at seeing her promise fulfilled and Laela on the floor where she belonged. Laela observed her body flinching as Frida neared her and kicked her with a pointed toe, but she remembered while wincing that this was a test, and she would not be falling into a pit of fear so easily. She looked down to hide this very determination from Frida, who took this as a recognition of her humiliated state.

"So, finally, the Princesses are coming to their senses. Prince Marl is prohibiting your bewitchment and troublemaking with his family. Finally! Well, it's back to the garden and bird services for you. You are not to speak with the Princesses or the children. If they approach you, you must politely decline to continue the conversation. They both know the new rules. Prince Marl will enforce severe retribution if you seek them out. Now, off to work."

Laela nodded and proceeded to the kitchen, where Nena, without a smile or glance, put a biscuit in Laela's apron pocket. Tomas also showed a calm and almost expressionless face, indicating the part of the garden where she should weed for the day. The day passed without incident, and Laela was grateful to be alone with her grief at ending another short-lived but compelling chapter in her stay in

Mergonland. The times of romancing her Prince with vows made under the boughs of evergreen trees and the carefree gatherings with friends she would love to have as her own family was ending. What was left for her here was to try and skirt the menacing predators couched around her in the deepening shadows—waiting to spring. She must return to her strategic thinking and finalize her escape plan soon.

That night, especially tired after being out of the habit of physical labor, she was surprised to see her little room made cozy with a small bed, two pillows, and a gray silk quilt covering it. There was a small chair at the foot of the bed for her to sit and dress. Tucked under her pillow, she found a note, "Dearest Laela, as you may imagine, it's not permitted for us to meet right now. I'm sending you this bedding as a small token of appreciation for your services." Merli.

She knew that Merli wanted to say more but should this note be intercepted, it had to suffice to say she wasn't at will to talk with Laela. Though most evidently thinking of her. Laela could only imagine Frida's irritation and protests over the bedding idea and Merli's courage in pressing forward to deliver this gift to her.

Laela embraced the pillow hoping for a trace of the scent of her sweet-smelling friend, who liked to bathe often and wear perfumes. Sinking her head into the pillow, she slept so much better.

Four days later, as she worked in the same berry patch where she had played with Timi, she heard a whispered hiss from the adjacent orchard. She saw a pale, delicate hand beckoning to her from behind a tree. Merli, her face wreathed in mischievous smiles, peeked quickly out at her and waved for her to come over. Laela hesitated, stricken, wanting to run and embrace Merli or run away as quickly as possible, for what was sheer danger for herself. Merli was behind the largest tree, and no guards were around. Laela's first thought was that Merli was one of the few women in the palace who could still be carefree and playful amid such menacing warnings.

The palace gloom had not yet snuffed out Merli's spirit. She found ways to do what she wanted. She cajoled and delighted her husband, Prince Roy. He treated her like a favored pet, quickly forgave her and Timi's mishaps, protected her from harsh consequences, and added restrictions. Merli had told Ellie and her that she admonished her husband when he was too strict. She asked if he wanted her to be a contented and adoring wife or a bitter-biddy one, the kind that always complains to their husband and finds everything either too salty or not enough for her tastes. A wife who constantly complains about her husband: Merli would point out to Prince Roy that she only praised him—in and out of his presence.

So here she was visiting Laela. Merli motioned again to Laela, who held her finger to her lips to say shush and crept toward the trees, looking around to see if anyone might be able to sight them.

Merli spoke softly and reassuringly, "We can talk, dear Laela. I snuck around the edges of the orchard, and we were alone. Prince Roy relieved me from the royal guard that Prince Marl wanted to set on Ellie and me. He is having Ellie's every step watched. No one can see us here, but as you know, we don't have long to talk. We're out of sight behind this tree. Merli gently stretched out a hand and twined Laela's fingers together through hers.

"My Treedle sister, things aren't going well with Ellie. She can't stop crying and can't eat. We have permission for Mateo to come and treat her with his sick nerve tonic. We didn't tell you, but we've spent much time thinking of a pretext to get Prince Mateo out of house arrest and here to the castle for a visit. Well, now one is approved. He'll visit you in the garden tomorrow. Stay attentive for a signal, a soft whistle, or a stone he may throw. Either way, he's to look at the medicinal herbs over there with Tomas present. The good news is that his conditions appear to be easing up. Word through the womenfolk is that he treats the families of all the guards with such great care they have no interest in making his life unpleasant.

"We have an idea to give you more time with him. He'll treat Ellie and surely need to return as she honestly is in a greatly perturbed state. We're all so worried about her. Her room servant was helping her dress and said she had some horrifying welts on her back. Still bleeding and not healing. Whipped like a slave."

Merli rolled her eyes upward, "Oh help me, powers that be not to wish death upon Prince Marl. But the head of our watch, of our persecution, is Frida. She's ailing with pain in her joints and swollen ankles. Curse her soul! We sent word for Mateo to prescribe some immediate bed rest, raising her feet on pillows, as he has done before. With Frida occupied, your visit will be even safer how; we hope that Mateo has made a good plan to free you. My darling sister, you must leave the Palace soon. I know you know that. Maybe I see things through rose-colored glasses, but I believe we'll meet in peace again one day. I will pray for you." Merli kissed her on the cheek and took Laela's face in with care.

Laela watched as she skirted out of sight and waited until there was no rustle or movement in hearing distance. She sensed that they were both safe, for the moment at least. Her heart was pounding so hard with joy at the thought of seeing Mateo that she wondered how she would be able to handle seeing him and letting them go. Without a secure plan, their meeting would provoke temptations in her that would require a level of self-restraint beyond anything she had to muster before. She wouldn't want to let go of him and wish beyond measure to go with him. But they mustn't be foolish or reckless. There was an unsettling aftertaste in thinking about how Merli was telling her goodbye in so many words, telling her she needed to leave the palace. Merli knew more than she was telling, and it would surely confirm what Laela intuited. The time was ripe to make bold decisions.

CHAPTER 23

Doctor's Visit

Nena's eyes glowed warmly for the first time in weeks as she appraised Laela for neatness and overall presentableness. "There there, you are looking fine. We're all looking forward to the treat in store for us—Prince Mateo's visit. Everyone is excited he will be visiting as a Court physician and bringing much-needed tonics and medicines for us. They don't suspect the main reason for him coming is how time changes things. He indicated he would visit the garden to survey the medicinal herbs. Merli spoke with me, and we will all plan this so you can be with Mateo alone for a short time." Nena lowered her eyes bashfully, "Even I have a romantic spot in my heart still, and I heard that the Prince is pining to see you. Tomas and I will act as guards. I will relay a signal to Tomas if anyone comes into the kitchen, though when I send out the snacks to the court, they're usually too busy eating to do that! And it is rare for the guards or other Mergons to walk through or inspect the kitchen gardens and orchard."

It was impossible to do any chores. Laela paced around the orchard, her stomach twisting and churning at every crack, rustle, or snap in the garden. They would meet in this spot, the least visited, enveloped in cool green shadows. The minutes dragged out, taunting her and testing her tiny amount of patience to its limit. Finally, she peered out from behind her hideout—the widest tree in the orchard—and saw her beloved stepping out of the kitchen and heading toward Tomas. Sunshine seemed to follow him in a warm golden aura—his wheat hair tousled and sparkling in the breeze. She bit her lip to think that he was hers, her Prince. It seemed like he was far away from her and only appearing in a dream. She was holding herself, arms wrapped around her waist, like a breathless servant girl fantasizing about a Prince that could never be hers. The feisty woman he praised as his equal was now hiding in the shadows of the palace where he grew up. In Mergon eyes, she was of no more value than an ant bred to feed its queen. A discardable servant. Would he see her differently? Sometimes she could barely remember who she was. Could their love survive her diminishment?

Mateo looked around the garden in a way that could just be a curious inspection of what was growing. But she knew he was trying to guess her whereabouts, and she waved her hand from behind the tree. Mateo nodded and continued to talk casually with Tomas. They all knew that eyes could be watching from the oddest of places.

Then, he sauntered over to the orchard, telling Tomas he would inspect it and gather leaves. From the vantage point Laela and Tomas had thought out, no one could see them. Other tree trunks from the orchards blocked them, and unless a guard were perched on a tree or looking out from a tower (there were none here), they wouldn't be seen. It was a spot and moment of blessed respite. Mateo didn't immediately embrace her or speak. He stood in front of her and then slowly took her in with his eyes. Tears fell involuntarily from the corner of his eyes which darkened with the weight of sadness. His expectant face drooped.

He had imagined how much she had suffered but seeing it was different from imagining a punch and receiving the blow itself. She still had the same overall features, but something had occurred in those lavender petal-lidded eyes—something deep and unfathomable. There was no trace of the free-spirited girl, just the look of loss and sorrow. Laela couldn't hide the ravages of despair, even trying to please Mateo.

Tearfully, Laela asked him, "How do you see me now?" She brushed her simple tunic and looked down at her feet wrapped in servant moccasins. She was no longer being held temporarily in a pit—but imprisoned for life. She couldn't shake this off like a sassy girl, as the threat was always there. Whether the jaguar was resting or out of sight, it was permanently close by, and its natural enemies would do well to fear every step near its lair.

Mateo took his time, looking her up with the most compassionate gaze she had ever seen on his face. He was quiet and still, and she sensed he was giving her the space he would provide a wounded animal cowering in fear to feel the gentleness of his intentions. He moved closer and tilted her chin to look up at him, sighing deeply, "I'm ashamed I haven't been able to protect you. I'll never forgive my father for this betrayal. I have always served him and cared for the health of all in the palace. I have thought of you day and night, but had I escaped the house guards and tried to visit you, it would have put you in more danger. I even chained Macecle so he would not make a scene in trying to find and see you. I am the more cautious of the two of us, and I wanted to have a solid plan before meeting with you. So I didn't even send notes, which could have been intercepted.

"So, you ask me what I see, and I will tell you. I see a woman whom I love more than ever."

Mateo pulled her tightly in his arms, and they rocked together in tears. It wasn't a romantic reunion but a comforting one as if they were mourning the death of a loved one together. Mateo ran his hands up and down her back and then began to kiss her tenderly all over her face, "I love every inch of you. I love your heart. Your suffering has made you even dearer to me if that is possible."

Hearing these words of comfort, Laela collapsed into wracking sobs. She sank into his arms and let out some of her pain—inner pain like silt that clouds clear water. The more she could let go, the more she could breathe, see, and appreciate this moment.

Mateo hesitated, afraid to ask, "I must ask you. Have they treated you very harshly?"

She chose her words carefully so as not to worry him about what he couldn't control or change, "The first days were very frightening for me. I had to wear leg chains, as you can see." His eyes followed to her still bruised ankles. "But I've been fortunate. I have one of the most pleasant duties a slave can have. And each day, Ellie and Merli find new ways to make my life brighter. We began to get so close they felt like dear family friends to me. They insisted I help with the boys, and we went on outings where I sometimes even forget I am a prisoner."

"I'll send you a healing lotion for the scars on your ankles from the chains," he said, not being able to continue looking at her in the eyes. "I try to imagine how each day, each new test must be for you, but it is worse than if it were happening to me. I love you that much, my darling."

Mateo wiped her tears with a large white handkerchief and adjusted his tone for a more practical conversation, "We haven't much time. I was able to come today because Ellie and Merli asked for a medical visit for their boys. The palace was reluctant to allow me in, but I'm still the only doctor the family fully trusts. My cousins said they were worried about the boys' indigestion. That is often why the family calls for me. They eat such heavy foods, and they do not walk enough or take fresh air. Then, it seems that Ellie might need medical care the most.

"I'll see her after our visit. Merli intercepted me at the entrance and told me a bit about the current situation with Ellie. It seems she has become quite ill of late. She asked me to treat Frida first." He winked conspiratorially at her, "I prescribed her some immediate bed rest and administered a relaxant that will have her sleeping all morning. Merli told me that Frida has been cruel to you.

"Of course, all of this was mainly a ploy to help me visit you. As you know, Ellie and Merli are your friends, my darling, and that is outstanding given the situation. They can now help us send messages."

Mateo continued with other news, "I traveled with Macecle. He's in a basket on my horse. When I leave, I'll show him how to arrive at the window of your room in the palace. He'll visit you later, and you must help him not be noticed. He will throw a nut or fruit from a tree when he enters the trees by the wall of your room. My darling, he'll be carrying messages from me in his pouch—the edible kind—and will bring a small blank parchment and pen for you to answer.

"I also have news of Macecle that will make you laugh. We were worried about him being lonely. Davi's family has a few marsupials like your Macecle on their farm that they got from the Trading Village. Davi brought one as a friend for him. We found out that she's a girl, by the way, an adorable one, and your Macecle now has a mate. Her name is Clara, and she's in training to be my totem as Macecle is yours. Macecle is teaching her how to understand our commands. She can't speak yet but follows all my basic commands."

Laela laughed at this, even though it was a bittersweet moment to think of Macecle bonding with someone else. No, this must only be joyful news. She quickly decided to release this momentary stab of jealousy.

Laela turned their conversation to the most pressing topic— survival. "Mateo, please understand that my days of safety here are counted. Your father won't have me be part of this palace life for long, and he might send me to a crueler job, like in the mines. Or worse. I plan to escape over the back wall of the garden but need Macecle to come with me. I need my backpack with its gear and for you to send Tan and Gibble. I must leave soon. I feel it in my heart." She pounded her heart with some of the old Laela emphasis.

Mateo mused for a moment, "I had thought we had a few weeks more to prepare as I want the escape to be foolproof."

Laela shook her head despondently, "It would take too long right now to explain all the details, but Prince Marl became enraged about me becoming so close to Ellie. We tried to hide our friendship, but he wouldn't have me serving his family so closely either way. We're sure he will seek revenge, and part of that will surely be to get rid of me once and for all." Laela gulped as she realized what she had said out loud wasn't just fear but reality.

Blood drained from Mateo's face. She could see his mouth tightening in distress.

"I will get on this immediately. We will move the date up to within the week. I have also done nothing but think of an escape plan as well. Davi and I are planning a way to smuggle you out after one of my medical visits. I have told some of the others at the palace that they must invite me back another day. There's quite a list now of those wanting tonics, treatments, and the like. I will bring a cloak to wrap you and put you in a sack to carry you out when I come. Davi has created a new form of purple gas. When we throw the canister and it hits the ground, it forms a temporary purple cloud and irritates the eyes so no one can stop us when we exit. From there, we would need to bolt to the nearest entry of the woods. And Laela, once I do something like this, I won't be able to return to my home. I'll need to go with you to Aerizon. It would be quite some time before I could visit Mergonland again. I would need to do so undercover. Davi will find ways to send messages and to see us in the future."

Mateo pulled her to her feet and seeing the surge of hope shining in her eyes, he picked her up and spun her around. Laela almost yelped in delight. Being lifted off the ground felt like her soul had ascended, a lifting of the wings of hope. She would lift the children like this when she was with them. It was a natural spring of joy.

One more gift came from this visit. He was leaping toward her. Macecle had raced over and around the palace walls dodging in and out of sight from guards, whom he was taught represent predators—enemies. He found the adjacent trees, bounded over the wall and down the first tree inside the garden. He was now in her arms and snuggling with her. Laela had to restrain herself from crushing Macecle in her embrace. She ran her fingers through his tufted ears and cried into his warm belly. Mateo circled his arms around them both, "Here, here. Is it my imagination, or are you more excited to see Macecle than me?"

Laela teased him, "I have to think about that!" Mateo looked about nervously. He would be expected to serve in the palace and not be in a deep conversation with Treedle servants, even the trusted Tomas. Laela understood and gave him a good-bye kiss on his cheek. "Make haste, my love."

She looked at Macecle and told him, "For now, you must leave with Mateo and then return with my backpack."

"My darling, please send Macecle before dusk to drop off my backpack. You can show him where the barred windows are to my room as you leave. My room isn't far from where they keep the horses. Please remind Macecle to be very careful and try to stay on the highest branches of the trees when moving from one place to another.

"I'm sure he can squeeze through them. If the backpack doesn't fit through the bars, he can take out items one by one and drop them through the bars until we get everything through. He should carry Tan and Gibble on his neck, though, in their travel pouch.

"It is extremely dangerous and risky to travel back into the forest with no moonline and other implements. This will be an escape and not an adventure, so even I know that I should be as prepared as possible."

Mateo nodded assent and planted a kiss fully on her lips, "You are my beautiful mate no matter what. Remember that."

He bade Macecle curl up in a sack and put the herbs he was to take home in another bag on top of Macecle. He hurried away, just turning as he went into the kitchen to give her a radiant smile.

Laela hugged herself, trying to hold onto the lingering warmth of Mateo's embraces and wishing she could stay right there, even spend the night breathing the air and touching the tree where they had been together. She thanked the 'One' and asked Him, "Please protect us, and may we one day bring joy and pride to both our peoples. And if I survive, may we be mated—if it is in your Plan." She had enough hope today to wish for something so far-reaching.

She was able to return to her room right after the evening meal. She asked Nena for permission to retire earlier from her evening work. Nena knew she wanted to savor the remnants of her delightful day alone. She smiled and sent Laela with a cloth sack filled with sweets to eat in her room.

Laela also wanted to be able to intercept Macecle before night. He was waiting outside a tree near her window. He was carrying the backpack over his belly with the straps over his shoulders. He would have looked quite the sight had he been detected. Laela made several shushing gestures for him to contain his excitement. She asked him to reach into the bag, pull out the blanket, and push it first through the bars of the window. She moved her bed by the wall under the window. Macecle was able to drop through the blanket, a jacket, boots, and her sling that Mateo had sent. Once he had passed these items into the room, the almost empty backpack followed. She found moonline and small pellets at the bottom of it.

Next, it was Macecle's turn to squeeze through the bars, and though he had to squeeze his belly a bit, he got through easily enough. He jumped into Laela's arms and just hugged her quietly and earnestly, putting his head next to her heart as a baby does to hear its mother's inner river pumping inside. They sat that way for a long time on Laela's bed. Then Macecle pulled away and proudly showed her the pouch on his neck.

Tan and Gibble weren't as eager or grateful to see Laela. Tan didn't understand her mistress's abandonment, even though she had been well cared for and had plenty to eat. It would take time to coax her back to normal. Gibble was just curious and, being mainly attached to his stomach, concerned about his next feeding. Laela would need to assure them of a safe corner under her bed and plenty of leaves that she would bring them from the garden. No one would care if she didn't clean under her bed.

She assembled the items in the back backpack to be ready for departure. Her stomach clenched, and a feeling of nausea overcame her as she finished packing it. Would Mateo, a gentle, kind-hearted doctor, be able to pull off an escape with her from a militarized court? She didn't doubt the magnitude of his love and devotion. But he wasn't here in the palace. Timing was essential: what if she couldn't wait to be rescued? What if she needed to escape on her own? A rivulet of dark dread snaked through any and every mental plan. Neither she nor Mateo could foresee the circumstances or know what plots her Mergon captors were up to at any given time.

She also felt compelled to have a plan to save herself should circumstances require it. It would certainly be safer for Mateo not to know of her plans and to remain in his own land if she ran off.

How would she know when to leave? How could she escape her locked room at night when it was time and go after midnight but well before dawn? How would she escape detection by the guards and conchos?

Among the bounty of possessions poured onto her bed, she found a note from Mateo and empty sheets of paper, a quill, and a bottle of ink should she want to send a return message with Macecle.

Mateo wrote, "Darling, you can eat this message after you read it, as it is made from a nourishing tree bark. Know that you are the love of my life and that no matter what test may occur, I'll seek to see you free and then seek to be with you. Let's trust in the 'One.' He's our ultimate and only Protector. May our love for Him and each other see us through. I'll be coming soon to get you out, and we will go to Aerizon together. I will marry you there. Stay strong. Love, Mateo."

Laela read the message until she memorized it while petting and stroking Macecle. She gave him the letter to eat as there was no joy in literally eating her lover's words. Laela did not fall asleep for a long time but cuddled with Macecle. Reliving the highlights of her day was better than rest. When she, at last, succumbed to sleep, it was deep and dreamless.

CHAPTER 24

The Black Jaguar

Laela instinctively woke earlier than usual to remind Macecle to leave and to return only near dusk time. She had hidden her backpack in the secret storage space in the wall behind the door.

She was still glowing with the memory of Mateo and then Macecle filling her with affection. She must not show any signs of such emotions right now—or draw any attention to herself. Now was the time to be a 'good' servant.

She had to put on the mask of humble dejection expected of servants and neither smile nor frown, neither laugh nor cry, but become an amorphous being. A Mergon Master wanted servants to be like sleek gray clay before it is hardened: easily moldable—shaped by their moods and needs, attending them with soothing expressions, obedience, and dispatch. Too much personality in a slave was a sign of an uppity and probably disloyal nature. It meant the slave had not entirely accepted their position and destiny. Such a slave would disrupt the quality of service of others who may be influenced by their independent attitudes. Laela had quickly learned that such slaves would suffer the worst possible fates.

The next two days passed without incident, but she could sense a mounting tension, nonetheless. She felt her royal predator lurking behind the columns in the recesses of the palace. The King was not after her, but his appointee, the enraged Prince, was surely debating a suitable punishment or even a way to snuff out her life quietly and quickly. Laela's hands felt clammy, and she moved through the motions of work, trying not to feel. She all but stroked the fur off of Macecle, and the night before, he had whimpered as she clutched him too hard. Macecle, who never showed sadness, was absorbing hers, and his eyes didn't light up with mirth when he saw her.

She had heard the Royal Family was planning a picnic by a pond, and there would be a day of festivities and games in honor of the summer solstice and Razi. Everyone would dress in yellow and gold. She saw servants confecting streamers and banners under the tutelage of Mergon seamstresses and craftsmen. That day was tomorrow, and Frida had told her to stay in the palace and work weeding the garden and then cleaning the birds' cages, feeding them, and bathing the large birds who were dirty.

She hadn't seen Merlie, Ellie, or the boys in many days. She increasingly felt that people were staring at her more maliciously or whispering about her, their contempt nipping at her heels as she walked away. Was she oversensitive? Whispering was the main palace pastime. Yet, she felt more alone and frightened than her first days at the palace. She knew too much and felt that interest in her had not waned since she had begun associating with the princesses.

The following day, she awoke early and bid Macecle stay in the trees by her room, well hidden, and not visit Clara or Mateo. It would help to have him nearby as the palace would be eerily quiet today when all set out for the festivities. The whole palace awoke at the same time, with sounds of hustle and bustle everywhere. Children were running around in a state of excited commotion, and adults were getting into their festival finery. The women in the Court had to dress to outdo and outshine one another, and the ones of marriageable age would take special care to attract attention with new and figure-enhancing day gowns. All had to be fed. But arranging even a simple breakfast and helping all get dressed had the servants running in fever pitch. Laela was on early duty in the kitchen to help pack the baskets of food in the wagons hitched to horses decked in golden-colored livery.

Laela was among the servants and guards who would stay behind. She was grateful to have a day for herself, though not without a certain anxious dread that hung over her mind like an immovable cloud.

She saw Merli from a distance, dressed in a yellow silk gown, cinched by a sparkling golden belt with a large topaz jewel in the center. There were strands of fine gold ribbons and pearls woven through locks of her hair that flowed over her shoulders. Mesmerized eyes followed her as she stepped around the horses with Timi, who was feeding them tubers. Merli saw Laela loading a basket into a wagon and walked by her, stopping for a minute behind.

"My sister, don't turn around so we won't be noticed." Laela immediately understood and kept moving her hands as if adjusting the baskets in the wagon.

"The plan is going forward soon, in two days. Ellie and I will be helping Mateo. Just lay low." Merli sounded like her throat was clutching, "We miss you dearly."

Merli walked off as if she were just passing by, and Laela headed in another direction returning to the kitchen. Just a few words from Merli were enough sunshine for her to get through another day.

Laela stood behind the guards and watched as the Royal Family and Court members got into colorfully painted coaches from a side gate. A few men mounted on top of the finest horses to lead the procession to the main garden. The garden featured covered pavilions, fountains, and a central area covered by tents where all would eat lunch together.

Laela ate her breakfast slowly in the garden and took her fill of her favorite berries. Nena had gone with the others as she would need to oversee all the food services the servants and slaves would provide.

Laela decided to dedicate the whole afternoon to cleaning up the aviaries. She used the morning to finish a patch of weeding work Tomas assigned to her. She could do this at a very leisurely pace and enjoy the warmth outside. The palace was chilly during the day and downright cold at night.

After the servants ate the sandwiches Nena had left for them, Laela took a short nap under the tree where she met Mateo. She awoke refreshed and looking forward to time with the birds.

She started with the raucous caw-caws, spraying them to release any dirt from their feathers and feeding them little treats as she cleaned their cages.

The bibidy birds reminded her of the giant butterflies at Aerizon. Their brilliant colors seemed to outweigh their delicate bodies: saturated orange, yellow, and azure. They were small and somewhat helpless, even to fly, but they managed to flutter from branch to branch in their large tree cage, chirping to one another the day-long. They would gather several times a day in small groups, forming sections of a chorus and then singing. Their melodic arias created whistling pirouettes of sound, always transporting her and dispelling her gloom. Laela would try to imitate them as she fed them. When she reached an exceptionally high pitch, they all responded with great excitement.

She had brought with her a metal bowl and a scraping tool to gather the bird droppings that she would later take to the palace apothecary as raw material for the coveted products to smooth and lighten Mergon women's skin.

Intent on scraping and listening to the birds, she paused in her musing state to pay attention to another presence that was entering the borders of her consciousness. She had barely noticed, and now it was clear. She heard quiet but firm footsteps—the kind made by bare feet. A pungent masculine smell charged the air. The man approaching was trying to move slowly, surreptitiously.

Why would anyone stay back from the day-long celebration? Tension shot through her neck and back. She realized why. It was a moment of advantage for her. Prepare. Only Prince Marl liked to walk around the house barefooted. The other men wore long, pointed felt slippers. Prince Marl wore rings on his toes and often had servants bow to kiss his feet before leaving the room. His hoarse breathing, from his pipe habit, clearly signaled it was him as he sidled closer to her. She could feel his purpose as he inched closer to her. She must act inoffensive, non-threatening. She remained bent over with the jars as if absorbed in her duties.

Treedle's instinct for foul play and danger was fine-tuned from birth. They were fragile in the body; they must be very adaptive and strong in mind. He could kill her with one twist of his large hands around her neck. He could overcome her with the weight of his body. He could tumble her down and cause damage to her internal organs even if pretending to play with her. She would need to rely on the one weapon she had. Cleverness. She instinctively grasped the piece of moonline in her pocket, with a metal foraging hook that she had fashioned from the coil of metal Mateo gave her when she was in his home. She often used it in the garden to cut herb stems or dig out a tiny object. She touched it with a prayer. 'One,' please save me. She willed herself to stay present, to think. He might do anything to her at all, even with witnesses, but his famed perversity was unlimited in private. And who in the end would question him at all about the welfare of a Treedle?

He sidled close to her back and grabbed her with one sizable thick hand encircling her waist and the other twisting her left arm behind her in a heavy clamp. The angle of her pinned arm caused sharp, unbearable pain. He leaned into her neck, smelling of sour sweat, fatty meat, and excessive ale. He brushed his damp, oily lips to her ear: "Stay as you are, as a lowly lizard. I have finally found you alone—where no one can bother us. We have some unfinished business, my dear." Then he raked her hair with his sharp nails in a gesture of ironic affection. "Now, our little self-important upstart, I'll show you who is who, what is what... what you are good for." He laughed to himself, "If even..."

"But why me, Prince? I am nothing, as you say. I'm just doing my job as a slave. Please let me go. Nothing good will come of this." Would appealing to his reason and his authority help? Laela knew deep down that anything she might say was only a temporary diversion of the inevitable.

Prince Marl jerked and twisted her pinned arm even more until she was near fainting. "Shut up. How dare you answer me back or tell me what's good for me to do. A woman's place is to please a man, her master, and a slave's place gives her life for her master. You need some lessons on how to be a woman and a slave."

"Your Prince orders you to hold completely quiet and still. Bend over. It's in your interest to cooperate fully. I will do what Prince Mateo is too cowardly to do; use you like the piece of rubbery rubbish you are. Lower than human, not even a real woman." He licked her neck. "You are neither sweet nor juicy like a Mergone woman, unworthy of my touch. If I split you in two with the 'tongue of fire,' you will be blessed to die in the service of the greatest Prince of Mergonland. I'll assume that your screams are ones of pleasure. Bend over more and prepare to serve your master."

Laela's throat constricted, her senses heightening painfully. Being caught in his heavy grasp was worse than being in the claws of a jaguar. This man would wrench apart both her soul and body. His hatred was engulfing her senses. She steeled herself to act despite the choking pain and fear. A thought of rapidly sinking the hook in his jugular popped into her mind. No, no. She dare not kill this Prince by the law of the land and, more importantly, the law of the 'One.' And if she tried, he might overcome her and enjoy the struggle, battering all her resistance to a pulp. Another idea? Focus. She had to marshal her mind and scale this seemingly insurmountable peak of fear. She couldn't run. Nor scream. No one would take her word over that of the Prince. She instantly knew she would rather kill herself than allow him to defile her.

Marl's breathing was getting heavier just at the thought of inflicting so much pain. Urging himself on with visions of her despair, he whispered, "Some women I let live, some I damage for life, and some I use again and again. Your reactions will help me decide how to deal with you. Fight, and I will break you and present the leftovers to my idiot brother. It would be an interesting end to a sick love story."

She prayed as she thought. Her only hope was in some way to unsettle his balance long enough to get out of his grasp. As he clutched her tighter, she leaned her right arm over his thick arm. She still had the metal hook in her hand and had momentarily forgotten it was with her and not in her pocket. He hadn't noticed her clenched fist. She tried to shift their combined weight further forward. She tilted her head around to show him her face contorted with pain. She must distract him from what she held in her right hand and what she would do with it. He wasn't interested in her hand, and this would help. However, if she failed in the maneuver, he would become extremely violent. Implacable. She sobbed with heartfelt agony while feigning weeping and passive acceptance. "Oh, great Prince, what have I done to offend you so? I have so little significance. I have seen over these past months how little I am worth. Please don't hurt me."

"Hurt you," he gurgled in a low voice. "My darling, it will be so much more than hurt." He began to pull up her jumper. Feeling like she was drowning in the force of his metal-like grip, she struggled to breathe. This was her only chance; she must try. If she failed? No time to think of that. With all her strength, she bent down quickly, snagging the hook under his large toe, just as he was trying to position himself. As he leaned into her while grasping her waist, she latched the hook on one of his toe rings—out of the line of his sight. Then as he was positioning himself holding her waist, she pulled on the hook attached to the ring and gave a jerk backward with all her might. He screeched loudly as the metal hook caught under his toe digging into his skin. He wavered in his balance and fell straight back, his head conking with a heavy thud on the palace floor. The force of the fall had flung her loose, and she lurched forward against the cage which was firmly anchored and just swayed with her weight.

Terror grew in her as she realized that the Prince was quite still. A rivulet of blood was trickling out from under the back of his head. His skin was brownish gray. His mouth was sagging.

Laela froze. She did not want to touch him. Was he even alive? Blood was flowing out in an uneven puddle now from his head. Heaven forbid he was dead. Had her clever plan just generated a greater tragedy—had she killed him with one blow after all? Then she may as well be dead. She could not run away. All evidence would link them together here. She must assess the situation, but she could barely drag herself to touch him. She hovered over him, noting that the blood seeping from under his head was ebbing. She grasped his wrists, and there was still a faint pulse. She saw a light twitching on his right hand. "Good," she said to herself, realizing she could not face killing Mateo's brother, even over her honor.

Laela placed a clean rag she had not used in cleaning yet under his head to soak up the blood. She quickly mopped up the area. An explanation was needed to save her life. She surveyed the scene of the would-be crime. What could have caused such a strong Prince to fall back, like a tree felled by a logger? What could she tell both the Prince and Court officials? She noted the bloody nick on his large right toe. She had aimed well indeed. What could have made his toe bleed? Why, he had tripped, even better than planned. Yes, indeed, he had tripped. She thought quickly and placed the sharp rim of one of the metal tops to the dropping jars by his foot.

While it wasn't likely that he would cut his toe on that top. Not likely, but then how likely would it be that a young Treedle girl knocked him out with no apparent weapons around. Well, there was the hook, and who knows how thorough an investigation would be carried out? She quickly buried the metal hook under a rock in the birdcage.

She paused and noticed that her teeth were audibly clattering in her head, she was shaking, and cold sweat was streaming down her body. Fear was breaking down her system as if a glass container were shattered and its contents poured out. She slumped onto the cool floor, empty, and her thoughts too dispersed to gather into a subsequent plan of action. The cold, hardness of the floor is a welcoming ground to stop. She may have lost time-consciousness she did not know. But she was aroused by distinct animal groans close to her.

The Prince was stirring and grasping his hands groggily to his head. Laela quickly stood up and went to tend the Prince, who had lost his power to attack for the time being.

The Prince looked at her with dazed eyes. "Where am I?" He glanced from Laela to the birdcage, to the bright red blood on his fingers as he had unconsciously swiped behind his aching head. His memory was not lost, and he quickly surmised the situation. "What did you do to me, evil girl?"

"Oh, Prince. I'm so sorry. You tripped on something, and we fell together on the floor. I wasn't able to stop your fall. It appears to have been the lid of this jar. You see, not only the back of your head is bleeding, but you have nicked your toe. It's what caused you to lose your balance."

The Prince narrowed his eyes, wincing from pain and disbelief. His voice trembled as he cursed her "You are a sorceress devil's spawn. The devil sent you to this Kingdom, and you will be purged from it. Soon." He groaned and now looked even whiter than before. He must be nauseous.

"Prince, tell me what to do to be of assistance," Laela asked, eyes cast to the floor. He started to lean on one elbow to get up. She gave him her hand, both loathful for the contact, he shaking and yet rigid, she shaking and without strength. She cautioned him, "Please sit up very slowly." Holding on to her hands, he gradually sat up and groaned with nausea. He tried to get up but slumped back.

He glared at her silently and then said, "Get my private physician right away. Tell no one of this accident. No one must see me like this. I might have died from this blow to the head. I blame you for this, as you cause misfortune wherever you go. I shouldn't have risked this as you may have lived to even sire a child by me. You are beneath the dirt we walk on. You will pay with every drop of blood in your body. I assure you."

They both knew he would never live down the shame of being downed by a Treedle girl and that he had no plausible story for a Treedle girl to oust him and bring him to blood.

She was able to locate the Court physician in the apothecary. She explained how the Prince had fallen, hit his head, and was bleeding. The physician's eyes widened in alarm. He quickly gathered some bottles, gauze, and towels and put them in a satchel, running with her to the aviary.

The Prince, lying prostrate still on the floor, looked tired and dizzy and did not speak much as the physician ministered to him. Laela flinched a bit as she saw how much gauze the physician wrapped around Prince Marl's head. It was a turban of shame for him and a sign that Laela's worst troubles were only beginning. There would be no time to celebrate escaping alive and with her maidenhood intact, but it did give her a secret reserve of energy to think of it.

Now she must escape and soon. She would spend tomorrow planning and get word to Mateo. She must leave on her own. There would be no time to wait for the approval of his friendly doctor's visit right now.

CHAPTER 25

Escape or Execution

Laela awoke, again and again, tossing and sweating—jolted into a semi-conscious state of terror between dreams. In her nightmares, the black jaguar and Prince Marl were chasing her through jungle-like mazes. At one time, she was running from the jaguar on the forest ground through cloying bramble trying to climb up a tree, and at another, she was tackling a smelly beast of a man with paw-like hands dripping with blood. The two were becoming indistinguishable in her dreams. She was always seconds away from being consumed by either predator.

Macecle clung to her side through the waves of unrest. He nuzzled her back as if to try and quiet her. He understood they were in danger.

Morning dawned, and no one came to open the door. Unease gradually became dread, making it hard to think or move with any energy. Laela knew the silence was not good news. She thought about sending Macecle to alert Mateo, but she could not be completely alone. She needed Macecle nearby for support and to be ready if they needed to flee together at a moments' notice. She would only send him off if she could gain a little more clarity in what she wanted to ask for or do. The particulars of escape seemed even less clear to her than when Prince Marl had her pinned.

Right now, the room was locked, and that indeed blocked off all avenues of escape. If they opened it during the day, it would surely be locked at night when she needed to escape. It seemed close to impossible to figure out an escape plan she could carry out in broad daylight. She would indeed need to alert Mateo—but when? If she called for him, he might come right away and walk into as much danger as her. She was aware of how little he knew of maneuvers to climb walls and trees, dart away from predators, and think of ways out if ambushed. She was the better warrior-adventurer of the two. And she would rather risk her own life and not his. She just couldn't visualize what to do next with any level of confidence.

The palace was hushed. No one unlocked her door, but Tomas quietly left her food that he dropped in small sacks through the slit in the door to her room. Alone with her thoughts, Laela went over her different scenarios of defense; should she be questioned. She didn't want to think of the direst possibility of torture and execution. But even so, she must. She would need to take an herb that would dull the pain and hope for a quick death. She had a small vial of a white powdery substance that she might be able to take if they took her to the dungeon for questioning. It would be easy to hide in the hem of her gown.

She spent the next few hours mulling over answers to all manner of questions and then revising them. "How did the Prince fall?" He was behind me and leaned over to look at something, tripped on the sharp edge of the rim of the jar top or scraping tool, lost his balance, and toppled over.

"He says you pushed him."

"How could I—a mere speck of a girl—push him over?"

It was late afternoon when Laela heard the sound of a key in her door. She braced to see Frida or a palace guard. But the person standing in the doorway and closing it swiftly behind her was Ellie—panting and out of breath. At first glance, she noticed the blood that had dripped over Ellie's delicate blue silk dress. She gasped when she saw Ellie's face. Both eyes were swollen, bloodshot, and encircled by purple bruises. Her face was transfigured by the beating she had suffered.

Laela stared. Macecle whimpered as if he knew.

"Laela, I can only stay a few minutes. You must listen to me carefully. I found a key to your room and will return it shortly to Tomas. I'm going to leave your door unlocked. As soon as night falls, you must escape somehow. I'm going to make sure the back door to the garden is left unlocked as well.

"Laela, they are planning to execute you in the morning. The King will have no more of this. You'll be called into his presence tomorrow. Merli and I can't help you right now. As you can see, the Prince all but killed me last night. He was weak but found enough strength to have me tied to a chair, and he beat me all over with a wooden paddle. He said that now I could be purple like my dear Treedle friend."

"The worst," she said, holding back a strange sob, "is that he beat my darling Aser, saying he deserved that and more for being a Treedle lover too. He said now you both can look like her. Aser dared to say he does love you. He showed a courage I've never seen before!

"But don't worry. Praise the 'One;' my brother came to the palace on Court business early this morning. When he stopped to visit me in my chambers, he saw what happened and was outraged. He called all our male family members to come and intercede with the King. King Malcolm is going to allow me to return to the countryside with my family. We must pay him additional tribute, but he has approved for Prince Marl to divorce me. My brother insisted upon this and found a way to save me from the wretched life I'd been condemned to live."

Laela started to cry and felt utterly helpless to see her friend beaten so severely after saving her own self from being raped.

Ellie spoke warmly to her, "Sister Laela, it's not your fault. Whatever you did to resist the Prince, I will always thank you. Yes, I got this terrible beating, but now I'll be freed. You freed me through your bravery and sacrifice, dear Laela. I'm going to pray for you as if you were my flesh and blood. I will beg the 'One' for your safe passage. But right now, I can't help you any more than this. Please forgive me. Merli sends her love."

Ellie hesitated as if afraid to tell her yet one more piece of terrible news, "And, when you return to Aerizon, which I know you will, you must warn your people. Prince Marl's next plan is to enslave all Treedles and have them work to expand and enrich the Mergon Kingdom. He's going to increase the number of slaves to double our Kingdom's mining capacity and build a much larger and greater fortified city. I can be killed for informing you of this state secret. But you are evidence of a beautiful people that must be saved. May the 'One' protect you so that you can prepare your people. The Prince and the military are advancing a plot for their entrapment or war to force all into slavery."

Ellie looked fearfully over her shoulder and left quietly, closing the door without locking it.

Laela sat on the bed, looking up at the small window and the dust floating lazily around in the few beams of sun that poked in through the forest leaves. How could things keep going from bad to worse for her? She now had a greater reason to survive than just her physical safety and desire to reunite with family and friends. But this challenge was beyond the scope of her imagination, of her capacity to comprehend. She decided to alert Mateo, but she knew she still must take the lead. She couldn't depend on anyone else to be responsible for warning her people. She must survive. She must trust the 'One' to guide and protect her. There was no other solution, and she felt no small measure of shame to seek Him fully only in the darkest moments of her life. If she had only been more aware of His guidance in lesser moments, she wouldn't be in this situation today. But no time to contemplate now.

Laela prostrated herself on the floor, and Macecle imitated her quietly by her side. She threw herself into the most ardent prayer and supplication of her life. She began by begging the 'One' for forgiveness. Too many faults and shortcomings came to mind, and there was too little time to explore each. She asked Him to please forgive her for all of them. He would know better than her what 'all' included. There wasn't time to list them in detail and consider how to make amends for them.

She simplified her prayer, "Please save the Treedles, and if I can serve as an instrument of good, please save me. If I am the one to alert my people, please help me escape and guide me safely to Aerizon. Please inspire Mateo to do what you Will him to do and protect him, Ellie, Merli, and the dear Treedles in Mergonland."

She remembered some of the teachings on tests and tribulations that she heard while growing up. Alvaro would explain how tests bring hidden blessings and opportunities if we're patient and open to how they appear. It often takes a long time before the secret benefit of a test becomes apparent. We can't avoid the suffering and pain that will take us to the new stage of growth and wisdom. The trees that are strongest and weather the most storms are gnarled and full of age lines. When they were young, they bent with the winds and were beaten by storms. They survived into grown trees only after being tempered by many natural trials. Then they became engrained with wisdom, grew tall and strong, and yielded many a fruit. She wondered if she would even survive, let alone become wise and understand the tribulations engulfing her.

For now, she was weak and couldn't stand strong on her own. The whole Court, not just the guards and militia, were involved in scheming and machinations against her and her people. She looked at her tiny lavender hands and thin, scarred legs. She was frail, a woman, a Treedle, and she had overestimated her ability to be self-reliant. She sobbed for a while, surrendering to her powerlessness. An image came to mind of the reed that Mergon's played as a musical instrument. She longed to empty her thoughts and become this instrument, a channel or instrument breathed into life and directed by the 'One.' She asked the 'One' to fill her hollow soul with His power and guidance. Whether it be to die with dignity or live on to serve her people, she offered her soul on the threshold of the ultimate source of power she must rely upon. He would move her and watch over her. She must trust whatever the voice deep inside her was telling her to say or do. She would act as the spirit guided her minute by minute, step by step.

She felt compelled first to write Mateo a message. She penned it quickly, telling him, "My darling, I send this message to you with Macecle and pray that no one intercepts it. Please have him return to me as soon as he gives it to you. I'll need to leave tonight. I can't wait for you, my darling. It is too late for you to intervene. If I survive, I'll find a way to get a message to you.

"Know that I will love you for all eternity, but that your life and happiness are more important to me than holding on to you. You must find another woman to mate. You mustn't be alone. You should have a family and bring good Mergon children into the world. We'll remain friends always, whether I live or go on to the next world." Love, Laela

Laela impressed upon Macecle the need to deliver the message to Mateo and head back to her as quickly as possible. She imagined that Mateo would want to write a note of his own. All of this would take some hours. Macecle set off with the message in his pouch, and she saw him disappear quickly through the treetops.

Laela dressed and prepared her backpack, hiding it again until it was time to leave. She put Tan and Gibble in the little travel pouch she used for them around her neck—with the promise ring tucked in the bottom of it. She fed them sleep-inducing leaves from a thistle plant Macecle brought her so they could hibernate for some days. She rehearsed in her mind, once again, the escape over the back garden wall. She envisioned what she would do if she encountered a concho or even a guard. She would use her sling and hope that the full moons would provide enough light to shoot pellets to stun, knock them out, or fell them without killing them. That would be tricky, but she must try to escape without adding to the many wrongdoings the Mergons would credit to her as a Treedle renegade. If she succeeded in escaping but did so by violent means, it would trigger motives of revenge and provide justifications for her Mergon captors to enslave more of her people. Murdering a Mergon would fuel endless retribution.

Macecle returned just as the moons were rising, silhouetting the peaks of the trees, and leaving the sky bright enough to seem like the first glow of dawn. Their light would allow her to see shapes and detect Mergon faces from afar but would make her more visible.

She read Mateo's message:

"My beloved. Do not leave. Wait. I will be there at the crack of dawn. We will get you out. Trust me." Love, Mateo

She ate the message gulping it down with a cup of water.

She considered waiting, but every impulse in her heart and body was commanding her to act. Not to wait. Not to involve Mateo, who would pay consequences for aiding and abetting her. He deserved a better life than an exile from his Kingdom: a rebel versus an honored and respected Prince, a true scion, and the only real hope for his people. He could influence many in the Mergon Kingdom toward building a more just and peaceful civilization. And, if he remained, she knew he would advocate for the Treedles.

She must think of her responsibility to her people first and foremost. Their romance was coming to a swift end, and they must each follow the path of service and duty.

Laela waited until the palace became utterly silent: no creaks, echoes, or distant laughter. It was well past midnight when she put on her backpack and dared to open her door. She tapped her mouth to give Macecle a quiet signal and then motioned him to follow behind. She tiptoed out ever so gently, trying to sideline the aviary and pass the chambers in the women's wing as soundlessly as possible. She was praying no bird would stir, and they didn't. She was also praying that no door would open, and they did not.

She felt a small sigh of relief as they all but floated through the warm kitchen, which smelled of bread loaves rising for breakfast the next day. The door to the garden opened easily. She paused by the side of the door jamb where she wouldn't be seen to survey the garden area and wall in the distance. Cor and Cora were full and resplendent casting a stream of light down the garden. She would need to skirt around the edges and not make too much sound as she set her feet down. She measured her steps carefully not to make crackling sounds over dry leaves and small twigs or trip on any shrubs.

It took longer than she wished to reach the two trees by the wall. She crept up and tied a lasso securely to a large branch so she could flip herself over the fence and rappel down the other side. Macecle stayed watching and helping unloose the moonline when she had descended over the wall. When she had lowered herself over the wall, rappelling down it smoothly with the moonline as an anchor, he untied the line, put it in his pouch, and jumped to the top of the wall. He positioned himself first, holding on to the ledge, then sliding down the other side bit by bit, slowing himself by dragging his fingernails against the wall and finally letting himself gently drop into Laela's arms. They were outside the perimeter of the palace but still on Kingdom grounds.

The next step was to edge around the wall until they could find the best way through the dense bramble bordering it. There was a small clearing beyond, and once past this barrier, they would be able to head toward the dark, hulking forest looming in the distance. Macecle found a burrow through the bramble, and they crawled through it, emerging onto flat and unobstructed ground. Now, they must dash to the nearest large tree and ascend. Laela felt exhilarated running. And to their good fortune, after passing a few smaller trees, they soon located a large and easily climbable tree. She signaled to Macecle to creep up and tie up a moonline to drop down for her. But suddenly, she heard faint thudding sounds not far in the distance that steadily increased into a crescendo of thumping, pounding feet. She turned to see the outline of the commotion behind her: the bobbing helmeted heads of guards outlined clearly in the moons' light. They had emerged from the west corner of the wall, where the orchard flanked the garden. On closer look, she surveyed the clearing they had just passed, and three conchos were racing in front of the posse.

She started to shimmy up the tree as fast as she could, using her hands to grasp the trunk and pinion herself with her knees so as not to slip. Macecle was still working on the moonline. Her stomach clenched in horror. A large concho was bounding toward her with ferocious strength, ahead of the group, and was only a few paces away. His shining snout seemed to point to her like a compass needle drawn to the north. Laela tried to ascend the tree, but the concho leaped up high, and with skillful aim, managed to reach her feet and grasp her leather shoed ankle in his teeth dragging her down. She twisted and turned on the ground, frantically trying to escape his iron jaws. As she did, her backpack came loose. She shoved it aside. She wouldn't be able to run.

As she tried to dodge and skirt the concho whose mouth was frothing with anticipation, she cried to Macecle to get her backpack and leave quickly. "Go to Mateo!" She had to alert him. The bag and Macecle needed to be out of sight. The conchos weren't trained to hunt marsupials, and Macecle would be able to take this incriminating evidence away. She could see Macecle scurrying away into the darkness with the backpack over his shoulders as she wrestled with the concho. Even as she fought off concho number one, the others were racing toward her. With the guards just paces behind, she was outnumbered and outpowered.

The whole militia must have been alerted and on-call about preventing her escape!

She tried to kick and push the concho away while reaching into her apron pocket. She pulled out a small knife and managed to jab the concho under his ear. He released her, yelping. It was only a momentary reprise as soon the other conchos were upon her. She sensed they were hungry and tormented by the ferocity of their barking. They would be rewarded with meat if they hunted well. She tried to guard her face to kick and flail. She could smell their pig-like musk and saw their glinting fangs and flashes of their rabid yellowish-green eyes as they lunged at her. They would eat her alive if the guards didn't call them off. It would be a painful and ignoble death, but she would defend herself as best she could and was aiming at one of the conchos with the small knife when rough hands pulled her up.

A tall, well-armed guard was holding her under the arms and yelling at the conchos, "Down! Good work, boys!" She had dropped her knife as he jerked her away. It had landed in a pile of leaves. Five other guards encircled her and grabbed her arms to tie them behind her back. She felt it was wise to have lost the knife.

They were quite excited and celebrating as if they had found a treasure. She heard one guard gleefully exclaim in the background, "Prince Marl is a genius. He thought well to train all the conchos with the Treedle rat's scent. He knew she would find a way to get to the trees. But she's too stupid to outsmart even a Mergon concho." She thought about how careless the guards were with their mouths. They mustn't worry about their methods or secrets ever escaping the Kingdom.

The guards pulled her roughly toward a waiting horse. They further bound her feet, and a guard bent her in half and deposited her in a side saddlebag. She would go on a ride similar to the one when she was removed from the pit. There would be no trial this time, and she shuddered to think of the night ahead and wondered if she would outlast it.

Then she heard two other guards talking behind them, "They'll put her in the dungeon for tonight, chained, of course. The King himself will execute her tomorrow. He was too merciful to her at the trial. Only special guards will be there. And since we're bringing her in, I'm sure we will get to watch. I can't wait. It should be the best execution of the year!"

When they arrived at the palace, the guard carrying her removed her and threw her over his shoulder. A guard flanked him on either side, and others formed a procession in front and behind. They entered the palace from a site unknown to her and began to descend steps, footsteps echoing, and cavernous, roughly hewn stone walls surrounding them to the sides. She could hear but not see them unlocking a heavy door and then descending further down into a dank underground corridor lit by flaming torches on the walls. The guard directly in front of her patted for a ring of keys and held up one he recognized, opening a heavy wooden door to her side that featured a barred slit for guards to peer into the room. The guards carried a torch inside with them and threw her on the floor. She tried to tumble with the fall but couldn't avoid the slamming and slapping effect of her body meeting the unyielding and icy stone.

She looked up and saw there was only a tiny window at the top of the wall. The room would be very dark when they closed the door. They unloosed her ropes and then chained her leg to a metal hook protruding from the wall.

The guard who had carried her held the torch to her face. Its flickers created menacing shadows around his prominent nose and beady dark eyes. He slapped her face hard and spit in it. "This is a message from Prince Marl. *You will pay for your crimes with a painful death tomorrow. And your people will also pay for your disrespect to Mergon Royalty. May you burn in hell forever.*"

Spitting in someone's face was the ultimate insult Mergons could enact on another. It was all but unheard of for a Treedle to do this, but that was the essential difference in their cultures. She barely felt the sting on her cheeks or the dripping spittle, thinking of how she could be associated as a cause of her harm to her beloved people. Laela would embrace death if that stopped the Royal plan to enslave them. However, she also knew that the appearance of a young albeit insolent and outspoken girl wasn't sufficient pretext to wage war on Treedles. For Prince Marl and the like, his very sense of privilege and entitlement as a royal Mergon would justify anything and everything he did to those who were 'inferior' to him. He would always be right no matter what he did to anyone, even his noble peers.

The guards left and shut the door, causing the room to become a chilling black void. She touched the floor with her hands and recoiled from its icy and unyielding hardness. She could smell the pungent layers of urine accumulated over time. Other smells, too, as if from the bottom of an old abandoned well.

As the minutes passed and her eyes accustomed to the inky darkness, she was relieved to see the faint glimmer of light coming from the little window above. A wan ray of light beamed through from the side of the windowsill. A moonline of hope. She would look at it to pass the hours with a focus. To remember. Her people and her love of the 'One.'

She wanted to curl up into herself, like a snail in a mollusk shell, shut herself into a smaller place and escape her body through a hatch in her mind. The impenetrable cold, the waiting, the worries for everyone she loved were pressing in on her so she could barely breathe. She willed herself to connect with the 'One' and felt there were two choices, giving in or giving up. She had nowhere to hide, but she could let all hope be extinguished or somehow hold on ember in a tender recess where no one could reach. The soul always had space for this ember. The soul could always receive the 'One' under any circumstances, even and especially to the last breath of life.

She would choose to give herself up to the 'One,' though utter despair was genuine and compelling. She would believe and hold hope there, deep in there. It was hard to pray. She repeated any words from the Writings that she could remember through the tiredness and terror. She tried to dwell on the hope that no pain and not even death could stop His Plan. She prayed to be aligned with that plan, imagining herself as the reed, not attached to any outcome, but the one ordained.

She became somewhat numb as she didn't have the body fat to withstand this cold without a blanket. She tried to move to circulate her blood; pray, move, beseech. She leaned against the wall, nodding her head and catching glimmers of sleep between long bouts of restless and clenching awareness of the approaching morning. As she relinquished herself in sleep one last time before the dawn, she had a dream of Denai, who whispered to her in a voice so loving and fragrant it was as if she were holding pera blossom under Laela's nose to breathe and infuse the words with sweetness. She stroked her head and said, "Trust in the 'One.' Speak from your heart to the King and say what comes from the Source. Be confidant and know that the 'One' is watching over you and Mateo. Peace be with you."

Laela woke up refreshed enough to think clearly, and though not without fear, she did trust that whatever would happen was meant to be. Her part was to be in grace with the 'One.' She could do that.

It was a few hours after dawn when she heard the rhythm of heavy boots stomping outside the door and the jangling of large metal keys. She breathed in and out slowly to calm herself.

A posse of guards came to open the cell in what must have been a few hours after dawn. The guard who had locked her up last night came in first and released her from the wall but fastened leg chains around her ankles and locked them. She would need to shuffle along. However, to speed things up, he threw her again like a sack over his shoulder. Then the group headed down the clammy, dark corridor toward an open stairwell. They climbed up the stone steps with her head bobbing downward, giving her a dizzying rush of blood.

She knew where they were headed, and after marching down a series of internal corridors, they opened a side door into the Great Hall and began dragging her across the marble floor on her knees. Then they stood her up on the viper pit pedestal. Guards flanked her on either side, tying a rope around each of her wrists. They positioned her as if she were in the middle of a tug of war.

King Malcolm and Prince Marl were seated on the two lofty thrones. They were dressed in regal finery. Prince Marl's crown was half the size of King Malcolm's, but he wore a most elegant purple robe trimmed in rare animal furs. There were enormous, bejeweled rings on all his fingers, and his beard was trimmed neatly for the occasion. She could feel his devouring gaze from the pit below, not many steps away. His was a mixture of pleasure and avid expectation of watching her writhe in pain soon.

She was surprised to see Mateo and Davi, dressed in large brown woolen capes, rushing in as though late for an invitation by the Court. They nodded and bowed to the King, who looked quizzically at Prince Marl. They whispered together for a moment. Then, King Malcolm announced to the small group of courtiers and guards present,

"The Prince and his friend are welcome to watch the execution if they remain to the side and don't speak. Prince Mateo should be present as justice is done. He, too, has been a victim of this sorceress. Stand by my son and watch as your father protects your royal dignity and heritage."

King Malcolm stood before his throne and announced in a booming voice that echoed around the almost empty Court, reverberating on the marble-clad walls.

"Today, justice will be done. I will complete the sentence that should have been carried out at the trial. Here stands a Treedle rebel who has mocked the sacred family and all that Mergons stand for. We were far too merciful and benevolent when I agreed to honor my son Mateo's petition to spare her life. She has been ungrateful for the kindness she was shown by the royal household. Now, she has attempted against the life and person of my son Prince Marl. She has brought nothing but trouble and dishonor to our family. Both my sons have been victims of this evil girl who is seeking our family's downfall.

"Treedle girl, this is your last day in our Kingdom and on earth. As one more sign of our munificence, you may speak your final words." King Malcolm held his hand to his heart, proud of his pledge of allegiance to his family and the victory he would be celebrating after the execution.

Laela lifted her head and looked directly into the Kings' eyes. She released herself into the moment and let the words flow through her. An inner Laela was speaking for her, clearly and confidently. She was a witness to words she hadn't consciously chosen,

"Your Majesty and Mergon citizens, I came to your country as an innocent girl. I was curious and wanted to see and know more about Mergonland. I had no other motive. I did not make an attempt on the life of Prince Marl, nor did I ever try to hurt anyone. I wanted to make friendships.

"Your Majesty, please know that Treedles are your brothers and not your enemies.

"Ages ago, we shared one homeland by the great ocean. Our four tribes were like flocks of different colored birds who shared the same forest and lived in harmony. The Prophet Asmea came to guide all four tribes. He brought the Teachings of the 'One' to us. He wanted us to live in peace and taught us about the power of unity.

"Treedles know that we can only be happy when we love and serve others. We have much to share with Mergons, and if you destroy our culture, you'll lose all the good that we can add to your lives. If you enslave and mistreat Treedles or any people, you will, in the end, become cruel and hardened people who have many things but no real peace or joy in your lives.

"There's more power in love and unity than hatred and war. If our people worked together, we could make the best possible life for all."

Laela had spoken far too long for a woman, let alone a Treedle, in the presence of the King. Her impassioned voice had lifted to rafters, and the Court was hushed. The guards and few courtiers surrounding her were mesmerized, and a few were gaping as if overwhelmed. Mateo was off to the side, so she could not see his face. However, the King and the Prince were narrowing their eyes and clenching their lips in rage. They exchanged meaningful glances.

She had a moment now to think of Mateo witnessing her execution and dearly wished that he and Davi hadn't shown up, but she must stay in a state of connection and prayer to make the next transition in her life.

King Malcolm raised his scepter like a shining gold torch and called out, "The 'One' has gifted to the world to the Mergon people and called upon the King of the Mergons to rule all peoples. Treedles aren't people like Mergons. They're inferior beings, animals who were created to be our servants.

"We will feed off the blood and bones of the Treedle people if they do not obey us.

"Treedle girl, your words and wishes will die with you. Soon to be forgotten—but Mergonland will grow more glorious than ever."

The King paced slowly to and fro on the podium holding the scepter like a sacred staff, "This is the scepter of justice. I will rid the Kingdom of this sorceress once and for all. The tongue of fire will devour all remnants of this pest, and all shall see what befalls an enemy of the Kingdom." He began to tap and shake the scepter rhythmically to alert the serpent. "This Treedle will suffer an agonizing death, and blood will ooze through every pore. Only with the sacrifice of her blood can she cleanse her crimes and leave the Kingdom of Mergon purified into ash."

He beckoned the guards to hold her arms apart wide spread. The guards on either side of Laela stiffened in fear and stepped out, tightening the ropes bound to her wrists stretching her arms out as if she were hanging upon a cross. They pulled the ropes tightly, as much to secure Laela and to ensure they were as far out of the way of the scepter as possible. Guards could suffer the same fate as the victim if too close. With her feet shackled, Laela was held in a stiff and unyielding position with her chest uplifted toward the King, so he could more easily aim the scepter at her juggler. The King began to take steps toward her holding the scepter like a golden sword pointing at her.

Then simultaneously, there was shuffling and shrieking. Macecle emerged from under Mateo's bulky cape, and with a wild cry, and bounded toward the King. The King's attention was drawn to the unexpected visitor popping out of nowhere. Macecle poised fiercely and sprung into further action. He made an extraordinary acrobatic leap onto the King's shoulder and placed his paws around the sides of the King's head, reaching over his eyes. The King instinctively reached up to push Macecle off, and guards began lunging toward them.

Laela, who was the closest to the King, was awestruck at the next turn of events. As Macecle jumped away quickly, the King fumbled with the scepter. He had his thumb on the mechanism to open the hood, which he had pointed directly at her. With Macecle still screeching at him and dodging the guards' spears, the King was distracted and lost his balance. As he stumbled, he inadvertently triggered the scepter to open. The brilliant green viper, his instrument of execution, shot out from the gold casing like a guided lance and fastened its fangs deeply into the King's throat.

At the same time, a bright purple rod flared and exploded on the floor between her and the King. She could see Clara running frantically about and tossing purple rods from her pouch. In the distance, she saw Davi aiming the same flares from a bag over his shoulder. The glass rods popped furiously and smashed into sparkling bits over the polished floors, igniting brilliant flares that turned into clouds of purple smoke and fog—with a foul smell like rotten eggs.

The King had now sunk into the purple fog on the floor. Laela stood motionless like a fixed point amid the pandemonium around her. She noticed a stream of dark red blood flowing among the shards of glass and seeping toward her. She could hear the serpent crunch and slurp its way into the King's body.

Mateo was moving up to a nearby guard who had locked her in the dungeon the night before. The guard was pale and dumbfounded by the commotion; he was unaware that Mateo had grabbed his key ring. Only a few of the King's guards were standing close to him, and even they seemed hesitant about handling the dire situation. This most lethal of vipers might jump onto them as well, and the King had fallen. Two guards moved forward to make motions to save the King, but it was too late. They knew within instants that the King was dead.

Mateo tried a few keys before he could unlock Laela's ankle chains. He whispered tersely, "Trust me. This is all part of our plan. A horse awaits us outside. We have to move fast before all the guards know what is happening. Your backpack is there. Davi will accompany us and throw more purple gas rods to get us on our way. We must hurry as the gas clouds don't last long."

Mateo put his cloak over Laela and took her hand. Laela, still a bit dazed, struggled to keep pace with him as they ran toward the entrance doors. The guards at the entrance were watching the spectacle occurring inside the Court. They didn't think about detaining the Prince or the hooded figure rushing along with him. Later they would regret that.

Mateo and Laela raced out to the side of the palace where the horses were stationed. They were followed by Davi, Clara, and Macecle bounding behind—throwing purple rods in front of the few guards not already drawn to the commotion in the palace hall. Noone stopped them for questions or to check Prince Mateo, though that would change shortly. Prince Marl wasn't pausing to grieve and wail but to assess the situation—rejoicing already in his heart to proclaim himself King. His first order of duty would be to hunt them down as fugitives from justice. As they left the hall, they heard Prince Marl screaming frantically about being the King and apprehending the devils who did this.

Mateo untied his horse, picked up Laela, and put her in a basket by the side of his saddle to be out of sight. The two riders on one horse could be a dead giveaway of the fleeing couple. Davi followed them on his horse with Clara and Macecle, and they moved as fast as possible down the pathway leading to the palace. They chose to skirt the town and areas filled with dwellings. They galloped in and out of fields and by little-traveled roads, horses glistening with sweat. Finally, they came close to the entrance of the forest where Laela and Macecle had first emerged. Few people lived or traveled among the wheat fields, and they might meet up with an occasional border guard, but not a posse. However, in a short time, the whole militia would be after them.

They stopped amid some thick full-grown wheat stalks that formed waving golden walls around them to confer briefly. Laela took a moment to look into Mateo's eyes and thank him for the rescue.

"There's someone else to thank, my darling," he said, nodding at Davi, who had sidled up close to Mateo's horse. Mateo's honey-colored eyes were dark with the silt of fear, and he looked over his shoulder as if potential enemies were hidden among the rippling shadows of the ripened stalks. "We're going to part ways with Davi here. He's the one who masterminded the flares and purple smoke. He trained Clara to carry and throw them and Macecle to jump out at the King and land on his shoulder. Macecle was supposed to have kicked the scepter out of my father's hands." Mateo controlled his involuntary sob at the word father. "More explanations later. We must hurry."

Laela reached over the basket cradled between the two friends' horses and extended her hand to Davi. "Thank you, dear friend. One day we'll be reunited, and I hope to show you my appreciation. I've never seen anything like those purple flares before."

Mateo was getting ready to move forward again, and pulling in the reigns, he said, "Davi is going to go to the Trader's Village to stay with a cousin. We must get word to him through your Treedle traders and find a way for him to join us later. We've decided to join our Treedle brothers in Aerizon for some time. Macecle and Clara will come with us now.

"May the 'One' protect you, my brother," he said to Davi with a constricted throat. "Thank you for your amazing heroism and sacrifice."

He and Davi leaned in toward each other for a final embrace, thumping one another on the back.

Then, Mateo put Clara and Macecle in the other side basket. Mateo gave her a look she hadn't seen before, like a question, "Now, Laela, we're in your hands. You must lead us on what to do next. We have some more gas rods, and you will need to assist me with your sling should we see conchos or a guard."

Laela had been decking herself in preparation with a moonline, knife, and sling she had taken out of the backpack, putting it in her apron pocket. She patted Tan and Gibble in their little sack and told them to hang on tight around her neck. She knew it was her turn now to be the scout and the rescuer. There was no time yet to rejoice until they were well out of the Mergon Kingdom and hidden in the Feral Forest. There was no time to ask about what had just transpired in the palace and what the future might hold. They must stay attentive for final hurdles or face capture and certain execution.

May they be guided.

CHAPTER 26

The Crossing

It was mid-morning, and the sun was not an ally to their cause. It was a peek farming hour. Both ground and tree birds had stopped their early dawn chatter and were feeding purposefully. Four-legged animals brayed in the distance, and farmers were tilling fields beyond the sea of wheat where they were slowly navigating forward on the horse. They could be easily spotted as they arrived near the borders of Mergonland.

Laela knew that Prince Marl was undoubtedly entertaining all possible hideouts and escape routes the pair might take. He could well imagine that they might be headed toward the forest after they fled the vicinity of the Palace.

The four of them moved cautiously through the field, trying to lean low on the horse. Not long before, a shadow rose over the horizon, and Laela could see the forest silhouetted against the impassive blue sky—the dark and great divide between the reaches of the Mergon Kingdom and her home. Laela restrained the urge to run out toward their hopeful harbor of escape.

She asked Mateo to stop, unmount, and confer in whispers that wouldn't rise above the rushing golden stalks. "We must let Macecle scout the area ahead. This is close to where we entered Mergonland. We'll ask Clara to go west and Macecle east over some meters to see if there are guards and conchos about and how many. I'll ask them to do this very quickly but quietly. The conchos shouldn't be alerted by their scents."

Laela gave Macecle, who gave Clara, basic instructions on the routine surveillance they might do on any hunting trip. Right now, the predators they needed to avoid were both human and animal. Macecle understood the gravity of the situation and saluted like the warrior he was becoming. The two rushed off, staying close to the ground, moving from place to place to avoid being in plain sight for very long.

Mateo gave her a wan smile in an attempt to hide his sense of helplessness at the moment, asking, "Next steps? What are you thinking? How can I help?" They both understood she was the leader and head of the escape expedition now.

Laela squinted, thinking out loud, "We'll need to find a tall tree with strong branches that are near others for the best getaway and to move as deep into the forest as possible to where the better ones are and where the conchos can't track us. We'll climb up the first tree quickly and then move from tree to tree. Sometimes we will use a vine and sometimes a moonline. Other times we will jump and periodically climb up and down to move onto other trees at strategic points. Just follow behind me and mimic my actions.

"I've tied a moonline around my waist and extended a rope to it, as you can see," she pointed to a rope behind her like a tail. "If you need an extra pull or to steady yourself, you can hold onto it. You are wearing a leather belt, and as needed, we can attach a line to it.

"But you are stronger than me and can use that strength to grip with your own hands and knees as we inch up. Try not to look down but only up or straight ahead. Just focus on climbing, pulling, or swinging—nothing else. The movements will be new to you, but you have all the natural capacities and alertness to learn quickly.

"If we meet up with a concho or guard, I will need to use my sling. We must escape." A concho could move faster than a guard, and she would shoot one of those first.

Waiting was also not an ally to their escape—with alerts rippling throughout the Kingdom about the band of renegades. Macecle and Clara returned just as she was about to run with Mateo out of sheer panic: imagining the swarm of guards and conchos unleashed around the borders. She was weakened from a night in prison and the execution attempt. Armed with a sling and a small knife, the four of them would be no real match if there were any skilled guards and conchos in the picture.

Clara had gone in the direction that would lead them toward the Trader's Village and Macecle toward the preferred route to Aerizon. Clara saw no signs of guards or conchos. Macecle saw one concho and two guards sitting and eating snacks under a huge tree.

Laela made her decision quickly and told Mateo, "We will need to leave the horse now. It is best to move on foot for a time heading west through the field, and then we will choose a spot to enter the forest. When I give the signal, run as fast as you can behind me. Backpacks on." She put her fingers to her lips and motioned her team to follow her graceful movements through the field.

Skirting near the edge of the field but still hidden, they walked along as quickly as possible. Finally, Laela sighted what looked like a trail into the forest and surmised that it might provide them a good running start to penetrate deeper into the woods and find the larger trees. Once they began to ascend the hill and the higher trees, they would be unreachable, mainly because they would start to swing out in some unpredictable patterns and move in ways that no one on the ground could catch them, unless they stopped to eat or sleep. Either way, Mergons had no training from all she had seen or heard about moving up and about in the forest and at treetop heights.

She gave the command, "Run now!"

As they ran, Laela could feel the energy of the wheat fields and the sun—a golden blaze behind them. The second they entered the forest, they moved through a whole other zone of climate and terrain.

It was cooler, and the air was pungent with oily evergreen sap and the earthy debris of what was once moving, settling into stillness—so many secrets buried on forest floors. Laela winced to hear the sticks and dry leaves crunching under their feet as they tried to find their escape tree. The earth was less steady and predictable where branches had fallen, and they swerved around mud hills full of thick-headed Mergon ants marching with jagged leaves in their mouths.

Laela focused on finding a cluster of trees to begin to make a route into the Feral Forest. They needed to dodge past the bramble and brush surrounding the smaller trees to the ones that were emerging canopy trees up ahead. She pushed forward now, getting some cuts and nips from bramble, but they had to go through and then beyond the hornet's nest of obstructing plant growth to get to the suitable trees.

They arrived at a tiny clearing and an ideal group of stately trees, with climbable gnarls surrounding them when Macecle sniffed and gave her a warning yipe. A concho was bounding toward them. It was headed toward Mateo behind her. Laela commanded Macecle and Clara to go up quickly and secure a moonline from a higher branch. They each had a store of moonlines, some rings, and hooks in their pouches. Laela quickly pushed Mateo in front of her and pulled out her sling. She had to kill the concho before it bit one of them or barked. She could only hope it was alone.

The concho was focusing its maddened hazel eyes on her now. She tracked it with her sling ready to shoot, and just as it lunged at her, she drew a breath in and exhaled fully to be steady while aiming. She had to get this perfect with one shot. She stretched back the slingshot band and sent a pellet that slammed into the concho's head, making a resounding crack. The concho yelped and dropped to the ground with a few last whimpering sobs.

Laela positioned Mateo to start shimmying up the tree and pointed out two gnarled bumps he could use to pinion himself to the trunk while Laela waited for a moonline she could attach to herself and help both of them climb up faster. Mateo was inching slowly, and she could tell he was somewhat dazed and shaky about the concho almost attacking her. "Darling, you must go faster." She pushed him a bit from his firm bottom—no time for niceties.

As she saw Macecle anchoring a moonline on a strong branch higher up, she grabbed it and was beginning to fasten it to her waistband. She could see that the concho hadn't been alone. They never were. A single guard on a horse had followed close behind it. As he broke into the clearing, she could feel his eagerness at having found both the Prince and her.

Mateo concentrated so hard on climbing the tree more quickly that he didn't pay attention until the horse stopped a few feet away from him. Laela watched as Mateo turned to see the guard, an expression of surprise, irritation, and familiarity evident on his face.

"Dromi," Mateo spoke in a kindly but commanding voice, "turn away. We need to leave now. We didn't kill the King. The King killed himself when he triggered his scepter, and the serpent struck him by accident.

"You must know that, but both of us will be executed if you turn us in. Dromi, we have been friends since childhood. I've cured your family members of so many diseases, and right now, your mother is making progress against the wasting disease. Think about that. Turn away."

Dromi's eyes widened, and he was pulling back on the reins of his horse, fidgeting as if to ask him for action. The young guard kept looking indecisively around and over his shoulder, his hand stroking the silver sword by his leg.

"What if they find out that I let you escape. I surely can't let myself be killed on behalf of you. I must do my job. I must bring you in. Sorry, Prince. The Court will decide the just thing to do."

Laela didn't hesitate now, there was no choice, and an argument or showdown of arms would prolong or impede their escape. She picked up her sling, and as she did, Mateo yelled, "No." She knew he meant, don't kill.

Laela aimed, and the large pellet whirred toward the mounted guard, hitting the horse's neck and causing the horse to rear up. The guard looked at Laela in surprise, not entirely understanding what was happening and that a young Treedle girl was aiming a potentially lethal weapon at him. It wasn't a scene he could ever have imagined. He lifted his arm as if to fend off the next pellet and fell. The pellet had hit precisely where she aimed. She hadn't lost her touch.

Laela sent a second pellet to thoroughly scare off the horse. To make it run. However, the wounded horse writhed in pain, distress, and panic, bucked up his hooves, and shook off the guard. The horse came down and inadvertently trampled on the guard's shoulder. The guard was so badly hurt he could only moan and then fainted. He would be very severely wounded but not killed.

There was no time to lose. Laela started climbing the tree and fastened the moonline that Macecle had dropped down. She used the moonline to brace her feet against the tree and ascend quicker. Once on the secure branch, she dropped a line to Mateo, struggling slowly along. He gripped it in his hand while continuing to climb. Laela coached him along using the line to give him a sense of safety and being anchored. But Mateo had to use how own body weight and balance to make his way up to the large branch where Laela and the totems were waiting.

Laela hoped to get them heading east to be on course toward Acrizon, but they would first need to get as far away from Mergonland as possible—and quickly. That would mean moving forward wherever and however it was easiest to do so—inland and away from the border. They needed to jump, swing, and move along from tree to tree as fast as possible. They should leave no ground trail and try to find trees with abundant foliage for camouflage if they were spotted from above or below by any potential enemy.

Once Mateo was safely up, Laela moved to the highest branch she could without danger of falling or snapping it off with her weight. She looked for a pattern of interconnected trees and found that moving slightly east, their preferred direction, they could go quite a distance. She also smiled to herself as she could see the outline of a small platform not far ahead. She surmised that Treedles had also visited this side of Mergonland, probably leaving themselves a comfortable hiding place to rest. Only her trained eye could make out that this was a structure nestling among the leaves.

It took time to move carefully across several trees. They descended up and down to reach out and grab onto stronger branches and move across to others. Laela planned out each move to ensure they anchored a safety rope around a sturdy branch for Mateo to move across and to save him from falling should he slip. They would have to move much more slowly than she envisioned, but his safety was foremost in her mind.

When they reached the broad, robust tree with the platform, a deep overhang of thick sculptural leaves created a cozy green shelter around it. The platform was ample enough for the four of them to sit, rest, and eat a small lunch. They were now all so hungry they wolfed down bread loaves and cheeses that Mateo had thoughtfully packed. There was a small barrel of rainwater with gourd cups on a ledge within the tiny fort, which would have to do to quench their thirst.

They all spoke up simultaneously, realizing they were now out of immediate danger with the nutrients of food and water and a place to stop and sit. The totems were making tiny shrieks of excitement and embracing each other. Mateo and Laela both chanted "thank the 'One'" several times. Laela asked that they all say a prayer to ask for the 'One's blessing for the rest of their journey. They sat in a solemn circle, and each said a short prayer.

They continued to rest a bit, and then Laela stood and explored the branches above the shelter. She was rewarded by yet another piece of good fortune. On the other side, she could spot the beginning of a tree-to-tree trail, which, while not as steady as a zip line, would have them heading east. Those who had been here before had fastened a strong vine connecting their tree to the next robust one ahead. Mateo could pass across hand over hand if they secured him with a moonline. Using her compass, they had high chances of eventually encountering the zip line route.

When she returned to tell everyone they needed to move on, Mateo was hiding something behind his back, beaming from ear to ear. He pulled out a harness with a clip attached, like the ones she had developed for the traders' route. She had told him about this invention, and he was admiring the handicraft used to make it. It was evident that either traders or spies had visited this spot and had left the harness behind.

Laela hugged him in delight, "Wherever did you find this?" Mateo pointed to a sack hanging over a branch within the shelter. They had been so hungry and tired they had not thought to explore what might be stored here, concentrating on eating and resting to restore their energy.

This revelation of a path forward was another confirmation of their journey.

"Please put it on, and I'll help you adjust it," Laela motioned to Mateo. He looked at her quizzically, "And why shouldn't you wear it instead of me. It will keep you safer, and you are leading us!" Laela nibbled her lip, trying to put things so that she could help Mateo understand without making him feel bad about his amateur climbing capacities. Mateo's inexperience was slowing them down considerably. She was terrified of the many accidents he could have, not knowing what to anticipate and how to respond to the natural hurdles they were encountering. He didn't know when to grip with his knees, when or where to use his hands, or the standing and sitting motions she used to climb without thinking.

"My darling, we're a team now. Your safety is mine and vice versa. I travel among trees as you do on land. It will save us time and much concern if you are in the harness, and we can send you across trees on vines or secure lines. It is the best use of the one harness for now."

Mateo smiled sheepishly and let Laela cinch him in the harness and received a warm hug of approval from her. She looked up at the sun, which seemed in a hurry to move across the sky today. "Time to go. Follow me!"

CHAPTER 27

The Moons Unite

Timid swirls of melon-pink and lavender, the first signs of sunset, were brushing across the paling blue sky. The sky would lose color as the warm and fiery waves began to arise and surge into full brilliance until the falling curtain of night steadily closed down over the last vestiges of the day.

They had to make camp and settle for the night now.

Laela climbed the tree they were on to reach the highest vantage point and used Mateo's looking glasses to survey their location better. She hoped to find a broader tree nearby and move there quickly. The branches of the tree on which they had stopped were not ample enough to house them for a good night's rest. Laela looked to the right and glimpsed telltale outlines of smooth wooden planks set in the crook of a tree not far ahead. She shrieked with excitement at what she was sure were the makings of a platform, a station for traders. She had not been in this area of the forest before. Some of the trees were new to her, and the terrain still wasn't as familiar as the Feral Forest. The Feral Forest was surrounded by a less ancient and lofty wooded region with large patches of open areas. The lower forests were as shores lapping into Mergon territory and outline trading villages. What she was viewing might be one of the stations between the Feral Forest and the woods that bordered the central Trader's Village. It would be beyond station four, where she and Macecle had made their detour to Mergonland. If this were a station ahead, it would be one of the three remaining ones built to ease the trading route.

Macecle had scurried behind Laela and was now hugging her from behind. She gave him a quick kiss on the furriest part of his cheek. "You've been such a great scout," she said, nuzzling him some more. "But now we need more food for dinner." She made some motions for him to bring seeds and nuts. If he could capture a small bird, all the better. She would leave Mateo with his heavier Mergon food, the little she had left, and she and the totems would do well on forest fare. "When you collect enough food for dinner, meet me over there." She pointed to the smudge of the platform, showing him through the glasses. He grunted with glee.

Next, she figured out a pattern of moves to get Mateo there safely and securely. She did not tell him about the platform, just that they needed to move to another tree for the night. He was the most delighted of all to land with Laela on the wide and welcoming platform, a real trader's station. The four of them could sleep on the platform or string up hammocks. Laela thought right away about unpacking both of their blankets and sharing them as a mattress over the floor. They would need to sleep close together to share their body heat. This first night, it would be too much for Mateo to rock in a hammock. She had noticed he was getting pale and straining to overcome dizziness. Trees swayed. Their skyworld was constantly in movement—not steady like the ground and the thick-walled Mergon houses.

Laela inspected the station with her trained eye. It was fenced in on two sides, and that would make a cozy corner for them to sleep on the floor without worrying about falling. On the other side of the platform was a small stove made of bricks and clay where they could make and contain a fire to cook food and warm themselves at night. There was a door at the bottom of the stove with kindling already in it. They need just to light it and cook their meal over the one burner. Next to it was a large jug of rainwater to douse the fire if needed and for drinking and light bathing. The traders had left a rudimentary cabinet nailed to the tree trunk. She peered in and found a metal pan, jugs, several plates, eating utensils, a few candles, a fire starter, and two hammocks.

She unpacked their small blankets, put them in the corner, and set out a candle in a jar, leaving Mateo to watch her curiously. She could see his face darkening with more than the shadow of approaching dusk but hurried ahead with starting the fire in the stove. She wanted to use the last minutes of daylight to get as many logistical tasks done as possible. Macecle returned with nuts, fruits, and two small birds. Plenty for dinner and even breakfast. Mateo would be able to try out some new foods. He had a few small loaves and some cheese left to complete his dinner.

Though Laela's body ached, enjoying the first evening meal in what seemed an uncountable number of days in freedom and in the company of loved ones was so invigorating she could climb hours more if needed. On the other hand, Mateo was unusually quiet and hunched over, stirring a small pile of nut husks with a stick. He was spent. He was not in the moment with her, not celebrating.

Laela sat close to him, reveling in the intoxicating newness of being alone with him out in the wild. She inched her nose close to his neck—savoring the smell of his wind-chapped skin—her fingers rasping through his hair to untangle small twigs and leaves. She whispered endearments, thanking him for how courageous he had been to help rescue and accompany her to a foreign land—taking so many risks.

Mateo started to speak, choked, and couldn't seem to clear his throat. Lacla, unsure of how to put him at ease, offered him some tea. She warmed some water on the stove and added some minty leaves Macecle had gathered for her in his cup.

"Look at the moons! I bet they'll be so bright we can't sleep tonight. Are you looking forward to our first night together in the sky?" Laela said cheerily.

Mateo looked at her trying to force a wan smile, "Please forgive me. This is a joyful moment for you, but not yet for me. I've never left my home, Mergonland, before. I need some time to pay respects to my father, if only in my mind. I will not be there for the funeral—to bury my father."

Laela winced, realizing how she had all but exalted the fall of the King and was anticipating a reunion with her loved ones.

She had assumed Mateo shared her excitement about this exodus but realized that her exodus was his exile. In his plans to meet her family, he probably had envisioned returning to Mergonland in the future. But with Prince Marl taking over the reins of the Kingdom, this would not be any time soon. And if he did return, his half-brother would want to eliminate any possible claim to King Malcolm's throne to protect his own. He was probably already blaming Mateo for sedition and the King's death.

Mateo continued in a low voice, "I'm sad my father, the King, died in such a violent way. I realized there was nothing I could do to save him once the viper attacked him. I feel terrible that our plan to surprise him and create confusion to free you caused his death. Davi made all the gas rods, and we trained Macecle and Clara to distract those around you. I didn't want anyone to die.

"My father is no saint, and he has done many terrible things. But he is my father. He raised me with much ease and comfort around me. He let my mother and I live a life that others only dream of. He made it possible for me to be a doctor and even help those in the royal Court and the poorest peasants in the countryside. I want to remember him with gratitude. And now, I'm running away and won't attend his funeral."

Laela had felt no pain or remorse for the King's suffering or his early demise. She couldn't squeeze out even one tear, not even for Mateo, as the thought of the King filled her with too much rage. She believed he had received justice for his actions, enormous arrogance, and his cruelty toward Treedles. However, she knew that guilt was clouding Mateo's thinking and understood all too well that she would have been dead had he not intervened. There was no way that interrupting the King's plans to execute her could have had a happy ending for all.

However, she had a father, and though he was a hero to others, not just herself, she understood that love for a parent was not based on the sum of their good deeds or their true merit. For Mateo, this was the loss not only of a parent but the sovereign of his land. The only father and King he had known. Even though their relationship was overshadowed by the poisons of scheming, greed, and malice at the core of the political engine moving the Kingdom, there was no less love, it was just more complicated.

Laela stroked his arm, "My darling, we'll have time for long conversations in Aerizon. Life is slower and calmer there. Many new and marvelous experiences await us, I'm sure. But we also have sad stories to share—tremendous grief and pain. We'll face this together. And we'll find a way to honor your father when we arrive in Aerizon.

Your father gave you life and, as your King, he opened the opportunity for you to become an outstanding doctor. I understand you have lost a considerable presence in your life and that you have a debt of gratitude to your father."

At this, Mateo collapsed with her onto the blankets and sobbed in her embrace. Mateo didn't need to justify his love for his father. He needed to cry. Macecle and Clara joined them on either side to give the affection that flowed so freely from their pure hearts and to help keep their masters warm through the night. Cuddling together, they all sank into deep sleep.

Although Laela woke up at the first hint of dawn, she decided to let Mateo sleep until he awoke naturally. She made a little shade tent for him, hanging her blanket over the fence and securing it with a brick. As she made breakfast, she planned today's trek and felt hopeful that the rest of their trip would be relatively smooth. Even without a map, the cable lines between stations, no matter how zigzag the route, were easily visible and connected from one sturdy tree to another. There were secure holds for crossing over to a new line. Mateo would be mainly riding now, not climbing. Thus, a delay of one day or even two, no matter how eager she was to see her family, might be in Mateo's best interest. They could move slower, rest more, and explore the beauties of the forest together. She didn't want her family to see a frazzled, frightened Prince. She wanted them to meet her beloved soulmate in the best possible light.

Mateo woke up and ate his breakfast with relish. As she was tidying up their camping area, he asked her what he could do. She said, "Don't worry, I'm not planning to become your maidservant. But now is not the time to show you how to set up and leave the stations. I wish for you to relax as much as you can. We're out of immediate danger." She turned her face away as a shadow of Marl's smirking face hovered over her thoughts. She hoped it was only a passing fear that somehow his tentacles of evil could reach them at these heights or extend as far as Aerizon. Mateo approached her from behind and wrapped his hands around her waist. He kissed the nape of her neck gently. "Turn around, my intrepid leader. She turned in his arms, and he rewarded her with a genuine smile and fully attentive honey eyes.

"I'm ready to thank you now for your kindness and patience with me. I'm quite impressed at how you got us to this base, especially with my total lack of climbing skills. I don't want to add to your burdens. You haven't had time to share your ordeals with me. I apologize for unloading so much on you yesterday."

Laela put her fingers to his lips, "Let's not apologize for showing sadness. We must be able to share our real feelings—everything. No secrets. We have both been through so much, and there's no easy way to handle it. As my mother Tara always says, we must let the tears of pain flow out for the healing ones of laughter and joy to come. Our key to happiness will be supporting one another."

Mateo pulled her head into the hollow of his neck, stroking her back lovingly, and then began to kiss her deeply and in earnest until she felt vanquished by love. She wanted to curl up with him and rest the entire day, but she shouldn't delay an arrival that could bring her family so much relief. In all, they would go slower but not stop for long until dusk.

The way east was now a sky path that any Treedle trader, hunter, or military man could easily follow. As they began to zoom smoothly toward the next station, it was Laela's turn to worry. The winds through the ziplines seemed to sweep the past away and speed her toward her future. She was getting closer and closer to home. She had shut down every reminder of Aerizon to get through her days in the Palace. The more she could numb herself and move mindlessly through the chill fog of enmity around her, the more bearable the unbearable became. The less she dwelt upon memories of family and friends, the smaller she could make herself and her pain. Recalling her loved ones awakened needs and wanting and doubled her fear because whatever misfortune happened to her would come to haunt them in the end.

She could dare to imagine them worrying and praying about her daily now. She could see her father bowed in prayer in his study room, her mother in the garden with more creases in her forehead, Oti swinging alone—wanting to share biscuits with her and hoping she was alive. And finally, Phips holding himself back to go search for her in Mergonland.

Because of her selfishness and lack of responsibility to the community, they suffered and worried every day about her. She had sent a note to her family a few days after her arrival in Mergonland. Did they ever get it? Banbo had said they heard of her story. Somehow the story of the Treedle girl going on trial at the Mergon Palace must have crossed borders—the news of the century! However, her family and friends must have been left wondering what became of her afterward. Would she be released back to her forest home? What did they imagine her fate to be during the long period of silence and no news?

She tried to picture their faces when she would arrive with no advance notice and a Mergon Prince in tow. She hoped the surprise would not be too overwhelming. She would need to approach the story of her adventure to Mergonland carefully. Except for the first days of idyllic friendship and budding romance and sharing her experiences leading to the trial and thereafter would be incredibly difficult. Everything that had happened to her was out of the realm of cogitation for Treedle women, young or old. It would be deeply shocking to tell the women closest to her heart how dangerous her situation had been. The specter of torture and death clung to her like a shadow she could not dodge. It would take hours just to explain the social reality of the Court and the Mergons' ways of thinking. She had entered a world unknown to them and was changed in ways they might never understand. She hoped that would not put up barriers to receiving the healing love she longed to feel.

On the other hand, what would be their responses to seeing her alive? She could almost taste the sweetness of the tears of joy.

Mateo was leaning back in his harness, and she could see him enjoying the refreshing winds—his streaming hair glinting gold as they passed into patches of sunny skies. He was a quick learner, open to the novel ways of moving and finding joy in each small bit of knowledge and new technique he learned as they went swinging to and moving away from tree after tree, line to line.

She was delighted when they arrived at camp before mid-afternoon. It was then that she changed her mind to take more time to arrive in Aerizon. Seeing a place that was now relatively close to her home and knowing they could finish the rest of the trip safely, she decided she wanted this night and one more, alone with Mateo. She did not want to plunge him into her world, the gentle but also very different society of Aerizon, until he had more time to reflect on the upcoming transition. He would need to be ready to be the only Mergon in a community full of innocent and curious Treedles. She knew that even when Mergons were welcoming and kind to her, like Mateo's family, Merli, and Ellie, there was discomfort in being the one strange person in a new land. The one who is different in color, voice, and thought—the one who is similar enough to communicate with, but who few would embrace as one of their own.

Laela left Mateo to get familiar with the camp and set off with Macecle and Clara trailing along to hunt for some food for dinner and breakfast. They descended a bit to where branches were the thickest and attracted the most animals. They hadn't gone far when they saw a net hanging with something alive trapped in it. Hunters sometimes left tree traps to catch small wandering mammals and birds with a net below to catch them. They saw movement within the net and pulled it up curiously. A baby jaguar was tangled in the net, mewing, and struggling. Laela forgot her usual caution. Empathy for this creature—captive and suffering—obliterated all concern for her safety. They could see that the cub was so enmeshed with the netting it was choking itself to death and could not tear the net with its teeth. Though delicate in appearance, Treedle netting was so strong only a very sharp metal knife could cut it. Laela pulled hers out hers.

Undoubtedly, a jaguar mother was tracking them nearby. But Laela, undeterred, decided to act. She carefully cut the net away as Macecle and Clara tried to restrain the cub so he would not get hurt by the knife. It took longer than Laela would have liked, but they all felt a celebratory moment when the cub licked Laela's hand, and she set him into the cradling shelf of a hole in the tree. They could see the mother, perhaps the very jaguar that had attacked Laela, watching stealthily behind the leaves of a branch from above.

Laela froze for an instant in terror, but Macecle pulled on her jumper, and they quickly climbed down and moved out toward a neighboring tree. They watched as the mother rescued her baby and sighed with relief that the cub took precedence over them. Even wild animals could be grateful if you saved their offspring.

When they arrived with some birds and two small mammals, she showed Mateo their upcoming meals. She didn't know that Mateo had observed her incident with the jaguar and was surprised when he chided her, only half kidding, "I was watching you with my looking glasses, my darling, and wanted to yell out to you that the mother jaguar was arriving. I thought I would faint from fear—no more heroics. If you get mauled by another jaguar, I won't be able to rescue you. And then, how would I get to Aerizon alone." He poked her in the ribs as if to say, 'seriously.'

That night Laela strung up two hammocks together, and she and Mateo lay on their backs, holding hands, gazing at the brilliant array of heavenly bodies and the three-quarter moons glowing melon and blue and seeming to wink at them occasionally. Laela had thought it would be a temptation for them to maintain her 'purity,' but it wasn't. They were both so tired from the journey, the build-up of fear and excitement leading to their escape, and the announcement they were bringing to Laela's family that there was no space for romance.

However, they did reach across their hammocks and whisper and then tickled each other, pretending to be each other's totem. This time Laela received a shower of endearments from Mateo and seeing him make ridiculous faces and grunts in her ear took her far away from the desert of abandonment and pain where she had been stranded for so long. He brought her into the present, immersing her in a refreshing shower of laughter and fun.

Mateo paused and then asked her, "Do you ever stop to think what might have happened if we had missed each other when you arrived in Mergonland? I hadn't planned to visit the fields so early in the morning that day. I just did for some reason. We could have missed each other by minutes depending upon where you had entered and I passed. The outcome would have been so different if you had crossed paths with another Mergon."

"Yes, I think about it often. I think how fortunate I was and that the gift of your love is more than I deserve. But there's more. I don't believe our paths crossing was just luck." Laela squeezed his hand significantly.

"Neither do I," Mateo affirmed, "I believe the 'One' brought us together and that our union isn't just for us, but for our people—a plan for us to unite Treedles and Mergons as promised in the Sacred Texts."

"My dream," Laela began hesitantly, revealing for the first time a deeper expectation she had for mating with him, is to save my people from enslavement—to stop Treedles from becoming enslaved and Mergons from enslaving others. We must work together to inspire understanding and bring about change."

Mateo completed her thought, "It won't be easy, but I must use my crown and capacity to heal and you—your bravery and leadership to protect our people. To stop a war. To start a new day of Mergon-Treedle relations."

"Imagine the possibilities of Mergon and Treedle collaboration? But first, my darling Prince, you need to get to know Treedles: real Treedle culture. While I was in Mergonland, it was like I was growing a new part of myself. Every day I learned something different and realized that Mergons have knowledge that we don't and vice versa, like pieces of a puzzle. Your mother and grandfather taught me more about the history of our faith in such a short time than I ever received growing up. Merli showed me how Mergon women cleverly handle the politics of the Court. Nena and Tomas showed me how dignified a Treedle could be living as a slave with no hope of freedom. I love how Ivan and Davi are advancing scientific knowledge in ways Treedles are only beginning to discover. I wish my people could benefit from Mergon culture, and I wish Mergons could learn from us about how to treat all living beings."

"You made friends and touched hearts under the worst circumstances," Mateo beamed at her with admiration. "You began to explore our culture fearlessly, just like you did with this forest. I know how much our friendship has changed my way of seeing things. I'm eager to spend a lot of time with your family and friends. That's the best way to get to know people and love them. Mergons have certainly learned nothing of value about Treedles through our history books or the traditional stories our Elders pass on to us."

"Well, Treedle children grow up fearing Mergons. Treedle children imagine all Mergons to be like Prince Marl—an insatiably cruel Mergon warrior. You have to know that some Treedles will fear you at first, pretty as you are," she laughed, tossing her hands through his hair.

They went to bed early, lying in their hammocks sharing stories of their confinement over the past months. Throughout it all, Mateo had thought only of how to get Laela released alive. Davi was a most enthusiastic accomplice and stopped work on all projects to design the purple gas rods and the entry and rescue plans for Laela.

Laela told Mateo they need not hurry tomorrow and should arrive at the very last station in the afternoon. She planned for them to spend one last night at station one so they could set out refreshed and well-rested in the early morning to enter Aerizon. If they pushed all the way through, they would not have the same energy to meet the curious gazes of a surprised community and answer the torrent of excited questions they would be showered with upon their arrival.

The group of four was now a coordinated team. They moved in synchrony through the zip lines, oblivious to the dangers of the Feral Forest. They were noisy—not stealthy—which scared off animals but easily alerted and attracted human attention. However, they need not think of human predators. Their Mergon enemies were far below, a long distance away. Laela felt a heavy burden cast off as if she were already home.

When they arrived at station one, she leaned against the central tree anchoring the platform around it and joyfully thanked the 'One.' Macecle was exhilarated and pointing to Aerizon.

"No, Macecle. Not today. First thing tomorrow." She rolled her hand over to show him the passing of the night. But she felt the same magnetic tug of family and friends, so close now.

She noticed a waxy soap flower plant growing up around the trunk and got an idea for preparing the group of them. She called out, "Set your things near the fenced area. We're all going to take a bath together. We will certainly make a better entrance smelling fresh and clean."

Laela could bathe in her jumper and get it and herself thoroughly clean. Then they would sit in a patch of sun to quickly dry the silky fibers. Mateo could bathe in his loin undergarment. The water collector was full, and they would use the gourds to rinse themselves.

They all set about squeezing and squirting the soap plants and oozing the clear, fragrant gel-like substance over one another. Macecle and Clara jumped on her and Mateo's heads and helped shampoo their hair. Laela did have time to notice Mateo's slim muscular torso, round bottom, and the sleek lines of his muscled chest and strong arms. His skin was glistening like gold satin under the soap lather. She would certainly want to explore that more if they were left alone in the jungle. As Mateo helped rinse her hair and back, the touch of his fingertips and caressing streams of water filled her with longing. She was grateful that they would be under the watchful supervision of her parents and then hopefully married very, very soon.

Laela helped Mateo wash out his clothes and hang them securely to dry on a branch. She took a peek in his backpack to see if he had another clean shirt, which he did, but he stopped her from reaching to the bottom, "Laela, I'm bringing a special present for your family, and it must remain a surprise. Promise you won't look further, please." Laela could tell from his face and tone of voice that this was a most solemn request, so she nodded, "Sure, I promise."

They didn't cook that night. Laela had packed some roasted brawn bird for Mateo. She and the totems filled up with nuts and fruits. And they celebrated their last night cupping their hands around Cor and Cora so bright in the fulness.

Laela told Mateo about some of the customs to expect that might be different from Mergonland: how they would take off their shoes before entering the house, kiss family and close friends on both cheeks when greeting, and that he should bow slightly to her father when meeting him. "Expect to be showered with questions, stared at, and have your intentions toward me thoroughly questioned."

They both had hoped for restful sleep as planned but often awoke—giggling about seeing the whites of each other's eyes glinting in the starlight. Dawn ambled in like a late guest. She, Mateo, and the totems were gulping down breakfast and clutching their stomachs with anxious excitement.

As they began to get ready to leave, they heard a whoosh behind them as someone jumped onto the platform from a nearby branch.

Laela gasped. It was Phips, looking more poised and statuesque than she had remembered him. Marriage had changed his bearing. He seemed to hold his chin higher, like a man to be reckoned with, not just an athletic youth anymore. He was draped with bags to store his catches after hunting.

They both yelled and leaped into each other's arms. Phips wiped away a tear, and Laela's face was streaming with them.

"You're alive! And well," he kept repeating, and Laela echoed back, "I'm alive and overjoyed to be home!"

Phips had been so excited to see Laela that he had not stopped to focus on the person by her side. He turned his gaze to Mateo and just stood, his mouth agape. He looked at Laela for a clue as to what to say or do.

Laela laughed, "Excuse me, this is Mateo, my soon-to-be mate. As you can see, he's a Mergon. I don't know if you all received my message, but he's the Mergon Prince who not only offered me hospitality but won my heart."

Phips shifted his feet awkwardly and bowed to Mateo. Mateo walked over to him and placed his hands gently on Phips' shoulders. "Please Phips, here in Aerizon, I'll be known only as Mateo. No Prince, no titles. I've heard so much about you and can't wait to meet and visit with you properly."

Phips looked at Mateo with the keen and penetrating gaze of a powerful Bouder man and then broke into a broad laugh. He gave Mateo a quick hug and two light thumps on the back with his fist, Treedle style for man-to-man friendship greetings.

"We'll have a lot of time to get to know one another, but I'll let you both move on. I don't want to delay your family reunion. I will just spend a few hours hunting, and then Oti and I will come whenever you send word. I know you need some time alone with your parents first. May it be well with you. Gloriously well. Ah, my sister and brother, what joy you have brought to us today!"

Mateo looked at Laela and nodded. He adjusted his backpack. "Ready, my love. Let's do this!"

Laela paused to think how Mateo would see the simple rhythms and pleasures of Treedle life over the following months. He was going where no Mergon had ever been. She would need to do everything to make this transition as kind as possible. But he was as ready as he could be. Just as a seed of the Mergon culture was growing in Laela's heart, one of Treedle culture was starting to root in Mateo's. Neither of them would ever return to 'home' as they had known it nor entirely fit into their native cultures anymore. Mergon and Treedle influences and elements were already mixing and could not be unmixed, just like flour and water when raised in bread. Love was a leaven spurring growth, changing their personalities and aspirations, and creating new possibilities through them.

They had overcome boundaries that others had not dared to imagine—connecting in spirit, crossing the frontiers of culture and allegiance to their lands to create a union that would change their lives and the lives of their people. From an unexpected encounter to intense attraction and turbulent tests, the moonlines of fate had enmeshed and bound them together. They would start a new era, a new race of people between her airborne community and his ground-rooted Kingdom. Laela took Mateo's hand and, together, they emerged from the Feral Forest into the welcoming morning light of Aerizon.